Robert Asprin Myth Series Omnibuses

ANOTHER FINE MYTH/MYTH CONCEPTIONS
MYTH DIRECTIONS/HIT OR MYTH
MYTH-ING PERSONS/LITTLE MYTH MARKER
M.Y.T.H. INC. LINK/MYTH-NOMERS AND IM-PERVECTIONS
M.Y.T.H. INC. IN ACTION/SWEET MYTH-TERY OF LIFE

M.Y.T.H. INC. IN ACTION

SWEET MYTH-TERY
OF LIFE

ROBERT ASPRIN

ACE BOOKS, NEW YORK

M.Y.T.H. INC. IN ACTION/SWEET MYTH-TERY OF LIFE

An Ace Book / published by arrangement with
Starblaze Editions of the Donning Company/Publishers

PRINTING HISTORY
Ace mass-market edition / October 2002

M.Y.T.H. Inc. in Action/Sweet Myth-tery of Life copyright © 2002 by Donning Company.
M.Y.T.H. Inc. in Action copyright © 1990 by Robert L. Asprin.
Sweet Myth-tery of Life copyright © 1994 by Robert L. Asprin.
Cover art by Walter Velez.
Cover design by Judy Murello.
Text design by Julie Rogers.

Visit our website at
www.penguinputnam.com
Check out the ACE Science Fiction & Fantasy newsletter!

ISBN: 0-441-00982-4

ACE®
Ace Books are published by The Berkley Publishing Group,
a division of Penguin Putnam Inc.,
375 Hudson Street, New York, New York 10014.
ACE and the "A" design
are trademarks belonging to Penguin Putnam Inc.

PRINTED IN THE UNITED STATES OF AMERICA

10 9 8 7 6 5 4 3 2 1

M.Y.T.H. INC. IN ACTION

Dedication

*With affection and apologies to my
many foreign translators
. . . especially those at my German publisher,
Bastei Lubbe!*

INTRODUCTION:

"What am I doing here?"

—ANY RECRUIT, ANY ARMY

"**N**ame?"

Now, in those circles within whose company I am accustomed to travelin', it is considered impolite to ask questions in general . . . and that question in specific. Unfortunately, I was currently well outside those circles, and as such felt compelled to answer the inquiry, however rude.

"Guido."

"Home address?"

"The Bazaar at Deva."

"What?"

"The Bazaar at . . . Oh! Uh . . . just say . . . 'varies.' "

The joker what was takin' down this information gives me a hard look before continuing with his questions. I give him my best innocent look back, which as any jury can tell you is most convincin', though deep down inside I am more than a little annoyed with myself. Bein' a smarter than average individual, I should have recalled that even though my travels and adventures with the Boss have accustomed me to other dimensions, to most folks here on Klah such places as the Bazaar at Deva are unheard of, and therefore suspicious. As I am makin' a specific effort to be inconspicuous, this is not the wisest answer to have given.

"Height and weight?"

This question makes me feel a bit better, as it serves to remind me that whatever I say or do, I will never be totally inconspicuous. You see, I am what is politely referred to as "a large person" . . . or less politely as "a knuckle-dragging monster." While this is of invaluable assistance considerin' my chosen profession, it does, however, make it difficult to blend with any given crowd. In fact, I would be the largest person in the line if it were not for Nunzio who is maybe an inch shorter, but a bit bulkier.

I can see the guy with the questions has noticed this all by himself, since he keeps glancin' back and forth between the two of us as he jots down my responses.

"Next of kin?"

"I guess that would be Nunzio, here," I sez, jerkin' a thumb at my colleague.

"You two are related?"

"He's my cousin."

"Oh."

For a second I think he's about to say somethin' more, but then he just shrugs and scribbles a little more on his pad.

"Do you have a criminal record?"

"Beg pardon?"

"A criminal record. Have you ever been arrested?"

"No convictions."

That earns me another hard look.

"I didn't ask about convictions. I asked if you've ever been arrested."

"Well . . . yeah. Hasn't everybody?"

"What for?"

"Which time?"

"How many times have you been arrested?"

"Oh, three . . . maybe four dozen times . . . but no convictions."

The joker has his eyebrows up now.

"You've been arrested nearly fifty times with no convictions?"

"No witnesses," I say, showin' him my teeth.

"I see," the guy sez, lookin' a little nervous, which is one of the customary side effects of my smiles. "Well . . . let's try it this way . . . are you currently wanted by the authorities?"

"No."

"Good . . . good," he nods, fillin' in that blank on the form in front of him.

"Okay . . . one final question. Do you know of any reason why you should not be allowed to enlist in the army of Possiltum?"

In the actualities of the situational, I knew of *several* reasons not to enlist . . . startin' with the fact that I didn't want to and endin' with the god-awful wardrobe that I would be forced to wear as a soldier-type.

"Naw."

"Very well," he sez, pushin' the form across the table at me. "Just sign or make your mark here, please."

"Is that all?" I ask, scribblin' my name in the indicated spot.

"Is that all, *sergeant*," the joker smiles, pickin' up the paper and blowin' on the signature.

Another reason for not joinin' the army occurs to me.

"Is that all, *sergeant*?" I sez, bein' careful not to let my annoyance show.

"No. Go to the next tent now and you'll be issued a uniform. Then report back here and you'll be assigned to a group for your training."

"Training?"

This is indeed somethin' what had never occurred to me or Nunzio, and could put a serious crimp in our projected timetable. I mean, how much trainin' does it take to kill people?

"That's right . . . training," the sergeant sez with a tight-lipped smile.

"There's more to being a soldier than wearing a uniform, you know."

Bein' a survival oriented individual, I refrain from speculatin' out loud as to what this might entail. Fortunately, the sergeant does not seem to expect an answer or additional comment. Rather, he waves me out the door as he turns his attention to the next unfortunate.

"Name?"

"Nunzio."

Now, those of youse what have been followin' dese books all along may be wonderin' just why it is that Nunzio and me is signin' onto Possiltum's army instead of performin' our normal duties of bodyguardin' the Boss . . . who you probably think of as the Great Skeeve, as you is not employed by him and therefore have no reason to think of him as the Boss.

This confusion is understandable, as this book is happenin' right after the book before the last one, *(M.Y.T.H. Inc. Link)* . . . and at the same time as the one before this *(Myth-Nomers and Im-Pervections)*. Add to that the fact that this is one of the M.Y.T.H. Inc. volumes, and is therefore bein' told from my viewpoint instead of the Boss's, and it becomes clear why your eyes is perhaps crossed at this point in the narrative. The only consolin' I can offer youse, is that if youse think my life whilst workin' for the Boss is confusin' to read, youse should try *livin'* it for a month or five!

Actually, to be totally honest with youse, dis book is not startin' where I was the last time you saw me, so let me refer youse back to the meetin' which started us on this particular chain of events . . .

I:

"What do you mean my characters talk funny?"

—D. RUNYON

It is indeed a privilege to be included in a war-type council, regardless of what war it is or who in specific is also attendin'. Only the very elite are involved, which is to say those who will be furthest from the actual fightin', as such gatherin's are usually concerned with which portions of one's forces are expendable, and exactly how and when they are to be expended. Since it is demoralizin' for those who are to be dropped into the meat grinder to know they have been chosen as "designated receivers," they are logically excluded from the proceedin's, seein' as how if they are made aware of their roles in advance, they are apt to take it on the lam rather than dutifully expiring on schedule, thereby botchin' up many hours of plannin' on both sides of the dispute in question. From this, it is easy to see that attendin' these borin' but necessary plannin' sessions is not only an honor, it greatly improves one's chances of bein' alive at the end of the fracas. To get killed in a battle one has had a hand in settin' the strategies for is an indication that one's plannin' abilities are sorely lackin' and will count heavily against youse when bein' considered for future engagements.

In this particular circumstantial, however, it was no special honor to be included in the plannin' session, as our entire force consisted of a mere five personages . . . six if you count the Boss's dragon. Needless to say, none of us was inclined to think of ourselves as fallin' into the "expendable" category. Realizin', however, that we was supposed to be trying to stop a renegade queen with a sizable mob of army-types at her disposal, one was not inclined to make book on our chances for survival . . . unless, of course, one was offered irresistible odds and maybe a decent point spread.

While there wasn't all that many of us, I, for one, had no complaints with the quality of our troops.

Tananda and Chumley are a sister and brother, Trollop and Troll team. While they are some of the nicest people it has ever been my pleasure to encounter, either of them is also as capable as any five knee-breakers ever employed by the Mob if they find it necessary to be unpleasant. In the Boss's absence, they have taken it on themselves to be the leaders of our expedition . . . an arrangement which suits me fine.

You see, my cousin Nunzio and me is far more comfortable takin' orders than givin' them. This is a habit we have acquired workin' for the Mob, where the less you know about why an order is bein' givin', the better off you are . . . particularly if at a later point you should be called upon to explain your actions under oath. (For those of youse who have failed to read about our activities in the earlier books in this series and are therefore ignorant as to our identities and *modus operandi*, our job description refers to us as "collection specialists" . . . which is a polite way of sayin' we're kneecappers.)

The fifth member of our little strike force is Massha . . . and if that name alone is not sufficient to summon forth an identifyin' image in your mind, then it is obvious you have not yet met this particular individual in the flesh. You-see, Massha has a singularly unique appearance which is unlikely to be mistaken for anyone else, though she might, perhaps, be mistaken for some-*thing* else . . . like maybe a dinosaurous if said saurous was bein' used as a travelin' display for a makeup and jewelry trade show. What I am tryin' to say is that Massha is both very big and very colorful, but in the interest of brevity I will spare you the analogous type comparisons. What is important is that as big and as tough as she is, Massha has a heart even bigger than her dress size.

We had been holdin' the start of our meetin' until she got back from droppin' the Boss off on Perv, which she had just done, so now we are ready to commence the proceedin's.

"So you're tellin' me you think King Rodrick was whacked by Queen Hemlock? That's why Skeeve sent you all here?"

This is Big Julie talkin'. While me and Nunzio have never met this particular individual before, we have heard of his reputation from the days when he also worked for the Mob, and it seems he and the Boss are old friends and that he's one of our main sources for information and advice in this dimension. In any case, we are usin' his villa as a combination meetin' point and base of operations for this caper.

"That's right," Tananda sez. "Hemlock's always been big on world conquest, and it looks like her new husband wouldn't go along with her schemes."

"Realizing she now has the combined power of her kingdoms' money and the military might of your old army," Chumley adds, "it occurred to Skeeve that she might be tempted to try to . . . shall we say, expand her holdings a bit. Anyway, he asked us to pop over and see firsthand what was happening."

"I see," Big Julie nods, sippin' thoughtfully at his wine. "To tell you the truth, it never occurred to me that the king's dyin' was a little too convenient to be accidental. I'm a little surprised, though, that Skeeve isn't checkin'

this out himself. Nothin' personal, but he never used to
be too good at delegatin'."

"He's busy," Massha sez, cuttin' it short like a casino
pit boss.

Tananda shoots her a look then leans forward, puttin'
a comfortin' hand on her knee.

"He'll be all right, Massha. Really."

Massha makes a face, then heaves one of her big sighs.

"I know. I'd just feel a lot better if he let a couple of
us tag along, is all. I mean, that *is* Perv he's wandering
around in. They've never been noted for their hospitality."

"Perv?" Big Julie scowls. "Isn't that where that weirdo
Aahz is from?"

"Where he's from, and where he's gone," Chumley
supplies. "He and Skeeve had a falling out, and friend
Aahz has quit the team. Skeeve has gone after him to try
to bring him back . . . which leaves us to deal with Queen
Hemlock. So tell us, Jules, what's the old girl been up to
lately?"

"Well, I'll admit there's been a lot of activity since the
king died," Julie admits. "The army's been on the move
almost constantly, and both they and the kingdom are getting noticeably bigger . . . know what I mean? It's kinda
like the old days when I was running the army, only on
a bigger scale. I get a postcard from one of the boys sayin'
how they're visitin' a new country, than ga-bing-ga-bang
that country's suddenly a new part of Possiltum."

"I see," the troll sez thoughtfully. "Well, what do you
think, little sister? You're the only one here who was
along the last time Skeeve stopped this particular army."

"Not quite. You're forgetting that Gleep was there . . .
and, of course, Big Julie."

She winks at that notable who responds with a gracious
half bow. Gleep, the Boss's dragon, raises his head and
looks around at the mention of his name, then sighs and
goes back to sleep.

" 'Course, I was on the other side last time," Big Julie
sez, "but it occurs to me that you got your work cut out
for you this time around."

"How so?"

"Well, last time we was the invaders, you know? The locals didn't like us, even though they didn't take much of a hand in the resistance Skeeve organized. This time, though, the army is the home team, and folks in the kingdom are pretty much behind 'em all the way."

"You mean the kingdomers are in favor of the queen's new expansion moves?" Tananda frowns.

"That's right," Big Julie nods, "and when you think about it, it stands to reason. The bigger the kingdom gets, the more people there are to share the cost, so the taxes get smaller. With their taxes goin' down with each new conquest, the citizens are positively ecstatic about the way things are going. If that weren't enough, unemployment is at an all time low what with so many goin' into the army, so pay scales are sky high."

"So Hemlock's running a popular war, eh?" Tananda sez, pursing her lips thoughtfully. "Maybe that's the route for us to go. What do you think, big brother?"

This last she directs at Chumley, who just shrugs.

"I suppose it's as good a place as any to start. Something about that analysis of the tax structure bothers me, though."

I tended to agree with Chumley, but Tananda is on a roll.

"Save it for the financial heavyweights," she waves. "For the time being, let's focus on doing what we're good at."

"And just what do you figure that is?" Massha interrupts. "Excuse me, but could you two run that by again slowly for the benefit of those of us who aren't used to your brother/sister shorthand?"

"Well, the way I see it, our best bet is to work on making Hemlock's expansion program unpopular. I mean, there's not much the five of us can do about stopping the army by ourselves, but if we can get the populace worked up maybe the queen will have to reconsider . . . or at least slow down."

"We could try to kill her," Massha sez pointedly.

"True," Tananda acknowledges, "and don't think I haven't given that option some serious thought. I think it's a little more drastic than Skeeve had in mind when he sent us on this mission, though. Anyway, I think I'd like to hold that option in reserve for now, or at least until Skeeve catches up with us and we have a chance to clear it with him."

"Well, if you don't mind, there's another possibility I'd like to try."

"What's that, Massha?"

"Tell me, Big Julie, is General Badaxe still running the army?"

"Hugh? Sure is. He's a fast learner, that one. Remembers mostly everything I've taught him about runnin' an army."

"Well," Massha sez, heaving herself to her feet, "I think I'll just wander off and try to find his headquarters. He had quite a thing for me the last time I was through. Maybe if I look him up again, I can get his mind off running the army for a while, or at least distract him enough that they won't be quite so efficient."

"I say, that's a good idea, Massha," Chumley sez. "Speaking of the army, Guido, do you think you and Nunzio can manage to sign up for a hitch? Remembering how you stirred things up at the Acme magik factory by getting the workers to unionize, you're the logical choice for demoralizing the troops, and that's best done from the inside."

"Yeah, sure," I sez with a shrug. "Why not?"

"Are you okay, Guido?" Tananda asks, peering at me sudden-like. "You and Nunzio have been awfully quiet since we started out on this venture."

"We're all right," Nunzio puts in quick. "We're just a little worried about the Boss . . . like Massha. Joinin' the army is fine by us, if you think it will help things. Right, Guido?"

"I said it was okay, didn't I?" I snaps back at him.

"So what are you and Chumley going to be doin' while we're playing solider?" Nunzio sez. It is obvious to me that he is out to divert the attention of the meetin' away from the two of us, but no one else seems to notice . . . except maybe Big Julie who gives me the hairy eyeball for a minute before turnin' his attention back to the conversation.

"We're going to see what we can do about stirring up the citizens," Tananda shrugs. "Tax reductions are nice, but there are bound to be some irritating things about life under Hemlock's new programs. All we have to do is root them out and be sure that folks see them as irritating."

"Do you blokes want Gleep, or shall we take him?" Chumley asked.

"Gleep?" sez the dragon, raisin' his head again.

"Aahh . . . why don't you and Tananda take him," Nunzio sez quick-like. "Truth to tell, he made me a little nervous the last time we was workin' together."

"Who? Gleep?" Tananda sez, reaching over to pet the dragon. "There's nothing to be nervous about with him. He's just a big sweetie and a snugglebug . . . aren't you, fellow?"

"Gleep!" the dragon sez again innocently while leanin' against Tananda.

"Good. Then you won't mind havin' him with you," Nunzio smiles. "That's settled."

"I suppose," Chumley sez absently, studyin' the dragon as he talks. "Well, I guess we might as well get started. Big Julie, do you mind if we relay messages to each other through you? Otherwise we're going to have trouble keeping track of things."

"No problem," the retired general shrugged. "To tell the truth, I figure you're all going to have enough on your hands, so you shouldn't be worrying about communications. I'll be here."

After sayin' our goodbyes to the others, Nunzio and I head off to try to find a recruiter for the army.

For a long time, neither of us sez anything. Finally, Nunzio clears his throat.

"Well, what do you think?"

"I think we got big trouble comin' our way," I sez,

tight-lipped, "and I *don't* mean with communications or even with Queen Hemlock."

"I know what you mean," Nunzio sighs, not lookin' around as he trudges along. "You want to talk about it?"

"Not just yet. I want a little more time to think things through. In the meantime . . ." I aims a playful punch at him which, bein' Nunzio, he takes without so much as blinkin'. ". . . let's occupy ourselves with somethin' easy . . . like disruptin' an army."

II:

"We want to make you feel at home!"

—L. Borgia

"*A h'd like to welcome you all to this man's army! The first thing you should know is that we're on a first name basis here ... and my first name is ser-geant ... Do I make myself clear?*"

At dis, the individual so addressin' our group pauses and glares at us. Naturally, there's no answer, as no one is particularly eager to call attention to themselves under dese circumstantials. It seems, however, dis was not the response the sergeant had in mind.

"*Ah asked you a question!! Do you think Ah'm up here running my mouth 'cause Ah like the sound of mah own voice?*"

It is clear that dis is a ploy to induce us new recruits into makin' a mistake which will further anger the sergeant, as at this point he has asked not one, but two questions callin' for opposite answers, and whatever answer is given is bound to be wrong. The other unfortunates in line with Nunzio and me seem to be unaware of this and blunder headlong into the trap.

"YES, SERGEANT!" they bleat eagerly.

"WHAT??!! Are ya'll tryin' to be funny?"

The sergeant, who I am glad I never had to compete against for a part in my old drama troupe, gives every impression of bein' on the verge of foamin' at the mouth and becomin' violent to the point of injurin' himself and anyone else in the near vicinity. Almost unnoticed, he has also asked a third question, placin' the odds of comin' up with an acceptable response well out of reach of the intellects in line with us.

"No . . . Ahh" . . . "Yes, Sergeant" . . . "Ahh . . . No?"

The attempt to shout an answer dissolves in a babble of confusion as the new recruits glance at each other tryin' to sort out what they're supposed to be sayin'.

"YOU!"

The sergeant's voice silences the group's efforts as he homes in on one unfortunate in the front row.

"What are you lookin at him for? Do you think he's cute??"

"No!"

"What?"

"Ahh . . . No, Sergeant?"

"Ah can't hear you!"

"No, Sergeant!"

"Louder! Sound off like you got a pair!"

"NO, SERGEANT!!"

"That's better!"

The sergeant nods curtly, then turns his attention to the rest of the formation again.

Viewed correctly, dis is a fascinatin' study in group-type dynamics. By focusin' on one individual, not only has the sergeant let the rest of the group off the hook of tryin' to come up with an acceptable response to his questions, he has impressed on them that they really don't want to ever be singled out by him.

"My name is Sergeant Smiley, and Ah will be your drill instructor for the next few days. Now, right away Ah want you to know that there are three ways of doing things in this man's army: the Right Way, the Army way, and My

Way . . . we will do things My way! Do I make myself clear?"

"YES, SERGEANT!!"

The group is gettin' into the swing of things now, bellowin' out their responses like a convention of beat cops goin' after a jaywalker.

"All right now, listen up! When I call out your name, sound off loud and clear so's I know you're here and not off wandering around somewhere. Understand?"

"YES, SERGEANT!"

"Bee!"

"Here!"

"HERE WHAT?"

The kid what has just answered is so skinny it is surprisin' he can stand without assistance, but he licks his lips nervously and takes a deep breath.

"HERE, SERGEANT!" he shouts, but his voice cracks in the middle of it, makin' his declaration less than impressive.

"That's better," the sergeant nods, apparently satisfied with the youngster's effort. "Flie, Hyram!"

"Here, Sergeant!"

"Flie, Shubert!"

"Here, Sergeant!"

The sergeant looks up from his roster with a scowl.

"Bee? Flie? What is this, a freaking Bug Convention?"

"We're brothers, Sarge," one of the two Flies supplies unnecessarily, as the physical similarities between the two broad-shouldered individuals would be obvious even if their names didn't link them.

"That's right," the other put in. "You can call me Hy for short, and Shubert there would rather be called Shu, 'cause otherwise . . ."

"DID I ASK?"

"No, sir."

"Sorry, sir."

". . . AND DON'T CALL ME *SIR!!!* I ain't no freakin' *officer*! It didn't take a grant from the crown to make me a gentleman . . . I was *born* one!! *DO YOU UNDERSTAND ME???"*

"YES, SERGEANT!!"

"Drop down and give me twenty push-ups just so you won't forget!"

"Umm . . . is that ten from each of us, Sarge, or . . ."

"TWENTY EACH!" Smiley roared. *". . . AND AN-OTHER FIVE EACH FOR CALLIN' ME 'SARGE'! MY NAME IS SERGEANT SMILEY OR SERGEANT, NOT SARGE OR SIR! YOU GOT THAT, TROOPER??"*

"YES, SERGEANT!!"

"THEN *HIT IT!!"*

The two brothers drop down and start pumpin' out push-ups as the sergeant turns his attention back to his list.

"Shu Flie and Hy Flie! My aching back! My God! here's *another* one! **Spyder!**"

"Here . . . *Sarge.*"

Smiley's head comes up with a snap like he has been poked in the ribs . . . which, of course he has. The use of the improper address so soon after it was forbidden *might* have either been by mistake or from stupidity were it not for the deliberateness with which it was uttered. As it was, however, there was no mistaking it for what it was: A challenge to the sergeant's authority . . . which is to say, stupidity.

The challenger is a sight to behold. She probably would have stood out in the line in any case, bein' the only female-type in our group, though one might have had to look a couple times to notice, as she stood in a habitual slouch. Her hair, however, made her a real showstopper. Cropped to a medium, mane-type length, it was dyed . . . somethin' I do not normally speculate on regardin' a skirt until we is on very close acquaintance, after which time I am too much of a gentleman to share such information with anyone who is not. In this circumstantial, however, I feel free to make said assumption, as hair, whether attached to a male or female-type bod, does not naturally come in that color . . . or, to be entirely accurate, colors.

Stripes of pink, white, blue, and green run across this broad's head from front to back . . . and not in subtle tones. These colors glow with electric-type vibrancy like they are bein' fueled by her glower, which would be truly intimi- datin' if it were, perhaps, pasted on a homelier mug . . . like, say my own. It has been some time since Nunzio and I hung out on the streets, but it is clear the type of punks they are currently breedin' is a strain mutated noticeably from our early days when "colorful" referred to our lan- guage, *not* our hair!

"Well, well," the sergeant sez, lickin' his chops a bit, "what have we here? It seems we are to be a part of the army's experimental program which is specifically testing the truth in the saying that the only thing meaner than a fighting man of Possiltum is a woman! Now I want all you *men* to watch your language during training. We have a *laaaadyyyy* in our midst."

From the way the skirt bristles, it is clear she is not used to bein' referred to as a lady . . . and doesn't care much for the idea. Smiley isn't through with her, how- ever.

"Tell me, little lady, what *is* that you've got on your head? If it's something that crawled up there and died, I hope you've had your shots 'cause it doesn't look like it was any too healthy!"

"It's called 'hair,' *Sarge!* What do you have on *your* head?"

"It isn't what I've got on my *head* that's important, 'cruit," the sergeant smiles, "it's what's on my sleeve!"

He taps the stripes that mark his rank.

"Three up, three down. You know what that means?"

"That you're a Master Sergeant, *Sarge.*"

"Close, but no cigar. It means you owe me *fifteen push-ups, 'cruit. Five for each time you've called me 'Sarge.' Hit it!*"

I expect the skirt to give him an argument at this, but instead she just drops down and starts pumpin' out push- ups like it's what she has been after all along . . . and maybe it was. I don't know what kind of breakfast-type cereal this broad patronizes, but she is doin' a notably better job of rackin' up her push-ups than the Flie brothers.

"One . . . Two . . . Three . . ."

Smiley watches her for a few moments, then turns his attention to the other figures on the ground.

"YOU TWO! I said give me twenty-five!"

This last was, of course, directed to the Flie brothers.

"We're . . . trying . . . Sergeant!"

"WELL I CAN'T HEAR YOU! *COUNT 'EM OFF!!"*

"Seventeen . . . eighteen . . ."

"YOU DON'T START COUNTING AT SEVEN-TEEN!! YOU START COUNTING AT ONE!!! DO YOU THINK I'M DUMB?!!"

"No . . . Sergeant! . . . One . . . two . . ."

"Now *listen up* 'cause I'm only gonna say this once!" the sergeant barks, turnin' his attention back to the rest of us. "When I'm talking, your ears are open and your mouths are *shut!* You don't say nothin' 'less I ask you a question, whereupon you answer it *briefly* then *shut up!* When I want questions from you, I'll say 'Any questions?'! *Do I make myself clear!"*

"YES, SERGEANT!

"All right then." He started to look at his roster again, then glanced at the struggling figures on the ground. "That's enough, you three. Get back in line. Now then, where was I? Guido!"

"Here, Sergeant!" I sez, 'cause I was.

"That's it? Just 'Guido?' No nickname like Cricket or anything?"

"No, Sergeant!"

He waited for a few seconds to see if I was gonna add anything, but I didn't, as I've always been a fast study. Finally he gives a little nod and moves on.

"Juney!"

"Here, Sergeant! . . . but folks call me 'Junebug.' "

Some people, on the other hand, never seem to learn.

"Twenty!" the sergeant sez without even lookin' up from the roster.

And so it went. By the time the sergeant is through

checkin' off the list of names, over half of our group has been called upon to demonstrate their physical prowess, or lack thereof, by performin' a number of push-ups, the exact count of which varies dependin' upon the sergeant's mood and their ability to remember to count out loud whilst performin' this exercise. This raises some serious questions in my mind as to the average IQ of the individuals who have chosen to enlist in the army, a rather disquietin' thought realizin' that I am one of said individuals. In an effort to maintain a positive-type frame of mind, I reassure myself that my enlistin' was a matter of followin' orders rather than any idea of my own.

"All right, *LISTEN UP!*" the sergeant bellows, havin' finished with his roll call. "In about half an hour, Corporal Whittle will take you across camp and get your hair cut to conform with army standards."

The little shrimp who has been lurkin' in the background draws himself up to his full insignificant height and smiles at this. Now Sergeant Smiley is a rather imposin' dude, though a touch out of shape around the middle, but the corporal looks like he would fail the entrance requirements to be a meter-type maid. That is, he looks to be the unpleasant kind of wimp who only pulls wings off flies when he has enough rank to back him up. Lookin' at his smile, I begin to have serious misgivin's about these haircuts.

"In the meantime," the sergeant continues, "you have a period of unstructured time, during which you may talk, sleep, or get to know each other. I suggest you take maximum advantage of this, as it will in all probability be the last time you will have to yourself until your training is completed. Now, before I dismiss you, are there any questions?"

To my surprise, two individuals raise their hands. This is a surprise first of all because I thought that most individuals would be cowed into silence by the sergeant's performance thus far, and secondly because one of the hands belongs to none other than my cousin Nunzio!

"You!" Smiley says, pointin' at the closest questioner. "State your name and question."

"Bee, Sergeant. I . . . I think there's been a mistake on my enlistment."

The sergeant shows all his teeth.

"The army doesn't make mistakes, son . . . except, maybe one." He shoots a glance at Spyder, who ignores him this time. "What's your problem?"

"Well . . . I shouldn't be here. I enlisted as a magician, and my recruiter said that . . ."

The sergeant's smile widens sufficiently to stop the recruit in mid-sentence.

"Son," he sez, in a voice that's more like a purr, "it's time you learned one of the harsh truths about the army. *Recruiters lie!* Whatever that sorry soul told you, son, unless you got it in writing signed by the queen herself, it don't mean squat! Now *I'm* telling you that every 'cruit that signs onto this man's army *will* learn basic infantry skills before receivin' his first assignment before active duty. You *might* get assigned as a magician, or you might not . . . it all depends on whether they need magicians or cooks when your number comes up for assignment, but you aren't gonna get assigned *anywhere* until I say your basic training is complete. *Next question!*"

"Nunzio, Sergeant! How long does it take to complete basic training?"

"That depends on how long it takes you unfortunates to learn the minimal skills required for you to wear the uniform of Possiltum. Usually it takes a week to ten days . . . but from the looks of you sorry souls, I figure you'll have the pleasure of my company for at least a month."

"You mean none of us gets assigned until everyone in this group completes their training?"

"That's right. Any other questions?"

My cousin glances down the lines at me, but I keep my eyes straight forward, hopin' his action isn't noticed. Luckily the sergeant misses this little blip in the formation, and as soon as he dismisses us Nunzio and I go into a huddle.

"What do you think?" he sez, worried-like.

"Same as you," I shrug. "We sure can't take no month gettin' trained if we're gonna by any help upsettin' the regular troops."

"That's for sure," he nods. "Looks like we're gonna have to push these recruits a little ourselves to be sure they pick up this training in double-quick time."

This realization puts my mood at an all-time low. It was bad enough that I was gonna have to do time as a soldier-type, but now I was gonna have to play nursemaid and coach to a bunch of raw recruits as well!

III:

"Just a little off the top!"

—A. BOLEYN

The haircut turned out even more ghastly than I had feared in my worst nightmare-type dreams. I would be tempted to lay in wait and inflict a little instructional-type revenge upon the individual what laid said haircut on me, but it would probably do no good as he was obviously brain damaged at birth and can't help bein' like he is. Instead, I should be thankful that society has found a place for a person what has only learned one style of haircut where he can serve a useful purpose. Further, I suppose it is only logical that that place is in the army, where his "customers" have no choice but to put up with whatever haircut they are given. My only puzzlement is where they managed to find an entire room full of mental deficients who have all only learned the same haircut.

The haircut under discussion is unique in its lack of imagination and style, consistin' of simply removin' as much hair from the victim as possible through the vigorous application of a pair of clippers. If they lowered their aim another quarter inch or so, the job would qualify as a scalpin' rather than as a haircut. Now, I have nothin' against baldness, and know a couple hard-type wiseguys in the Mob what shave their heads to look especially mean. What we ended up with, however, was not enough hair to look stylish, but too much to look tough.

Now this in itself was annoyin', but the haircut in conjunction with the uniforms which was foisted off on us bordered on bein' intolerable. For those of youse which are fortunate enough not to have viewed the Possiltum army uniforms first hand, they consist of somethin' like a short-sleeved flannel nightshirt, which is worn under a combination breastplate and skirt made of hardened leather. That's right, a skirt. At least, I can't think of any other way to describe a bunch of leather strips hangin' down to about knee length with no semblance of legs built in. As a final insult, we was each issued a pair of sandals, which to my opinion did not even come close to replacin' the spiffy wing-tipped black and white shoes I normally favor.

The overall impression of our trainin' group once we had been shorn and uniformed, was that we looked like a pack of half-dressed department store mannequins waitin' to be fitted for wigs.

"Nunzio," I sez, surveyin' the damage what has been done to my hitherto head-turnin' image, "tell me again about how nothin' is too desperate when it comes to guardin' the Boss or carryin' out his orders."

Now, this is a mistake. While my cousin is a first-rate partner when it comes to rough and tumble, lurkin' in the depths of his sordid resumé is the fact that he did time as a schoolteacher for a while, and the lingerin' effect of that experience is that he has a tendency to deliver lectures on nearly any subject at the drop of a hat or a straight-type line.

"You just don't understand the psychology involved in converting civilians to soldiers, Guido," he sez in that squeaky voice of his that can be so irritatin' at times . . . like now. "Hair styles, like fashions in clothing, are dis-

tinctive marks of one's previous social and financial
standing. The whole idea of the haircuts and uniforms is
to reduce everyone to a common denominator, as well as
giving them a traumatic, but harmless, experience to
share, thereby encouraging bonding."

Normally, I would not dream of arguin' with Nunzio,
as I not only am inclined to lose, it only gives him an
excuse to prolong and embellish upon whatever half-
baked theory he is emotin' upon. This time, however, I
feels compelled to take umbrage with his assertions.

"Cousin," I sez, "can you look around at our fellow
unfortunates and tell me honestly that you can't tell who
comes from where without committin' such blatant perjury that even the most bought judge would have to call
youse on it?"

I mean, shorn and frocked as we are, it is still pretty
easy to spot who the players are and where they're comin'
from. The Flie brothers have that well muscled, robust
glow of health what only comes from puttin' so many
hours a day into farm work that doin' time in the army
has to look like a resort vacation to them. Bee, with or
without hair, looks like a fledgling geek, and as for the
Spyder broad . . . well, givin' a wolf a poodle cut doesn't
make it look like a show dog, just like a pissed off wolf!
It was clear to me that wherever that junior sociopath went
to school, it couldn't have been more than a block or two
from the alma mother what gave Nunzio and me our head
start on the other head bashers in the Mob.

As usually occurs, however, just when it looks like I'm
gonna finally win an argument with Nunzio, somethin'
intervenes to change the subject.

"Do you believe this?" the tough broad spits . . . literally . . . lettin' fly with an impressive jet of fluid from between her teeth to punctuate her anger. "Military Law!
It's bad enough that we have to put up with these haircuts
and flaky uniforms, but now we have to sit through lectures on crud like Military Law! When are they gonna get
around to teaching us something about fighting?"

This does not come as a particularly startlin' revelation

to me, as I have long suspected that Spyder did not enlist for the cultural-type benefits that the army offers. I am, however, more than a little taken with the distance she gets with her spittin'. It occurs to me that I haven't tried spittin' that way since Don Bruce promoted us and hinted strongly that we should class up our act a little, and, realizin' this, decide not to try to match her performance, as distance spittin' such as hers requires constant practice if one is to remain in form. For the educatin' of those of youse what has been raised too proper and upright to have ever experimented with this particular form of self-expression, let me caution youse against tryin' this for the first time in front of a critical audience. If your technique is anythin' less than flawless, the odds are that your effort will dribble down your chin and onto your shirt rather than arcin' away in the picturesque display you are expectin', leavin' the viewers with an impression of youse as a chump rather than whatever it was youse was tryin' to pass yourself off as.

All of this passes through my mind in a flash, as I am a fairly quick thinker despite the impression given by my size, whilst I am tryin' to think of an appropriate response to Spyder's kvetchin'. Nunzio comes up with somethin' before I do, however, as he is no slouch himself when it comes to thinkin' . . . particularly when there is a skirt involved.

"I think you should listen *real* close to what they tell us about Military Law, Spyder," he sez, "it'll pay some solid benefits in the long run."

"How so?"

"Well," he smiles, settlin' into his lecture voice again, "speaking from long personal experience, it is often much easier to continue doing exactly what you want to do right under the noses of authority if one is aware of exactly what those authorities consider to be antisocial behavior. When you stop to think about it, it's real nice of the army to give us official advance warning of exactly what rules they plan to enforce and, by exclusion, what is fair game. If they didn't, or we were dumb enough to sleep through

this particular lecture, the only way to figure out what
activities can be done openly and which should be per-
formed in ... shall we say, a less public manner, would
be to act blindly, then wait to see what they came down
on us for."

"Just how long is that 'personal experience,' fellah?"
one of the Flie brothers pipes up.

"Yeah, I was just wondering the same thing," the other
chimes in. "Aren't you two a little *old* to be joining the
army?"

Now, it is clear to me what is goin' on. The two farm
boys have been hopin' to put some moves on Spyder, but
then Nunzio gets in the way. Rather than backin' off like
any sane person would do, they was tryin' to score their
points by pickin' a fight with him. To say the least, I have
seen better plans to continue one's good health.

Of course, Nunzio can spot it too, and he knows that
we should be avoidin' any kind of trouble if we want to
complete our training quick instead of sittin' in the stockade for a few days. He also knows, however, that he is
bein' made to look like a fool in front of the only skirt
we is likely to be associatin' with for a while, and while
he has considerable tolerance at soakin' up abuse from a
boss what is payin' our wages and expenses, his ability
to put up with bein' hassled without blowin' his cool
drops in direct proportion to the standin' of the hassler in
the peckin' order, and the Flie brothers don't stand very
high at all.

"Are you boys sayin' you think we're too old to be any
good in a fight?" he sez, turnin' to face his critics while
flexin' his hands slightly.

If I didn't recognize the dangerous tone in his voice, I
could sure recognize that flexin' action of his as I was the
one who taught it to him in the first place, and figure I
had better step in before things get too messy.

"Before proceedin' with the discussion at hand," I sez,
"I think youse should all perhaps take notice of the attention which is bein' paid to our intellectual-type conver-

sation by the corporal who is standin' not twenty yards behind youse."

" 'Intellectual-type discussion'?" Shu brays, punchin' his brother on the arm. "What kind of talk is that, Old Man?"

"Paw told us big city folk talked kinda funny," Hy grinned, "but I ain't never heard *nobody* who sounds as weird as this guy."

"He's talked that way ever since he played one of the leads in 'Guys and Dolls' while we was in college," Nunzio sez, quick-like. "Beyond that, I strongly suggest you drop the subject."

That's when I realize that I have commenced to flex my own hands a bit . . . an action which has the tendency to make Nunzio nervous. While I am not particularly sensitive to callous or ignorant remarks about my size or how I'm gettin' older, I *can* get a little touchy if anyone tries to poke fun at how I talk. You see, I have spent considerable time perfectin' this particular style of expression as I feel it enhances my believability as a rough and tumble leg-breaker, thereby minimizing the number of times I have to actually partake of the violent-type actions which so offend and depress my sensitive soul. Therefore, anyone who tries to state or imply that talkin' like dis is easy or stupid is issuin' an invitation to waltz with me which would best be withheld unless his or her hospitalization insurance is substantial, detailed, and paid up. This is, of course, the very button the Flie brothers is tinkerin' with, and I find their efforts sufficiently clumsy as to require immediate instruction as to the error of their ways and perhaps a little behavioral adjustment. The fact that I am still annoyed over the haircuts and uniforms and sorta lookin' for someone to take it out on has completely nothin' to do with my reactions.

"Were you in that musical, too?" Junebug sez, unwittingly steppin' between us in his eagerness to start a conversation. He is a good-lookin' kid with the kind of soft, unblemished features usually associated with male fashion-type models. "I got to play Sky Masterson, myself. What was your major, anyway? I got my Bachelor's in Dance."

"BusAd . . . a Master's," I sez, tryin to ease around him.

Unfortunately he has given the Flie brothers a face-savin' out from the buildin' confrontation with Nunzio and me. Whether motivated by any native intelligence or simply saved by animal survival instinct, they switch their harassment to this new target without so much as pausin' for breath."

"A college man? . . . And a dancer! Ooooo! Did you hear that, Hy?"

"Sure did," his brother responds and commences to make kissey noises at Junebug. "No wonder he's so purdy."

"Leave him alone, you guys!"

This last comes from Spyder, who for some reason has seen fit to deal herself into the situational.

"Oh yeah?" Shu sneers, turnin' his attention toward this new front. "And who's going to make me?"

"If I have to, I will," Spyder shoots back.

"Oh yeah?"

"Yeah!"

"Well then, why don't you show us . . . OW!"

By now I have cooled off enough to take advantage of the situational as it presents itself. As they puff up and start to strut toward Spyder, the two brothers have thoughtlessly and rudely turned their backs on me. Before they can close on her, I have stepped in behind and between them, and dropped a friendly arm around their shoulders.

"Excuse me, Spyder," I sez with a smile, "but I need to have a few words with these boys in private whilst they are still able to stand and walk without the aid of crutch-type assistance. Right boys?"

"OW! . . . Right!"

"Yeah . . . Aaah! . . . Sure!"

The sudden cooperative nature of the Flie brothers is in no small way influenced by the fact that I have casually dug a thumb into the hollow of a collarbone on each of them and tend to tighten my grip another notch each time I asks them a question . . . regardless of how rhetorical it might be. The real trick to this maneuver, in case any of youse is interested in technical-type details, is not to loosen your grip once you start tightenin' it. That is, it isn't squeeze . . . release . . . squeeze . . . release . . . , it's squeeze . . . tighten . . . tighter . . . *grind*. . . . See what I mean? Now if, perhaps, youse have developed your grip to a point where you can crumble bricks with it . . . like I have . . . this will prove to be a most convincin' punctuation to the weakest of logic durin' a difference of opinion.

Anyhoo, returnin' to my oration, I draws the two brothers aside for a little chat, all the while keepin' a wary eye on the hoverin' corporal.

"Now, don't you think it would be a good idea for you boys to lighten up a little? (squeeze)" I sez softly so's we are the only ones who can hear. "There are two things you should be considerin' here. First, dis collection of individuals we is goin' through trainin' with constitutes a group, and within a group it is always better to be nice than nasty. With nice, you got friends who will cover your back in a fight . . . with nasty, youse gotta watch your back from them. You got that? (tighten)"

"Right, Guido!"

"OW! Sure Guido!"

"Good. Now second, I want youse to keep in mind that if you does *not* abandon your querulous habits, and those habits slow or otherwise interfere with this group completin' its trainin' in the shortest possible time . . ." I sneak a glance at the corporal, then lower my voice while takin' great pains to keep a smile on my face. ". . . then I will *personally* rip off each of youse guy's heads and spit down your neck! (tighter) You got that?"

"Gaah! Yeah! Got it!"

"Anything you . . . Owww . . . say, Guido!"

"Oh yeah. Just one more thing. I *don't talk funny.* (grind) Agreed?"

"Aaaahhh . . ."
"God . . ."

I noticed the corporal is comin' our way, thereby sig-
nalin' an end to our playtime.

"I'll take that as a 'yes,' " I sez, and releases my grip
all at once.

I have neglected to mention durin' my previous instruc-
tional oration that if youse relaxes the aforementioned grip
suddenly and completely, the resultin' rush of blood to
the area which has been assaulted by said grip causes
additional discomfort to a point where some subjects have
been known to faint dead away. The advantage of this is
obvious, in that you are not actually even touching them
at the moment the effect takes hold.

The Flie brothers are in exceptionally good shape, as I
have noted before, so they merely stagger a bit. It is clear
to them, however, as it is to me, that for a while they will
have extreme difficulty movin' their arms with any degree
of speed or strength . . . like say, in a fight. This, of
course, has the originally desired effect of mellowin' their
previously bullyin', swaggerin' behavior noticeably.

"What's going on here?" the corporal demands, burstin'
in on our little group.

I blinks innocent-like and gave him a helpless shrug
like he was a DA during cross examination.

"We was just discussin' the logical-type benefits of social over antisocial behavior in a group situational."

"Oh yeah? Is that right, you two?"

The Flies try to match my shrug, but wince halfway
through the gesture and have to resort to nods.

The corporal glares at us suspiciously for a few, then
turns to the rest of the group.

"All right, everybody form up in two lines!" he hollers
in a poor imitation of the sergeant. "It's time we move
out for the classrooms!"

"Did our agitators respond properly to applied logic?"
Nunzio murmurs, easin' up beside me.

"Sure did," I nods. "What's more, I think they got it

in one lesson. I don't know why you keep sayin' that youth today is slow learners."

He rolls his eyes at this and fakes a mock swing at me.

"Maybe we should start calling you 'Fly Swatter,'" he grins.

Some of the other recruits laugh at this, which makes me a tad nervous, as I know from the Mob just how easy it is to get saddled with a screwball nickname after some dumb incident or other. The corporal saved me the trouble of havin' to change the subject, however, as he chose that moment to start hollerin' and wavin' for us to get together for the next round of trainin'.

"Come on," I sez, bouncin' a punch off his arm that was notably harder than the one he had taken at me. "We gotta go learn how to be effective fighters."

IV:

"Squeeze, don't jerk, the trigger."

—R. ROGERS

Unfortunately, the "Fly Swatter" moniker Nunzio hung on me stuck . . . or at least the "Swatter" part did. What was even more discomfortin' was the fact that I got tagged by the sergeant to be Actin' Squad Leader for the little group of recruits I have already named, which is much of why I named them. This position consisted of nothin' more than playin' sheepdog for the "Bugs," as everyone seemed to take great delight in callin' 'em, while they was bein' herded from one trainin' session to another. Still, it was a leadership position, which, as I have earlier noted, I tend to avoid like I would a subpoena.

The stuff we had to learn as part of our basic-type trainin' wasn't really too bad, though. Most of the information they passed along was indeed necessary when considered as an overview, and it was presented simply, but with a real effort toward makin' it interestin' enough to hold the attention of us recruits. This was a pleasant change from my college profs, most of whom seemed to

feel they was the greatest experts on the most interestin'
subjects and that the students should feel lucky to pay
substantial hunks of money for the privilege of worshipin'
at their feet. What's more, they tested the loyalty of said
students on a regular basis by the simple process of
makin' the presentation dull enough to bore a stone and
seein' who managed to stay awake long enough to absorb
sufficient data to pass their finals.

The army, in direct contrast, started with the basic assumption that recruits would be totally ignorant and
couldn't care less about the subject at hand, unless it was
made interestin' enough to hold their predictably short
attention, often by graphically demonstratin' at a personal
level how vital said subject was to the continued functioning of their bodies.

(Out of courtesy to those of youse who are currently
investin' large hunks of your or your kid's time in college,
I will refrain on commentin' on which system I think is
better for passin' information, much less the actual life
value of that information which is bein' passed, and con-
fine myself to the simple observation that instruction in
the army is neither mindless nor lackin' in value. What's
more, *they* pay *you* while you're learnin'. Of course,
things might be quite a bit different if corporations other
than fast-food franchisers took it upon themselves to take
an active hand in the trainin' of their employees . . . but
that is a whole 'nother subject and a definite digression
from the subject at hand, which is army trainin'.)

For the most part, Nunzio and I had no complaints with
the lessons, and even found them uniquely informational.
As youse are probably aware, the Mob is big on individual
tactics or free-for-all-type brawls such as is usually the
case in ambushes, so learnin' to fight from formations was
a genuinely new experience for us. Of course, we had
some difficulty acceptin' that this would ever be of actual
use to us.

Firstus, as I have just so previously mentioned, bodyguardin' usually involves ambushes and what is known in
sports as "scramble defense," raisin' serious doubts in our

mind that formation fightin' would be utilizable in our civilian life after the service, seein' as how we would lack the warm-type bodies for such maneuvers, and it is doubtful those throwin' the surprise party would give us sufficient time to gather the necessary quantities of warm bodies, as the entire purpose of their ambush is to catch us with our tactical pants around our ankles.

Secondous, and more to the point, however, it was unclear how we was supposed to use these tactics while *in* the army. You see, at this point it was no secret that the army of Possiltum was the largest, best equipped force around, so few kingdoms or towns chose to buck the long odds by confrontin' them in the field where formation-type tactics would come into play. Consequentially, there was little actual fightin' goin' on when they moved into a new neighborhood, an any opposition offered was more on the order of covertous resistance of the stab-em-in-the-back or slit-their-throats-while-they're-asleep-type variety. As formations were of absolutely no use in dealin' with this kind of petty harassment, it was hard for us to understand why we was havin' to spend so much time learnin' about them.

Somehow, however, Sergeant Smiley neglects to ask our advice as to the content of his trainin' program, so we are spared the discomfort of havin' to figure out how to share our views with him without hurtin' his feelin's.

Similarly, when it is explained to us that we has to learn marchin' as it is "the best way to move a group of soldiers from one point to another in the shortest period of time," we are not given a chance to ask if the army in general or the sergeant in specific has considered the benefits of rapid transit.

While there are numerous points like this of dubious logic throughout our trainin' there is only one point which we take serious exception to. While we take great pains to keep this variation from army thinkin' from becomin' obvious, it finally escapes into the light of public notice one day while we are at the firin' range.

The army is havin' us train with crossbows . . . which

is understandable, as the trainin' time necessary for usin' a longbow with any degree of proficiency in a combat situational is considerable, thereby makin' it a dubious subject of study for basic trainin'. Slings is even worse, as until one has reached near expert familiarity with one, the best odds of inflictin' injury with this weapon is that of hangin' oneself with said weapon whilst tryin' to get the rock to fly somewhere near the general direction of the target. The most physically inept of klutzes, however can attain a minimal level of effectiveness with a crossbow in a single afternoon, which is doubtlessly why the army chose this particular weapon to introduce the recruits to the intricacies of projectile combat.

"You will notice that you will be firing at full sized, man-shaped targets for this exercise," Sergeant Smiley says, havin' already bellowed at length on range safety and proper handlin' of the weapons. "The army has chosen to have you train on these as opposed to bull's-eyes, as it will better prepare you mentally and emotionally to fire your weapon at a live opponent. At all times during this exercise, you will fix it in your minds that the dummy facing you is a live enemy who wants to kill you, and conduct yourselves accordingly. Do I make myself clear?"

"YES, SERGEANT!!"

The crew has this response down pat now . . . and it only took 'em a few days of trainin' to master it. Nunzio and me joins in at the proper cue, though there are some questions which could have been raised at this point.

For example, while the idea behind usin' these targets was interestin' and maybe even admirable, in all my years with the Mob I have never seen an opponent who would do you the favor of standin' rock-still, in the open, upright, with his shoulders square to you while he was tryin' to shoot you. They are more inclined to be crouched or flattened behind cover and movin' around whilst sendin' you the message, specifically to minimize the chances of your cancelin' their stamp before they reach the final salutation. In light of this, thinkin' you can shoot because you can pump arrows or quarrels into a straw dummy of any shape struck me as a dangerous case of over-confidence and not to be encouraged. I kept quiet about this, though, figurin' that this was only the first round to familiarize everybody with their weapons, and that the *serious* trainin' would be covered at a later date.

Soon, the crew is scattered along the firin' line, takin' turns sprayin' quarrels downrange whilst the sergeant and corporal prowl back and forth behind them, qualifyin' some and hollerin' at the slow learners. This is one managerial style I have noticed the army and the Mob have in common, which is to say the belief that if you shout loud enough at someone who is doin' somethin' wrong, they will respond by doin' it right.

Nunzio and me hang back from the first bunch of shooters, as we have little fear of passin' this particular test. We focus instead on how the rest of the crew is doin' so's we can help out the ones what is havin' trouble.

The Flie brothers are surprisingly good shots, each of them not only hittin' the target with every shot, but holdin' a shot group you can cover with a double handspan. Realizin' that the targets are close enough to hit with a rock, however, this display of marksmanship fails to impress me a great deal. Sergeant Smiley, on the other hand, seems genuinely pleased with their performance.

"Now *that's* how the army likes to see you handle those weapons!" he sez loud so's everyone can hear him. "Who taught you boys to shoot like that, anyway?"

"Our dad did," Shu Flie grins. "You may have heard of him. They call him Horse Flie."

"Mom can outshoot him, though," Hy Flie adds. "They call her Dragon Flie."

At this point, I stopped followin' the conversation, both because it was makin' my stomach hurt, and because Nunzio was beckonin' me to huddle up with him.

"We got problems," he sez, which wasn't surprisin', as knowin' him as well as I do I could see he was worried.

"Like what?"

"It's Spellin' Bee," he sez, which is what we've taken to callin' our junior magician. "I don't think he could hit the broadside of a barn if he was inside it."

I snuck a look over his shoulder, just in time to see Bee loose a quarrel which misses the target by fifteen feet, give or take a mile. The corporal was right there beside him, offering helpful suggestions at the top of his lungs.

"I see. Well, it's not like he's gonna do much shootin', what with him bein' a magician."

"Maybe not," Nunzio shrugs, "but we're *all* supposed to qualify today or the whole group gets held back ... remember?"

"That could be a problem," I nods. "Doesn't he have a spell or somethin' that could help him out?"

My cousin rolls his eyes and snorts, disgusted-like.

"Are you kidding? He only knows two spells, and neither of them are gonna be of any help to him on the firing line."

"Two spells? What are they?"

"Let's see, he knows Dispell, which lets him see through disguise spells."

"That's not much help," I admits. "What's his other spell?"

"Datspell," Nunzio grimaces, "which is nothing more than the disguise spell the Boss uses with a silly name."

"So all he can do is disguise himself and see through other disguises," I sez, turnin' it over in my mind.

"That's it. Nothin' that's gonna help him qualify today."

"Maybe ... maybe not," I sez, thoughtfully. "Tell you what. Is there any chance you can get him alone for a few minutes?"

"No problem. When he finishes blowin' this round, he'll have to wait to take another turn. I can get him then. Why? You got an idea?"

"Uh-huh," I grins. "Just convince him to use his disguise spell ... what does he call it? Oh yeah, Datspell ... so's you can change places. Then *you* qualify for him, you switch back, and no one will be any the wiser."

"I dunno," Nunzio sez, rubbin' his chin. "We might be able to fool the corporal, but the sergeant there's a pretty sharp cookie. He might spot there's somethin' different about the Bee."

"I'll take care of distractin' the sergeant when the time comes. Just be careful not to shoot *too* good . . . just good enough to qualify. Got it?"

Then there isn't much to do whilst waiting for the plan to unfold. Finally the corporal gets fed up with shoutin' at our young magician and sends him off the line for a "break" until he has rested his voice a bit.

Tryin' not to pay too much attention, I watch out of the corner of my eye while Nunzio drapes an arm around Bee's shoulder and begins to talk to him in an earnest-type fashion, all the while leadin' him casually behind the weapon storage tent and out of general sight. After what seems like an intolerably long time, "Bee" re-emerges, walkin' in a rollin' stride that is very familiar to me, and I know the power of reason and logic has triumphed again. I wait until he is steppin' up to the firin' line for yet another try, then commence to create a diversion.

"You're tryin' too hard, Spyder," I sez, loud-like, step-pin' up behind that notable where she is standin' at the far end of the firin' line from "Bee."

Both Spyder and Junebug are sporadic in their marks-manship, keepin' their shots in the vicinity of the target, but only hittin' it occasionally.

"You're keepin' your left arm way too tense . . . you gotta loosen up a little and just cradle the weapon in your hand. Ease up on the trigger, too. Just use the tip of your finger instead of tryin' to wrap it all the way around the trigger. Otherwise, you'll pull your shot off to the left every time you squeeze off a round."

"Like this?"

"Yeah, only . . ."

"WHAT THE HECK YA THINK YOU'RE DOIN??!!"

It should have been gratifyin' to know that I was correct in my appraisal of Sergeant Smiley's boilin' point. Up until now, Nunzio and me have been real careful to do our coachin' of the other recruits out of his sight and hearin', so's not to conflict with the authority-type image he is workin' so hard to maintain. I figure that this open display will not sit well with him, and this figurin' proves to be dead on target. I should be glad, but as he comes stompin' toward me I have to fight off the sneakin' feelin' that this has not been the wisest tactic to pursue.

"Guido was just giving me some pointers on handling this thing, Sergeant," Spyder sez, innocent-like, her polite manners a testimony to her hard learned lessons that Smiley is not someone to hassle unnecessarily.

"Oh, so now the Bug Swatter's an expert on crossbows, is he?" the sergeant snarls, puttin' the crosshairs on me. "Thinks he's better'n me or the range instructors at teaching marksmanship, does he?"

While trackin' this with great attention, I nonetheless see over his shoulder that Nunzio, disguised as Bee, is firin' his qualifyin' round . . . right under the nose of the corporal, who is more interested in watchin' the sergeant and me than in payin' attention to what's happenin' at his end of the range.

"Why don't you just show us how good you are with this weapon, *acting* Squad Leader Guido," Smiley sez, snatchin' the crossbow away from Spyder and thrustin' it at me. "*If* you can qualify, then *maybe* I won't bust you back into the ranks."

Now I have been threatened by experts . . . literally . . . so this effort by the sergeant fails to generate in me the obviously desired nervousness. If anything, I am tempted to deliberately blow these shots, thereby gettin' myself off the leadership-type hook which, as I have noted earlier, I am not particularly happy to be danglin' from. Still, my professional abilities have been openly challenged . . . and in front of a skirt, even if it's just Spyder. Besides, Nunzio has now finished qualifyin' for Bee, so there is no incentive to prolong this diversion any longer.

I spare the crossbow no more than a cursory glance, havin' a weak stomach when it comes to substandard weapons. It is obviously the work of government contractors, and bears the same resemblance to the custom weapons from Iolo that I normally use that a plow horse bears to a thoroughbred. Ignorin' this, I holds a quarrel in my mouth while cockin' the crossbow by puttin' the butt in my stomach and jerkin' the string back with both hands (which is quicker'n usin' the foot stirrup to do the same thing), drop the quarrel into the groove ahead of the drawn string, and squeeze off a quick shot down range.

Not surprisin'ly, the missile *thwacks* into the dummy's right shoulder.

"A bit lucky, but not bad," Smiley sez, grudgin'-like. "You'd get better accuracy, though, if you shot from the shoulder instead of the hip. Trying to show off will only . . ."

By the time he gets this far in his critique, I have recocked, reloaded, and loosed a second shot . . . again workin' from the hip.

This shot hisses into place not more than two finger widths from the first.

The sergeant shuts his mouth so fast you can hear his teeth click together, which is fine by me, and watches in silence whilst I snap a third shot off that makes a neat triangle with the first two.

"Pretty sloppy," comes the sneerin' squeak of Nunzio, as he joins our group, free of his disguise now. "I warned you that crushing stuff with your hands was gonna ruin your touch for a trigger!"

"Izzat so!!??" I snaps, more than a little annoyed at havin' my handiwork decried. "Let's see you do better with this thing!"

I lob the crossbow to him, which he catches with one hand, then squints at the bindings.

"Government contractors," he sez in the same tone he uses to announce he's stepped in somethin' organic and unpleasant. "It sure ain't Iolo's work!"

"The quarrels are about as straight as a barroom pool cue, too," I sez, givin' him the rest of the bad news. "But like the Boss sez: 'Ya does the best ya can with what ya got.' Right?"

He makes a face at me, then snaps off his three shots, also shootin' from the hip. I notice that even though he works the dummy's other shoulder to avoid confusion, his groupin' is not a noticeable improvement over mine.

"Okay, it's the weapon . . . *this* time," he admits, handin' the crossbow back to Spyder. "If we were working a longer range, though, I still think . . ."

"Just a minute, you two!"

We turns our attention to the sergeant, both because he sounds upset over somethin', and because we've been havin' this particular argument for years, so it's doubtful we would have resolved anythin' even if we had continued the discussion uninterrupted.

"What are you trying to pull, here?"

"What's wrong, Sergeant?" Nunzio sez, expressin' the puzzlement we both is feelin'. "Two out of three hits qualifies, right?"

"What's wrong?" Smiley smiles, showin' too many teeth for comfort. "Shot groupings like those mean you've both got excellent control of your weapons. Now, correct me if I'm mistaken, but doesn't that also mean you could have put those groupings anywhere on the target you wanted?"

"Well, sure . . . Sergeant."

"So how come you shot the dummy in the shoulders instead of in the head or chest?"

"That would kill him," I sez before I've had a chance to think it through.

"YOU'RE SUPPOSED TO KILL HIM! THAT'S WHAT BEIN' A SOLDIER IS ALL ABOUT!!!"

Now, in hindsight I know I shoulda' gone along with him, but he caught me by surprise, and my old Mob-type habits cut in.

"What kinda cheap barroom shooters do you take us for??" I barks right back at him. *"Me and Nunzio is professionals!! Any jerk can kill somebody, but it takes SKILL to leave 'em in a condition where they can still pay protection . . . OR give you information . . . OR . . ."*

"What my cousin *means* to say," Nunzio sez, steppin' between us quick-like, "is that wounding an enemy takes *three* opponents out of the action instead of just one, since someone's got to help him get back to . . ."

It was a good try, but too late. The sergeant was still into takin' me on.

"Are you calling the trained soldiers of Possiltum jerks?" he hollers, steppin' around Nunzio to come at me again. *"What are you? Some kind of PACIFIST?"*

"What . . . did . . . you . . . call . . . me . . . ?" I sez in my softest voice, which I only use on special occasions.

The trainin' area around us suddenly got real quiet and still . . . except for Nunzio who gave a disbelievin' whistle through his teeth as he stepped back.

Somethin' in my voice or the way I was drawin' myself up to my full height must have triggered the sergeant's survival instinct, 'cause all of a sudden he looked around nervous-like as if he were tryin' to find an emergency exit door.

"WHAT ARE YOU ALL DOING JUST STANDING AROUND??!!!" he bellows, turnin' his attention from me to the crowd which has gathered around us. *"YOU'RE SUPPOSED TO BE QUALIFYING!! MOVE IT!!! NOW!!!"*

This interruption gives me time to get my temper under control, and, after coolin' down a bit, I decide it is just as well the episode has drawn to a close. It seems, however, that the sergeant has a few last words for me.

"Guido!" he sez, just loud enough for me to hear, not lookin' me in the face.

"Yeah, Sergeant?"

"This isn't the time or the place, but we *will* continue this discussion . . . later."

The way he said it, it wasn't a challenge or a threat . . . just a statement.

V:

*"When I travel, nobody knows me . . .
and I like it that way!"*

—S. KING

Nunzio and me was tryin' to figure out what it was they had put on our plates under the laughin' title of "dinner," when Spyder plops down next to us. We're a little surprised at this, as we're normally left to ourselves when dinin', but the reason for her forwardness is not long in comin'.

"You guys are with the Mob, aren't you," she sez, without so much as a "Hello" or "Nice evening."

Now, way back in the intro, I mentioned that we are not real big on bein' asked questions in general, and this specific question is a definite no-no.

"Are you a cop?" Nunzio shoots back, automatic-like.

This is a "Must Learn" question for anyone whose livelihood depends on extra-legal activities, as if one asks it of a cop, however undercover they might be, they have to acknowledge their profession. Otherwise, any attempt to use the followin' conversation as evidence is dismissed as entrapment.

"Me? Are you kidding? No, I'm not a cop. Why do you ask?"

"Why do you want to know if we're in the Mob?" Nunzio shoots back.

You will notice that at this point, Spyder has answered our question, but we have not yet given a "yea" or "nay" to hers. Like I say, one has an inclination toward caginess in our line of work. Maybe it's a habit resultin' from our regular and prolonged discussions with DAs and Grand Juries.

"I've been thinking of trying to join up with them once I get out of the army," she sez with a shrug. "I thought maybe you guys could give me a little information about what it's like workin' for the Mob, if not give me a recommendation or at least a contact."

"Connection."

"What's that, Swatter?"

"I said 'Connection.' In normal business you have contacts. In the Mob, the first step is to get 'connected.'"

". . . Or so we've heard," Nunzio sez quick-like, givin' me one of his dirty looks. "I dunno. We might be able to share a few rumors with you. What do you want to know?"

As you can see, my cousin is still bein' cautious, havin' less faith than I do in a "hearsay" defense. With his "rumor" gambit, however, he has opened the door for us to answer a few questions 'bout the Mob *without* actually admittin' to any affiliation on our part.

"Well, what's it like?"

"The hours are lousy," I sez.

". . . And the retirement plan leaves a lot to be desired," Nunzio adds.

". . . But the pay's good. Right?" Spyder urges.

I have mentioned before that my cousin has few loves greater than the desire to lecture, and this chick has just pushed one of his favorite buttons. While he does not relax completely, he defrosts a bit.

"Not as good as you'd think from what the media says," he squeaks. "You see . . . remember what Guido said a second ago about being connected? Well, for a long time, when you first join the Mob, you actually have to pay us . . . strike that . . . *them* instead of the other way around."

"How's that again?"

"It's easier to understand if you think of it as a franchise system. The Mob gives you permission or license to operate, and you give them a share of your profits. You have to give a percentage, say half, to the guy over you, who in turn has to split with the guy over him, and so on right up to the top. Of course, the guys at the top pull down a bundle, since there's a whole pyramid under them feeding 'em percentages."

"Wait a minute!" Spyder frowns. "The last time I heard something like this, they were trying to get me to sell cosmetics . . . or was it cleaning products?"

"There are similarities," Nunzio agrees. "But there are some major differences, too."

"Like what?"

"Like the cosmetic pyramids don't break your face or your legs if you try to operate independently," I sez.

"What I was going to say," Nunzio sez, glarin' at me, "was that the cosmetic chains don't supply you with lawyers, much less alibis, if the authorities take offense at your activities . . . or your tax reports."

"Oh yeah?" I bristles, gettin' a little fed up with Nunzio's know-it-all attitude. "Well the soapsy folks don't whack you if they think you're shortin' them on their take, either!"

"Well what do you expect 'em to do?" he snaps right back at me. "Have 'em arrested?"

"What's with you, Swatter?" Spyder sez, cockin' her head at me. "You sound like you're really down on the Mob."

"He's just a little edgy," Nunzio puts in quick before I can answer myself. "We were having a bit of an argument when you joined us."

"Oh, I'm sorry," she blinks, poppin' to her feet. "I didn't know I was interrupting anything. I can catch you guys later. Just think about what I was asking, okay?"

We watch her walk away, which is a real treat, as feminine company has been notably lackin' since we started our trainin'. Then Nunzio turns to me.

"Okay. What's eating you?"

"The same thing that's been eatin' me since the Boss sent us on this assignment," I sez. "Talkin' about the Mob makes it harder than usual to ignore. Know what I mean?"

"We wasn't assigned, we volunteered."

"We was *asked* to volunteer by the Boss, which for us is the same as bein' ordered."

Nunzio heaves one of his big sighs and droops a little.

"I guess we might as well have this out right now," he grimaces. "You're talking about us being here in Possiltum right?"

"I'm talkin' about us declarin' war on the Mob," I corrects. "Seein' as how we're currently holdin' the bag at ground zero, this is of some concern to me. Sorry, but I tend to get a bit nervous about overwhelmin'-type firepower when it is apt to be directed at me . . . especially when all we've got is government issue crossbows . . . and leather skirts for armor!"

If, perhaps, this concern of mine has taken youse by surprise, allow me to enlighten youse, startin' with a brief history lesson. For those of youse already aware of the danger cousin Nunzio and I are in, however, feel free to skip to the next asterisk-type punctuation mark.

Nunzio and me first met the Boss about five books back [*Hit or Myth* (Myth Adventures #4)] when we was assigned to tag along with one of the Mob's mouthpieces whilst he was looking for the same Big Julie we was conversin' with in the first chapter. To be more precise, he was lookin' for the army which Big Julie was supposed to have been leadin' in a little fund-raisin' venture for our organization, and which, accordin' to reports, had disappeared into thin air after encounterin' a bit of resistance led by the Boss. Of course, in those days we didn't call him the Boss as we weren't workin' for him at the time. All we knew was that there was some bad news-type sorcerer named Skeeve the Great givin' the Mob grief and we was supposed to keep him off Shyster's back whilst the investigation progressed.

In the interest of brevity not to mention the preservin' of our royalty income from the backlist of this series, I will refrain from narratin' all the intriguin' details of that assignment. What is crucial that you understand, however, is that at the conclusion of that first encounter, a deal was struck between the Great Skeeve and Don Bruce, the Mob's Fairy Godfather. By the terms of that agreement, Don Bruce and the Mob was to lay off the Kingdom of Possiltum in general and Big Julie and his boys specifically, in exchange for the Great Skeeve givin' the Mob access to another dimension . . . to wit, Deva, complete with its rather famous bazaar.

Shortly thereafter, Don Bruce hired the Great Skeeve to oversee the Mob's interests on Deva, and assigned Nunzio and me to him as bodyguards . . . which is when we started callin' him Boss.

With me so far?

Okay, now review the circumstantials with me again, and see if youse can understand the dilemma facin' us.

First of all, the Boss is working for the Mob.

Second, he has sent us to deal with the situation in Possiltum while he goes after Aahz.

Now, as he works for the Mob and we all work for him, the entire strike force which is currently movin' on Queen Hemlock can be considered to be in the employment of the Mob.

Unfortunately, there is a deal in effect, one personally negotiated by Don Bruce himself, which says that no one in the Mob is to move against Possiltum! This means that our current operation is in direct violation of Don Bruce's sworn word . . . and while I can't say that notable has never gone back on his word, to do so is a decision he usually reserves for himself personally and tends to get

more than a little peeved when someone else undertakes
to break his word for him.

As you may have noted from followin' whatever type
of media is in vogue where you're readin' this, when
someone of Don Bruce's level in the Mob gets peeved, it
is not usually expressed by an angry memo. If he feels
his position or authority in the Mob is bein' challenged
by some overly frisky underling, his usual response is to
squash said underling like a bug. Of course, in our position as bodyguards to the Boss, this places us between the
Squasher and the Squashee, resultin' in the edginess I was
referrin' to a couple pages back which necessitated this
explanation.

Understand now? If not, just trust me that I know more
about these things than youse, and that our whole crew
will be in trouble with the Mob when and if Don Bruce
finds out what we're doin'.

"I've been giving it a lot of thought," Nunzio sez like
he never left the conversation, which of course, he
hadn't, "and I'm not sure the Boss *knows* he's crossing
Don Bruce by sending us back here."

Now this set me back on my heels a bit. I had been
assumin' all along that Skeeve sendin' us here was a premeditated move. The idea that he might be ignorant of
the consequentials of this action had never occurred to
me.

"How do you figure that?"

"Well, the way I see it, the Boss is a real sharp cookie . . .
except in two areas: the Mob, and broads."

"That's true," I sez, 'cause it was. While I have nothin'
but the highest regard for the Boss overall, in those two
areas he tends to be what we refer to in the Mob as "dumb
as a stone."

"Also," Nunzio continues, "there's the fact that he
didn't consult with us about the advisabilities of startin'
a ruckus with the Mob, or even warn us to be careful of
anything except Hemlock . . . which is not like him at all

if he was expecting trouble from Don Bruce."

Again he has hit on a valid point. Skeeve has easily been the most considerate Boss we have ever worked with and has always been sensitive to our feelin's . . . especially those which is attached to parts of us which bleed or break. This has a lot to do with the loyalty and genuine affection we hold for him . . . along with his pay scale which is both generous and dependable.

"Now that you mention it," I sez, "it wouldn't make much sense for the Boss to get into a power struggle or try to take over from Don Bruce, as he has never expressed any interest in or desire to elevate his standin' in the Mob."

Nunzio shrugged. "If that were his inclination, all he'd have to do is marry Bunny and let Don Bruce hand him the whole organization on a platter as an inheritance."

He is referrin' to the fact that not only is Bunny Don Bruce's niece, she is head over heels in love with the Boss . . . somethin' which seems to have escaped his notice entirely. Like we said earlier . . . The Mob and broads . . . Stone stupid.

"You may be right . . ."

"Of course I'm right! It all fits!"

". . . But even if you are, I'm not sure what difference it makes," I finish, ignoring his rude interruption. "Whether we're breakin' Don Bruce's word by accident or on purpose, we will still be in the line of fire when that notable decides to put things right."

"The difference is that if we assume the Boss *doesn't* want trouble with Don Bruce, we aren't obligated to stand and fight. More specifically, we're free to try to act as peacemakers between the two of them before blood starts to flow."

This reasonin' has a certain appeal to it, particularly as if said blood does indeed begin to flow, the odds are that it will be the two of us at the source of said flow.

"Okay," I sez. "*Assumin'* that you're right about the Boss not wantin' trouble, and *assumin'* that Don Bruce lets you get a word in edgewise before the shootin' starts, what are you gonna say to cool him down?"

"That part," Nunzio hesitates, ". . . that part I'm still working on."

It occurs to me that until my cousin comes up with a surefire sales pitch to settle things, all that takin' a peace-maker role is accomplishin' is committin' us not to shoot back when the trouble starts!

VI:

"Boards don't hit back!"

—B. LEE

Pre-inhabited as I was with my worries about Don Bruce and the Mob, the altercation between Sergeant Smiley and myself slipped my mind completely. As it turned out, however, this did not matter, as the sergeant took steps to remind me of it, and the way it was sprung on me, it wouldn't have done me no good to have used up a lot of time and energy thinkin' about it.

We had reached the portion of our trainin' in which we was to learn how to relate to the enemy at close quarters ... preferably without surrenderin'. That is to say, hand-to-hand type combat.

Sergeant Smiley was teachin' this section himself, which did not strike me as odd until later, as he obviously had more than passin' familiarity with the techniques we was to learn. He homed in on the Flie brothers as his demonstrator/victims, and had great fun showin' us all that size was not a factor in hand-to-hand combat by tossin' and punchin' 'em both around with impressive ease . . . or, put differently, he really made them fly.

While all this was great fun to watch, I could not help thinkin' that the lesson he was attemptin' to drive home stank higher than the "Realistic Doggie Doodle with Life-like Aroma that Actually Sticks to Your Hands" that I was so familiar with. I mean, I wonder if he really thought he was foolin' anyone with his "size doesn't make a dif-ference" spiel. It doesn't take a genius to figure out that size can make a *considerable* difference in a physical-type difference of opinion, as one honest to goodness fight will usually demonstrate this fact clearly enough to convince even the dimmest of wits. The only time skill triumphs over size is if the little guy is *very* skillful and the big guy is very *unskillful* . . . not to mention slow and maybe has a glass jaw. If they are at all matched for skill, the big guy is a good bet to make strawberry jam of the little guy if he is so inclined. This is why professional contact, sport-type athletes, not to mention kneecappers like Nun-zio and me, are on the extra-large side. It isn't because our employers figure we are cheaper if cost justified on a "by the pound" rate, it's because we tend to win.

Of course, even if one accepts the "skill over size" con-cept, there is still a glarin' flaw in the sergeant's logic. Remember how long I said it would take to train someone with a longbow? (No, this isn't gonna be a test . . . I was just askin'.) Well, it takes even longer to train someone to be skillful at Hand-To-Hand. A *lot* longer. The idea that someone like the Spellin' Bee could absorb enough skill in one afternoon to be effective against one of the Flie brothers, *however* unskilled, is laughable. Realizin' this, it was clear to me that even though he *said* we was bein' prepared for combat with the enemy, all he was doin' was showin' us a few tricks to help us survive the inevitable barroom type brawls which seem to naturally gravitate toward people in uniform who are tryin' to have a quiet drink around civilians durin' their off-duty hours. Simply put, we was bein' trained to deal with unskilled civilian-type fighters, preferably blind staggerin' drunk, rather than against skilled soldier-type fighters in the field.

"*. . . Of course, these are techniques which will enable you to dispatch an unarmed opponent!*" Sergeant Smiley was sayin', which was again misleadin' as none of the countermoves he was demonstratin' were lethal enough to "dispatch" anyone, confirmin' my belief that *someone* was figurin' we'd only use them on civilians.

"*. . . To deal with an ARMED opponent, however, is a different matter entirely! Fortunately, we have an EXPERT with us to demonstrate how that is done! GUIDO! Front and center!*"

"Me, Sergeant?" I blinks, as I had not expected to be called upon.

"That's right," the sergeant sez, showin' some extra teeth in his smile. "At the firing range you made a big point that only jerks have to kill people. Well, here's your chance to show everybody how to 'gentle' an enemy into submission when he's trying to kill you."

Needless to say, I don't care for the sounds of this, but as I have been summoned, I have little choice but to step forward into the clear space bein' used for the demonstrations. My discomfort grows as the sergeant gestures to Corporal Whittle, who tosses him a short sword. That's right, a real short sword . . . with a point and sharpened edges.

"What's with the sword, Sergeant?" I sez.

"I *said* this was going to be a demonstration against an armed opponent," he grins. "What we're going to do is I'm going to try to kill you, and you're going to try to stop me without killing me."

". . . And if I don't?"

"Then I guess we'll have us a little 'training accident' . . . unless, of course, you'd rather just back out now and admit you can't do it."

Needless to say, I did not obtain my current lofty position as bodyguard by backin' away from fights. What's more, the sword wasn't my real worry as it is nothin' more than a long knife, and I've dealt with knives often enough.

"Oh, I can do it," I shrugs. "The trouble is it might

involve striking a non-commissioned officer . . . which I seem to recall from our Military Law lesson is a no-no."

The sergeant's smile fades a bit, and I realize he has been expectin' me to withdraw from this exercise when he feeds me the cue. Unfortunately for both of us, this realization comes a little late to do us any good.

"Don't worry about that, 'Cruit,' " he sez, though I notice his voice has gotten tighter. "Even if you get *real* lucky and tag me, you're acting under orders so no charges will be brought."

That was all I needed to hear. As a last precaution, I glance back at Nunzio where he's standin' in line, and he gives me a little nod with his head.

"Your cousin can't help you now, Guido," Smiley snaps, regainin' a bit of confidence. "This is between you and me."

That wasn't why I was checkin' with Nunzio, but I have no trouble goin' with the flow, bein' real adaptable when the music is startin' and I am one of the designated dancers.

"I was just wonderin'," I sez with a shrug. "It's nice to know *you* know I'd be under orders. The question is whether or not that officer knows it."

Now the sergeant is no dummy and I really don't expect him to fall for the old "there's someone behind you" gag . . . but he does. It isn't until much later that I find out non-coms have a real thing about officers. That is, they are comfortable runnin' the army . . . unless there is an officer somewhere in witnessin' range. Anyway, Smiley starts cranin' his neck around tryin' to spot the officer to which I am referrin', and when his head is turned away from me, I glide in on him.

If this tactic sounds a little strange to you, realize that if someone waves a sharpened hunk of metal at you, the last thing they are expectin' is for you to charge them. What you are *supposed* to do is freeze up, or better yet run, thereby givin' them ample leisure time to carve their initials on whatever portion of your anatomy is handiest. When you move forward instead of back, it tends to startle them, and they usually react by pokin' at you with their weapon to try to get you to back off like the script says. This is really what you want, as it has put *you* in control of their attack and lets you bring it in where and when you want it instead of just standin' and hopin' they'll go away while they play around on their own timetable.

The sergeant sees me comin' out of the corner of his eye, and, just like I expect, he sticks his sword out like he's hopin' I'll run into it and save him the trouble of havin' to plan and execute an attack of his own. This makes it easy for me to weave past his point and latch on to the wrist of his sword arm with my left hand, which keeps the weapon out of mischief and me, whilst I give him a medium strength pop under the ear with my right fist.

It was my genuine hope that this would end the affair without further waltzin', but the sergeant is still a pretty tough old bird and it only crosses his eyes and drops him to one knee. I realize the situation has just become dangerous, as he still has hold of his sword and in his dazed condition may not remember that this is only an exercise . . . if that was his original intention at all.

"Give it up, Sarge," I hisses quiet-like, steppin' in close so's only he can hear me. "It's over."

Just to be on the safe side I wind his arm up a little as I am sayin' this to prove my point. Unfortunately, he either doesn't hear me or chooses to ignore what you must admit is excellent advice, and starts strugglin' around tryin' to bring his sword into play.

"Suit yourself," I shrugs, not really expectin' a response, as at that moment he faints, mostly because I have just broken his arm . . . for safety sake, mind you. (For the squeamish readers, I will hasten to clarify that this is a clean break as opposed to the messier compound variety, and that it probably wouldn't have put the sergeant out if he hadn't been woozy already from the clout I have just laid on him. As I have noted before, *controlled* violence is my specialty . . . and I'm *very* good at it.)

"WHAT ARE YOU DOING TO . . ."

These last words come from Corporal Whittle who has come alive far too late and tries to intervene after the dance is already done. The incomplete nature of his question is due to the fact that, as he is steppin' forward, he runs into a high swing from Nunzio's elbow goin' in the opposite direction, which effectively stretches him out on his back and turns his lights out . . . and also stops his annoyin' prattle. For the record, this is what the earlier exchange between Nunzio and me was all about . . . my makin' sure he was in position and willin' to cover my back while I dealt with the sergeant.

There is a moment's silence, then someone in the ranks lets out a low, surprised whistle, which seems to cue everyone to put in their two cents worth.

"Wow!"

"Nice goin', Swatter!!"

" 'Bout time someone taught him to . . ."

Hy Flie starts nudgin' the corporal's nappin' form with his toe.

"They don't look so big lying down, do they, Swatter?" he grins, like he took the two of 'em out all by himself.

"AT EASE! ALL OF YOUSE!!" I bellows, cuttin' the discussion off short. "If you touch that man again, Hy, you and I are gonna go a couple rounds. YOU UNNER-STAND ME??"

He looks surprised and hurt, but nods his agreement.

"I can't hear you!!!"

"YES, SAR . . . *I mean,* GUIDO!!"

"THAT GOES FOR THE REST OF YOUSE TOO!" I snarls. "I DON'T WANT TO SEE YOU KICKIN' EI-THER OF THESE TWO, *OR* MAKIN' FUN OF THEM *UNLESS* YOU'RE WILLIN' TO DO THE SAME THING WHEN THEY'RE AWAKE AND ABLE TO HIT BACK. *DO I MAKE MYSELF CLEAR??"*

"YES, GUIDO!!!"

As might be noticed in my manner, I am a bit annoyed at this point, but mostly with myself. I am genuinely irked that I was unable to squelch the sergeant's move without havin' to break his arm, and am quite willin' to take my anger out on the crew. If my speech pattern when addressin' my colleagues seems uncharacteristic, it is because I discovered quickly that the army's non-coms have a point . . . it *is* the easiest way to shout at an entire formation at the same time.

"Okay, now LISTEN UP!! As Actin' Squad Leader, I am the rankin' individual present until such time as the sergeant and corporal regain consciousness. I want one volunteer to get a medic for these two, while the REST OF US CONTINUE WITH THE TRAININ' EXERCISE!!"

This strikes me as the logical course to follow, as I am not eager to lose a day's trainin' whilst waitin' for our non-coms to wake up. At this point, however, I notice my cousin has raised his hand politely for my attention.

"Yes, Nunzio? Are you volunteerin' to go for a medic?"

"Not really, *Acting Squad Leader* Guido, sir," he sez, sarcastic-like. "I was just thinking that, before you assumed command, it might be wise for you to check in with the officer over there who is the ranking individual present."

Now, as youse will recall, when I pulled this gag on the sergeant, it was a ploy to divert his attention. I've played Dragon Poker with Nunzio though, and I can tell when he's bluffin' . . . and this time he wasn't. With a sinkin' feelin' in my stomach, I turn to look in the direction he is pointin'. Sure enough, there is an officer there, the first I have seen outside of our lectures. What is worse, he is comin' our way with a real grim look on his face.

"**S**tand easy, Guido."

I switch from Attention to At Ease, which is not to say I am at ease at all. I have been summoned to the Officer's Tent, which is not surprisin' as it is obvious I am gonna take some kinda flack for the afternoon's skirmish. What does take me off guard is that Sergeant Smiley is there as well, sportin' a sling for his arm and a deadpan expression.

"Sergeant Smiley here has given me his version of what's been going on with your training group that led up to the event I witnessed this afternoon. Would you like to tell me your side of the story?"

"I'm sure the sergeant's account is complete and accurate . . . sir," I sez, crisp-like.

Normally, I would have just clammed up until I had a lawyer, but so far no charges have been mentioned, and I somehow don't think this is a good time to make waves.

"Very well," the officer nods. "In that case I feel compelled to follow the sergeant's recommendation in this case."

It occurs to me that maybe I should have offered up some defense, but it is too late now, as the officer has already swung into action. Pickin' up a quill, he scribbles his name across the bottom of a series of papers that have been sittin' on his desk.

"Do you know what an army that's been growing as fast as ours needs the most, Guido?" he sez as he's writin'.

I start to say "Divine Intervention," but decide to keep my mouth shut . . . which is just as well as he proceeds to answer his own question.

"Leadership," he sez, finishin' his signin' with a flourish of his quill. "We're always on the lookout for new leaders . . . which is why I'm so pleased to sign these orders."

For a change, I have no difficulty lookin' innocent and dumb, as he has totally lost me with his train of thought.

"Sir?"

"What I have here are the papers promoting you to sergeant and Nunzio . . . he's your cousin, isn't he? . . . to corporal."

Now I am really lost.

"Promotions, sir?"

"That's right. Sergeant Smiley here has told me how the two of you have taken it on yourselves to lead your squad during training . . . even to the point of giving them extra training during off-duty hours. After seeing for myself how you took command after . . . that mishap during training today, I have no problem approving your promotion. That's the kind of leadership and incentive we like to see here in the army. Congratulations."

"Thank you, sir," I sez, not bein' able to think of anything else to say.

"Oh yes . . . and one other thing. I'm pulling your entire unit out of training and assigning them to active duty. It's only garrison duty, but it's the only thing available right now. I figure that anything more they need to learn, you can help them pick up on the job. That's all . . . Sergeant Guido."

It takes me a minute to register he is addressin' me by my new rank, but I manage to come to attention and salute before turnin' to go.

"If I may, sir," I heard Sergeant Smiley say, "I'd like to have a word outside with Sergeant Guido before he rejoins his unit."

I am half-expectin' Smiley to try to jump me, bad arm and all, once we get outside, or at least lay some heavy threats on me about what would happen the next time our paths cross. Instead, he is all grins and holds out his good hand for me to shake.

"Congratulations, Guido . . . sorry, I mean *Sergeant* Guido," he sez. "There was one thing I wanted to say to you away from the other recruits."

"What's that, Sergeant?"

"I wanted to tell you that you were right all along . . . it *does* take more skill to handle a combat situation without killing . . . and I'm glad to see we're getting men of your abilities enlisting on our side. Just remember, though, that we only have limited time to train the recruits . . . which is why we focus on getting them to think in terms of 'kills.' If they're at all squeamish about killing, if they think they can get by by disarming the enemy, they'll try to do that instead . . . and they don't have the skill and we don't have the time to teach it to them, so they end up dead themselves and we end up placing second in a two army fight. Try to keep that in mind the next time you're working with a group of raw recruits. In the meantime, good luck! Maybe we'll get a chance to serve together again sometime."

I am so surprised by the sergeant turnin' out to be a good Joe, not to mention givin' careful consideration to the thoughts he laid on me, that I am nearly back to the unit before the full impact of my promotion sinks in.

Then, I feel depressed. My entire career has been geared toward avoidin' bein' an authority-type figure, and now I am saddled with what is at least a supervisory post . . . permanent this time instead of temporary. My only consolations are that a) I can potentially do more damage havin' a higher rank, and b) Nunzio has to suffer the burden of extra stripes right along with me.

Perkin' up a little from these thoughts, I go lookin' for Nunzio, wantin' to be the first to slip him the bad news.

VII:

"To Serve and Protect..."

— TRADITIONAL MOTTO OF
PROTECTION RACKETS

As eager as we are to get on with our assignment, which is to say demoralizin' and disruptin' the army, both Nunzio and me are more than a little nervous about doin' garrison duty.

Not that there is anything wrong with the town, mind you. Twixt is a bigger'n average military town, which means there is lots of stuff to keep us amused during our off-duty hours. The very fact that it is a sizable burg, however, increases the odds of our presence bein' noticed and reported to Don Bruce...which, as we have mentioned before, was not high on our list of desirable occurrences.

The duty itself was annoyin'ly easy, annoyin' in that it's hard to stir up the troops when the worst thing facin' them is boredom. The situation is readily apparent even when I put Nunzio to work settlin' our crew in whilst I report in to the garrison commander.

"Our only real job here is to maintain a military presence . . . show the flag so's folks remember why they're paying their taxes."

The individual deliverin' this speech is average height, about a head shorter than me, and has dark tight-curly hair with a few wisps of grey showin' in spots . . . which might have made him look dignified if he didn't move like a dock worker tryin' to finish early so's he can go on a heavy date. He has a rapid-fire kinda speech pattern and rattles off his orders without lookin' up from the papers he is scribblin' on. I can't help but notice, however, that what he is workin' on so hard looks a lot like poetry . . . which I somehow don't think is covered by his official orders.

"All you and your boys gotta do is spend a certain number of hours a day patrolling the streets in uniform so's folks can see the army is here. The rest of the time, you're on your own."

"You mean like *policemen?*"

The words just sorta popped outta my mouth, but they must'a had a note of horror in them, as the commander broke off what he was doin' to look at me direct.

"Not really," he sez, quick-like. "We used to be responsible for patrolling the streets, but the town's grown to a point where it has its own police force, and we try not to interfere with their authority. They watch the citizens, and our own Military Police watches our troops. Clear and separate. See?"

"Yes sir."

". . . which brings us to another point," the commander continues, startin' to scribble on his papers again. "There's a non-fraternization rule in effect for our troops. We don't enforce it too strictly, so you don't have to worry if one of the . . . ah, ladies makes advances toward you or your men, but let them come to you. Don't start messing around with the ordinary civilian women. It's liable to get the civilian *men* upset however it goes, and our main directive here is to *not* incite any trouble with the civilians. Be nice to them . . . show them we're just plain folks, like they are. If you can do that, then they're less inclined to believe any wild stories they might hear about what our troops are doing on the front lines. Got that?"

I didn't think it would really matter what I said or did, as the commander is rattlin' all this off like it is memorized while he fiddles with his writin'. I didn't think it would be wise to test this theory, however.

"Yes sir," I sez. "No fraternizin' with the women . . . No fightin' with the men. Got it."

"Very well, report back to your unit and see that they're properly settled in. Then take the rest of the day to familiarize yourselves with the town, and report here for assignment tomorrow morning."

"Yes sir." I draw myself up and give him a snappy salute, which he returns without even lookin' up.

I can't help but I feel I have kinda gotten the bum's rush on my briefin', so on the way out I pause to have a few words with the commander's clerk . . . a decision which I'll admit is in part due to the factual that she is the only skirt I have seen in uniform except for Spyder, and I am beginnin' to feel a little desperate for the sound of a female-type voice. Besides, I outrank her, and figure it is about time my new stripes work a little *for* me instead of against me.

"What's the deal with the commander?" I sez, friendly-like, givin' her one of my lesser used non-intimidatin' smiles.

Instead of respondin', however, this chick just stares at me blankly like she's still waitin' for me to say somethin'. Now, she is a tiny little thing, a bit on the slender side, so her starin' at me with those big eyes starts makin' me feel a little uncomfortable . . . like she's a praying mantis tryin' to decide if she should eat me before or after we mate.

"I mean, how come he's writin' poetry?" I add, just to get some kinda conversation flowin'.

"Lyrics," she sez, in a flat sort of voice.

"Excuse me?"

"I said 'lyrics' . . . as in 'words for songs.' He likes to

perform in the local clubs at their open stage nights, and
he writes his own material . . . constantly."

"Is he any good?"

This gets me a small shrug.

"I suppose he's not bad . . . but he doesn't play guitar,
so mostly he has to sing a cappella. That makes his performance sound a little thin after listening to an evening
of singers with instrumental accompaniments."

I notice that for all her apparent disinterest, this chick
seems to know a lot about what the commander does on
his off-hours . . . even to the point of sittin' through a
whole evenin' of amateur singers to listen to his set when
she doesn't really like his singin'. From this I deduce that
I am not likely to get much of anywhere with her as a
sergeant, so I settle for bein' friendly.

"Maybe he should try keyboards," I sez.

"Try what?" she blinks, suddenly takin' more interest
in the conversation.

"Key . . . Oh! Nothin'. Hey, I got to be goin' now. Nice
talkin' with you."

With that I beat a hasty retreat, a little annoyed with
myself. Again my time on Deva has almost gotten me in
trouble. For a second there, I forgot that this dimension
not only doesn't have keyboards, it does not have the
electricity necessary for the pluggin' in of said instrument.

"Hey Guido!" comes a familiar voice, interruptin' my
thoughts. "What's the word?"

I looked around to find Nunzio and the rest of the crew
bearin' down on me.

"No big deal," I shrugs. "We don't even go on duty
until tomorrow. The commander's given us the rest of the
day to settle in and check out the town."

"Sounds good to me," Hy Flie sez, rubbin' his hands
together like . . . well, like a fly. "What say we get something to eat . . . and at the same time see if we can find a
place to hang out on our off-duty hours."

"How about the spaghetti place we passed on the way
here?" Spyder sez, jerkin' her head back in the direction
they had come from.

I shoot a quick glance at Nunzio, who is already lookin' at me. As so often happens when we're workin' together, we are thinkin' the same thing at the same time, and this time we're both thinkin' that the best way to avoid runnin' into someone with Mob connections is by *not* usin' a spaghetti place for a base of operations.

"Ah . . . let's see if we can find someplace less likely . . . I mean, *closer*," I suggest, casual-like.

"Well, how 'bout we try right here?" Nunzio chimes in, pickin' up on my general train of thought.

I look where he is pointin', and have to admit that it is probably the last place someone from the Mob would think of lookin' for us. The sign over the door of the joint reads, ABDUL'S SUSHI BAR AND BAIT SHOP.

"Sushi?" Shu Flie scowls. "You mean like raw fish?"

"At least we know it's fresh," Junebug sez, gesturin' at the second part of the sign.

"Oh, don't be a bunch of babies" Spyder grins, givin' Shu a poke in the ribs. "Wait 'til you've tried it. It's good! Come on."

Now, I am no more enthusiastic than the Flie brothers about eatin' this stuff, even though Nunzio has been after me for some time to give it a try. I mean, I'm used to fish in a tomato sauce or somethin', served with pasta—not rice. Still, there seems little option than to follow Spyder and Nunzio as they merrily lead the way into the place.

"Ah! Members of our noble fighting forces!" the proprietor sez, slitherin' up out of the dim depths to greet us. "Please, come right in. We give special discounts for our men . . . and ladies . . . in uniform!"

"Can we have a table close to the window so's there's more light?" Nunzio sez, giving me a wink.

I know what he is thinkin' and normally would approve. The proprietor is makin' me feel a little uneasy, however. Despite his toothy smile, I have a strong feelin' he can tell within a few pieces of small change how much money our crew is carryin' . . . and is already tryin' to figure how much of it he can glom onto before we escape.

In short, I haven't felt this sized up by a merchant since we left the Bazaar at Deva.

Despite my growin' discomfort, I join the crew as the proprietor ushers us to a window table and distributes menus. Everybody gives their drink orders, then start porin' over the menus with Spyder and Junebug servin' as interpreters . . . everyone except Nunzio, that is.

Ignorin' his menu completely, my cousin starts fishin' around his belt pouch.

"While we're here, anyone care for a couple quick hands of Dragon Poker?" he sez innocent-like, producin' a deck of cards and a battered, dog-eared book.

The whole crew groans at this, a sure indication of their familiarity with the game, which is not surprisin' as Nunzio and me have been takin' great pains to teach it to 'em. Despite their apparent reluctance, however, I notice that their stakes money appears on the table in a quick ripple of movement, which is in itself a testimony to the addictin' nature of this particular pastime. I can speak from my own experience in sayin' that there is nothin' like watchin' a pot you've built on a nice hand disappear into someone else's stack because of some obscure-type Conditional Modifier to convince a new player that it is definitely in his best interest to learn more about the game as it is his only chance of winnin' some of his money back, much less show a profit. That is, you play your first game of Dragon Poker for the fun of it, and after that youse is playin' for revenge.

"Okay . . . ante up!" Nunzio sez, givin' the cards a quick shuffle and offerin' the deck for a cut.

"Not so fast, cousin," I interrupts, fishin' my own copy of the rulebook out. "First, let's settle what the Conditional Modifiers are."

"Why bother?" Shue Flie grimaces. "They change every day."

"Every day? You mean every hour!" his brother sez.

"Whatever," Spyder shrugs. "Start dealing Nunzio. Swatter here can fill us in on the high points."

For those of youse unfamiliar with Dragon Poker, it is

a very popular means of redistributin' wealth throughout the dimensions. You can think of it as nine card stud poker with six card hands . . . that is, if you don't mind gettin' your brains beat out financially. You see, on top of the normal rules of card playin', there are Conditional Modifiers which can change the value of a card or hand dependin' on the dimension, hour of the day, number of players, position at the table, or any one of a multitude of other factors, makin' Dragon Poker the most difficult and confusin' card game in all the dimensions.

Nunzio and me got fascinated by dis game whilst everyone was tryin' to teach it to the Boss in time for his big match with the Sen-Sen Ante Kid, and it isn't really all that hard . . . providin' one had a copy of the rules applicable to the dimension youse is in at the time. (Of course, the Boss couldn't use a book durin' the big match, as he was supposed to be an expert already.) Before leavin' the Bazaar for this particular caper, both Nunzio and me included pickin' up copies of the rulebook for Klah (our home dimension where dis narration is takin' place) as part of our preparations. If youse perhaps think that buying two copies of the rulebook is a needless expense, let me give youse a free tip about playin' Dragon Poker: Your best defense at the table is havin' your own copy of the rules. Youse see, one of the standin' rules in *any* Dragon Poker game is that the players are individually responsible for knowin' the Conditional Modifiers. Put simply, this means that if you don't know a particular modifier which would turn your nothin' hand into a winner, no one is obligated to announce it to you. This is a tradition of the game and has nothin' to do with the honesty of them what plays it. If anything, it avoids accusations that a player deliberately withheld information to win a hand rather than a particular modifier simply bein' overlooked amidst the multitude of modifiers in effect at any given time. In short, as much as I trust my cousin Nunzio to cover my back in a brawl, I feel it wisest *not* to count on him lookin' out for my interest at a Dragon Poker table, and therefore figure havin' my own copy of the rulebook is a necessary expense, not a luxury or convenience.

"Let's see," I sez, thumbin' through the book, "the sun is out . . . and we're playin' indoors . . ."

". . . and there's an odd number of players . . ." Spyder supplies, showin' she's gettin' the hang of the modifyin' factors.

". . . and one of them is female . . . sort of . . ." Junebug adds, winkin' at Spyder.

"Sorry to take so long with your drinks, my friends," the proprietor sez, announcin' his presence as he arrives back at the table with a tray of potables. "Now, who has the . . . *HEY! WHAT IS THIS???!!!*"

It suddenly occurs to me that there may be some local ordinance against gamblin' . . . which would explain why the proprietor is suddenly so upset.

"This?" I sez, innocent-like. "Oh, we're just havin' a friendly little game of cards here. Don't worry, we're just usin' the coins to keep score and . . ."

"Don't give me that!" our host snarls, with no trace of his earlier greasy friendliness. "That's Dragon Poker you're playing! No one plays that game unless . . ."

He breaks off sudden-like and starts givin' each of us the hairy eyeball.

"All right, which one of you is a demon? Or is it all of you? Never mind! I want you all out of here . . . *RIGHT NOW!!!*"

VIII:

"It takes one to know one!"

—Jack D. Ripper

To say the proprietor's accusation caused a stir at our table is like sayin' it would cause raised eyebrows to have Don Bruce as the guest speaker at a Policeman's Banquet. Unfortuitously, everyone had different questions to ask.

"What's he mean 'demon'?" Spyder demanded.

I started to answer her, as I knew from my work with the Boss that a demon is the commonly accepted term for a dimension traveler, but there was too much cross-talk for rational-type conversation.

"Are we supposed to leave?" Spellin' Bee sez, scared-like as he peered at the retreatin' figure.

"What's wrong with Dragon Poker?" Shu Flie put in.

"Nothin'," I sez to him. "You see, Spyder . . ."

"Then what put the burr under his saddle?" Shu pressed, startin' to get under my skin.

Fortunately, in trainin' I have discovered there is one way to shut this particular individual up when he gets on a roll.

"Shu Flie," I sez, "don't bother me."

It was an old joke by this time, but it still got a laugh . . . which is not surprisin' as I have found that the vast majority of army humor pivots on old jokes.

"Watch yourself, brother," Hy Flie sez, pokin' Shu in the ribs. "The Swatter there is lookin' to squash a fly again . . . and he might not be too picky about which of us he swats."

Under the cover of this new round of laughs, Nunzio leans forward to talk to me direct.

"Are you thinking what I'm thinking, cuz?"

"That, of course, depends upon what it is you are thinkin', Nunzio," I sez, reasonable-like. "If, perchance, you are thinkin' that you can color our cover 'blown,' then we are, indeed, thinkin' along the same lines."

To my surprise, instead of agreein' he rolls his eyes like he does when I'm missin' something which to him is obvious.

"Think it through, Guido," he sez. "He thinks we're from off-dimension, because we know about Dragon Poker . . . right?"

"Yeah. So?"

"So how does *he* know about it?"

To me, this question is as trivial as wonderin' how a cop happens to know about a particular ordinance . . . which is to say it is beside the point, totally overlookin' the immediate dilemma of dealin' with the aftermath of us gettin' caught breakin' it.

"I dunno. I guess someone showed it to him. So what?"

For some reason, this seems to get Nunzio even more upset.

"Guido," he sez, clenchin' his teeth, "sometimes I wonder if all those knocks on the head you've taken have . . . oops! He's coming back. Quick . . . Bee?"

"Yes, Nunzio?" our junior magician sez, blinkin' with surprise at havin' been suddenly included in our discussion.

"Get your Dis-spell ready, and when I give you the nod . . . throw it on the proprietor."

"The proprietor? Why?"

"Bee . . . just do it. Okay?" I interrupts, havin' learned from experience that the only thing that takes longer than listenin' to one of Nunzio's lectures is tryin' to pry a straight answer out of him when he's tryin' to let you discover the point yourself.

Bee starts to say somethin', then shuts his mouth, shrugs, startin' to mumble and mutter like he does when he's gettin' ready to use magik.

The others at the table look at Nunzio expectant-like, but he just leans back in his chair lookin' confident and smug. I, of course, imitate his action, though I have no more idea what he is about to pull than the rest of the crew. You see, past experience has taught me that one of the best times to act confident is when youse is totally in the dark . . . but would just as soon no one else is aware of your ignorance.

"Are you still here?" the proprietor demands, materializin' beside our table again. "I don't want to have to tell you again! Now get out before I call the cops!"

"I don't think so," Nunzio sez, starin' at the ceilin'.

"WHAT???!!"

". . . In fact, I was thinkin' we might want to make your place our home away from home . . . If you know what I mean."

"Izzat so?! Think just 'cause you're in the Army you can do anything you want, do you? Well, let me tell you something, soldier-boy. I happen to be a tax paying member of this community in good standing with the authorities, and soldiers or not they don't take too kindly to demons in these parts. In fact, I can't think of one good reason why I shouldn't call the police right now and have them drag you all right out of here!"

"I can," Nunzio smiles, and nods at Bee.

At the cue, Spellin' Bee squares his shoulders, purses his lips, and lets fly with his Dis-Spell, and . . .

"What the . . ."

"MY GOD!!!"

"Lookit . . ."

The reason for this outpourin' of surprise and disbelief on the part of our crew is that, despite our time with them, Nunzio and me has failed to brief or otherwise prepare them for acceptin' the concept of demons . . . which is what they're suddenly confronted with. That is, as soon as Bee completed his spell, there was a ripplin' in the air around the proprietor, and instead of a greasy local type, he now looked just like . . .

"A Deveel!" I sez, hidin' my own surprise.

Actually, I am a little annoyed at myself for not havin' figured it out on my own. I mean, no matter what he looked like, I had been thinkin' that he was actin' like a Deveel since I first set eyes on him.

The reaction of our crew to this discovery, however, is nothin' compared to the reaction we gets from the proprietor.

"WHAT ARE YOU DOING!!??" he screeches, lookin' around the place desperately, only to find we are the only ones present. *"YOU TRYIN' TO GET ME LYNCHED???"*

With that, he goes scuttlin' off, leavin' Nunzio and me to deal with the confusion caused by the removal of his disguise.

"THAT WAS A DEVIL!!!"

I miss who exactly it is who observes this particular utterance, as it is said behind me and the choked, gargley nature of the voice makes positive identification no easy task. Still, I have no difficulty comin' up with a response.

"I know. That's what I said before," I explain.

"No, you said he was a Da-veel," Junebug sez frownin'.

"Same difference," I shrugs.

"Look," Spyder sez, holdin' up a hand to the others for them to be quiet. "Are you guys going to tell us what's goin' on here or not?"

"Guido," Nunzio sez, jerkin' his head in the direction the proprietor has gone. "Why don't you go do a little negotiating with our host before he gets *too* recovered from our little surprise, whilst I try to explain the facts of life to our colleagues."

This is fine by me, as I do not share my cousin's love of lengthy and confusin' explanations and am glad to be excused from what promises to be a classic opportunity for him to pontificate. Besides, it is not often that one has a chance to really stick it to a Deveel, and as in those few occasions I have been present for, I have usually had rank pulled on me by the financial types of the M.Y.T.H. Inc. team, I am lookin' forward to a rare opportunity to demonstrate my own negotiatin' talents. Of course, it occurs to me that the only witness I will have for this exercise will be the individual upon whom I am turnin' the screws, and he will doubtless be less than appreciative of my finesse. Doin' one's best work in the absence of witnesses is, however, one of the unfortunate and unjust realities of my chosen profession, and I have long since resigned myself to the burden of anonymity . . . tellin' myself that if I had wanted to be a *well-known* crook, I should have gone into politics.

The proprietor has vanished like a cat burglar at the sound of a bell, but I soon discover him in a small office behind the bar. He is holdin' one of those small foldin' cases with a mirror in it like broads use to check their makeup, only instead of powder and colored goop, his just seems to have a couple dials in it. Starin' into the mirror, he twiddles with the dials a bit . . . and slowly the disguise he was wearin' before came into focus again, leadin' me to conclude that it is some kind of magik device. If it seems to youse that it took me a long time to reach this conclusion, you are makin' the mistake of underestimatin' my speed of thinkin'. Included in my observational analysis was a certain amount of speculation of whether such a device might be handy to have for my own use . . . as well as whether it would be better to obtain one on my own or simply include this one in my negotiations.

Apparently the gizmo also functions as a normal mirror, as the proprietor suddenly shifts the angle he is holdin'

it at so's we are starin' at each other in the glass, then he
snaps it shut and turns to face me.

"What do *you* want?!" he snarls. "Haven't you done
enough to me already?"

I do not even bother tryin' to point out that I am not
the one what stripped him of his disguise spell, as I have
learned durin' my residence on Deva that unless they are
actively sellin', which fortunately is most of the time, Deveels are extremely unpleasant and unreasonable folks
who do not accept that simple logic is sufficient reason to
stop complainin'. They *do*, however, respond to reason.

"I have come as a peace emissary," I sez, "in an effort
to reach an equitable settlement of our differences."

The Deveel simply makes a rude noise at this, which I
magnanimously ignore as I continue.

"I would suggest you meet our offer with equal enthusiasm for peace . . . seein' as how continued hostilities between us will doubtless result in my colleagues and me
trashin' this fine establishment of yours . . ."

"What? My place?" the proprietor blinks, his mouth
continuin' to open and close like a fish out of water.

". . . As well as spreadin' the word about your bein' a
Deveel to the authorities you was so ungraciously threat-
enin' us with . . . and anyone else in this town who will
listen. Know what I mean?"

Now, I have this joker cold, and we both know it. Still
he rallies back like a punch-drunk boxing champ on the
downslide, fightin' more from guts and habit than from
any hope of winnin'.

"You can't do that!" he sez, gettin' his mouth workin'
well enough to at least sputter. "If you turn me in as a
demon, then I'll incriminate you, too! We'll *all* end up
getting killed, or at least run out of town."

"There is one major difference in our circumstantials
which you are overlookin'," I sez, grinnin' at him. "While
I will admit that my cousin and me have done some dimension travelin', this particular dimension of Klah happens to be our home territory. The appearances you see
are legit and not disguises, so any attempt to accuse us of

bein' from off-dimension would be difficult to prove, as we are not. On the other hand, *you*, bereft of disguise, would encounter extreme difficulty in convincin' a jury or lynch mob that you was from around here."

I thought this would bring any resistance on the proprietor's part to an end, but instead he straightens up and frowns, his eyes takin' on a mean glitter.

"You're from this dimension? You wouldn't happen to know a local magician and demon by the name of *Skeeve*, would you?"

As I have said before, I have not reached my current age and position by panicking under cross-type examination *or* by overratin' the necessity for voicin' the *whole* truth. I can see that this Deveel has some kind of grudge against the Boss, so while habitually avoidin' any false statement which could lead to perjury charges, I am careful not to acknowledge my actual relationship with the individual in question.

"Skeeve?" I sez, frownin' dramatically like I learned to do in theater. "I think I may have heard the name while I was workin' at the Bazaar, but I ain't heard it recently."

"Too bad," the Deveel mutters, almost to himself. "I owe that Klahd a bad turn or two. I spent a couple of years as a statue under a cloud of pigeons because of him. In fact I'd still be there if it weren't for . . . but that's another story, if you know what I mean."

Of course, from workin' with the Boss, I knew *exactly* what he meant . . . that the story of his escape was gonna be marketed separately sometime as a short story to generate additional revenue whilst promotin' these books at the same time. Of course, admittin' this understandin' would have been a dead giveaway, so I decide to change the subject instead.

"Yeah, sure. Say, speakin' of names, what's yours, anyway? I mean your *real* name, not this Abdul alias."

"What? Oh! It's Frumple . . . or it used to be back when I was welcome in my own dimension of Deva."

That had a familiar sound to it, but I decide enough is enough, and take a firm grip on the subject at hand.

"Well, I'm Guido and my cousin what was talkin' to you back at the table is Nunzio . . . and I believe we was discussin' the terms of our peaceful coexistence with youse?"

Frumple cocked his head to one side, studyin' me close-like.

"You know," he sez, "you sound like you work for the Mob. In fact, now that I think about it, I seem to recall hearing something about the Mob trying to move in on the Bazaar."

"Yeah? So?"

"So I'm already making yearly protection payments to the Mob, and I don't see why I should stand for being shaken down for anything extra."

This information that the Mob is operatin' in these parts is disquietin' to say the least, but I manage not to show any surprise or nervousness.

"Really?" I sez. "Tell me, does your local Mob sales rep know that you're a Deveel?"

"Okay, okay! I get the point," Frumple says, throwin' up his hands. "What do you want to keep *that* information quiet?"

"Well, since we're lookin' to make this our hangout for a while, I figure we can protect your little secret as a courtesy."

"Really?"

"Sure," I smiles. "Of course, in return, it would be nice if you extended the hospitality of your establishment to us and our friends . . . as a courtesy."

"I see," he sez, tightenin' his lips to a crooked line. "All right, I guess I don't have much choice. It'll be cheaper to give you free drinks than to have to relocate and start building a business up from scratch. I'll give you free drinks, and maybe an occasional meal. The rooms upstairs are out, though. If I start letting you use those for free, I'll go out of business anyway. They're the profit margin that keeps this place afloat."

"Rooms?"

"Yeah. I've got a few rooms upstairs that I rent to the

customers by the hour so they can . . . have some privacy with any interesting people they happen to meet here. You see, this place gets pretty lively evenings. It's one of the more popular singles bars in town."

"You mean you got broads workin' the joint at night?"

"Certainly not! The women who hang out here have regular high-paying jobs and wouldn't dream of charging for their company."

"So the customers pay you for the rooms, but not the broads," I sez. "Sounds like a sweet setup to me."

"Not *that* sweet," Frumple amends, hastily. "Still, it helps pay the rent."

"Okay. I think we can settle for drinks and food," I shrugs. "Come on out front, Frumple, and I'll let you buy me a drink to show there's no hard feelin's."

"You're too kind," the Deveel grumbles, but he follows me out of the office.

"I think champagne would be appropriate to seal our agreement, don't you?" I sez. "White champagne."

"White champagne?"

"Of course," I smiles, glad for a chance to show off my knowledge and culture. "This here is a sushi bar, ain't it? You think I don't know what color champagne to have with fish?"

IX:

"Manners are acquired, not inherited!"
—S. PENN

Things are pretty sweet for a while after I make our arrangement with Frumple. The reduced costs of our off-hour drinkin' are a real boon on the scut wages the army is payin' us, and the Deveel sure had the right of it when he said his sushi bar was a happy huntin' grounds when it came to broads.

Of course, "broads" is perhaps a mis-no-menclature for the type of women what hang out at this establishment evenings. These was not the usual gum-snappin, vacant-eyed skirts we are used to associatin' with, but rather the classy, fashion-wise young female executive with a lot on the ball what normally wouldn't give lunks like us the time of day. It seems that once we invaded the sanctuary of these upwardly mobile females, however, they was open-minded enough to give us serious consideration in their own deliberations. While I will not try to comment on which of these two types of females actually makes for better companions, there are things to be said for each . . . though not all those things are complimentary.

There are two flies which mar our enjoyment of this ointment, however, and here I am not referrin' to the Flie brothers. First, there is the ever-present danger of runnin' into someone from the Mob, as Frumple's comments have confirmed our suspicion that they maintain some kind of presence here. Second, there is the annoyin' detail that we are supposed to be working on an assignment, not havin' a good time. Naturally, this is the subject of no small amount of conversation between Nunzio and me.

"The trouble is, we can't really do a good job of disruptin' without movin' around town," I was sayin' durin' one such discussion, "and if we move around town, then the odds of our runnin' into someone from the Mob goes way up!"

"Then we'll have to see what we can stir up from right here," my cousin sez. "When you stop to think about it, this is a pretty good setup for it . . . makin' trouble, I mean. Most of these women have husbands at home, and even the ones that don't have sufficient standing in the community that if it comes to an altercation, the local authorities will have to take her side of it."

"Why do you say that? I mean, why should messin' with *these* broads cause any more hassle than any others?"

Instead of answerin' right away, Nunzio leans back and gives me the hairy eyeball for a few minutes.

"Guido," he says at last, "are you tryin' to be stupid just to get a rise out of me?"

"What do you mean?"

"I mean that you yourself said that our commander told us that it was okay if we messed with bimbos, but to leave the respectable women alone. Yet now that I am tryin' to put together a specific course of action, you are actin' like it is a brand-new concept to you."

"It just seems to me that it is a revoltin' form of class bias and bigotry," I sez, "assumin' that a woman's respectability is a matter of her financial standin' and education. Wouldn't it be better if it were the other way around? I mean, if a woman's respectability determined where she stood in the financial order instead of the other way around?"

"There are two problems with that," Nunzio sez. "First of all, the same unfair standard is applied to men as well . . . meanin' it holds for everyone, not just women. Them what is rich and educated is always deemed more respectable . . . if for no other reason than they wield more power and pay more taxes."

"That's true," I sez, noddin' thoughtful-like.

"The second problem is that it's completely off the subject of what we was discussin' . . . which is to say how to cause disruption."

"It is?"

"What is more, any time you try to start a philosophical discussion with me, it is to be taken as a sure sign that you are deliberately tryin' to divert my attention . . . as normally you avoid such conversations like a subpoena."

I say nothin' when he pauses, as he seems to have me cold. I *had* been tryin' to change the subject.

"All of this, the attempt at stupidity and the lame effort at philosophical discussion, leads me to believe that for some reason you are stalling and do not wish to commence working on our assignment. Am I right?"

I avoid his eyes and shrug kinda vague-like

"Come on, Cuz, talk to me," Nunzio urges. "Are you really havin' so much fun playing soldier that you want to prolong the experience?"

"That is not only silly, it is insultin'!" I sez, my annoyance overcomin' my embarrassment at havin' been caught.

"Then what is it? . . . If you don't mind my asking?"

"Well . . . to be honest with youse, Nunzio, I feel a little funny stirrin' up trouble at this particular location, seein' as how it was me what did the negotiatin' with Frumple to not cause him any grief."

Nunzio throws back his head and gives a bark of laughter . . . which to me is a dubious way to express his sympathy at my plight.

"Let me get this straight," he sez. "You're worrying about dealing fair with a Deveel?"

"You may laugh," I sez, "though I suggest you not do it often when I am the subject of your amusement. Allow me to remind youse, however, that even though Deveels are notoriously hard bargainers, it is also true that once a deal has been struck, they are equally scrupulous about stickin' to the letter of said agreement. As such, it occurs to me that failin' to honor one's own end of such an agreement is to place oneself in a position of bein' even less trustworthy than a Deveel . . . which is not a label I relish hangin' upon myself."

"Okay . . . let's examine the letter of said agreement," Nunzio shrugs. "What you agreed to was that we would neither trash his establishment, nor would we reveal the true nature of his identity as a Deveel. Correct?"

"Well . . . yeah."

". . . Neither of which conditions is broken by us directing our attentions to the lovelies which have taken to making this establishment their after-hours habitat . . . even if our attentions should turn out to be unwelcome."

"I suppose . . . but don't you think that such activity would violate at least the spirit of our agreement, by which I mean the implication that we would not make trouble for our host?"

"That is the portion of your discomfort which I find the most amusing," Nunzio sez with an infuriatin' grin. "Realizing that Deveels make their living as well as their reputation by honoring the letter rather than the spirit of their agreements, I think it is ironic that you are recoiling from dealing with them with the same ethic that they deal with others."

I consider this for a few minutes, then take a deep breath and blow it out noisily.

"You know, cousin," I sez. "You're right. I mean, when you're right, you're right . . . know what I mean?"

"I do," Nunzio frowned, "which is in itself a little disturbing."

"So . . . when do you think we should start?"

"Well . . . how about right now?"

While my cousin has convinced me that it would be within the bounds of ethical behavior to launch our campaign, such an accelerated-type timetable catches me unawares.

"Excuse me?"

"I said how about starting right now. Opportunity should be seized when it presents itself . . . and right now there is a young lady at the bar who has been checking you out for the last several minutes."

I sneak a peek in the direction he is lookin', and sure enough . . . there is one of those classy broads I have been tellin' you about, a blonde to be specific, perched on a bar stool and starin' right at me. I know this to be true, 'cause though for a minute I thought she was lookin' at someone else, as soon as our eyes meet, she closes one eye in a broad wink and smiles.

"Nunzio," I sez, duckin' my head and turnin' my back on her. "There is one more problem I have neglected to mention to you."

"What's that?"

"Well, though my manners with broads are perhaps not as polished as they should be, they are nonetheless the best I have managed to acquire over the years. That is to say, I am normally on my best behavior with females, so the idea of tryin' to act so offensive that they call for help is not particularly comfortable to me. Mind you, I am sayin' I would have difficulty doin' this with the ordinary broads I am accustomed to dealin' with, and to tell you the truth, I find the kind of classy broads that hang out here more than a little intimidatin'. I'm not sure I can start a conversation with one, much less summon the courage to try to be offensive."

"Well, I don't think that starting a conversation is going to be a problem," Nunzio sez.

"Why not?"

"Because the lady in question is on her way over to our table already."

Surprised, I swing my head back around to check

things out for myself . . . and come dangerously close to plantin' my nose in the broad's cleavage, as she is much closer to our table than Nunzio had indicated.

"Oops . . . Sorry!" I sez, though it occurred to me as I said it that it was not a great start to bein' offensive.

"No problem," she sez. "A girl likes to feel appreciated. Mind if I join you?"

Somethin' about the way she grins while sayin' this is familiar . . . or at least, decidedly unladylike. Before I can comment, however, Nunzio has taken over.

"Certainly. In fact, you can have my chair . . . I was just leaving anyway. Catch you later, Guido . . . and remember what we were talking about."

With that, he gives me a big wink and wanders off, leavin' me alone with the skirt . . . who wastes no time plantin' her curvaceous bottom on the chair my cousin has so graciously vacated.

"So . . . I haven't seen you in here before."

"What?"

I have been so busy thinkin' about what I am goin' to do to Nunzio to repay him for his "graciousness" that I nearly miss the broad's openin' gambit.

"Oh. No, we just got into town this week. This seems to be turnin' out to be our main hangout, though."

"Hey, that's terrific! This is one of my favorite spots. It's my first time in this week, though. Girl's got to do the rounds to keep up with what's going on in town . . . like when new soldiers arrive."

Although I have been feelin' self-conscious about meetin' one of these high-class skirts, this one seems real easy to talk to . . . like I'd known her for years. What's more, she is certainly not at all hard on the eyes, if you know what I mean.

"Say," I sez, "can I get you somethin' to drink? A wine spritzer, maybe?"

"Bourbon. Rocks. Water back."

"Say what?"

I mean, it isn't just that she drinks stronger hootch than I would have expected, it is the way she rattled it off. I decide it is not this chick's first time into a bar . . . a decision made easier by the fact she has already told me as much.

"Better still," she sez, "isn't there somewhere else we can go?"

This is a rough one. Abdul's is the only joint in town I have frequented so far.

"Ummmm . . ." I sez, thinkin' fast, "I have heard of some place around here where there's open stage entertainment."

Mind you, I am not wild about takin' this skirt somewhere where I might run into my commandin' officer, but I figure she'll be impressed with my willingness to spring for a good time.

"I was thinking someplace more like the rooms upstairs," she sez, leanin' forward to smile at me real close.

I am taken a little aback by the forwardness of this suggestion, though I suppose I shouldn't be surprised. When a high-class babe like this approaches a low-brow Joe like me in a bar, she is not usually after witty conversation . . . which, in my case, is fortunate.

(AUTHOR'S NOTE: It has been brought to my attention by some of my test readers that the concepts in this chapter and those that immediately follow are a marked change of pace from the normal MYTH content. In this, I fear it may be my sad duty to introduce to some readers for the first time the horrifying reality that there *are* a few sick, twisted, perverted individuals who approach members of the opposite sex in singles bars for purposes other than pleasant conversation! I feel free to identify them as such in this book, since it is a well-known fact that such blots on the shining history of mankind *do not read,* making me relatively safe from legal action. Incidentally, this is also why the question "Read any good books lately?" has become such a popular way of screening whom one does or doesn't talk to under such circumstances. I will

leave it to you how to answer if the question is ever
addressed to you. Meanwhile, back to the story . . .)

As I was sayin' before I was so *rudely interrupted*, I
am at a bit of a loss as to how to respond to this advance.

"Right now?" I sez. "Don't you want to talk for a while
first?"

"What's wrong? Don't you like me?" she sez, startin'
to pout a little. "Should I go peddle my wares somewhere
else?"

"Peddle?"

"Watch it," she sez, flat and nasty. "It's a figure of
speech."

"Oh."

I am vastly relieved to hear this. The only thing more
depressin' to a sensitive guy like me than learnin' that a
female is interested in him for his body and not his mind
is learnin' that her *real* interest is in his wallet.

"Well?" she sez, cockin' an eyebrow at me.

Though I am, perhaps, a little dense at pickin' up cues
from a skirt, let it never be said I am slow once the message has gotten through. Scant seconds later I have acquired the key to a room from Frumple and am leadin'
this vision of loveliness up the narrow stairs . . . well, followin' her, actually, as experience has taught me that this
gives one an excellent view of the sway of her hips, which
is to me still one of the most beautiful and hypnotic sights
in any dimension.

In a masterful display of control, I manages not to fum-
ble with the key whilst unlockin' the door, and even stand
aside to let her enter first.

Bein' a broad, she whips out one of those foldin' mir-
rors and starts checkin' her makeup even before I finish
lockin' the door behind us.

"So," I sez, over my shoulder, "What do you want to
do first?"

To be honest with youse, at this point I have no interest
at all in creatin' a hassle. Instead, I am thankin' my lucky

stars that a skirt like this would give a lug like me a second look, and hopin' we can get on with things before she changes her mind.

"Well," she sez, "You could start by bringing me up to date on how you and Nunzio have been doing."

It takes a moment for this to sink in, but when it does, I knows just what to say.

"Say what?" I sez, spinnin' around.

The skirt what I come upstairs with is nowhere to be seen. Instead, I've got a different broad in the room with me. One with green hair and . . .

"Hi, Guido!" she sez. "Great disguise, huh?"

X:

"Now, here's my plan!"

—R. BURNS

"Tananda? Is that you?"
    My surprise is not entirely due to my not havin'
spotted who it is what has been cadgin' drinks from me
all evening . . . though I hadn't. Rather I am more than a
little startled by her appearance, which has changed considerably since we parted company at the beginnin' of this
mission.

Tananda is normally a spectacular lookin' skirt with
an impressive mane of green hair. While she has never chosen to present the formal, every-hair-in-place-self-
presentation favored by most of the broads what hang out
at the sushi bar, optin' instead for a casual windblown
look, I am sufficiently versed in the secrets of the female
gender to be aware that the latter look is as, or more,
difficult to establish and maintain as the former, and often
harder to carry off. All of which is to say Tananda is
usually very attractive to and careful of her looks.

What I am currently seein', however, is someone who

looks like she has been on the wrong end of a bad accident. Most of the hair is missin' from one side of her head, along with the correspondin' eyebrow, and the other side of her face is marred by a big bruise which seems to be fadin', but still looks painful. Havin' both given and received more than my share of the latter type of injury, I can estimate with fair accuracy the force of the blow necessary to produce such spectacular results . . . and it must have been a doozey.

"Sorry for the horror show," she sez, puttin' away her disguise mirror after takin' one last peek, as if to see whether things have changed since the last time she looked, "but it's been a rough assignment so far."

"What . . . What happened to you?" I sez, findin' my voice at last. "Who did this to you?"

I mean, we had all known there might be some trouble associated with this mission, but nobody likes to see a beautiful skirt get worked over.

"Would you believe it was our own team?" she sez, flashin' a quick smile, though I knew it hurt.

"Come again?"

"The hair is courtesy of Gleep," she explained. "I guess it was an accident. I must have gotten between him and dinner or something. Anyway, it's not as bad as it looks . . . or could have been. Chumley saw it coming even if I didn't and got me out of the way of the worst of it . . . which is both where the bruise came from and why I'm not complaining about it. Honestly, you should see what happened to the wall that was behind me at the time."

"Speakin' of which, where are Chumley and Gleep?"

For the first time in our conversation, Tananda starts lookin' uncomfortable.

"They've . . . ah . . . headed back to Big Julie's. Actually, big brother's in a bit worse shape than I am, so rather than have him trying to work with his arm in a sling, I told him to take Gleep somewhere out of the action and stay with him for a while. It's funny, you know? I still can't figure what set Gleep off . . . but until we can get a handle on it, I figure he's more of a danger than a help on this assignment. Anyway, I decided to stay on and use this disguise gizmo to see if I could do anything to help the cause on my own. I sure couldn't do much worse than we were doing as a team."

Somethin' was tuggin' at the back of my mind . . . somethin' that Nunzio had said about his last assignment and bein' nervous about workin' with Gleep again. I couldn't put my finger on it, though, and seein' as how the discussion was makin' Tananda uncomfortable, I decided not to pursue the subject. I did, however, make a mental note to talk with Nunzio about it when we had a chance.

"Sounds like things weren't goin' too well even before the accident," I sez, pickin' up on her last aside.

"You can say that again," Tananda sez, heavin' a little sigh. "We were trying to work a variation on the old badger game . . . you know, where I give a soldier the come-on, then Chumley bursts in and raises a ruckus because the guy's compromising his sister's honor?"

"I know the scam," I sez, 'cause I do . . . though I've never run it or been victimized by it myself. Still, it's a time-tested, classic gambit.

"Well, it wasn't working anywhere near as well as we would have hoped. Most of the soldiers around here are under orders to keep their hands off the local women, and if I upped the voltage to make them forget their orders, then the locals would spot what I was doing and take the position that I was asking for whatever attentions I got."

"Gee, that's tough," I said. "It musta been hard on you . . . particularly if you was workin' injured."

I still didn't like the way that bruise was healin', and it must have shown in my voice 'cause Tananda leans forward and puts a hand on my arm.

"I'm all right, Guido, really . . . though it's sweet of you to be worried. I've gotten a lot worse just rough-housing with Chumley . . . honest."

Realizin' that her big brother is a troll, I can well believe that Tananda is used to gettin' dinged up a bit in family squabbles. Right now, however, there is somethin' else weighin' on my mind.

You see, Tananda's touch was real soft and warm when she laid her hand on my arm, and it gets me to thinkin' again about the original reason I had for bringin' her up to this room. As I said before, it has been a long time since I have been alone with a skirt on anythin' resemblin' an intimate basis . . . But Tananda is *still* a business associate, and as with any profession, it is unwise at best to allow oneself to become intimately involved with a fellow worker. Besides, she has never indicated to me any interest beyond friendship . . . or maybe a big sister. Still it was *real* nice to have a woman touchin' me . . .

"Umm . . . All right. If you say so," I sez, movin' slightly to break the physical contact between us. "We was just assigned here ourselves, so we haven't had a chance to do much of anythin'. I think maybe we should try to figure out how Nunzio and me can work the same area as you without us gettin' in each other's way."

"Don't be silly, Guido. Since you're here, we can all work together!"

"Come again?"

"Think about it," she sez, gettin' all bouncy in her eagerness. "I've been having trouble finding soldiers to take the bait on my little routine, but *you're soldiers*, so it can make both our jobs easier. If we're working *both* sides of the game, we can control exactly how we want things to go."

I make a sincere effort to ignore her bouncin' whilst I try to think of a good reason not to go along with her suggestion. Somehow I am not sure my actin' skills are up to *pretendin'* to be physically forward with Tananda . . . but I am even less enthusiastic about havin' Nunzio take the part.

"I dunno, Tananda," I sez, reluctant-like. "I'm not so sure that's a good idea. I mean, we might pull it off once . . . but if we're successful in our play-actin', then Nunzio and me end up in the stockade and out of action for the duration."

"Oh yeah?" she sez, cockin' her remainin' eyebrow at me. "So what were you thinking would happen when you brought me up here this evening?"

"Ummm . . ." I sez, recallin' that, unfortuitously, takin' the Fifth Amendment only works in court.

"Never mind, Guido," she grins. "I withdraw the question. Tell you what, though. If being directly involved makes you uneasy, just line me up with one of your army buddies. You've been in long enough that you should have a pretty good idea of who we can sucker."

I find that I am not wild about this idea either; first, because it seems like a dirty trick to play on any of the crew what's been workin' with Nunzio and me the last few weeks, and second, because I find I am not overjoyed with the idea of *anybody* pawin' Tananda. Still, I had to accept that we was gonna have to break *somebody's* eggs to get this omelette made, and that Tananda is right, it would be easier and quicker to do if we set the thing up ourselves.

"Okay, Tananda," I sez. "We'll try it that way."

"Are you okay, Guido?" she sez, peerin' at me concerned-like. "You sound a little flat."

"I'm all right. I'll tell youse though, Tananda, this assignment is gettin' me down a little."

"Well cheer up, things may have been rocky so far, but working together, we should be able to make some progress. Tell you what, find Nunzio and fill him in what we're doing. Then we'll meet back here and give it a try . . . say, tomorrow night?"

"Sure, why not?"

"In the meantime," she sez, openin' her disguise mirror again and startin' to fiddle with the knobs, "come on downstairs and *I'll* buy *you* a drink or two."

For a minute that sounds like a good idea. Then I remember Frumple.

"I think we'd better cool it, Tananda. We gotta be careful about how much we're seen together here."

"What do you mean?"

"The reason we're hangin' out here is we found out that the proprietor's a Deveel. The trouble is, he seems to know the Boss and has some kind of grudge against him.

So far, he doesn't know we're connected with the Boss, but if he gets suspicious . . ."

"A Deveel?"

"Yeah. Says his name is Frumple."

"Frumple? So he's back in operation again, is he?"

"You know him?"

"Sure. He teamed up with Isstvan against us back when I first met Skeeve . . . and you're right, if he gets suspicious, a disguise spell wouldn't keep him from figuring out who I am."

"Maybe we should wait and try to run our gambit somewhere other than here," I sez, tryin' to keep the hope out of my voice.

"No need," Tananda grins. "As long as he doesn't make the connection between us beforehand, we should still be able to pull it off tomorrow night. In fact, it'll be killing two birds with one stone, in a manner of speaking. I don't mind doing Frumple a bit of dirt in the course of action, but it looks like his place will be at ground zero when the fireworks start. By the time he puts it together, we'll be long gone."

"Swell," I sez, with more enthusiasm than I am feelin'. "Then we're all set. Youse go ahead and leave first. I'll stay up here awhile and give youse a head start."

As soon as she is gone, I settle myself to try to sort out my misgivin's about how things are goin' on this assignment. It doesn't take long to figure out that I am sufferin' under a burden of conflictin' loyalties.

Youse may find this surprisin' from someone in my line of work, but loyalty and betrayin' trust counts very high up in my books . . . which is one of the things I have always admired about the M.Y.T.H. Inc. crew as they all seem to value the same thing.

In the past, I've managed to balance my loyalties between the Boss and the Mob, as the strange approach the Boss takes to things has not directly threatened any of the Mob's interests. This current situational, however, is turnin' out to be a horse of a different caliber.

In plannin' to stir up trouble between the civilians and the army, I am violatin' the trust placed in me as a representative of the army . . . but I have managed to rationalize this as it is my *reason* for joinin' the army in the first place, so in this matter I am actin' kinda like a spy with my loyalty clearly with the Boss.

Nunzio has convinced me that I am not violatin' my deal with Frumple by usin' his place as a site for our mischief, as it falls outside the agreement we made. This strikes me as a little shaky, but I can be flexible when the occasion calls for it.

This latest plan, though, of settin' up someone in your squad to be the fall guy is *real* hard to see as anythin' except betrayin' a friend. Still, Tananda is right . . . it *is* the best way to be sure that things go the way we want 'em to.

Thinkin' it over real hard, I finally come up with an answer: What I gotta do is think of it as a joke on a buddy. Okay, maybe it's a dubious joke . . . like poppin' a paper bag behind someone who's gettin' ready to blow a safe . . . but as long as the notable in question does not end up permanently damaged or incarcerated as a result, it can be passed off as a joke.

Now, my only concern is tryin' to make sure that whoever we pick has a sense of humor . . . a real *good* sense of humor!

XI:

"That's why the lady is a tramp!"

— B. MIDLER

"Hoooo-ey! The place is sure jumpin' tonight!" Shu Flie exclaims, leanin' back in his chair to survey the room.

"You kin say that again, Shu," his brother sez. "Hey! Lookit that one over there!"

Any way youse look at it, the Flie brothers run a class act . . . though politeness will forbid my commentin' on *which* class. For a change, however, I am inclined to agree with them.

This is our first weekend in Twixt, much less here at Abdul's, and the bar is packed to overflowin'. In fact, if we hadn't been drinkin' here since early afternoon, it's doubtful we would have a table at all. As it is, we are entrenched at our regular table with a good view of the bar . . . or, to be more specific the de-rears arrayed along the bar . . . as well as the de-fronts when they turn around. Believe me, speakin' as a well-traveled demon, youse don't get scenery like this just anywhere!

Unfortunately, my enjoyment of the view is marred by my distraction over the comin' events.

"Whatdaya think Swatter?" Shu sez, turnin' his attention to me. "You ever see women like this before?"

"Oh, they're not bad," I sez, cranin' my neck to scan the crowd.

It has occurred to me that Tananda will probably be in disguise when she arrives, and it will therefore be difficult for me to recognize her unless she gives me some kind of signal.

"Not bad? Listen to this, guys! All this beautiful woman-flesh, and all Swatter can say is 'They're not bad'!"

"Really, Swatter," Junebug sez. "You just don't see beautiful women like this in the army!"

This earns him a dangerous scowl from Spyder, but he misses it completely as he is feelin' his drinks more than a little at this point.

"Nice crowd for a fight. Know what I mean, cuz?" Nunzio murmurs in my ear low enough so no one else can hear.

"I dunno," I sez, scannin' the crowd again. "I don't see a single one of these white collar types that even Bee couldn't take without half tryin'."

"That's what I mean," Nunzio grins, and helps himself to another swallow from his drink.

As you can maybe tell from his behavior, the hesitations I have been experiencin' about settin' up one of our buddies has not bothered my cousin in the least. If anything, he seems to be lookin' forward to a bit of trouble.

"Watch my chair," I sez, standing up. "I'm goin' to the bar for a refill."

Like I said, the place is mobbed, and in typical tight-fisted Deveel type fashion, Frumple has not incurred the added overhead of puttin' on extra help, so if youse wants to get a drink sometime *before* the next Ice Age, it is necessitated that youse belly up to the bar to get your refill directly from the bartender. If youse is wonderin' why someone as greedy as Frumple is willin' to miss the extra

income generated by a higher turnover of drinks, let me re-
store your faith by explainin' that he makes it up both by
waterin' the hootch *and* by increasin' his unit revenue . . .
which is to say he raises his prices as the crowds get bigger.

Strangely enough, neither the weaker drinks nor the
sky-high prices seem to faze this crowd in the least. I
figure this is because they feel that payin' three times the
normal goin' fare for a drink will screen out the rabble
one usually has to tolerate when drinkin' in a public place,
thereby insurin' that they are makin' their passes at folks
of an equal or higher income bracket, and as to the wa-
tered drinks . . . well, the only reason I can come up with
that they aren't complainin' about this is that they probably figure that booze is unhealthy, so a weak drink is
somehow healthier than a strong one.

You see, I have ascertained through eavesdroppin' that
health, and specifically healthy consumables, is a *very* big
issue with these upwardly mobile folks. It's like they're
used to thinkin' that you can get anythin' with enough
money . . . and they've gotten it into their heads that by
spendin' more for health foods and health drinks, they is
never gonna die. Of course, they spend so much time
worryin' and naggin' each other about good health, that
they tend to generate sufficient stress to keel over and
croak from heart attacks . . . but this seems to be an acceptable, if not desirable, option as it is generally viewed
as "the high pressure which is the mark of a successful
career person" and therefore has become somethin' of a
badge of status. What is somehow overlooked in all this
is that much of the stress is needless anxiety they inflict
upon themselves by worryin' about such things as status
and health foods.

Perhaps it is because of the high-risk nature of my chosen profession, but I personally have no illusions of my
own immortality. The way I see it, there are enough unpredictable things in life that can kill you that the only
rational approach to life is to take what little pleasures
youse can as they presents themselves, so that when your

number comes up, you can at least die knowin' you've had a full and happy life. I think that life should be more than an exercise in self-denial, and even if I was guaranteed that I could live forever by abstainin', I'd probably continue my occasional indulgences. I mean, who wants to live forever . . . particularly if that life has been designed to be borin' and devoid of pleasure?

I am reflectin' on this when a broad elbows her way in next to me at the bar. At first I think she is just really desperate for a drink, which as I said is understandable considerin' the slow service, and step aside, usin' my not inconsiderable bulk to make room for her.

"Got my target picked out for me?"

It takes a second for me to realize that I am the one this question is bein' addressed to, as she sez it casual without lookin' at me direct.

"Tananda?" I sez, lookin' at her hard.

She is wearin' a different disguise tonight . . . a shoulder length cloud of dark curls and a dress made of some clingy fabric that . . . well, shows off everything she's got underneath it.

"Don't look at me!" she hisses, quietly grindin' a heel onto my toe to emphasize her point while glancin' at the ceilin'. "We aren't supposed to know each other . . . remember?"

"Oh, right . . . sorry."

I go back to starin' into my glass, doin' my best to ignore her presence . . . which is not easy as the crowd is pressin' a considerable amount of her against me as we're standin' there.

"Okay, who's our pigeon?"

"You see the two broad-shouldered guys at our table? The loud ones? I figure the one on the left will do you just fine."

Guido and I have decided on Shu Flie for our victim. Of the crew, we're probably the least fond of the Flie brothers, and while either of them would probably serve our purposes, Shu is the more dominant and might start trouble if Tananda made a play for his brother instead of

him. As our objective is to cause trouble between the
army and the civilians, fighin' within our own ranks
would be counter-productive.

"Who's the yummy one across the table from the animals?"

I sneak a peek behind me to be sure who she's talkin'
about.

"That? That's Junebug. He used to be an actor or a
dancer or somethin'."

"He'll do," she sez firmly, a predatory note creepin'
into her voice.

I refrain from lookin', but have a strong suspicion she
is lickin' her lips . . . mentally, if not physically.

"I don't think that's such a hot idea. Tananda," I sez.
"There's sort of a thing goin' between him and Spyder.
At least, she's got a thing for him."

"Who?"

"Spyder. The chick in uniform sittin' next to him."

"That's female?"

While, as you know, I had much the same reaction the
first time I met Spyder, for some reason it bothers me
hearin' it from Tananda.

"Don't let the hair fool you," I sez, "She's pretty
tough."

"That's sweet of you, Guido," Tananda sez, misunderstandin' what I was sayin', "but the day I can't hold my
own against *that*, I'll hang it up. Well, off to work."

"What I mean is . . ." I try to say, but Tananda is already gone, slitherin' after Junebug like some kind of fe-
line snake sidlin' up to a drunk canary.

This is just swell! While I suppose our "army vs. civilians" objective could be achieved by a catfight between
Tananda and Spyder, it wasn't exactly what we had in
mind when we planned this scenario.

As it turns out, though, I needn't have worried.
Watchin' from the bar, I see Junebug respond to Tananda's come-on like a first offender latchin' onto his lawyer, and instead of startin' a fight, Spyder just stands up

and stomps out of the place with a scowl on her face and her ears laid back in her multicolored hair.

"Who's that talking to your buddy?" Frumple sez, materializin' in front of me.

I make a big show of lookin' back at our table.

"Just a broad," I shrug casual-like, signallin' for a refill. "Why?"

"No reason. For a minute there I thought she looked familiar is all."

He heads off down the bar to fetch my drink, leavin' me a little uneasy. I tell myself there is no reason why the Deveel should recognize Tananda, as her current disguise bears no resemblance to her regular appearance. Still, he is an unstable element in the current equation, and I would just as soon keep him out of it entirely, if possible.

"I thought we were targeting Shu Flie," Nunzio sez, easin' in beside me at the bar. It may have been crowded where we were, but people usually manage to make room for someone Nunzio's size, especially if he's talkin' to someone my size.

"We were," I sez. "But Tananda has her own ideas on the subject."

"Well it sure put Spyder's nose out of joint. I don't think I've ever seen her so mad. Unless it was the time . . ."

"Hey . . . Abdul!"

It was Junebug, standin' right behind us tryin' to get Frumple's attention. He has his arm draped around Tananda's shoulders, but if you look real close youse can see that she is actually holdin' up most of his weight.

"Yeah? What do you want?"

Though he wasn't particularly pleasant about it, the speed with which any of our crew could get the Deveel's attention was evidence that he hadn't forgotten we all knew his secret.

"I . . . we need . . . a room."

"There aren't any available."

Frumple starts to turn away, only to find his movement

is restricted . . . specifically by my cousin who has reached across the bar and taken hold of his shoulder.

"Give him a room," Nunzio sez, soft-like.

Now, when Nunzio talks quiet like that, it usually means he is about to lose his temper . . . which, in this case, is understandable. I mean, we have put an awful lot of trouble into this setup to have it thwarted by anything silly like room availability.

"But there aren't any . . ."

"Give him the room you keep for yourself. You're going to be too busy down here to use it for a while."

"I'm not *that* busy," the Deveel argues, tryin' to twist out of Nunzio's grip. "And if . . ."

"You *could* be a lot busier . . . if you know what I mean," Nunzio sez, startin' to tighten his hand.

"All right! Okay! Here!" Frumple sez, producin' a key from his pocket and passin' it to Junebug. "Last door on the right!"

"Thanks, Nunzio," Junebug calls over his shoulder as he and Tananda weave their way toward the stairs.

My cousin waits until they are out of sight before he bothers to release his grip on Frumple.

"Now, see how nice it makes you feel to bring a little happiness into someone else's life?"

The Deveel bares his teeth in a silent snarl, then heads off down the bar to tend to the growin' number of shouters.

"Well, *that* didn't take long," I sez, lookin' at the stairs where Tananda and Junebug have vanished.

"Not surprising, really," Nunzio sez with a leer. "I mean, how long would *you* dawdle around if Tananda invited you into her room?"

If you surmise from this that I have not given my cousin a *complete* account of my meetin' with Tananda, you are correct. I decide to change the subject.

"One question, cousin," I sez, takin' a sip of my drink. "How are we supposed to know when to intrude on the proceedin's?"

"I dunno, I guess we wait until we hear Tananda start callin' for help."

I swivel my head around and stare at him.

"Nunzio," I sez, "has it occurred to you that with the racket goin' on down here, she can shoot off a cannon and we won't be able to hear her?"

This brings a scowl to his face.

"Good point," he sez, borrowin' a sip from my drink.

"Good point? Is that all you got to say?" I am startin' to get worked up now. "What do you think is gonna happen if we miss our cue and *don't* break things up?"

"Hmmm . . . well, if we don't rescue her, then Tananda's gonna have to deal with Junebug herself."

". . . Which means one of our squad ends up in the hospital," I finishes for him. "Either that or *Tananda* takes a bunch of lumps waitin' for us to show up like we said we would."

"Like I said . . . good point."

"Well, *I'm* not gonna just sit here," I sez, standin' up. "You comin' with me?"

"You mean bust in on 'em right now?"

"That's *just* what I mean. Why not? They've already been up there for a while."

At this point, I am besieged by mental images of Tananda bein' pawed by Junebug . . . all the while callin' vainly for us to help her.

"Just a second, Guido," Nunzio sez, then raises his voice. "Hey! Bee!"

Our junior magician comes scuttlin' over to us.

"What is it, Nunzio?"

"I want you to go out and find some police and bring them back here."

"Police? But why . . ."

"Just do it! Okay?"

"Sure Nunzio. City police or Military Police?"

"Both, if you can manage it. Now get going."

He turns to me as Bee goes sprintin' out into the night. "All right, Guido. It's party time!"

XII:

"It sure looks to me like a big night to-night!"

—ARTHUR, REX

In our plannin', we had neglected to establish a means by which Tananda was to let us know which room they was gonna be in. (Oversights such as this is why I am usually willin' to let someone else ... like the Boss ... do our plannin' for us!) Fortuitously, the Deveel had given them directions loud enough for us to hear at the same time as he was handin' them the key, so we have no trouble findin' where we are supposed to be.

"I don't hear anything ... do you?" Nunzio sez, cockin' his head outside the door.

By now, however, I am gettin' a head of steam up and am in no mood to quibble over details.

"Maybe you should have thought of that *before* you sent Bee for the cops," I sez, backin' up to get a runnin' start. "But since you did, we are kinda committed to be there when the waltz starts ... know what I mean?"

"Well, just remember that the key to this working is to try to promote confusion whenever possible."

"That shouldn't be hard," I snarl, and launch myself at the door.

I have specifically mentioned our objective of "confusion" so that youse folks readin' this will not think your brains have suddenly gone Fruit Loops while tryin' to sort out this next series of events . . . that is, it's *supposed* to be confusin'!

Anyway, the door goes down, as doors are inclined to do when I hit them goin' full tilt, and the two of us pile into the room . . . which I am not too busy to notice is considerably nicer than the room Frumple gave me yesterday.

To our startlement, there is no altercation occurrin' in the room . . . at least, not until we arrive. Tananda and Junebug are in a huddle on the sofa, but any noise she is makin' is not screams of outrage. Still, as we have made our entrance, my cousin and me have little choice but to continue with the script as originally planned.

Nunzio latches on to Junebug, liftin' him clear of the sofa whilst I turns my attentions to Tananda.

"*Are you okay, lady??*" I sez in my loudest voice, which projects pretty well thanks to my old drama coach. "*Just take it easy!!*"

"Damn it, Guido! Not yet!!" she hisses, glarin' at me as she struggles into a sittin' position.

Now, this is not part of our planned dialogue, and I glance over at Junebug quick-like to see if he has noticed that Tananda has let it slip that we know each other. I need not have concerned myself.

Nunzio is holdin' Junebug high enough that his feet are not touchin' the floor, hangin' onto him by the front of his uniform while shakin' him hard. Of course, on the out-stroke, he is also slammin' our colleague into the wall in a repeated manner solidly enough to shake the buildin'. He has done this to me on a couple of occasions, so I can state from personal experience that while it may *look* like he is tryin' to help you clear your head, the actualities of the situational is that after hittin' the wall a few times, you're lucky to remember your name, much less why he is carryin' on in this manner.

"Calm down, Junebug!" my cousin is shoutin'. *"She isn't worth it!! We don't want no trouble!!!"*

Seein' as how Junebug is distracted, which I can tell by the way his eyes are rollin' around independent-like in his head, I turn my attention to Tananda once more.

"Look, Tananda," I growl, lowerin' my voice so's only she can hear me, "I apologize if our timin' is less than exact. You can beat on me for it later. In the meantime, might I point out that the curtain is already up and you have been entrusted with a rather important role in our performance?"

"But we were just starting to . . ." she pauses here and draws a long, ragged breath. "Oh . . . All right!"

With this, she reaches up, takes hold of the shoulder of her dress, and rips it diagonally across her body down to the hip . . . in doin' so givin' me a quick glimpse of a lot more of Tananda than it has previously been my privilege to view.

"He was going to . . . Oh, it was just awful! What kind of people are you, anyway?"

She pauses in her hysterics.

"Guido!" she sez, urgent-like.

I am still starin' at the portion of the dress she is now tryin' to hold together with one hand.

"Hmmm? Oh . . . Yeah! *Just take it easy, lady!!*" I sez, avertin' my eyes as I am a little embarassed. *"He didn't mean nothin'!!"*

"Get him away from me!!! Just get him away!!!"

That cue I can remember.

"Come on Nunzio," I sez. "Let's get him out of here!"

With that, we each grab Junebug by one arm and usher him out of the room through the crowd that's startin' to gather. I look back at Tananda and give her a wink, but she just sticks her tongue out at me quick-like before continuin' her hysterics.

"WHAT KIND OF A PLACE IS THIS?" she screams

after us. *"Letting animals like that mix with decent people . . ."*

I lose the rest of her performance as we are carryin' Junebug down to the main floor by now.

The crowd what has been outside the room was nothin' compared to what was waitin' for us in the bar. Everybody in the place is crowdin' around to see what is goin' on . . . well, crowdin' at a distance like folks do when they don't want to be right up close to the action. Toward the back, I can see the uniforms of some of the local constabulary, though they are havin' trouble reachin' us through the heavy traffic. Of the Military Police there is no sign . . . so I figure we will just have to start without them.

"What's going on up there?" Frumple demands, appearin' at my side.

"Here," I sez out of the side of my mouth, pushin' some money into his hand. "Take this."

"What's this for?" he sez, scowlin' at my offerin'.

"That should cover the bar bill for our table since this afternoon."

"Your bar bill?" he frowns. "I don't get it. We had a deal. I give you free drinks, and you don't bust up my place or tell anyone . . . my secret."

"Don't worry," I sez, showin' him a few teeth. "Your secret is safe."

"Then what . . . Hey! Wait a minute! You aren't going to . . ."

Just then, the police reach us.

Now, earlier Nunzio and me was commentin' how there wasn't anyone in the bar who could give us a run for our money. This situational changes when these cops roll in. There are four of them, and while none of them looks particularly tough physically bein' uniformly soft around the middle, there is a steadiness in their eyes that anyone in the business can spot as the mark of someone what don't get particularly rattled when trouble starts.

"All right!" the biggest one of 'em says, steppin' up to us. "What's going on here?"

As you might guess, people of Nunzio's and my profession are not overly fond of the authorities of the law, particularly the street variety, and we usually give them wide berth. So in actual confrontation such as this, it is not too difficult for us to act unpleasant.

"What kind of town is this?" Nunzio bellows, glarin' around at the crowd. *"A man in uniform tries to have a quiet drink . . . and the next thing you know, some bimbo is trying to set him up for a bum rap!!"*

"Just take it easy, soldier," the cop sez, friendly-like. "You're among friends now. There are a couple of us who were in the service ourselves once."

This is somethin' we hadn't counted on. The last thing we need right now is for the cops to act reasonable. I figure it is about time I take a hand in the proceedin's personally.

"Oh, yeah?" I sneers. *"What happened? You chicken out when it looked like there might actually be some fightin' to be done? Figured it was safer hasslin' drunks than gettin' shot at?"*

"Cool down, soldier," the cop smiles, but I can see his lips are real tight. "Let's just step outside and discuss this."

"You hear that?" Nunzio shouts to the Flie brothers who are still holdin' down our table. *"They don't mind taking our money for drinks . . . but when we catch 'em tryin' to roll one of our boys, THEN they try to send us packing!"*

"Oh yeah?" Shu Flie bristles and stands up, crowdin' toward us followed close by his brother. "Well if they want us out of here, they're gonna have to *throw* us out!"

Caught between us on one side and the Flie brothers on the other, the cops start gettin' nervous, swivelin' their heads back and forth tryin' to keep an eye on all of us.

"Now hold on a minute!" the cop we was talkin' to sez. "Who are you saying was trying to roll you?"

"That floozie upstairs!" Nunzio snarls, jerkin' a thumb back over his shoulder. *"She gave our buddy the big come-on . . . crawlin' all over him, you know? Then when we*

*go up to see if he's all right 'cause he's been drinkin',
she's goin' through his pockets!"*

"That's right!" Hy Flie sez. "We were sittin' right over
there when this bombshell starts playing up to Junebug
here!"

"Of course, they stick up for each other!" one of the
guys in the front of the crowd snorts to the fellow next
to him.

I don't think he meant to be heard, but Shu Flie was
standin' right beside him and caught it.

"Are you callin' my brother a liar?" he sez, startin'
for the loudmouth.

I'm thinking we got the fight in the bag, but one of the
cops gets between 'em holdin' them apart with a hand on
each of their chests.

"Back off! *Both of you!*" he orders. "We're going to
get to the bottom of this . . ."

"GET YOUR HANDS OFF THAT SOLDIER!!"

The Military Police have arrived and come pushin'
through the crowd to join our discussion group.

*"Military personnel are to be handled by the MPs and
not pushed around by some cop with a chip on his shoulder!"*

The sergeant in charge of the MPs is a real bruiser and
just the kind of Joe I wanted to see . . . not too bright and
dog-stubborn. He has three of his buddies with him, so
we *really* outnumber the cops. Then I see some more police uniforms comin' through the door and have to revise
my count again. It looks like a real party shapin' up.

"We *weren't* pushing him around!" the first cop sez,
steppin' in nose to nose with the MP sergeant. "What's
more, this investigation involves a civilian, so until we
find out what happened . . ."

"We caught some bimbo tryin' to roll one of our boys!"
Shu Flie shouts at the MP. *"And now they're all tryin' to
cover up for her!"*

"Is that so!" the MP scowls, glarin' around at the bar.
"These soldiers risk their lives to keep things safe for you,
and *this* is the thanks they get?"

What a great guy, I think. What a great, gullible, thick-headed guy. He could probably get this fight started all by himself . . . if we let him.

"I resent that remark!" our cop snarls, finally startin' to lose it. *"We risk our lives too, you know!"*

"Oh excuse me! I forgot!" the MP smiles nasty-like. "You're in constant danger of choking to death on a doughnut!"

"Doughnut, is it?" the cop sez, lookin' around slow at the other cops . . . maybe to count heads and check the odds before decidin' what to do or say next.

I turned my head to sneak a wink at Nunzio, just in time to see Tananda make her entrance from the stairs.

"THERE THEY ARE!!!" she shrieks. *"Those are the soldiers that attacked me!!"*

It would seem that she has been busy with her disguise gizmo, because the bruise I have earlier commented on is now clearly in evidence . . . although to an experienced eye such as my own, it is obvious that it is not a recent injury. Of course, bein' Tananda and havin' a flair for the dramatic, she has not stopped there. While the dress she is wearin' is the same color as the one she had on earlier, its hemline and fit are a lot more modest than the hot outfit she used to get Junebug's attention . . . a *lot* more. On top of that, her wild, sexy hairdo now looks more like some librarian's maidenly bun what has been pawed to pieces. The *real* beauty of all this, however, is that she is standin' where the cops can see her, but the MPs can't! Of course, the crowd can see her, too.

"*That's* no floozie!" the guy what mouthed off earlier sez.

"Hey! I think she works with me!" someone else chimes in.

"See what happens when they let *soldiers* in here?"

The crowd is startin' to get ugly, but to give the cop credit, he tries to calm things down.

"Just relax, everybody!" he hollers. **"We're** handling this!"

Then he turns back to the MP, his face all grimlike.

"We've got to get to the bottom of this, sergeant," he sez. "I want you to hold *those* three men . . ."

As he's sayin' this, he raises his hand to point in our direction.

Now there is a gag that Nunzio and I have pulled so often that we don't even have to look at each other now to know what to do. We are still holdin' Junebug up by his arms, and the cop is close enough that when he tries to point at us, it's an easy matter for us to move Junebug sideways in front of his hand . . . then let go!

Unless you are watchin' real close at the right moment, this looks exactly like the cop took a poke at Junebug and decked him!

Realizin' the already tense nature of the situational, this is a little like beatin' on a blastin' cap with a hammer.

The MP starts to reach for the cop, but I get there first . . . mostly 'cause I know what is comin' and have a head start.

"Let me!" I sez, then I do somethin' I've been waitin' to do all my life.

I lay my best punch on a cop . . . in front of witnesses!

XIII:

"Weren't you expecting me?"

—J. RAMBO

Me and Nunzio have a bit of a wait before the company commander shows up at his office. This is fine by me, as it gives me a chance to stop my nose from bleedin' quite so much, and we even talk the MPs guardin' us into gettin' some disinfectant to put on our knuckles.

If from this youse infers that it was quite a brawl, youse is correct. It was . . . and what's more we are the clear winners. Now, the civilian cops may have different opinions regardin' this, but we was still standin' at the end of it and they wasn't so I feel we are justified in claimin' the victory.

As I mentioned, our guards are okay guys and in a pretty good mood to boot, which is understandable as they was fightin' on our side in the fracas under discussion. We have a pretty good time with them while we are waitin', swappin' tales from the fight that were at least partially true, interruptin' each other all the time with comments of "Did you see it when I . . . ?" and "Yeah, what about when that big cop. . . ." In fact, we are gettin' downright chummy with 'em, but then the captain walks in.

All our talkin' stops when he appears, though he musta heard us long before we saw him, so there isn't really any point tryin' to pretend we have been this quiet all the time. Still, he doesn't look happy, so without any kind of spoken agreement we all drop back into our appointed roles. By this I mean the guards stand at parade rest and look stern, whilst me and Nunzio just sit and look uncomfortable . . . which isn't too hard since, as I said, we have not emerged from the fracas unscathed.

We watch in total silence as the captain sits down at his desk and starts studyin' the report which has been placed there. I suppose I could of looked at it myself when we was talkin' with the guards, but to tell you the truth it hadn't occurred to me until I see the captain readin' it and realize the fates of Nunzio and me might well be decided by what is in it.

Finally, the captain looks up as if seein' all of us for the first time.

"Where are the others?" he sez to one of the guards.

"At the infirmary tent, sir," the guard sez.

The captain raises his eyebrows.

"Anything serious?"

"No sir. Just a few bumps and bruises. Besides . . ."

"The guard hesitates and glances at me, and I knew I was on.

"I told 'em they should get patched up and let me talk to you first, Captain . . . sir," I sez. "You see, it was Nunzio and me what started the fight, and the squad just pitched in later to help us out . . . so I figured that . . . well, since we was responsible . . ."

"Can you verify this?" the captain sez to the guard, cuttin' my oration short.

"Yes sir."

"Very well. Send word over to the infirmary. Tell the rest of the squad they are free to return to their quarters

after their wounds are treated. Sergeant Guido and Corporal Nunzio are taking full responsibility for their actions."

"Yes sir," the guard sez, then salutes and leaves.

This is a bit of a load off my mind, as I have been
worryin' a bit about gettin' the crew into trouble with our
gambit. A bit, but not all . . . as there remains the question
of what the captain is gonna do about me and Nunzio.
This is a for real question, as the stare the captain is lev-
elin' at us is real noncommittal, which is to say he neither
looks happy nor upset . . . though I'm not sure what he
would have to be happy about in this situational.

"Are you aware," he sez finally, "that I was called off
stage to deal with this matter? One song into my final set,
no less?"

"No sir," I sez, 'cause I hadn't been.

This simple statement did, however, settle two things
in my mind. First, there is the matter of his rather flashy
outfit . . . which while it is indeed quite spiffy, is decidedly non-regulation. Second, it removed any doubts I
might be havin' as to the level of benevolence the captain
is feelin' toward us . . . noncommittal stare or not.

"According to this," he sez, lookin' at the report again,
"you two were involved in, if not the actual instigators of
a barroom brawl, not only with civilians, but with the
local police as well. Is there anything you'd like to add
to that?"

"One of those civilians tried to roll one of our squad,"
I sez.

I figure that now we have accomplished our mission, it
is time to start lookin' out for ourselves.

"Then, when we try to get him out, the others try to
say he has assaulted her. As far as the cops . . . I mean,
the local police go, well, they was tryin' to arrest us all,
even though our own military police were right there on
the scene of the alleged crime, and we was taught in basic
trainin' . . ."

"Yes, yes, I know," he waves. "Soldiers are to be tried
in military, not civilian court, so you two took on a whole

room full of civilians over a point in the Military Code.
Is that it?"

"Yes sir. That and to try to help one of our squad."

"Very well," he sez, and looks over at the guards. "You
men can go now. I'll handle this from here."

We wait quiet-like until the MPs file out of the room,
then a little longer as the captain is studyin' our files
again.

"You two have only been assigned to me for about a
week . . . and only enlisted a few weeks before that. Is that
correct?"

"Yes sir."

"So you're fresh out of Basic and already a sergeant . . .
and corporal. And now this."

He goes back to starin' at our files, but I am startin' to
feel a little less anxious. While there is no question of us
beatin' the rap, as we have confessed, it's startin' to sound
like we might get off with nothin' more than losin' our
stripes . . . a possibility which does not distress me overly
much. Not bad for not havin' a mouthpiece to do our plea
bargainin'.

"The civilian authorities are recommending you be disciplined severely . . . that you be made an example of to
discourage other soldiers from following your example."

I start feelin' anxious again. This does not sound so encouragin', and after a career unblemished by a single con-
viction, I am not eager to spend time in an army stockade. I
wonder if it is too late to withdraw our confession . . . and
whether the MPs are still outside.

"Very well," the captain sez finally, lookin' up from
our files. "Consider yourselves disciplined."

We wait for him to say more, then realize that's all
there is.

"Sir?"

The captain gives a tight little smile at our reactions.

"Do you men know what an army that's growing as
fast as ours needs the most?"

I experience a sinkin' feelin' in my stomach, as I have

heard this speech before. Nunzio, however, was not present the last time it was run past me.

"A better tailor," he sez.

The captain blinks in surprise, then erupts in a quick bark of laughter.

"That's pretty good," he sez. "A better tailor. You've got a point there, Corporal Nunzio . . . but that wasn't what I was referring to."

He drops his grin and gets back on track.

"What we need are leaders. You can train men to shoot, but you can't train them to lead. Not really. We can show them the procedures and tell them the principles so they can at least go through the motions, but *real* leadership . . . the charisma to inspire loyalty and the guts to act in a crisis . . . that can't be taught."

He picks up the report and tosses it back down carelesslike.

"Now, publicly we have to discourage our soldiers from fighting with civilians, whatever the provocation. Any other position would endanger our welcome in the community . . . such as it is. We are aware, however, that there are those who try to exploit our men at any opportunity, and many who frankly resent us . . . though I never could understand why."

I am willin' to let this pass, but Nunzio doesn't.

"Maybe it's because the army is the major recipient of their tax money," he sez.

"But their taxes are being lowered, not increased by our campaigns," the captain frowns.

Just as it did the first time I heard it, this statement strikes an impure note in my mind. Again, however, I am not allowed time to pursue it.

"Whatever," the captain sez, shakin' his head. "The truth of the matter is, that while we cannot publicly condone incidents such as the one you were involved in, there are far worse things in the army's eyes than to be willing to fight for your men *and* the Military Code. The fact that you were willing to take this stand against civilians, police even . . . and after only three weeks in the army too . . .

Tell me, have you men given any thought to going Ca-reer? Of making the army your permanent occupation?"

This takes us a little aback, as we have given this idea about the same consideration we would give pokin' our-selves in the eye with a sharp stick.

"Ummm . . . to be honest with you, sir," I manage at last, "we was gonna see how things worked out in our first tour of duty before tryin' to reach any decision."

This struck me as a diplomatic answer, as it is not wise to tell a man you think his career choice stinks on ice . . . especially when he is in a position of control over your immediate future. For some reason, however, the captain seems to take my response as an encouragin' sign.

"Perhaps I can make the decision a little easier for you," he sez, startin' to scribble in our files. "I'm promoting you both. Nunzio, you're a sergeant now . . . and Guido, you're getting another stripe. Of course, we can't have you wan-dering around town now . . . or your squad either, for that matter. It might get our civilian hosts upset. Tell you what. I'm going to transfer you and your squad to Headquarters Staff. There's always opportunity for advancement there. That's all, men. You can go now . . . and congratulations!"

I would like nothin' more than a little time to think over this latest development, but it is not to be. Nunzio barely waits until we are clear of the commander's office before he starts on me.

"Guido," he sez, "am *I* crazy, or is the army?"

"Probably both," I sez, "though I'll admit I think the army has an edge on you in the 'foo-foo land' depart-ment."

"I don't get it. I just don't get it," he continues like I hadn't said anythin'. "I mean, we disobeyed standing or-ders . . . even roughed up the *cops* for cryin' out loud. And we get promoted for *that*?"

"It would seem," I sez carefully, "that we're bein' re-warded for 'action against the enemy.' I guess we just miscalculated who the army sees as 'the enemy,' is all."

We walk on in silence for a few, each of us reflectin'
on what has occurred.

"I guess there is a good side to this," I sez at last. "If
we are gonna continue our attempts to disrupt the army,
headquarters is probably the best place to do it from."

"True enough," Nunzio sighs. "Well, Guido, let me be
the first to congratulate you."

"On what?"

"Why, on your promotion, of course," he sez, glancin'
sideways at me. "I know *exactly* how much it means to
you."

I think of hittin' him, but he has deliberately stepped
out of range as he lays this on me.

"Nunzio," I sez, "let us not forget your own . . ."

"Hey guys!! Wait up!!"

We look around to find Spyder comin' up behind us.

"Oh, hi Spyder."

"So what happened?" she sez, tryin' to get her wind
back as she catches up to us.

"Well, there was a bit of a fight after you left, and . . ."

"I *know* that," she interrupts. "I heard. Sorry I missed
it. I meant afterward. Are you guys in trouble?"

"Naw," Nunzio shrugs casual-like. "In fact, we're all
being transferred to Headquarters Staff . . . oh yeah, and
Guido and me got promoted."

He sez this real easy, expectin' her to be as surprised
as we was. Strangely enough, however, she lets it skate
on by her.

"What about the civilian authorities? What are you
gonna do about them?"

"Nothin'," I sez. "Why should we?"

"Are you kidding? The way I heard it you punched out
a cop! They aren't gonna just ignore *that!*"

"They're gonna have to," I shrugs. "As soldiers, we are
subject to discipline by the military, *not* civilian courts."

"We are?" she frowns, stoppin' in her tracks.

"Sure. Don't you remember? They told us about that back in Basic."

"I *told* you you should pay attention to the Military Law lectures," Nunzio sez, grinnin' at her.

"Gee," she sez, chewin' her lip. "Then I guess you don't need the help I brought you."

"Help? What help?"

"Well, I thought you were gonna be in trouble with the civilian authorities, and since I knew you guys was connected, I figured I should find somebody to pass the word to so . . ."

Until now I had only been listenin' casually. As Spyder spoke, however, a loud alarm began to sound in the back of my mind . . . a *very* loud alarm.

"Connected?" I sez, interruptin'. "You mean like with the Mob?"

"Of course," she sez.

"You went lookin' for the Mob?" Nunzio sez, catchin' on at last.

"That's right. Found 'em too."

"Wait a minute," I frowns. "When youse said you 'brought back help,' were you sayin' you've got somebody along *now*?"

"That's right," she sez, lookin' around. "He was with me when I spotted you a second ago. I may have gotten a little ahead of him, but he should . . ."

"Hello Guido . . . Nunzio . . . long time no see."

The owner of this new voice melts out of the shadows close to us . . . too close.

"Hello, Snake," I sez, edgin' a little away from Nunzio so we both have lots of room for whatever is gonna happen next.

"You remember me!" he sez, though his mockin' smile makes it clear he is not surprised. "I wasn't sure you would."

I don't think anyone would have trouble rememberin' Snake . . . except for maybe, witnesses . . . as he is what you would call highly memorable. He is tall and real thin, and has a habit of dressin' all in black like he is now, which is why he was able to ease up on us in the shadows.

"You guys know each other?" Spyder sez, hesitant-like lookin' back and forth between us.

"Oh, we're old friends," Snake sez in that smooth, purrin' voice of his.

"Actually, it's more like 'associates,' " Nunzio corrects, easin' even farther apart from me.

While both Nunzio and me know Snake, we have never pretended to like him. He is one of the top enforcers for the Mob, but tends to like his work a little too much for our tastes. You have perhaps noticed that when the occasion calls for it, neither Nunzio nor me are adverse to the judicious application of violence, but as it goes against our delicate natures we have trained ourselves to terminate such encounters in the briefest possible time. Snake, on the other hand, likes to prolong and drag out his work as much as possible . . . and he works with a knife. He can be as fast as his moniker when the situation calls for it, however, and though Nunzio and me had been confident about roustin' a room full of normal people earlier this evening, there is a serious question in my mind as to whether both of us workin' together can take Snake if things get ugly.

"Why don't you head on back to the barracks, Spyder," I sez, not takin' my eyes off Snake. "Our colleague here probably has some things he wants to discuss with us . . . privately."

"Not me!" Snake says, holdin' up his hands palms out in what to my eye is an exaggerated show of innocence. ". . . Though I'll admit I think a conversation between us would be . . . interesting. No, I'm just here to escort you to another old friend."

"And who would that be?" Nunzio sez.

Snake's smile slips away and his voice drops a dozen degrees.

"Don Bruce wants to talk to you . . . he wants to talk to you *real bad*."

XIV:

"You countermanded me on whose authority?"

—POPE JOHN

"That's quite some babe you got there."

I shoot a sideways glance at Snake when he sez this, but his manner seems as respectful as his tone, so I decide he is sincere and not tryin' to be sarcastic.

"She's okay," I sez, noncommittal-like.

Realizin' we are in trouble with the Mob, it does not seem like the best idea to seem *too* close to Spyder.

"So what happened to her hair?"

"I think she likes it that way," I shrugs. "Who knows with broads. Of course, it looked better before the army cropped it short."

"That reminds me of a joke I heard once," Nunzio sez. "It seems this guy takes an alligator, then cuts off its nose and tail, and paints it yellow . . ."

"You know," Snake interrupts, "while we were looking for you, she was asking me about joining the Mob after her enlistment is over."

I realize now why Snake is bein' so talkative. He is

checkin' politely to see if either Nunzio or me has any claim on Spyder . . . professionally or personally. This is understandable, for while I do not think he is afraid of us, every guy knows that messin' with another guy's moll—or, in the Mob, his recruit—is apt to be considered a challenge, so it is wisest to check things out carefully before proceedin'. While it is not exactly gettin' permission, havin' the courtesy to ask is a good way to avoid blunderin' into somethin'; thereby avertin' hurt feelin's, not to mention needless bloodshed.

"She's got her own mind," I sez cautious-like. "Of course, she was askin' me and Nunzio the same thing a week ago, so *we* was kinda figurin' to sponsor her if it came to that."

"Okay, got it," Snake nodes. "Of course, that depends on where you guys are going to be in the future."

He sez this easy enough, but it is a cold reminder of the realities of our situational. He is actin' friendly, like he has no grudge against us other than, perhaps, professional rivalry. There is no doubt in our minds, however, that if Don Bruce gives him the word to whack us, he will do his best to carry out that order.

"Speaking of our future," Nunzio sez, "where are we going?"

I have a pretty good idea of the answer from the direction we have been walkin', and Snake confirms it.

"Back to Abdul's Sushi Bar and Bait Shop," he sez. "Or, as Guido here would say, the scene of the perpetration."

"Snake," I sez, drawin' myself up a little, "are you tryin' to make fun of the way I talk?"

"Me?" he sez, all innocent-like. "Heavens no. I've always admired your command of the language, Guido, as does everyone else in the Mob I know. Besides . . ."

We have reached the doorway of our goal, but he pauses briefly to finish his sentence.

"I . . . *certainly* wouldn't want to offend anyone as tough as you . . . or you either, Nunzio. By the way, I *love* your new outfits. They really show off your legs, know what I mean?"

Now, I have been expectin' some kinda wisecrack about our uniforms ever since Snake stepped out of the shadows. It is oblivious to me, however, why he has waited until now to mouth off, as it allows him to duck through the door before we can reply by beatin' his head in . . . which is exactly what he does, leavin' us little choice but to follow him in.

"There they are now. Come in, boys! Come in!"

The scene which greets us can be taken in at a glance, but what that glance shows is none too promisin'.

The place is a wreck, with overturned and broken tables and chairs scattered everywhere. I had known we made a bit of a mess in the course of the altercation I mentioned earlier, but whilst it was in progress my attention was much more occupied with inflictin' damage on *people* whilst avoidin' receivin' damage from the same, so I had not been takin' close note of what was happenin' to the place itself. Lookin' at it now without the distractin' activity, however, it is clear that housekeepin' is gonna have their work cut out for them.

Don Bruce is leanin' against the bar drinkin' wine from one of the few remainin' bottles . . . drinkin' directly from the bottle as there are no unbroken glasses remainin' that I can see. Though his greetin' was real friendly, there is no pretendin' that this is a social call, as scattered around the room, leanin' against the wall in the absence of chairs, is no less than half a dozen Mob goons.

"Hi guys! Come join us!"

This comes from Tananda who is standin' on one side of Don Bruce. She has dumped her disguise for the occasion, but is wrapped in Don Bruce's lavender coat. While he maybe doesn't care for females the way Nunzio and me do, Don Bruce is always the finest of gentlemen when it comes to dealin' with them. Standin' next to him on the other side, is . . .

"**That's the ones!** Those are the guys that busted up the place! I thought I was paying you for *protection!!*"

Frumple is there. For a minute I think he's dropped his disguise as well, but then I realize that he's still disguised as a local and that his face is bright red 'cause he's hoppin' mad.

"All right, *all right!*" Don Bruce sez, soundin' a little annoyed. "We'll consider that a firm identification. Just get your place fixed up and send us the bill . . . better still, give us a list of what you need in supplies and repairs. We can maybe get you some *discounts* from the distributors and contractors . . . know what I mean?"

"I should think so," Frumple snorts, reachin' for the wine bottle.

"In the meantime," Don Bruce sez, movin' the bottle out of his reach, "why don't you take a little walk or something. There are a few things I want to discuss with the boys here."

The Deveel hesitates for a second, then nods his agreement.

"All right," he sez, but he shoots us a black look as he starts for the door. "I should have known that double-crossing Skeeve was behind you two . . . I suspected it from the start. Him and this floozie of his . . ."

"Hold it!!"

Don Bruce's voice cracked through the place like a whip, and I knew Frumple had made a mistake . . . a bad mistake.

"What did you just say about Skeeve? . . . And Miss Tananda here?"

The goons have come off the wall and are startin' to drift forward.

"I . . . um . . . that is . . ." the Deveel sez, lookin' around desperate-like.

"Perhaps you should consider being a bit more careful in your selection of words when describing an associate of mine . . . *or* a lady who is a personal friend *and* present at the time."

"Well . . . you see . . ." Frumple tries, but the Don isn't finished yet.

"I've reconsidered my settlement offer," he sez. "I

don't think that fixin' this place up again will do . . . considering the damage to your reputation. I think we'll have to set you up in a whole new place."

This confuses the Deveel, but he is scared enough to remember his manners.

"That's nice of you," he sez. "But I don't think . . ."

". . . On Deva!" Don Bruce sez, droppin' the other shoe.

For a second Frumple's eyes snap wide open. Then he turns on us like a cornered rat.

"You . . . you gave me your word!" he screeches. "You said you wouldn't tell anyone . . ."

"They didn't have to tell me nothin'," Don Bruce snaps. "I got ears in a lot of places . . . *includin'* the Bazaar."

"But I can't go back there!"

"I know that, too," Don Bruce sez cold-like. "Still, that's our offer. Either we set you up on Deva . . . *or* you stay right here and pay for your own repairs. Take it or leave it."

Now, I hadn't known that Don Bruce knew that Frumple was a Deveel, just like I was unaware that the Deveel was unwelcome in his own dimension for some reason. My surprise, however, was nothin' compared to Frumple's reaction. He looks like he's in shock.

"I . . . I can't go back there," he manages to repeat, finally.

"Good. Then it's settled." Don Bruce is suddenly friendly again. "Now why don't you go ahead and take that walk . . . and by the way . . ."

The Deveel turns to find the Don starin' at him real hard-like.

". . . Remember what I said . . . I got ears in a lot of places. If you start runnin' off at the mouth, *or* do anything to give Skeeve, Miss Tananda, or the boys here any grief, I'll hear about it. Remember that. Now, get outta here."

Frumple slinks off, and as soon as he's gone, Don Bruce jerks his head at the goons.

"You boys take a walk, too," he sez. "What we got to talk about is private . . . and Snake?"

"Yes, Boss?"

"Keep an eye on that joker, will you? Make sure he doesn't talk to anyone . . .'cause if he tries, I'm afraid he might have a little accident. Know what I mean?"

"Got it, Boss," Snake says, and follows the others out into the night.

"Well, boys," Don Bruce sez, turnin' to us at last. "Now that we're alone, I think it's about time we had us a little talk."

He is real friendly as he says this, but as you yourselves can see from the preceedin' incident with Frumple, this is not as reassurin' as it would appear. It occurs to me that I would not like to sit in on a Dragon Poker game with Don Bruce, as he would doubtless make you a friendly loan so's you could keep playin' while at the same time havin' a whole extra deck of cards hidden in his lap.

"Miss Tananda here was just tellin' me about your current operation . . ."

"That's right," Tananda sez. "Don Bruce didn't . . ."

" . . . and realizing, as you have just heard, that I pride myself in being informed," the Don continues, talkin' right over Tananda . . . which is a bad sign, "it was a little embarrassing to have to admit my ignorance until your little friend came to me this evening for help. Now, what I want to know is . . ."

"What are you doing operating in the kingdom of Possiltum . . . especially considering the agreement we made?"

"Agreement?" Tananda sez in a small voice.

"That's right," Don Bruce sez, turnin' to her. "You weren't around at the time, but way back when I first met Skeeve, we made a deal and I gave him my personal word that the Mob wouldn't move on the kingdom of Possiltum."

"But what does that . . ."

" . . . and since Skeeve . . . and through him, all of you . . .

are now on the Mob's payroll as employees, *your presence here is breakin' my word. Capish?*"

"I see," Tananda sez, glancin' over at us with new understandin'. "But tell me, Don Bruce, if the Mob isn't
operating in this kingdom, then what are you doing taking
protection money from merchants like Frumple? In fact,
what are you doing here at all?"

This is a good question, and one which has not occurred
to me . . . though I suspect I know the answer. The Don
has enough grace to look a little embarrassed, though,
when he gives it.

"All this is from *before* I gave my word," he sez. "I
never said we was going to give up the operations we
already had in place."

"Hmmm . . ." Tananda frowns, "it sounds like a pretty
fine distinction to me."

Of course, the Mob makes a lot of money from such
fine distinctions . . . but this does not seem like the time
to bring it up.

"That may be," Don Bruce sez, his voice hardenin' up
again. "But it's beside the point. I'm still waiting to hear
what *you're* doing here!"

"Oh that," Tananda smiles. "Well, you see . . .
umm . . ."

Though Tananda is no slouch at Dragon Poker and is
actin' very confident, I can see she is stuck and trying to
bluff.

"Relax, Tananda," Nunzio sez, speakin' for the first
time since we came in. "I can explain it."

"You can?" I sez, slippin' a bit in my surprise.

"Sure," my cousin insists, lookin' at me hard like he
does when I'm supposed to be ready to provide him with
an alibi.

"All right, Nunzio," Don Bruce sez, settlin' back
against the bar, "start talking."

"Well, you see, Don Bruce," Nunzio sez, "the Boss is
unhappy with the agreement you referenced regarding the
Mob's relationship with Possiltum."

"Oh he is, is he?" the Don snarls, but Nunzio holds up a hand and continues.

"The way it is," he sez, "is the Boss figures that circumstances have arisen which *neither* of you took into account in the original negotiation . . . specifically, the new expansion policy that's pushing the borders out."

"Go on," Don Bruce sez, but he's nodding now.

"The *spirit* of your agreement was that the Mob wouldn't infringe on the kingdom's territory, but the way it's going, the *kingdom* is pushing into the Mob's territory. What's more, the *letter* of your agreement is keeping the Mob from protecting what's ours."

"So I noticed," the Don sez, sarcastic-like.

"Now, the Boss doesn't think this is right. What's more, *he* feels personally responsible since it was his sloppy negotiating for the kingdom that has placed you in this predicament. The problem is that as he is now working for the Mob and not for the kingdom, he is not in a position to renegotiate the terms to make things right again."

"Yeah," Don Bruce sez thoughtful-like, "I can see that."

"Now, you may not know it, Don Bruce," Nunzio continues, "but the Boss thinks the world of you and would never do anything to hurt you or your reputation. Because of this, and because he feels responsible for your current difficulties, he has taken it upon himself to correct the situation by mounting a covert operation to halt the kingdom's expansion. In fact, the reason he has been keeping this secret from you is for a little extra insurance. This way, if anything goes wrong, you can swear under oath that you knew nothing about it, and certainly never took a hand or gave an order against Possiltum. What he's doing, Don Bruce, is setting himself up to be a scapegoat . . . all to take the pressure off you!"

While I am occasionally less than complimentary when referrin' to Nunzio's long-winded tendencies, there are times when I am truly grateful for his talent for shovelin' . . . like now. Even bein' as aware as I am of the truth of the matter, that the Boss has probably overlooked his agreement with Don Bruce completely when givin' us this assignment, I am not sure I could separate fact from guff in my cousin's rendition, even with the aid of a pry bar.

"That Skeeve!" Don Bruce laughs, hittin' the bar with his fist in his enthusiasm. "Can you see why I love him? He's really trying to do all this on his own . . . just for me? I'll tell you, boys . . ."

He glances around, then hunches forward before continuin'.

"You have no idea how much grief the other Mob bosses have been giving me because of that agreement. Especially the boss of the Island Mob."

"You mean Don Ho?" I sez.

"That's right," Don Bruce nods. "Even the boss of the senior citizens' Mob . . . Don Amechie! They've all been on my case. I'm just surprised that Skeeve was aware of it. I keep telling you, that boy's got real promise. You know what an organization as big as ours needs the most?"

"Leadership," Nunzio and me answer at the same time.

"Lead . . . Hey! That's right!" the Don sez, blinkin' at us in surprise. "You know, you boys have been shaping up pretty well yourselves since you started working for Skeeve. Maybe I should start giving some thought to setting you up with your own operations."

It occurs to me that this promotion thing is gettin' totally out of hand.

"Ummm . . . We're pretty happy with things the way they are, Don Bruce," I sez, quick-like.

"Yeah," Nunzio chimes in. "We figure the way things are going, the Boss is gonna need all the help we can give him."

"Hmmm . . . I suppose you're right," the Don sez, makin' us both a little uncomfortable with how unwillin' he seems to give up the idea of advancin' us in the ranks. "Tell you what, though, like Skeeve says, I can't take an open hand in this thing you got going, but if you want I can assign a few boys to give you a hand!"

A picture flits across my mind. A picture of me tryin' to sleep, much less operate, with Snake loiterin' about in the near vicinity.

"I . . . don't think so," I sez. "we're pretty used to workin' with the crew we got already. Besides, any of the boys you assigned to us would have to enlist . . . and there's no guarantee where they'd get assigned."

". . . And most of them would quit before they'd be seen in public in those outfits you're wearing," Don Bruce laughs, winkin' at Tananda. "Yeah. You got a point."

Me and Nunzio force smiles, which is as close as we can manage to joining in the merriment.

"Well, be sure to let me know if there's anything I can do to help."

"Sure, Don Bruce."

"Thanks, Don Bruce."

"Oh yeah! One more thing. How's Bunny doing?"

"Bunny?" Tananda sez, comin' off the bar like a prize-fighter. "That little . . ."

"Sure! You remember Bunny," I interrupts quick-like. "Don Bruce's *niece* who's workin' with us?"

"Oh! Right!" Tananda blinks, and settles back again.

"She's working out real well, Don Bruce," Nunzio supplies hurriedly. "In fact, right now she's holding down our office while we're out in the field."

"Yeah, right," Don Bruce waves. "But how is she getting along with Skeeve?"

Even though we can maybe snow him from time to time, the Don is pretty quick, and he catches our hesitation and glances at Tananda.

"Say . . . *you* aren't interested in Skeeve yourself, are you, Miss Tananda?"

Tananda thinks for a second, then wrinkles her nose.

"Not really," she sez. "I guess he's kind of like a kid brother to me."

"I see," Don Bruce nods. "Well, as a favor to me, could you take Bunny under your wing, too? She likes to talk tough and comes on like she's real experienced and worldly, but inside she's still just a kid. Know what I mean?"

In response, Tananda just nods slow-like. To my eye, she seems less than thrilled with the idea . . . especially after hearin' how serious Don Bruce takes promises.

"You know how the Boss is when it comes to dames," I sez, quick-like. "Slower'n a bail bondsman what's been stung three times runnin'."

I am tryin' to draw attention away from Tananda, but the Don is ignorin' me and starin' at her instead.

"Say . . . are you okay?" he sez, misreadin' her signals. "It looks like you've been takin' more than your share of lumps in this operation."

"I'm just a little tired," she sez, flashin' a quick smile. "You're right, though. I'm not getting any younger, and I'm not sure how many more nights like this I can take."

"Why don't you head on back to Big Julie's and hook up with Chumley?" I sez. "We're gettin' transferred out of here, and there's not much you'll be able to do on your own realizin' the shape you're in."

"Transferred?"

"That's right," Nunzio sez. "We've been promoted and transferred to headquarters. It seems the Mob isn't the only ones who can spot leadership potential."

As an indication of the physical and nervous stress of the night we have been through, I do not have the energy to even *think* about throttlin' him.

XV:

"An army travels on its paperwork!"

—J. CARLSON

"Well, Sergeant Guido, you and your squad come highly recommended. Yes, highly recommended indeed!"

"Yes, sir. Thank you, sir."

Okay, so I am layin' it on a little thick. Considerin' the number of officers I'm seein' here at headquarters, however, it seems like the wisest attitude for an enlisted type like me to assume . . . which is to say one step up from grovelin'.

"Well," he sez, settin' our files to one side and startin' to rummage through the other stacks of paper on his desk, "let's see what we can find for you in the way of assignments."

Actually, I would be surprised if he can find his *feet* in this office. It has only been a few times that I have seen so much paper stuffed into as little space as there is in this office . . . and most of the other times was in the offices I poked into while lookin' for this one. There is paper stacked *everywhere*, on the chairs and on the floor, on the window ledges and on the tops of file cabinets . . . not to mention the stacks set on the top of already filed paper in the open drawers of said cabinets. There are also, of course, assorted piles of paper on the desktop of the officer I am speakin' to, and it is through these stacks he is currently rummagin'.

"Ah! Here's something," he sez, pausin' to peer at one of the sheets he has been rifflin' through. "What would you say to my assigning you and your crew as sanitation engineers."

"As what?"

"You know," he sez, "digging and filling latrines."

It occurs to me that while there might be *some* potential for disruptin' the army from such a position, it is not a route I would be particularly eager to take. You see, Nunzio still ribs me about my work with the Realistic Doggie Doodle with Lifelike Aroma that Actually Sticks to Your Hands on my last assignment for M.Y.T.H. Inc., and I would therefore prefer to avoid workin' with variations on the real thing this time around.

"It sounds like a stinkin' detail . . . sir," I sez, the words sort of slippin' out.

I try to recover by addin' ". . . if you'll forgive the play on words . . . sir."

That's so he'll know I read.

I expect him to get a bit upset at my forthrightness, but instead he just gives a little shrug.

"Of course it is," he sez with refreshin' honesty. "But remember where you are, Sergeant. This is Headquarters . . . the brains of the army. It only stands to reason that most of that brain power is devoted to finding nicer, cushier assignments for the owners of those brains . . . which is to say the place is armpit deep in politics . . . if I make myself clear."

"Not really, sir."

The officer sighs.

"Let me try to explain it this way. Here, everybody knows somebody, and uses their connections to get the best jobs. The higher the connections, the better the jobs. You and your squad, on the other hand, have just arrived and consequently know nobody . . . which means that for a while, you'll have to content yourselves with the jobs no one else wants. I expect that as you make connections, you'll get better duties, but for the time being that's the way it is."

I consider mentionin' my connections with the Mob, but decide they will be of little value in this circumstantial and may even be construed as a threat. Then something else occurs to me.

"Is General Badaxe available, sir?"

This gets the officer's attention.

"You know General Badaxe?" he sez from under sky-high eyebrows.

"Not to any great extent, sir," I admit. "We just met once in passin'."

"Oh. Well, he *is* here at Headquarters, of course. I think you'll find that he's indisposed, however . . . at least he has been for the last couple of weeks."

"Would that indisposition by any chance be female, sir? Extra, extra large . . . a lot of makeup and jewelry?"

This earns me a lot harder look from the officer before he answers.

"As a matter of fact, yes," he sez at last. "You seem remarkably well informed for someone who has just arrived at Headquarters . . . or do you know the . . . young lady as well?"

For several reasons I figure it would be wisest *not* to admit the true relationship Nunzio and me has with Massha.

"She was with the general when I met him at court, sir," I sez, sorta truthfully.

"You've been to the Royal Court?"

"Yes sir . . . but it was a while back . . . just before the king married Queen Hemlock."

"I see," the officer sez, thoughtful-like, then sets the paper he was holdin' aside and starts rummagin' again.

"Well in that case, perhaps I *can* find something a bit

more pleasant in the way of an assignment."

"Take your time sir," I sez. "I can understand how things can be a bit disorganized with the general gone so much."

"Not really," the officer sez, absentminded-like. "If anything, they're going smoother."

"Excuse me? . . . sir?"

"What? Oh," he sez, returnin' his concentration to the situational at hand. "Well, I probably shouldn't say anything, but since you already know some of the personalities involved . . ."

He pauses to glance around like someone might be loiterin' among the stacks of paper . . . which considerin' their height is a real possibility.

"If you know General Badaxe, then you probably already know that while he is a more than adequate leader, he is rather inflexible in his attitudes as to how things should be done. That is, he wants things done *his* way, whether there is a better way of doing things or not."

This description sounds like everyone in the army I've met above the rank of corporal, but I content myself with noddin' in agreement.

"Well, a lot of us officers who came on board during the current expansion drive originally served under Big Julie back when he led the invasion of Possiltum. In some ways it's nice because it guaranteed us rank in the Possiltum army, but it also means we know there are other ways of doing things than the way General Badaxe wants . . . lots better ways. The trouble is, until now we haven't been able to implement any changes or improvements without disobeying orders from the general."

"And now?" I urge, not even botherin' to add a "sir" to it.

"Now, with the general 'indisposed,'" the officer smiles, gettin' a little lost in his own thoughts, "we're left pretty much on our own, which means we get to do things *our* way for a change. If Badaxe stays out of our hair for another few weeks, we should have this army whipped into shape so we can *really* get down to business. I'll tell

you, serving under Big Julie might have been a pain from
time to time, but that man sure knows how to run an army.
I wonder how he's doing now that he's retired?"

"Last time I saw him, he was doin' great."

If I had said God himself was walkin' through the door
I couldn't have gotten a bigger reaction from the officer.
He sits up straight sudden-like, and his eyes lose their
dreamy focus and center on me . . . though I notice they
are buggin' out a little.

"You know Big Julie?" he sez in kind of a reverent
whisper. "When was the last time you talked with him?"

"A couple weeks back," I sez. "Just before Nunzio and
me enlisted. We was sippin' some wine with him and
some friends over at his villa."

"You were a guest at his villa? Tell me, is it . . ."

The officer breaks off and shakes his head like a dog.

"Excuse me, Sergeant," he sez, in much more normal
tones. "I didn't mean to pry. It's just that . . . well, Big
Julie is something of a legend around Headquarters. I was
a junior officer when I served under him, and never met
him personally . . . just saw him a couple of times during
reviews and inspections."

"That's too bad," I sez, with real sympathy. "He's really a great guy. You'd like him . . . sir."

I finally remembers I was talkin' to an officer, and my
"sir" seemed to remind him of why I was in his office in
the first place.

"Now that I think of it," he sez, pullin' some papers
off the top of one of his stacks, "there *is* something here
that I could assign you and your crew to. Would you like
to take over running one of our supply depots?"

This sounds like just what we need to do the most damage to the army's attempts to reorganize. I also notice that
the officer is now *askin'* me about which assignment I
want.

"That sounds fine, sir."

"Good," he sez, startin' to scribble on the sheets. "We
have a whole supply crew in the infirmary right now—
got a bad batch of chili or something. Anyway, I'll just

put you and your squad in there as replacements, and when they get out, they can take the sanitation engineer slots."

It occurs to me that these other guys are gonna be less than thrilled with their new assignment, but that, of course, is not my problem. Still, it will be a good idea if for a while we keep a lookout for anyone tryin' to sneak up on us from the downwind side.

"Thank you sir," I sez, and mean it.

"Just report to Supply Depot Number Thirteen and you'll be all set."

"Yes sir . . . ummm . . . is it far? I mean, I got my crew outside and we got all our gear with us . . ."

"Just flag down one of the wagons going your way and hitch a ride," he sez. "One of the nicer things about working at Headquarters . . . with the supply depots right here is that there are *lots* of wagons around. You'll rarely have to walk anywhere."

"Yes sir. Thank you again, sir."

"Oh . . . Sergeant Guido?"

"Sir?" I sez, turnin' back to him.

He is pushin' a stack of papers across his desk toward me that must weigh more than twenty pounds.

"Since you'll be riding, you might as well take this with you instead of waiting for it to be delivered by courier."

"I . . . I don't understand, sir," I sez, eyein' this mountain of dead weight suspiciously like it was a distant relative arrivin' unannounced. "Do you want I should store this for you over at the depot?"

"Of course not," the officer sez, givin' a little laugh. "This is for your requisition and inventory forms."

I am likin' this less and less the more I hear.

"You mean we gotta fill all this out just to move somethin' in or out of the depot . . . sir?"

"You misunderstand me, Sergeant," he sez quick-like. "These aren't the forms themselves."

I experience a quick flood of relief.

". . . These are just the *instructions* for filling out the forms!"

The relief I had been feelin' disappears like a single shot of whiskey in a big bowl of watered-down punch.

"The instructions," I echoes weakly, starin' at the pile.

All of a sudden this assignment is not lookin' as good as it had a few minutes ago.

The officer notices the expression on my face.

"Come, come now, Sergeant," he sez, givin' me what I guess is supposed to be a fatherly smile. "It's not as bad as it looks."

"It isn't?" .

"No. It's really quite simple once you get the hang of it. Just read these instructions all the way through, then follow everything they say to the letter, and everything will be fine."

"If you say so, sir," I sez, unconvinced.

"Yes, I *do* say so . . . *Sergeant*," he sez, givin' up his sales effort. "I *told* you we were going to get things under control and to do that, proper documentation is vital. It may look like a lot of needless hassle, but believe me, unless all the paperwork for supplies is filled out correctly, the best of armies will bog down and become ineffective."

"Yes sir. Thank you, sir."

With that, I salute and get out of his office quick . . . takin' the stack of paper with me, of course. All of a sudden, my depression over seein' the massive list of instructions disappears. Instead, I am feelin' a degree of optimism I have not felt since the Boss sent us on this assignment without realizin' what he was doin', the officer has just made our job a lot easier.

"Without proper paperwork," he had said, "the army will bog down and cease to be effective . . ." and, as you know, the effectiveness of the army was a matter of no small concern to me and Nunzio.

XVI:

"So what's wrong with following established procedures?"

—M. GORBACHEV

The warehouse which was Supply Depot Number Thirteen was truly immense, which is to say it was big. In fact, it was so huge that youse got the feelin' that if the weather turned bad, they could move all the stuff out of here and have the war indoors. The only trouble with that idea was that by the time they got everythin' moved out, odds are they would have forgotten what it was they was fightin' about in the first place . . . but even if they could remember, they'd probably be too tired to want to fight about it.

There was racks of stuff everywhere, with aisles big enough to drive a wagon down scattered around so as to carve everythin' into a series of islands, and *lots* of tunnels and crawl spaces twistin' their way into each of the islands. It occurred to me upon first viewin' this expanse that it was gonna be a perfect base of operation for us, as when and if anythin' went wrong, it would make one whale of a hideout. This thought was amplified when we discovered that the crew what had worked here before us had apparently opted to live on-site, as there were a lot of "nests" and hole-ups around the warehouse furnished with cots and hammocks and pillows and other stuff obliviously filched from the piles of supplies.

In short, it was a sweet setup, and the crew loses no time settlin' in, after some of them scattered and went explorin' to find out just what sort of stuff we have inherited to ride herd on while a couple of us tried to make sense out of the paperwork and charts heaped up on the desks.

"Hoo-ey!" Shu Flie sez, emergin' from the stacks with his brother at his side. "I've never seen so much stuff in one place! They got everything here!"

"A lot of it's pretty old, though," Hy Flie sez. "We had newer stuff than some of this junk back on the farm . . . and most of that stuff is still around from Pop Flie."

"Pop Flie?" I sez before I has a chance to think about whether or not I really wants to hear the answer.

"That's our grandpa," Shu explains. "Course, sometimes we call him . . ."

"I get the picture," I sez, interruptin' before he can explain any more.

It occurs to me to make a point of *not* ever visitin' the Flie residence.

"What I can't figure," Junebug sez, joinin' our discussion, "is how they keep track of all this stuff. I mean, there doesn't seem to be any order or scheme to how things are stored. It's like they just keep pushing the old pile further back and stack the new stuff in front as it comes in without any effort to group things by category."

This sounds uncomfortably like the beginnin' of an idea which could improve our efficiency . . . which is, of course, the last thing my cousin and me want to see happen. Sneakin' a glance at Nunzio, I can see he's thinkin' the same thing, and catchin' my eye he gives a little shake of his head to confirm that observational.

"Ummm . . . I don't guess it is such a bad system, Junebug," I sez, thinkin' fast. "I mean, would *you* want to rearrange all this stuff to make room for each new shipment as it comes in?"

"You could get around that by leaving extra room in each storage category," he sez, not backin' off from his idea. "We gotta do *something* to organize this mess. Otherwise, we'll be spending all our time just trying to locate each item when we have to fill an order. I can't see how they've been operating around here without some kind of system."

"They've got a system all right," Spellin' Bee sez, lookin' up from the Forms Instruction Manual he was readin'. "The problem is, they've got so much duplicate paperwork to fill out they probably never had any time left over to try to organize the warehouse itself! I can't believe they expect us to fill out all these forms for every item in and out of inventory."

What the officer told me flashes across my mind, and it gives me an idea.

"Do you think you can come up with a better trackin' system, Bee?" I sez.

"Probably," he sez, shuttin' the instruction manual. "Let's see . . . we'd need some sort of floor map . . . two of them actually, one so we know what's already here and where it is, and a second to establish the redefined areas . . . and then a simple In/Out Log so we could track the movement of items . . ."

"Okay," I interrupts, "get started on it. Figure out what we're gonna have to do and what you'll need in the way of information."

This, of course, earns me a hard look from Nunzio.

"I . . . If you say so, Guido," Bee sez, hesitantly, glancin' at the instruction manual. "But shouldn't we be following the established procedures?"

"Just go ahead and work up your plan," I sez. "We'll worry about fillin' out the army paperwork *after* we get this place functionin' the way we think it should."

"Okay," Bee shrugs. "Come here a second, guys, and I'll show you what I need. If you can start mapping out what's already here, I can start roughing out an In/Out Log, and . . ."

"Excuse me, *Sergeant* Guido," Nunzio sez. "Can I have a word with you . . . in private?"

"Why certainly, *Sergeant* Nunzio," I smile, givin' it right back to him, and follow him as he moves a little ways away from where the crew is huddlin'.

"What are you trying to do?" he hisses, as soon as we are alone. "Maybe I missed a loop, but I was under the impression that improving efficiency was the *last* thing we wanted to do here!"

"It is," I sez, "except everyone on the crew is thinkin' just the opposite. I'm just stallin' for a little time by insistin' that Bee come up with a complete plan before we actually have to *implement* any changes."

"Okay," Nunzio nods, "but what happens after he finishes comin' up with a new setup?"

"Then we either stall some more . . . *or* see if things will actually get fouled up more if we go ahead and try to go against army procedures. The officer what was briefin' me seemed pretty certain that the whole army will grind to a halt if all that paperwork Bee is talkin' about doesn't get filled out. At the very least we should have a chance to find out whether or not he is right."

"I dunno," my cousin frowns. "It seems to me that . . ."

"Guido! Nunzio!!"

We turn to find an apparition bearin' down on us. At first, I think it is one of those new armored wagons the army has been experimentin' with . . . only done up as a parade float. Then I look again, and see that it's . . .

"Massha!"

By the time I get this out, our associate has reached us, wrappin' one meaty arm around each of us in a humongous hug.

"I *heard* you guys were here and just *had* to come by and say 'Hi'!"

Because I am sorta to one side of her instead of directly in front of her, I can see past her to where our crew has stopped what they are doin' to gape at us . . . which is the normal reaction of folks what is seein' Massha for the first time.

"H . . . Hi, Massha," Nunzio sez, managin' to squirm loose. "How are things going? Any word from the Boss?"

"Not a peep," Massha sez, lettin' go of me. "There were some funny signs coming through a while back on the monitor ring I gave him, but they settled down and since then everything seems to be normal."

"Do you think he's okay?" I sez. "He's been gone nearly three weeks now."

"Maybe . . . maybe not," she shrugs. "Remember that time doesn't flow at the same speeds on all dimensions. It may only have been a few *days* where he is."

"I get it," Nunzio nods solemn-like. "Like in Moorcock's *Eternal Champion* books."

"That's right," Massha beams. "As to your other question, things couldn't be going better. Hugh and I are hitting it off like a house afire. I'll tell you boys, I don't like to brag, but I've got him so lovesick, I don't think he remembers that he's *in* the army . . . much less that he's supposed to be running it."

Now, I haven't read the book they was chattin' about a second ago, but this is somethin' I *can* comment on.

"Ummm . . . Massha?" I sez. "That may not be such a good thing."

"What do you mean?" she sez, her smile fadin' as she looks back and forth between Nunzio and me. "That was my assignment, wasn't it?"

"Tell her, Guido," Nunzio sez, dumpin' the job of givin' Massha the bad news in my lap.

"Well, the way *I'm* hearin' it," I sez, wishin' I was dead or otherwise preoccupied, "the army is functionin' better without him."

"But that doesn't make sense!"

"It does when you consider that the layer of officers directly under him trained and served under Big Julie," Nunzio sez, redeemin' himself by comin' to my rescue. "The more you keep him away from his troops, the more those officers get to run things their way . . . and it seems they're better at this soldierin' than General Badaxe is."

"So you're saying that the best thing I could do to louse up things is to let Hugh go back to commanding the army?" Massha sez, chewin' her lower lip thoughtful-like. "Is that it?"

"So it would seem," I sez, relieved at not havin' to be the first to voice this logical conclusion. "I'm really sorry, Massha."

She heaves a hugh sigh, which on her is really somethin', then manages a wry grin.

"Oh well," she sez. "It was fun while it lasted. Nice to know I can still distract a man when I set my mind to it, though."

Politeness and self-preservation convince me to refrain from makin' any editorial additions to this comment.

"I guess I'll just say my goodbyes and head back to Big Julie's," she continues. "Any word from the other team?"

"They've called it quits, too," Nunzio sez. "You'll probably see them when you get to Big Julie's and they can fill you in on the details."

"So it's all riding on the two of you, huh?" she sez, cocking an eyebrow at us. "Well, good luck to you. I'd better get moving and let you get back to work. It looks like your friends are waiting for you."

I glance over where she is lookin' and sure enough, the whole crew is standin' there, alternately glancin' at us and mutterin' together.

Wavin' goodbye to Massha, we ambles over to join them.

"Who was that?" Spyder sez, kinda suspicious-like.

"Who, that?" I sez, tryin' to make it casual. "Oh, just an old friend of ours."

"Scuttlebutt has it that she's the general's girlfriend," Junebug sez in a flat voice.

"Where'd you hear that?" Nunzio sez, innocent-like.

"Here and there," Junebug shrugs. "Face it, there can't be many people around Headquarters who would fit her description."

He had us there.

"Isn't it about time you guys told us exactly what is going on?" Spellin' Bee sez.

I realize, far too late, that we have been seriously underestimatin' the intelligence of our crew.

"What do you mean by that?" Nunzio sez, still tryin' to bluff his way out of it.

"Come on, Nunzio," Junebug sighs, "it's been pretty obvious since Basic that you and Guido here don't really belong in the army. You've got too much going for you to pass yourselves off as average recruits."

"You fight too good and shoot too good for someone who's supposed to be learnin' all this for the first time," Shu Flie sez.

". . . And you've got too many connections in high places," Spyder adds, "like with the Mob."

". . . And with devils," Bee supplies.

". . . And now with the general's girlfriend," Junebug finishes. "All we want to know is, what are you guys *really* doing in the army? I mean, I suppose it's none of our business, but as long as we're servin' together, what affects you affects us."

"Bee here thinks you're part of some secret investigation team," Hy Flie sez, "and if that's what's going on we'll try to help . . . unless it's us you're supposed to be investigating."

"Well, guys," Nunzio sez, shakin' his head, "I guess you found us out. Bee's right. You see, the army wants us to . . ."

"No," I sez, quiet-like.

Nunzio shoots me a look, but keeps goin'.

"What Guido means is we aren't supposed to talk about it, but since you've already . . ."

"I said 'No,' Nunzio!" I sez, squarin' off with him. "The crew's been playin' it straight with us all along. *I* say it's time we told them the truth . . . the *real* truth."

Nunzio hesitates, as he is not real eager to go head to head with me, then glances back and forth between me and the crew.

"Okay," he sez finally. "It's your funeral . . . go ahead and tell them."

Then he leans against the desk with his arms folded while I fill the crew in on our assignment . . . startin' with how the Boss's plan to keep Queen Hemlock from tryin' to take over the world fell apart when King Rodrick died, right up to our current plans to try to use our position in the supply depot to mess up the army's progress. They're all real quiet while I'm talkin', and even when I'm done no one sez anythin' for a long time.

"Well," sez Spyder, breakin' the silence, "the way I see it, we can't mess up *every* shipment or the army will just jerk us out of here. We'd better hold it down to one in five for a while."

"One in ten would be better," Junebug sez. "Otherwise . . ."

"Wait a minute! Stop the music!" Nunzio explodes, interruptin' the conversation. "Are you guys sayin' you're willin' to *help* us screw things up?"

"Sure. Why not?" Shu Flie sez, puttin' a hand on my shoulder. "You and the Swatter here have been lookin' out for us since Basic. It's about time we did something for you for a change."

"Besides," his brother chimes in, "it's not like you're trying to bring down the kingdom or destroy the army. You're just out to slow things up a little . . . and that's fine by us."

"What it boils down to," Spyder smiles, "is that after working with you two all this time, we know you well enough to trust you to not hurt us . . . or anyone else for that matter . . . unless it's absolutely necessary. I think I speak for all of us when I say we've got no problem putting our support behind any plan you think is right. Am I right, guys?"

There is a round of nods and affirmative grunts, but I am only half payin' attention. It is occurrin' to me that I am buildin' a better understandin' of what the Boss means when he sez he's nervous about commandin' more loyalty than he deserves. While the crew is sayin' they don't be-

lieve we would do anythin' to hurt them, I am thinkin' about
how we set them up for the barroom fight in Twixt . . . a detail I omitted when I was testifyin' about our recentactivi-
ties. This makes me feel a little low, and while I am not
about to refuse their help, I find it strengthens my resolve
to avoid such leadership and decision makin' positions in
the future.

"What about you, Bee?" Nunzio is sayin'. "You aren't
lookin' too happy. You want out?"

"N . . . No. It isn't that," Bee sez, quick-like. "I'm willing to help as much as I can. It's just that . . . well, I was
sort of looking forward to trying to get this place organized."

"You can still do that, Bee," Junebug sez, winkin' at
him. "We still need to know what's going on, even if we
only use the information to slow things up."

"It's just too bad we don't have our own teamsters,"
Shu Flie sez. "Then we could *really* mess things up."

"What was that, Shu?" Nunzio sez, suddenly lookin'
real attentive.

"What? Oh. Well, I was thinking that if we could have
our own drivers to do the delivering instead of using army
wagons, we could scatter our shipments all across the
kingdom."

"No . . . I mean what did you say about teamsters?"

"Teamsters," Shu repeats. "You know. The guys that
drive freight wagons . . . at least, that's what we called
'em back on the farm."

I look at Nunzio and he looks at me, and I realize from
our smiles we is thinkin' the same thing.

"Spyder," I sez, "you found the Mob once in Twixt . . .
do you think you could do it again?"

"Sure," she shrugs. "Why?"

"I got a message I want you to get to Don Bruce," I
smiles. "I think we just found somethin' he can do to help
us."

XVII:

"Ya gotta speak the language."

—N. WEBSTER

"**H**ey, Swatter," Shu Flie sez, lookin' out one of the warehouse windows, "do you know there are a buncha wagons and drivers sitting outside?"

"No," I sez, "but if you hum a couple bars, I'll fake it."

Okay, so it's an old joke. Like I've said before, the army runs on old jokes. Unfortuitously, this particular joke is apparently a little *too* old for our farm-raised colleague.

"Say what?" he sez, lookin' kinda puzzled.

"Strike that," I sez. "Are they army or civilian?"

While it is procedure to have army wagons and drivers take shipments out of the supply depot, deliveries from suppliers is done by the supplier's own transports, and are therefore civilian.

"Civilian," Shu sez.

"Are the wagons full or empty?"

"They look empty from here."

I look over at Nunzio.

"Think it might be the teamsters we're expectin'?"

"Easy enough to check," he shrugs. "Hey Shu! What are they doing?"

"Nothing," the Flie brother reports. "They're just sitting around and talking."

"Sounds like them," Nunzio smirks. "I think it's your deal, Junebug."

As you might be able to detect from this last comment, we're all occupied with our favorite pastime, which is to say, Dragon Poker.

"Shouldn't one of you go out and talk to them or something?" Shu sez, wanderin' over to our table.

"It wouldn't do any good," I sez, peekin' at my hole cards. "They'll talk to us when they're good and ready . . . and not before. Pull up a chair and relax."

As it turns out, it is several hours before there is any contact with the drivers. When it finally comes, it takes the form of a big, potbellied individual with a tattoo on his arm who comes waddlin' through the door and over to our game.

"Hey, *hey!*" he snarls, "is somebody gonna talk to us or what?"

Now, just because Nunzio and me is big guys what get our way by tossin' our weight around does not mean we are particularly tolerant of anyone else who does the same thing.

"We figured you guys would talk to us when you were good and ready and not before," Nunzio sez, gettin' to his feet. *"You got a problem with that?"*

"Oh yeah?" the guy hollers, goin' nose to nose with Nunzio. *"Well for your information, we'll talk when we're good and . . .* and . . . oh. Yeah."

It takes a little doin', but I manage to hide my smile. This guy is already at a disadvantage in the negotiations, as my cousin has beaten him to his own punch line. Havin' lost the edge in the bluster department, he retreats to his secondary defense of indifference.

"We . . . ah . . . heard around that you guys was lookin'

for some civilian transport, so we thought we'd drop by
and see what the score was for ourselves."

"The stuff's over there on the loadin' dock," I sez, jerkin' a thumb in the appropriate direction. "And here's the
list of where it's supposed to go. Bill us."

I nod to Bee, who hands the guy the papers for the
shipments we have selected. Like I say, we'd been expecting them.

The guy looks at the list he's holdin' like it's a road-
kill.

"Just like that, huh?" he sneers. "Don't you wanna talk
about our haulin' rates?"

"No need for that," I shrugs. "I'm sure you'll charge
us a fair price."

"You are?" he sez, squintin' suspicious-like.

"Sure," I sez, givin' him my best collection agent's
smile, "especially seein' as how the rates is gonna be re-
viewed . . . and if they look outta line, there's gonna be
an investigation."

"An investigation," the driver sneers. "We get Royal
Investigations all the time . . . and we ain't changed
nothin' yet. If they give us too much grief, we just
threaten to shut down haulin' all over the kingdom."

"We wasn't talkin' about a Royal Investigation," Nunzio sez. "We was thinkin' of another judgmental body."

"Oh yeah? Like who?"

Nunzio winks at me, and I take a deep breath and give
it my best shot.

"Don . . . de don don. Don . . . de don don Bruuuuuce!"

Though my singin' voice is not what you would call a
real show stopper, the guy gets the message. His smile
droops, and he swallows hard . . . but he's a fighter and
tries to rally back.

"Yeah, okay, so you get our 'special' rates. Just don't
expect any express delivery."

Now it's Nunzio's turn to show off his grin.

"Friend," he sez, "if we wanted efficiency, we wouldn't
have sent for the teamsters."

"What's that supposed to mean?" the guy bellows,

gettin' back some of the color he lost when we mentioned Don Bruce.

"Just that your normal delivery schedules will suit us fine," I sez, innocent-like. "Know what I mean?"

"Yeah . . . well . . . I guess that's settled," the guy sez, lookin' back and forth between Nunzio and the men. "We'll go ahead and get started."

As he is goin', I find I cannot resist takin' one last dig at him.

"Say, Nunzio," I sez in a loud voice. "What do you call a teamster in a three piece suit?"

"The defendant!" Nunzio shoots back just as loud.

This humor goes right past the others in the crew, but the driver gets it. He breaks stride, and for a second I think he's gonna come back to "discuss" it with us at length. Instead, he just keeps on goin' and contents himself with slammin' the door for his witty response.

"You know, Guido," Nunzio sez, goin' back to studyin' his cards, "special rates or not, eventually we're going to have to pay these jokers . . . and we do not currently have access to the funds we are accustomed to operating with in M.Y.T.H. Inc."

"Relax, cuz," I sez, seein' the current bet and raisin' it, "I got an idea for that, too."

I have a chance to try out my plan that afternoon when a shipment arrives from one of our suppliers. I wait until the unloadin' is almost complete, then amble over to the driver.

"Say . . . you got a minute?" I sez, friendly-like.

"Okay," the driver shrugs. "What's up?"

"Well," I sez, lookin' around like I'm expectin' a cop, "I got some information you should pass back to your outfit."

"What's that?"

"There's a rumor goin' around that the queen is callin' for an audit on military spendin'," I sez. "Somethin' about a lot of our suppliers chargin' us more for supplies than they do civilians."

"An audit?" he repeats, suddenly lookin' real nervous.

"Yeah, scuttlebutt has it that any outfit caught gougin' extra profits out of army contracts is gonna get shut down and their entire inventory confiscated by the government."

"Is that legal?"

"Hey, we're talkin' the queen here. If she sez it's legal, it's legal."

"When is this gonna happen?"

"Not until next month, the way I hear it," I sez. "I just thought you might like to know a little in advance. You know, so just in case any of youse guys' prices should need some quick readjustin', youse could do it *before* the audit started."

"Hey thanks! I appreciate that."

"Yeah? Well, let your management know about it and see if they appreciate it, too. If they do, then maybe it would be a good think if in addition to adjustin' their prices, they made a little *refund* to postdate the price change . . . like maybe you could drop it off here when you make your next delivery?"

"I'll do that," he sez, noddin' vigorously. "And thanks again. We won't forget you."

Things went pretty smooth after that. We only had to plant our audit rumor a couple times for the word to spread through the suppliers, and soon there was a steady arrival of "refunds" . . . more than enough to pay off the teamsters. What's more, Bee's plan for reorganizin' the warehouse worked well enough that we ended up havin' a fair amount of leisure time each day, which we devoted to sharpenin' our Dragon Poker skills . . . as well as to our new hobby: Creative Supplyin'.

This pastime proved to be a lot more fun than any of us had anticipated, mostly because of the rules we set for ourselves. Since we agreed to only botch up one out of every ten orders, we have a lot of time to decide exactly which orders will get botched up and how. You see, to keep ourselves covered, we decide that it is best to switch items that either had identification numbers close enough to each other that the error would seem like a simple mis-readin', like a 6 for an 8 . . . or that were of a similar nature or appearance so it would just look like we pulled the wrong item, like sendin' summer weight uniforms to an outfit requestin' winter weight gear.

My personal favorite was when we sent several cases of Propaganda Leaflets to an outfit that was desperately askin' for toilet paper. It seemed somehow appropriate to me.

Like I say, it was a lot of fun . . . so much fun, in fact, I had a sneaky feelin' that it couldn't last. As it turned out, I was right.

The end of the festivities came when I got an order to report to our commandin' officer.

"**S**tand easy, Sergeant Guido. I've just been reviewing your unit's efficiency rating, and from what I'm seeing, it looks like it's time we had a talk."

I am more puzzled than nervous at this, as we have not been forwardin' the required copies of our paperwork . . . mostly because we have not been fillin' out the required paperwork at all. This is confirmed by the officer's next words.

"It seems your squad is not overly fond of filling out the supply forms required by regulations, Sergeant."

"Well, sir, we've been pretty busy tryin' to learn the routine. I guess we've gotten a little behind in our reports."

" 'A little behind' hardly describes it," he sez, tightenin' his lips a little. "I can't seem to find a single form from your supply depot since you took over. No matter, though. Fortunately there is sufficient cross-reporting to give me an idea of your progress."

This makes me a little uneasy, as we have figured there would be several rounds of requests and admonishments on our negligent paperwork performance before any attention was paid to the actual performance of our jobs. Still, as I am not totally unaccustomed to havin' to explain my actions to assorted authority figures, I have my alibis ready to go.

"Are you aware, Sergeant, that your squad is performing at ninety-five percent efficiency?"

"Ninety-five percent?" I sez, genuinely surprised, as our one-in-ten plan should be yieldin' an even ninety percent.

"I know it sounds high," the officer sez, misunderstandin' my reaction, "especially considering that sixty-five percent is the normal efficiency rating, even for an experienced supply crew. Of course, a practiced eye can read between the lines and get a pretty good idea of what's happening."

"Sir?"

"Take this one shipment, for example," he sez, tappin' one of the sheets in front of him. "It took a shrewd eye with attention to detail to spot that this request for winter weight uniforms was actually several months old, and to realize that substituting summer weight uniforms would be more appropriate."

A small alarm started goin' off in the back of my head, but the officer was still talkin'.

". . . or take this item, when you substituted cases of these propaganda leaflets for toilet paper. Everybody's heard about the morale problem of that unit, but it seems you not only had an idea about what to do, you acted on it. It's worked, incidentally . . . word is, their *esprit de corps* is at an all-time high since receiving your shipment."

As he is speakin' I am starin' at the leaflet he has shoved across the desk. Now understand, we had sent this stuff out without openin' the cartons, so this is the first time I am seein' one of the actual leaflets. It features a large picture of Queen Hemlock, who is not a bad lookin' broad normally, but looks particularly good in this picture as she is wearin' little more than a suggestive smile. Underneath the picture in large letters is the question: WOULDN'T YOU RATHER BE ON *MY* SIDE? Though I do not pretend to be a sociology expert like my cousin Nunzio, I can see where this would perk up a depressed soldier.

". . . But I'm getting bogged down in details," the officer is sayin'.

"In addition to your shipping efficiency, are you aware that the turnaround time for an order at your depot is less than a third the time it takes to get an order through any other depot?"

I am startin' to see the direction this interview is goin', and needless to say I am not enthused with it.

"That's mostly Private Bee's doin' sir," I sez, tryin' to get the focus off me. "He's been experimentin' with a new organization system in our warehouse . . . as well as a new 'reduced paperwork' trackin' system."

"Private Bee, eh?" the officer sez, makin' a note on his pad. "Tell him I'd like to see him when you get back to your unit. I'd like a bit more information about this experimental system of his . . . and speaking of experiments . . ."

He looks up at me again.

"I understand you've been using civilian transports for some of your deliveries. Is that another experiment?"

"Yes, sir," I sez.

I figure he'll be upset about this, so I am willin' to take the blame. It seems, however, that once again I have misjudged the situational.

"You know, Sergeant," he sez, leanin' back in his chair, "the army considered using civilian transports for the disbursement of supplies, but abandoned the idea as being too expensive. From the look of things, though, you may have just proved them wrong. Of course, you should have cleared it with me before implementing such an experiment, just as it was beyond your authority to authorize Private Bee to change established procedure, but it's hard to argue with your results. Besides, it's a rare thing these days to find a soldier, especially an enlisted man, who's not afraid to show a little initiative."

I experience a sinkin' feelin' in my stomach.

". . . And if there's one thing an organization that's growing as fast as ours needs . . ."

I close my eyes.

". . . it's *leadership*. That's why it gives me such great pleasure to approve your promotion to lieutenant, and . . ."

My eyes snap open.

"Wait a minute!" I sez, forgettin' all about the proper modes of addressin' a superior. *"You're makin' me an officer??"*

My reaction seems to take the officer by surprise.

"Well . . . yes," he sez. "Normally we'd require your attending officers' school, but in this situation . . ."

"That does it!" I snarl, losin' my temper completely. *"I QUIT!!"*

XVIII:

"Has anybody got a plan?"

—G. A. CUSTER

To say the least, our reunion with the rest of the
M.Y.T.H. Inc. team at Big Julie's was somethin' less
than a celebration.

Oh, we are all glad to see each other, and our host is
more than generous with the wine from his vineyard, but
contrary to popular belief, drinkin' does not necessarily
improve one's mood. To my experience, what it does is
to *amplify* whatever mood youse is already in . . . so if
youse is happy, youse gets *very* happy, and if youse happens to be depressed, youse gets *very* depressed . . . and
the unfortuitous circumstantial was that we was not very
happy.

There is no gettin' around the fact that we have failed
dismally in our efforts to stop Queen Hemlock, and while
we could try to convince ourselves that it was an impossible task for five individuals and a dragon to achieve, this
is the first time since we incorporated that we have failed
to come through on an assignment. Realizin' that it wasn't

a *real* job, as in one we had been commissioned for, but just a favor for the Boss didn't help much . . . as, if any-thin', we felt worse about lettin' the Boss down than we would about refundin' a client's fee.

"Did you have much trouble getting out of your en-listment?" Tananda was sayin' after we finish explainin' why we are back.

"Not really," Nunzio sez, refillin' his goblet from a pitcher of Big Julie's wine. "Oh, eventually we had to call in General Badaxe to approve it, but after we told him we were on a special assignment for Skeeve, he signed the papers without asking any more questions. The only prob-lem we had was that they *really* wanted us to stay . . . right, *Lieutenant?*"

He starts to grin at me, then notices from the look on my face that I am not in a mood to be kidded.

"Fortunately," he continues hastily, "the bait they kept offering was to promote us even higher . . . which, to say the least, was a temptation we had no difficulty resisting."

What my cousin is carefully omittin' from his report is that the *real* problem we had with leavin' wasn't with the army . . . it was with our crew. Speakin' for myself, I hadn't realized how much they all meant to me until our discharges had been approved and we was ready to say goodbye. I guess it wasn't until then that it hit me that I'd probably never see any of them again.

"Goodbye, Guido," Spellin' Bee had said, shakin' my hand solemnly. "I really appreciate the help you've given me with my magik. I guess I've been so caught up learn-ing the techniques that I've never stopped to think of all the ways it can actually be applied."

"That's nothin'," I sez, feelin' a little embarrassed. "When you get out, look us up and I'll introduce you to the Boss. He knows a lot more about that magik stuff than I do, and I don't think he'll mind givin' you a few point-ers."

"Do you really think that would be all right?" Bee sez. "I haven't said anything before, but the Great Skeeve has always been sort of an idol to me. I . . . I'm not sure I can learn enough about magik here in the army to where he'd want to bother with me."

"There's magik and there's magik," Nunzio sez, puttin' a hand on Bee's shoulder. "I think he'd like to meet you even if you don't get any more magik training than you've got right now. That was a pretty impressive system you came up with for organizing the warehouse, and our outfit is always on the lookout for . . . ah, *administrators*."

I roll my eyes and he shrugs at me, apologetic-like.

The commandin' officer had been impressed with Bee's system . . . so much, in fact, that he was bein' promoted and transferred into the task force assigned to improvin' the army's efficiency. Consequently, there was some question in the minds of Nunzio and me if he would ever actually see any further magik trainin' . . . which was, I guess, why Nunzio said what he did.

Personally, I wasn't sure we could use Bee if he *did* show up, as the M.Y.T.H. Inc. operation is service-oriented and therefore doesn't have any warehouses, but I kept this thought to myself.

"Gee, thanks guys," Bee sez, blinkin' a bit more than usual. "Well . . . see you around, I guess."

"You guys take care of yourselves . . . you hear?" Spyder sez, standin' on her tiptoes to give each of us a big hug.

"Sure, Spyder," I sez, blinkin' a little myself. "And listen . . . when you get out . . . if you're still interested in joinin' the Mob, you come see us first . . . got that?"

"Got it," she sez, noddin' vigorous-like.

". . . and stay away from Snake," Nunzio sez, "you want help . . . you come to *us!*"

"Sure thing . . . and you guys remember, if you need any help . . . well, if there's anything you think I can help you with, you let me know and I'll be there. Okay?"

"That goes for the rest of us too, Swatter," Shu Flie sez, grabbin' my hand and pumpin' it once. "You give the word, and we'll come runnin'."

"I'll remember," I sez. "Just let us know when you all

get out. We wouldn't want to interfere with your army duties."

I meant this as a kind of a joke, but they all seemed to take it serious.

"Don't worry about that," Junebug sez, lookin' me in the eye hard-like. "We know where our first loyalties lie . . . and you do, too."

Like I said, it wasn't an easy partin'. The hardest part, though, was knowin' that whatever we said about them lookin' us up, the odds were that if they did try, they probably wouldn't be able to find us. As soon as this assignment is over, we'll be headin' back to our head-quarters at the Bazaar, and unless they learn how to dimension-travel . . .

"So what do we do now?" Tananda sez, pullin' my mind away from my memories and bringin' it back to the present. "Pack it up and head for home?"

"I believe there *is* one more option which I brought up at the beginning of this assignment," Massha sez slowly, starin' into her wine.

It takes me a second to remember, but finally it comes back to me.

"You mean, whackin' the queen?" I sez.

She nods. Then there is a long time when no one sez anything as each of us thinks it through.

"Well," Nunzio sez finally. "I suppose we should give it a shot . . . at least then we can say we tried *everything* before we gave up."

I hesitate a second longer, then nod my agreement.

"All right, cuz," I sez, "you're on. Big Julie, if you can find that gear we stored here before we enlisted, Nunzio and me can . . ."

"Whoa . . . stop . . . HOLD IT!!" Massha sez, holdin' up a hand. "Who said you two were going to be the ones to go after the queen?"

"Well . . . it's oblivious, ain't it?" I sez, a little annoyed that my attempt to grab the assignment has been thwarted, but willin' to try to bluff my way through. "I mean, this is right up our alley ... seein's as how it is what we are trained to do."

"... And from what you've said about your disagreements with your drill instructor, that training is geared more toward enforcing than killing."

"Don't you worry about that," Nunzio sez, givin' her a tight little smile. "We're just against *unnecessary* killing. In this case, it seems that it's necessary."

"Well, when I suggested it, I figured that *I* was going to be the one to go after her," Massha sez, with no trace of her normal "happy-fat-lady-vamp" act.

"You?" I sez. "Excuse me for pointin' it out, Massha, but though you're more than a little intimidatin' physically, I don't think that physical acts are your forte."

"Who said anything about getting physical?" she sez, holdin' up her ring-laden hands. "You think I wear all this stuff for decoration ... or ballast? I've got a few toys here that should take care of things just fine."

Although she is still a beginner in the *natural* magik department, Massha held her own as a city magician for a long time before she signed on as the Boss's apprentice on the strength of the *mechanical* magikal gear she has collected ... most of which is in the form of jewelry. While I have suspected as much ever since we first met, this is the first time that she has confirmed that at least some of her baubles are of a lethal variety.

"Besides," she finishes, crossin' her arms decisively. "I'm Skeeve's apprentice ... so the job falls to me."

"... And *we're* his bodyguards who are specifically supposed to eliminate any threats to the Boss's well being," Nunzio snaps back. "While I don't doubt your sincerity *or* the reliability of your toys, Massha, whackin' somebody takes *experience* ... and Guido and I are the only ones on the team with experience in that area."

"Aren't you forgetting something, boys?" Tananda purrs, breakin' into the argument.

"What's that, Tananda?"

"While you two may be trained and experienced as *generalists* in controlled violence, part of *my* background is specifically as an assassin. By your own logic, then, it looks like the unpleasant task falls to *me*."

"Not to spoil your fun, little sister," Chumley sez, "but I was rather counting on giving it a go myself."

"You?" Tananda laughs. "Come on, big brother, you've still got your arm in a sling."

"What . . . this?" the troll sez, glancin' down at his arm. "It's hardly worth mentioning, really."

He pulls his arm out of the sling and wiggles his fingers, then sets his elbow on the table beside him.

"Do any of you want to try arm wrestling with me? Or will you concede the point?"

"Really, Chumley," Tananda sez, ignorin' the challenge, "just because that thick hide of yours is hard to get through . . ."

". . . Is the exact reason why *I'm* the logical choice for the assignment," the troll finishes with a smile.

". . . Except for the minor detail of your appearance," Massha adds. "Sorry, Chumley, but you're the last of us I'd figure for the assignment. Any of the rest of us could pass for natives, but you'd stand out like a sore thumb without a disguise spell."

"So I borrow little sister's makeup mirror."

"Not a chance," Tananda sez, stubborn-like.

". . . Or I simply borrow a hooded cloak or something for a disguise," Chumley continues smoothly as if she hasn't spoken. "How about it, Big Julie? Have you got anything lying around in an extra-extra large?"

"As a matter of fact," the retired general sez, "I was thinking of doing the job myself."

"What?"

"You?"

"That's . . ."

". . . BECAUSE," Big Julie continues, silencing us all with the simple technique of raisin' that voice of his to an authoritative level, "because I'm an old man and therefore the most expendable."

We all sink back into our chairs, too embarrassed to look at each other. With these few words, he has gotten to the heart of what was prompting our apparently blood-thirsty argument.

"I've been listening to all of you," he sez, takin' advantage of our uneasy silence, "and what nobody seems to want to say out loud is that trying to assassinate the queen is pretty much a suicide mission. Political leaders . . . and particularly royalty . . . are the best guarded folks in any nation. Even if you can get to them, which is uncertain at best, the odds of getting away afterward are so small they aren't even worth considering."

He looks around the gatherin'.

"Of course, I don't have to tell you this because you all know it already. That's why each of you is so eager to take the job . . . to let the others off the hook by nobly sacrificing yourself. Well, my advice, as your tactical advisor, is to forget the whole thing and go home . . . since I don't believe Skeeve ever intended for things to go this far . . . or, if you're determined to have the queen killed, then to let me do it. Like I said before, I'm an old man who's doing nothing but idling away my retirement with petty self-indulgences. All of you are contributing more to life, and are therefore more valuable, than I am. Besides," he lets a little grin play across his face, "it might be kinda fun to see a little action just one more time. I never really figured on dying in bed."

"That's sweet of you, Big Julie," Tananda sez, "but it's totally out of the question. Even though you've worked with us as an advisor, you're not really part of the team . . . and I'm *sure* this is one job Skeeve wouldn't want us to subcontract."

"I think we're agreed at least on that," Massha sez, glancin' around our assemblage. "If it's going to be done, it's going to be done by one of us."

"Then you still figure to try for Hemlock?" the ex-general frowns.

"I think," Chumley announces, standin' up and stretchin', "I think that we're all too tired and have been drinking far too much to make a rational decision. I suggest we all retire for now and pick up this discussion in the morning when our heads are clearer."

"You know, that's the first sensible idea I've heard in the last half hour," Tananda sez, stretchin' a bit herself . . . which would be fun to watch if I wasn't still thinkin' about the problem at hand.

"Good thinking, Chumley," Nunzio sez.

"Right."

"Sounds good to me."

With everyone in agreement, the party breaks up and we all start to drift off to our rooms.

"Nunzio," I sez, as soon as the others are out of hearin' range. "Are you thinkin' what I'm thinkin'?"

"That we should figure on getting up a little early tomorrow?" he sez.

". . . Because if anyone goes for the queen, it's gonna be us," I declare.

". . . And if we leave it to the group to decide, someone else might get the job . . ." he adds.

". . . Whereas if we simply present them with a *fait accompli*, it'll be too late to argue," I finish. "Right?"

"Right," he answers.

Like I say, though Nunzio and I sometimes have our differences, we work together pretty well when the stakes are high . . . which is why we are both smilin' as we wave good night to the others.

XIX:

"We must hurry . . . it's almost over!"

—P. FOGG

As I mentioned, Nunzio and me have brought along a few accessories on this assignment which we stored at Big Julie's for fear the army might be less than appreciative if we showed up to enlist already equipped . . . especially as our personal gear tends to be of a much better quality than that which the army issues.

Bein' true professionals, we spend considerable time sortin' through our travelin' kits for items which would be of specific use for the job at hand. The knuckle dusters, sawed-off pool cues, lead pipes and such we set aside . . . as they would normally be used for much more subtle ventures, and attemptin' to apply them in a fatal manner would be both time-consumin' and messy. Though it broke our hearts, we also decide to leave behind our Iolo crossbows. While they are great in an open confrontation, they are a bit bulky to be considered as concealable weapons which counts against them as whatever we use will have to be carried in under the noses of the queen's guards. While these deletions shorten our equipment list somewhat, we are still left with a fair assortment of tools from which to make our final selection.

Nunzio finally settles on a pocket, pistol-grip crossbow and a length of piano wire . . . just in case . . . while I opt for a blowgun and a nice set of throwin' knives. For those of youse who may be surprised by the latter choice, I would note that while I might not be as good as Snake is, I am still no slouch when it comes to shivs. Unfortunately I cannot provide youse with references to this fact, as those who would be in a position to testify on the degree of my skill from firsthand experience are, unfortuitously, no longer with us . . . but I digress.

"You know, Guido," Nunzio sez, startin' to stash his gear in the spiffy civilian clothes we're now wearin' again, "there *is* one problem with us taking this contract on ourselves."

"What's that?"

"Well, if we get caught afterwards, which as Big Julie points out is a definite possibility if not a probability, then we are again faced with a situation where it looks like the Mob is interfering with the kingdom of Possiltum."

"Come on, Nunzio," I sez. "We have been workin' for the Mob for a number of years now, and in all that time the authorities have not even come close to provin' there is any direct connection between ourselves and that august organization."

"I wasn't thinking about the authorities," my cousin sez, grim-like. "I was thinking about Don Ho and the other Mob bosses to which Don Bruce referred."

"Oh . . . Yeah."

I had not considered this, but it is definitely a point worth reflectin' upon. However, I am still unwillin' to let one of the others on the M.Y.T.H. Inc. team take the fall instead of us.

"Tell you what," I sez. "Chances are, only one of us will do the actual whackin' . . . right?"

"Well, yeah. So?"

"So if it looks like he's gonna get caught, then the

other one whacks *him*. Then the survivor can say that the
one what whacked the queen was a renegade, and was
eliminated for violatin' the Boss's orders."

"Sounds good to me," Nunzio sez. "Let's get going."

If, perhaps, our attitude toward dyin', not to mention
the possibility of maybe whackin' each other, sounds a
little callous, I would suggest youse consider anew what
it is Nunzio and me do for a livin'. We is bodyguards . . .
which means that along with our jobs, we accept the possibility that at some point one or both of us might have
to die so that the person what we are protectin' does not.
I repeat, it is part of the job . . . and we'd be pretty dumb
bunnies if that part of the job description came as a surprise to us after all this time.

As to the possibility of one of us havin' to whack the
other . . . well, I don't relish the thought of droppin' Nunzio any more than I like the idea of him droppin' me.
Still, once one has accepted the above referenced possibility of dyin' on the job to protect the Boss's body or
reputation, then it requires little additional justification to
accept that dead is dead and afterwards it doesn't really
matter exactly who it was what did the number on youse.
If anythin', if Nunzio did me or vice versa, then at least
we would be assured of it bein' a neat, professional job
with a minimum of fuss and bother.

Anyhow, it is just after dawn as we sneak out of the
villa, openin' the door an inch at a time in case it squeaks,
then easin' onto the patio as soon as it's open far enough
for us to slip through. At this point seein' as how it seems
we have effected our exit without arousin' the others on
the team, I pause to give Nunzio a wink and a thumbs-
up sign.

"Morning, boys!" comes a familiar voice from the far
side of the patio. "Care for a bit of breakfast?"

Big Julie is sprawled on a recliner, soakin' up the morning sun as he picks at the food laid out on the table next
to him.

"Shhh! Could you keep it down?" Nunzio hisses, puttin' a finger to his lips as he hurries over to our host.

"What for?" Big Julie sez, still speakin' in that loud, projectin' voice of his.

"Well . . . ummm . . ." I sez, shootin' a glance at Nunzio who just shrugs. "To tell you the truth, Big Julie, we are takin' it on ourselves to bring yesterday's argument to a close by goin' after the queen before there is any further discussion. This effort will, of course, go to waste if the others hear you and emerge before we have made our departure."

"Oh . . . it's too late to worry about that," he sez, casual-like.

"Excuse me?"

"They've already gone . . . one at a time, of course."

"They did? When?"

"Well, let's see . . . Tananda was the first . . . she left last night . . . then Chumley took off when he woke up and realized she was gone. Massha . . . well, she lit out about an hour ago when she found out the others had gone . . . you know, that woman moves pretty fast considering the weight she's carrying."

"So they're all ahead of us," Nunzio sez, disgusted-like. "And here we thought we were being clever getting an early start."

"Well, there *is* one detail I notice your teammates neglected to mention yesterday," Big Julie sez. "You see, today is the day the queen holds her public court and hears cases and complaints from anybody . . . first come first served. That makes it perfect for the kind of questionable deed you were discussing . . . but the lines form early, both for those seeking an audience and those who simply want to be *in* the audience."

"Oh that's just swell!" I sez. "Tell me, Big Julie, if you don't mind my askin', why didn't you try to stop them?"

"Me?" he blinks, innocent-like. "I had my say yesterday . . . and as I recall was unanimously told to butt out. That makes it none of my business . . . though I'll admit I'd be no more eager to try stopping any of the others than I'd be to try to stop you two. Know what I mean?"

"Yeah, I guess I see your point," Nunzio sez quick-like, lookin' grimmer than I've seen him in a long time. "Well, come on, Guido! We've gotta hurry if we're gonna be in this game at all!"

Just as Big Julie predicted, the palace throne room was packed to the walls with even more folks waiting outside to get in if anyone left early. As I have mentioned before, however, Nunzio and me is of sufficient size that most folks give ground when we crowd them, so we are able to eventually elbow our way in to where we can at least see.

The crowd what has shown up just to watch is linin' the walls about twenty deep or jammed into the balconies, leavin' the center of the room open for those havin' business with the queen. Seein' as how that pack is standin' in a line which stretches back out the door, we have little choice but to join the audience . . . which hides our presence to a certain extent, but greatly reduces our chances of a quick withdrawal after we finishes workin'.

"There's Massha," I sez, though it's kinda needless, as she is standin' in the line waitin' to go before the queen and is *very* noticeable in that company. "Can you see the others?"

Nunzio just shakes his head and keeps scannin' the audience on our right, so I start doin' the same for the crowd on the left.

Of course, I realize it is unlikely I will be able to spot Tananda, since with that disguise mirror of hers she can look like anyone she wants. I suspect though, knowin' her to be more than a little vain, that even disguised she will be both female and attractive.

Chumley, however, is another matter entirely. All I gotta do is look for a good-sized figure in an outfit that hides its face, and . . .

Nunzio gives me a quick elbow in the ribs to get my attention, then jerks his head up toward the ceilin'. It takes me a minute to figure out what he's tryin' to point out to me, but then somethin' moves in the shadows of the raf-

ters and I see her. It's Tananda, and she's flat on one of
the heavy timbers easin' her way closer to the throne. At
first, I'm afraid she'll fall, but then I realize that she's . . .

"Quit looking at her," Nunzio hisses in my ear. "Do
you want the guards to spot her?"

I realize I have been starin' up at her like some kind
of a tourist, and that if I keep doin' it, other people . . .
like the guards . . . are gonna start wondering what I'm
lookin' at and start checkin' the rafters themselves.

"So what do we do now?" I whispers back, tearin' my
eyes away from Tananda's progress.

"We move," Nunzio sez, ". . . And fast, if we're gonna
score before she makes her try. With this crowd, though . . .
tell you what. You try easin' up on the left there and I'll go
up this side."

"Got it!" I sez, and put a gentle elbow into the kidney
of the guy ahead of me, thereby openin' up a route to the
other side of the throne room.

Sayin' we'll get close to the throne, however, proves
to be considerably easier than actually gettin' there. At
first I am worried about movin' too fast and catchin' the
guards' eyes as someone tryin' too hard to get close to
where the queen will be. After a few minutes of fightin'
with the crowd, though, I am more concerned with bein'
able to move at all. It seems like the closer to the front
of the room I gets, the more determined the people are to
not give up their place.

By the time I am halfway to the throne, I am startin'
to get desperate over how long it's takin' and look around
to see where Nunzio is. As it turns out, he is havin' even
more trouble than me, havin' progressed a mere six steps
before gettin' boxed in behind a gaggle of old biddies.
They are not about to give ground for anyone, and it appears that short of punchin' his way through them, he isn't
gonna make it to the front at all.

Of course, this leaves it to me to beat the others to the
queen . . . which suits me just fine. Redoublin' my efforts,
I sneak a peek upward to check Tananda's progress, only
to find I can no longer see her at all.

Just then, someone lets loose with a blast of brass horns . . . and the queen appears.

For a moment, I am too stunned to keep pushin' forward . . . in fact, I lose a couple steps.

You see, I met Queen Hemlock back at the same time I met the Boss, and more recently had a chance to refresh my memory while gazin' at a propaganda leaflet. While she is not what you would call a knockout, neither is she exactly plain. The woman easin' herself onto the throne, however, looks so much different than those images that if they hadn't hollered out her name as she walked in, I probably wouldn't have recognized her. Of course, even just passin' her on the street, the crown would have been a pretty strong clue.

She looks like she hasn't been sleepin' very well, as there are big dark circles under her eyes, and it looks like she's been off her feed . . . well, more so than normal as she's always been a bit on the scrawny side. Then the first guy in line starts yammerin' about how he thinks his business is payin' too much taxes, and for a minute I think she's gonna burst into tears.

It occurs to me that however successful her expansion may look from the outside, it doesn't look like it's makin' Queen Hemlock any too happy.

Just then I spot Chumley . . . or at least a big figure in a hooded cloak . . . edgin' along the wall behind the guards not ten feet from where the queen is sittin', and know I have run out of time. Slidin' one of the throwin' knives down my sleeve, I start eyeballin' the distance between me and Hemlock. It's gonna be one heck of a throw, but it won't get any easier by my starin' at it, so I step back for balance and . . .

. . . And all hell breaks loose at the back of the room!

At first I think the guards have jumped Nunzio, but when I look his way he is standin' clear of the action, lookin' right back at me and pointin' desperately out the door, mouthin' somethin' I can't make out over the hub-bub. I crane my neck tryin' to figure out what he's pointin' at, but all I can see is the crowd outside the throne

room is partin' ... makin' way for something or somebody.

There's a ripple of noise spreadin' forward from the
back of the crowd, buildin' in volume as more and more
voices join in. Abandonin' my efforts to see what's goin'
on, I bend an ear to try to sort out what it is they're sayin'.

"... *magician* ..."

"He's back!"

"HE'S COMING!"

"... COURT MAGICIAN!!!"

"LOOK!! THERE HE IS!! IT'S ..."

"THE GREAT SKEEVE!!!"

... And it was!!

Just as I make out the words, the crowd at the back of
the throne room parts, and the Boss comes walkin' in ...
and Aahz is with him!! They seem to be arguin', of
course, and are totally ignorin' the crowd around them
which first surges back, then presses forward like a wall.

I am out of the audience before I am aware that I have
trampled several of Possiltum's citizens in my haste, and
pass Massha who is always a little slow off the line because of her size. I see Nunzio comin' through the crowd,
knockin' people down like duckpins, and am vaguely
aware that I am doin' the same ... but I don't care. I am
just happy to see the Boss here and in one piece.

"SKEEVE!!"

I hear someone shout in a voice that sorta sounds like
the queen's, but by now I am six steps out and closin'
fast.

Now, I have never been fond of the Mob tradition of
men huggin' each other, but this time I figure to make an
exception.

"BOSS!!" I hollers, and throws my arms wide and ...

... And the room spins ... then everythin' goes black!

XX:

"I want a rematch!"

—M. TYSON

"**G**uido! Hey! Come on! Wake up!"
I can hear Nunzio's voice, but decide to keep my eyes closed a little while longer. Havin' had numerous similar experiences in the past, I have no difficulty figurin' out what has happened . . . which is to say I have been knocked cold. The difficult part is recallin' the circumstantials which led to this condition, a task which is not made any simpler by the fact that my brain is still a little scrambled from the experience . . . which is why I have chosen to pretend I am still out to lunch whilst I composes myself.

We were in the throne room . . . then the Boss walked in with Aahz . . . I started over to greet him . . . Nunzio was comin' over to do the same thing . . . then . . .

I get a fix on Nunzio's location from his voice, then open my eyes and sit up quick-like, grabbin' him by the throat as I do so.

"Did you just sucker punch me, cousin?" I sez, curious-like.

The world starts to spin again a little, makin' me reconsider the wisdom of havin' tried to move so fast so
soon after regainin' consciousness, but I blink a couple
times to clear my vision and it settles down. I also notice
that Nunzio is turnin' a little purple, so I loose my grip
on his throat so's he can answer me.

"It . . . wasn't me!" he squeaks.

Seein' as how Nunzio is usually very proud of his
work . . . particularly on those occasions when he has just
worked on me . . . I figure he is tellin' the truth and open
my grip the rest of the way.

"Well if *you* didn't do it," I frowns, still blinkin' a little,
"then who . . ."

"Meet Pookie," he sez, pointin' over my shoulder with
his left thumb, as his right hand is busy rubbin' his throat.
"She's the Boss's new bodyguard."

"New bodyguard?" I sez, takin' a look behind me
and . . .

The world stops . . . as does my heart and lungs.

Now, when I say this chick is stunnin', it has nothin'
to do with the fact that she just knocked me cold. She has
the smooth, strong lines of a panther . . . except for a few
pleasant roundin's one does not normally find on a cat of
any size. She also has green scales and yellow eyes which
are regardin' me levelly.

"Sorry about the mix-up," she sez, not soundin' at all
sorry, "but you came in so fast that Skeeve didn't have a
chance to tell me you were on our side. Anyway, pleased
to meet you . . . I guess. Here's your knife back."

I look at the throwin' knife she is holdin' out and realize it is indeed one of mine. I musta still been holdin'
it in my hand when I went to greet the Boss, which is an
embarrassin' oversight. One of the troubles with havin'
big hands is that sometimes one forgets one is holdin'
things.

"New bodyguard, huh?" I sez, not bein' able to think
of anythin' wittier to say as I accepts the knife and stashes
it.

"We met on Perv," she sez, a little frosty. "Skeeve

needed a bodyguard . . . and it seems he didn't have one with him."

Now I am not so far gone that I can't spot a professional rebuke when I hear one.

"We didn't like it, either," I growl, "but the Boss *ordered* us not to go along with him and *asked* us to lend a hand here instead."

Pookie thinks about this for a second, then gives a small nod.

"That explains a few things," she sez, unthawin' a little. "Skeeve's being alone had me wondering about you two, but I guess you really didn't have much choice in the matter."

There is no reason why her approval should mean anything to me . . . but it does.

"So, you're from Perv, huh?" I sez, tryin' to prolong the conversation.

"She's my cousin," Aahz sez, and for the first time I become aware that he is standin' nearby.

In fact, the whole team is standin' here, and I . . .

"Your cousin!" I sez, the words finally sinkin' in.

"Don't worry," Pookie sez, givin' me a small smile and a wink. "We aren't at all alike."

"Can you guys keep it down?" Tananda hisses at us. "I'm trying to eavesdrop on this!"

Wrenchin' my attention away from Pookie, I finally start to focus in on what's goin' on.

We are still in the throne room, but the crowds are gone. In fact, the whole place . . . floor and balconies . . . are empty of people and guards except for us. Well, us and the Boss, who is sittin' on the throne steps chattin' with Queen Hemlock.

". . . so everything was going pretty well, until Roddie caught some bug or other and died," she is sayin'. "When I didn't die, too, I realized those rings you gave us didn't *really* link our lives . . . incidentally, I'd get my money back on those if I were you . . ."

"You mean the King really *did* die of natural causes?" I whispers.

"So it seems," Tananda murmurs back. "Now put a sock in it. I want to hear this."

". . . and you *know* I've always wanted to expand our borders just a teensy tiny bit, so I figured, 'Why not give it a try?' . . ."

"From what I hear," the Boss interrupts, "the expansion goes way past 'teensy tiny' in anyone's definition."

"I know," the queen sighs, deflatin' a little. "It just seems to have gotten away from me. My advisors . . . you remember Grimble and Badaxe? . . . well, they keep assuring me that everything is fine . . . that as long as I keep lowering the taxes, the people will support me . . . but I keep having this feeling that I've lost control of . . ."

"Lowering the taxes while you expand your borders?" the Boss breaks in. "But that can't be done! A bigger kingdom means *more* expense, not *less!* You still have the cost of local government, *plus* the cost of extra layers of bureaucracy to manage the local bureaucracies."

It finally dawns on me what has been botherin' me about this "lower taxes" thing every time I hear about it. I also remember that I had to take Econ. 101 three times.

"I know," the queen sez. "I've been covering the extra cost from my old kingdom's treasury, but that's almost gone. Grimble keeps saying that things will level off eventually when the kingdom gets big enough, but . . ."

"It's not going to happen," the Boss sez, shakin' his head. "You can't beat the mathematics of the situation. You're either going to have to raise the taxes or pull your borders back . . . or go bankrupt."

"Oh Skeeve!" Hemlock sez, givin' him a quick hug. "I *knew* you could figure it out. That's why I sent for you."

"Sent for me?"

"Of course, silly. The ring. Didn't you get it?"

"Well, yes. But . . ."

"I never was much good with letters," the queen continues, "but I was *sure* you'd get the message when I sent you Roddie's ring . . . of course, I had to send a little of *him* along with it . . . you were right about the rings not coming off, by the way."

"That was *Rodrick's* ring?"

"Of course. You don't think I'd cut off *my* finger, do you?"

She holds up her hand and waggles her fingers at him . . . all of them, includin' the one with her ring on it. The skin on the finger we had gotten had been so soft and smooth, we had all *assumed* it was a woman's finger. Of course, stoppin' to think about it, kings don't work much with their hands, either.

"Anyway, you got the message, and you're here now . . . so everything's going to be all right."

"The message," the Boss sez, lookin' a little confused . . . which to my mind is understandable. "Umm . . . just to be sure we understand each other, would you mind saying what you wanted to tell me in words instead of using . . . graphic communications?"

"Isn't it obvious?" the queen sez. "I need your help to manage things, so I'm offering you a position."

"Well . . . I'm kind of busy these days," the Boss sez, "but I guess I can spare a little time to help you straighten things out as your advisor . . ."

". . . as my *consort*," the queen corrects.

The whole team flinches at this, and we swap a few worried looks back and forth between us.

The Boss, however, is a little slower on the uptake.

". . . of course, the first thing you'll have to do is to order the army to stop advancing until we figure out what to do next."

"Consider it done . . . and then Grimble and I will . . . *CONSORT??!!*"

As I have said, the Boss can be a bit slow from time to time, but eventually he catches on.

"Of course," Hemlock beams at him. "I figure we can get married, then if we divvy up some of these bothersome duties, we'll still have time to . . ."

"*CONSORT???*"

The Boss seems to be stuck on the word.

"That's right," the queen says, cocking her head at him. "Why? Have you got a problem with that?"

The temperature in the throne room seems to drop along with the chilly tone in her voice.

". . . Because if you do, there *is* another option. I can do what you suggested back when Roddie and I got married."

"Which was . . . ?" the Boss sez in a small voice.

"Abdicate." Somehow the queen manages to make the one word sound like a sentence . . . a death sentence. "I can step down from the throne and name *you* my successor. Then you can try to run this whole mess all by yourself!"

Check and mate.

This whole conversation is makin' me more than a little uneasy . . . but that is nothin' compared to what it is doin' to the Boss. He looks absolutely panicky . . . not to mention sorta green around the gills.

"I . . . I . . ." he stammers.

". . . But don't you think it'll be so much nicer if you just go along with my original idea?" Hemlock sez, all kittenish again. "That way, you get the whole kingdom *and* me!"

"I . . . I don't know," the Boss manages at last. "I've never thought about getting married."

"Well think about it," the queen sez, gettin' a bit of an edge on her voice.

"No . . . I mean, I'll need some *time* to think about it."

"Okay," Hemlock nods. "That's fair."

"Maybe in a year . . ."

". . . I'll give you a *month*," the queen sez, actin' like the Boss hadn't said anythin'. "Then I'll expect your answer one way or the other. In the meantime, *I'll* order the army to stop and *you* can start going over the books with Grimble. I mean, that will be a good idea whatever decision you make, won't it?"

"I . . . I guess so."

This is not lookin' good. The Boss has never been

good with skirts, and it looks like Hemlock is gonna be able to lead him around by the nose.

"I think I've heard enough," Tananda sez. "I'll see you guys later."

"Where are you going, little sister?" Chumley sez, voicin' the question for all of us. "It looks like Skeeve is going to need all the help we can give him . . . and then some."

"Actually," she sez, "I was going to head back to the home office. I figure I need a little break, so I thought I'd tend the home fires while my hair grows back."

"Really?" Chumley frowns.

"Of course," she purrs, flashin' a wide smile, "that will free *Bunny* from her duties. I think I'll send her back here to lend a hand."

"Bunny?"

"Well you can't expect Skeeve to straighten things out here without his administrative assistant, can you?" she sez, innocent-like. "Besides, Bunny's a lot better at dealing with figures than I am."

She pauses and sends one last dark look at the queen.

". . . at least, I figure in *this* situation she will be."

NEXT: Skeeve tries to unravel the puzzle of the opposite sex in . . .

Sweet Myth-tery of Life.

AUTHOR'S NOTE

for the 1990 edition of
M.Y.T.H. INC. IN ACTION:

I am not a fast writer,
I am not a slow writer,
I am a half fast writer!

—R. L. ASPRIN

The fan mail I've received has been pretty much split on the subject of my last Introduction; some found it interesting and insightful, while others thought it was boring and a waste. If you are of the latter group, please feel free to jump ahead directly into the story, since there is nothing in this message you need to know to understand (and, hopefully, enjoy) the book.

For the rest of you, this note is mostly an apology . . . or, more accurately, a string of apologies.

Back in *M.Y.T.H. Inc. Link*, I optimistically stated that I would be trying to write two Myth episodes a year . . . and things have not been the same since. I, my publishers, and many bookstores and dealers have been flooded with queries and demands for "the next Myth book," with each reader being *sure* the books were in existence somewhere because of the schedule I had so foolishly "committed to" in that introduction.

To belabor the obvious, I haven't been able to write at the speed I anticipated at the time. While the popularity of the series and the loyalty of its readers is both gratifying and profitable, any publisher can tell you that trying to get a book out of an author when "it isn't happening" is like pushing on a rope. You see, when I made my writing "guesstimate," I had just finished writing *MIL*, and the speed with which the prose goes onto the page when I'm closing on the end of a book was still fresh in my mind. That is, when it's flowing, it flows very fast. What I had overlooked was the months of outlining and false starts that go on *before* things get flowing. (These books only *look* spontaneous and easy to write. Honest!) Anyway, the cruel realities of the situation surfaced when I tried to meet my promised schedule, and I fell far behind my anticipated timetable. As the queries and demands from the readers grew, the tolerance of the publishers for late delivery grew less and less, and the pressures on me increased "to get the manuscript in" with less and less time for rewrites and polish.

Finally, in 1988, things blew up. I got into a dispute with Donning/Starblaze (the prime Myth publisher . . . the mass-market [small paperback] editions from Ace are sub-contracted reprints) over royalties. The dispute has been settled, and the only reason I mention it here is that it lasted the better part of a year . . . delaying my writing that much more.

In addition to the negotiated terms of that settlement, however, there is an additional apology that I owe the management of Donning. You see, part of the settlement was that the next book (the one you're holding) would not be advertised nor orders taken until the manuscript had been delivered. This was an effort to take some of the "deadline" pressure off my writing as I tried to get back into stride. There were two unfortunate side effects of that condition, however. First, I was unable to reply to the many readers and fans asking when the next book would be out . . . as it would be less than fair to insist that Donning not advertise a release date, then banter it about myself. Secondly, at one point I gave my assurance to Donning on the phone as to when the manuscript would be completed . . . then promptly forgot that I had done so. This meant that when I encountered problems with my writing, I neglected to warn Donning of the delay, and in that absence of revised information, they launched an extensive and expensive advertising campaign for the release of the book in late '89 . . . only to suffer embarrassment and loss of credibility when the manuscript failed to appear for production.

While I am not in a position to repair the financial damage caused by the "false start" advertising campaign, I feel it only honorable to offer public apology to Donning for the professional embarrassment which my memory lapse caused. For the record, the late appearance of this volume is due to delays at the author's end, not the publisher, distributor, bookstore, or dealer. Writers are often quite loud in voicing horror stories about having their works mishandled by the publishing industry, yet not so vocal when it comes to admitting their own shortcomings. Folks, this time the confusion and delays were **my fault**, and the distress I feel because of that will only be compounded if I allow others to take the blame by remaining silent.

While I'm prattling, let me try to head off another potential round of misunderstanding and confusion. In July of '90, another humor series of mine, science fiction this time, will premiere with the publishing of *Phule's Company*. Please do not panic. This new series is *in addition to, not replacing*, the MYTH novels. As promised back in *MIL*, the MYTH novels will continue *at least* through #12.

(More than) Enough said. While this intro hasn't been as much fun as the last, look at it as a different sort of insight into the "carefree life of an author" and the frus-

trating complexities of the publishing industry. Enjoy the
book. I only hope it justifies the wait.

Robert Lynn Asprin
February 1990

SWEET MYTH-TERY
OF LIFE

This volume is dedicated to my friends and counselors who helped me break through a two-and-a-half-year writing block, including (but not restricted to):

> Mystia Deemer
> Todd and Mary Brantley
> Darlene Bolesney
> Randy Herbert
> Roger Zelasny
> The NO Quarter Sword Club

To the publishers and readers who have waited so patiently and loyally while I worked my way through this difficult period in my life, I feel the best way to express my thanks is to keep writing!

R.L.A.

I:

"Is it just me, or does it seem to you I get more than my share of troubles?"

—JOB

"... **A**nd so, to recap, the situation is this ..."
I ticked the points off on my fingers, giving my audience a visual image to reinforce my words.

"First, Queen Hemlock wants me to be her consort. Second, she's given me a month to think it over before I reach my decision. Third ..."

I tapped the appropriate finger for emphasis.

"If I decide *not* to marry her, she says she'll abdicate, naming *me* her successor and sticking me with the whole mess. Got that?"

Despite my concern over my predicament, I was nonetheless proud of my ability to address the problem head-on, summarizing and analyzing it as I sought a solution. There was a time in the not too distant past when I simply would have lapsed into blind panic. If nothing else, my adventures over the years had done wonders for my confidence in my abilities to handle nearly any crisis.

"Gleep!" my audience responded.

Okay . . . so I wasn't all *that* confident.

While I knew I could muddle through most crises, the one situation I dreaded the most was making a fool of myself in front of my friends and colleagues. While they had always been unswerving in their loyalty and willingness to bail me out of whatever mess I blundered into, that didn't mean I was particularly eager to tax our friendships yet another time, even if it was just for advice. At the very least, I figured that when I *did* approach them, I should be as level-headed and mature about it as possible, rather than babbling hysterically about my woes. Consequently, I decided to rehearse my appeal in front of the one member of our crew I felt truly comfortable with . . . my pet dragon.

I've always maintained that Gleep is quite bright, despite the one-word vocabulary that gave him his name. According to my partner and mentor, Aahz, my pet's limited vocal range was merely a sign of his immaturity, and it would expand as he edged toward adulthood. Of course, realizing dragons live several centuries, the odds of my ever having a two-way conversation with Gleep were slim. At times like this; however, I actually appreciated having someone to talk to who could only listen . . . without helpful asides regarding my inability to walk across the street without landing myself and the crew in some kind of trouble.

"The trouble is," I continued, "what with all the problems and disasters I've had to cope with over the years, not to mention trying to be president of M.Y.T.H. Inc., I haven't had much time for a love life, like, none at all . . . and I *sure* haven't given any thought to getting *married*! I mean, I haven't ever really reached a decision on whether or not I want to get married at *all*, much less *when* or to *who*."

Gleep cocked his head to one side, to all appearances hanging on my every word.

"Of course, I *do* know I'm not wild about the alternative. I had a chance to play king once . . . and that was *twice* too often, thank you. It was bad enough when I was just being a stand-in for Roderick, but the idea of trying to run the kingdom by myself, *as* myself, and forever, not just for a few days, well, that's flat out terrifying. The question is, is it more or less terrifying than the idea of being married to Queen Hemlock?"

My pet responded to my dilemma by vigorously chewing at an itch on his foot.

"Thanks a lot, Gleep old boy," I said, smiling wryly despite my ill humor. While I obviously hadn't really expected any glowing words of advice from my dragon, I had at least thought my problems were serious enough to hold his attention. "I might as well be talking to Aahz. At least *he* looks at me while he's chewing me out."

Still smiling, I picked up the goblet of wine I had brought with me for moral support and started to take a sip.

"Oh, Aahz isn't so bad."

For a startled moment, I thought Gleep had answered me. Then I realized the voice had come from behind me, not from my pet. A quick glance over my shoulder confirmed my worst fears. My partner, green scales, pointed teeth and all, was leaning against the wall not ten feet from where I stood, and had apparently been listening to my whole oration.

"Hi, Aahz," I said, covering my embarrassment with a forced smile. "I didn't hear you come in. Sorry about that last comment, but I've been a little . . ."

"Don't worry about it, Skeeve," he interrupted with a wave of dismissal. "If that's the worst you've had to say about me over the years, I figure we've been doing pretty well. I *do* lean on you kinda hard from time to time. I guess that's gotten to be *my* way of dealing with stress."

Aahz seemed calm enough . . . in fact, he seemed to be *suspiciously* calm. While I wasn't wild about his shouting at me, at least it was consistent. This new display of reasonability was making me uneasy . . . rather like suddenly noticing the sun just rose in the west.

"So . . . what are you doing here, partner?" I said, trying to sound casual.

"I was looking for you. It occurred to me that you might need a sympathetic ear while you figured out what to do next."

Again, a small warning gong went off in the back of my mind. Of all the phrases that might occur to me to describe Aahz's interaction with me in the past, "a sympathetic ear" wasn't one of them.

"How did you know where I was?"

I was dodging the issue, but genuinely curious as to how Aahz found me. I had taken great pains to slip down to the Royal Stables unnoticed.

"It wasn't hard," Aahz said, flashing a grin as he jerked his thumb at the door. "You've got quite a crowd hanging around outside."

"I do?"

"Sure. Pookie may be a bit mouthy for my taste, but she knows her stuff as a bodyguard. I think she's been tailing you from the time you left your room."

Pookie was the new bodyguard I had acquired during my recent trip to Perv . . . before I knew she was Aahz's cousin.

"That's funny," I scowled. "I never saw her."

"Hey, I said she was good," my partner winked. "Just because she respects your privacy and stays out of sight doesn't mean she's going to let you wander around unescorted. Anyway, I guess Guido spotted her and decided to tag along . . . he's been following her around like a puppy ever since they met . . . and, of course, that meant Nunzio had to come, too, and . . . Well, the end result is you've got all three of your bodyguards posted outside the door to see to it that you aren't disturbed."

Terrific. I start out looking for a little privacy and end up leading a parade.

"So, what do you think, Aahz?" I asked.

I knew I was going to get his opinion sooner or later, and figured I might as well ask outright and get it over with.

"About what?"

"About my problem," I clarified.

"What problem?"

"Sorry. I thought you had been listening when I explained it to Gleep. I'm talking about the whole situation with Queen Hemlock."

"I know," my partner said. "And I repeat, what problem?"

"What problem?" I was starting to lose it a little, which is not an unusual result of talking to Aahz. *"Don't you think . . ."*

"Hold on a second, partner," Aahz said, holding up his hand. "Do you remember the situation when we first met?"

"Sure."

"Let me refresh you memory, anyway. Your old mentor, Garkin, had just been killed, and there was every chance you were next on the hit list. Right?"

"Right. But . . ."

"Now *that* was a problem," he continued as if I hadn't spoken. "Just like it was a problem when you had to stop Big Julie's army with a handful of misfits . . . realizing that, if you were successful, Grimble was threatening to have you killed or worse when you returned to the palace."

"I remember."

"And when you decided to try to clear me of that murder rap over on Limbo, a dimension which just happens to be filled with vampires and werewolves, I'd say that was a problem, too."

"I don't see what . . ."

"Now, in direct contrast, let's examine the *current* situation. As I understand it, you're in danger of getting married to the Queen, which, I believe, includes having free run of the kingdom's treasury. The other option is that you decide not to marry her, whereupon she abdicates to you . . . leaving you again with a free hand on the treasury, only without the Queen." He showed me his impressive array of teeth. "I repeat, what problem?"

Not for the first time, it occurred to me that my partner had a tendency to appraise the pluses and minuses of any situation by the simple technique of reducing everything to monetary terms and scrutinizing the bottom line.

"The problem is," I said tersely, "that in order to *get* that access to the treasury, I have to get married or become king. Frankly, I'm not sure I'm wild about either option."

"Compared to what you've been through in the past to scrape together a few coins, it's not bad," Aahz shrugged. "Face it, Skeeve. Making a bundle usually involves something unpleasant. Nobody . . . and I mean *nobody* . . . is going to fork over hard cash for your having a good time."

Of course, those "few coins" we had scraped together over the past years added up to enough to make even a Pervish banker sit up and take notice, but I knew the futility of trying to convince Aahz that there was *ever* such a thing as enough money.

"Maybe I could just write about having dubious adventures instead of actually doing anything," I muttered. "That always sounded to me like a pretty cushy job to cash in on the good life."

"You think so? Well, let me educate you to the harsh realities of the universe, partner. It's one thing to practice a skill or a hobby when you feel like it, but whether it's writing, singing, or playing baseball, when you've *got* to do something whether you're up for it or not, *it's work!*"

I could see this conversation was going nowhere. Aahz simply wasn't going to see my point of view, so I decided to play dirty. I switched to *his* point of view.

"Maybe I'd be more enthusiastic," I said, carefully, "if the kingdom's finances weren't at rock bottom. Doing something unpleasant to acquire a stack of debts doesn't strike me as all that great a deal."

Okay. It was hitting below the belt. But that just happens to be where Pervects such as Aahz are the most sensitive . . . which is to say where they keep their wallets.

"You've got a point there," my partner said thoughtfully, wavering for the first time in the conversation. "Still, you managed to finagle a whole month before you have to make a decision. I figure in that time we should be able to get a pretty good fix on what the *real* financial situation around here is . . . *and* if it can be turned around."

"There's just one problem with that," I pointed out. "I know even less about money than I know about magik."

"Just off hand, I'd say you were doing pretty well in both departments."

I caught the edge in my partner's voice, and realized that he was on the brink of taking my comment personally . . . which is not surprising as he was the one who taught me nearly everything I know about magik *and* money.

"Oh, I'm okay when it comes to personal finances and contract negotiations . . . more than okay, in fact . . . and I have you to thank for that." I said hastily. "What we're looking at now, though, is *high* finance . . . as in trying to manage the funds for a whole kingdom! I don't think *that* was covered in my lessons, or if it was, it went over my head."

"Okay. That's a valid concern," Aahz conceded. "Still, it's probably the same thing you've been doing for M.Y.T.H. Inc., but on a larger scale."

"That's fine, except Bunny's been doing most of the heavy financial work for M.Y.T.H. Inc.," I grimaced. "I only wish she were here now."

"She is," Aahz exclaimed, clicking his fingers. "*That's* the other reason I was looking for you."

"Really? Where is she?"

"Waiting in your room. I wasn't sure what kind of sleeping arrangements you wanted set up."

One of the changes from my previous stay at the palace was that instead of sharing a room with Aahz, I had a room of my own. It's a tribute to how worried I was, however, that the implications of what he said went right over my head.

"Same as always," I said. "See if we can find a room for her that's at least in the same wing of the palace as ours, though."

"If you say so," Aahz shrugged. "Anyway, we'd better get going. She seemed real anxious to see you."

I only listened to this last with half an ear, as something else had momentarily caught my attention.

I had turned away from Aahz to give Gleep one last pat before we left, and for the barest fraction of a second saw something I had never noticed before. He was listening to us!

Now, as I noted earlier, I've always maintained that Gleep was bright, but as I turned, I had a fleeting impression of intelligence in his expression. To clarify, there *is* a difference between "bright" and "intelligent." "Bright," as I'd always applied it to my pet, means that he is alert and quick to learn. "Intelligent," on the other hand, goes beyond "monkey see, monkey do" tricks, all the way to "independent thought."

Gleep's expression as I turned was one of thoughtful concentration, if not calculation. Then he saw me looking at him and the look disappeared, to be replaced with his more familiar expression of eager friendliness.

For some reason, this gave me a turn. Perhaps it was because I found myself remembering reports from the team about their efforts to disrupt the kingdom in my absence. Specifically, I was recalling the claim that Gleep had nearly killed Tananda . . . something I had dismissed at the time as being an accident that was being blown out of proportion in their effort to impress me with the difficulties of their assignment. Now, however, as I stared at my pet, I began to wonder if I should have paid closer attention to what they were saying. Then again, maybe it had just been the light playing tricks on me. Gleep certainly looked innocent enough now.

"Com'on, partner," Aahz repeated testily. "You can play with your dragon some other time. I still think we should try to sell that stupid beast off before he eats his way through our bankroll. He really doesn't add anything to our operation . . . except food bills."

Because I was already watching, I caught it this time. For the briefest moment Gleep's eyes narrowed as he glanced at Aahz, and an almost unnoticeable trickle of smoke escaped from one nostril. Then he went back to looking dopey and innocent.

"Gleep's a friend of mine now, Aahz," I said carefully, not taking my eyes off my pet. "Just like you and the rest of the crew are. I wouldn't want to lose *any* of you."

My dragon seemed to take no notice of my words, craning his neck to look around the stable. Now, however, it seemed to me his innocence was exaggerated . . . that he was deliberately avoiding looking me in the eye.

"If you say so," Aahz shrugged, heading for the door. "In the meantime, let's go see Bunny before she explodes."

I hesitated a moment longer, then followed him out of the stables.

II:

"It's good to see you, too."

—H. LIVINGSTON, M.D.

As Aahz had predicted, my three bodyguards were waiting for me outside the stables. They seemed to be arguing about something, but broke off their discussion and started looking vigilant as soon as I appeared.

Now, you may think it would be kind of fun to have your own bodyguards. If so, you've never actually had one.

What it really means is that you give up any notion that your life is your own. Privacy becomes a vague memory you have to work at recalling, as "sharing" becomes the norm . . . starting with the food on your plate and ending with going to the john. ("Geez, Boss! You know how many guys got whacked because someone was hiding in the can? Just pretend we ain't here.") Then, too, there's the constant, disquieting reminder that, however swell a fellow *you* may think you are, there are people out there waiting for a chance to bring your career to a premature conclusion. I had to keep telling myself that this latter point didn't apply to me, that Don Bruce had insisted on assigning me Guido and Nunzio more as status symbols than anything else. I had hired Pookie on my own, though, after getting jumped during my recent trip to Perv, so I couldn't entirely discount the fact that bodyguards were occasionally necessary and not just an inconvenient decoration.

"Got a minute, Skeeve?" Pookie said, stepping forward.

"Well, I was on my way to say hello to Bunny . . ."

"Fine. We can talk as we walk."

She fell in step beside me, and Aahz graciously fell back to walk with my other two bodyguards.

"What it is," Pookie said, without preamble, "is I'm thinking of cashing in and heading back to Perv."

"Really? Why."

She gave a small shrug.

"I can't see as how I'm really needed," she said. "When I suggested I tag along, we thought you were coming back to a small war. The way I see it now, it seems like the crew you've already got can handle things."

As she spoke, I snuck a glance back at Guido. He was trudging along, his posture notably more hangdog than usual. It was clear both that he was infatuated with Pookie, and that he wasn't wild about the idea of her moving on.

"Umm . . . Actually, I'd prefer it if you stuck around for a while, Pookie," I said. "At least, until I've made up my mind what to do about this situation with Queen Hemlock. She's been known to be a bit nasty when things don't go her way."

"Suit yourself," Pookie said, giving another shrug. "I just wanted to give you an easy out if you were looking to trim the budget."

I gave a smile at that.

"Just because we're going to be working on the kingdom's finances doesn't mean there's anything wrong with our treasury. You should know your cousin well enough to have faith in his money managing."

"I know Aahz, all right," she said, shooting a dark look at that individual, "enough to know that before he'd part with money unnecessarily, he'd cut off his arm . . . or, more likely, someone else's."

"He's mellowed a bit over the last few years," I smiled, "but I know what you mean. If it makes you feel any better, though, I hired you, so I figure you're reporting directly to me and not to him."

Pookie cocked an eyebrow at me.

"If that wasn't the case," she said, "I wouldn't have come along in the first place."

I could have let it go, but my curiosity was aroused.

"What's the problem between you two, anyway? More specifically, what's your problem with Aahz? He has nothing but the highest praise for you and your work."

Pookie's features hardened, and she broke eye contact to stare straight ahead.

"That's between him and me," she said stonily.

Her attitude puzzled me, but I knew better than to pursue the subject further.

"Oh. Well . . . anyway, I'd like you to stick around if that's okay."

"No problem from my end," she said. "Just one thing . . . to ease my mind. Could we adjust my pay scale? The prices you've been paying are my premium rates for short term work. For long term employment, I can give you a discount."

"How much?" I said quickly. As I noted before, Aahz had taught me most of what I know about money, and I had picked up some of his reflexes along the way.

"Why don't we knock it down to the same rate as you're paying those two," she said, jerking a thumb at Guido and Nunzio. "If nothing else, it might avoid some hard feelings between us professionally."

"Umm . . . fine."

I didn't have the heart to tell her that Guido and Nunzio were actually earning more than her premium rates. Realizing she was not only from the same dimension, but the same family as Aahz, I wasn't sure how she'd take the news. With everything else on my mind, I decided to sort it out at a later date . . . like, payday.

"Well, that takes care of me," Pookie said. "Any general orders for us?"

"Yes. Tell Nunzio I'd like to have a word with him."

One thing about living in a palace is that it takes a long time to walk from anywhere to anywhere, giving us lots of time to have conferences on the way to other conferences. Hey, I didn't say that it was a nice thing about living in a palace . . . just a thing.

"So what's the word, Boss?" Nunzio said, falling in step at my side.

"Is she stayin' or goin'?"

"What? Oh. Staying, I guess."

"Whew! That's a relief!" he said, rolling his eyes briefly. "I'll tell you, I don't think Guido would be livable if she left right now . . . know what I mean?"

"Uh huh," I said, glancing back at his cousin . . . who, judging by the grin on his face, had already heard the news. "He seems quite taken with her."

"You don't know the half of it," Nunzio grimaced. "So, what did you want to talk to me about?"

"Well, you know how you've been saying that Gleep has been acting strange lately?"

"Yeah. So?" he said, his squeaky voice taking on a cautious note.

"I want you to try to spend more time with him. Talk to him . . . maybe take him out for some exercise."

"Me, Boss?"

"Sure. You get along with him better than anyone . . . except, maybe, me . . . and I'm going to be tied up with the kingdom's finances for a while. If there's anything wrong with Gleep, I want to find out about it before anyone else gets hurt."

"If you say so."

I couldn't help but notice an extreme lack of enthusiasm in his voice.

"Yes. I say so," I repeated firmly. "It's important to

me, Nunzio, and I can't think of anyone I'd trust more to
check things out for me."

"Okay, Boss," he said, thawing a little. "I'll get right
on it."

I wanted to give him a bit more encouragement, but
just then we arrived at the door to my quarters.

"I'll wait out here, Boss, and make sure nobody else
comes in for a while," Nunzio said with a faint smile as
he stepped back.

This surprised me a little, as the crew usually followed
me into my room without missing a step or a syllable of
conversation. Then I noticed that the others of our group
had also halted short of the door and were watching me
with a smile.

I couldn't figure what was going on. I mean, so Bunny
was waiting inside. So what? It was just Bunny.

Nevertheless I took my cue, nodding at them vaguely
as I opened the door.

"SKEEVE!!"

I barely turned around from shutting the door when
Bunny charged across the room, slamming into me with
a huge hug that took my breath away . . . literally.

"I was so worried about you!" she said, her voice muffled by my chest.

"Ahh . . . ack!"

That last comment was mine. Actually, it wasn't so
much a comment as a noise I made while trying to force
some air into my lungs. This proved easier said than
done . . . and it wasn't all that easy to say!

"Why didn't you come by the office on your way back
from Perv?" Bunny demanded, squeezing even harder and
shaking me slightly. "I was going out of my mind, thinking about you all alone in that terrible dimension . . ."

By ignoring what she was saying and focusing my entire consciousness on moving, I managed to slowly force
one hand . . . then an arm . . . inside her embrace. Sum-
moning my fast fading strength, I levered my arm sideways, breaking her grip and allowing myself a desperately
needed rush of air.

Okay. So it wasn't particularly affectionate, or even polite. It's just that I've picked up some annoying, selfish habits over the years . . . like breathing.

"What's the matter, Skeeve?" Bunny said in a concerned voice, peering at me closely. "Are you all right?"

"UUUUH hah . . . UUUUH hah . . . ," I explained, realizing for the first time how sweet plain air could taste.

"I knew it!" she snarled. "Tananda kept saying you were all right . . . every time I asked she kept saying the same thing . . . that you were all right. The next time I see that little. . . ."

"I'm . . . fine . . . Really, Bunny. I'm . . . fine."

Still trying to get my lungs working on their own, I reached out a tentative finger and prodded her biceps.

"That was . . . quite a 'Hello,' " I said. "I never realized . . . you were so . . . strong."

"Oh, that," she shrugged. "I've been working out a little while you were gone . . . like every night. Not much else to do evenings. It's an easier way to stay in shape than dieting."

"Working out?"

My breathing was almost back to normal, but my head still felt a little woozy.

"Sure. You know, pumping iron?"

I had never realized that simple ironing could build up a woman's arms that much. I made a mental note to start sending our laundry out.

"I'm sorry I didn't think to check in with you," I said, returning to the original subject. "It's just that I assumed you were okay there at the office, and was in a hurry to see if the crew was okay."

"Oh, I know. It's just that . . ."

Suddenly she was hugging me again . . . gentler, this time.

"Don't be mad at me, Skeeve," she said softly from the depths of my chest. "I just get so worried about you sometimes."

I was surprised to realize she was trembling. I mean,

it just wasn't that cold here in my room. Especially not huddled together the way we were.

"I'm not mad at you, Bunny," I said. "And there was nothing to worry about . . . really. Everything went fine on Perv."

"I heard that you nearly got killed in a fight," she countered, tightening her grip slightly. "And wasn't there some kind of trouble with the cops?"

That annoyed me a little. The only way she could have found out about the trouble I ran into on Perv would be from Tananda . . . except I hadn't told Tananda anything about it before she headed back to the Bazaar to relieve Bunny. That meant that either Aahz or Pookie was telling people about my escapades . . . and, to say the least, I wasn't wild about that.

"Where did you hear that?" I said casually.

"It's all over the Bazaar," Bunny explained, burrowing further into my chest. "Tananda said you were fine, but I had to see for myself after everything I heard."

Com'on, Bunny," I said soothingly, mentally apologizing to Aahz and Pookie. "You know how everything gets exaggerated at the Bazaar. You can see I'm fine."

She started to say something, then turned her head as sounds of an argument erupted through the closed door.

"What's that?"

"I don't know," I admitted. "Guido and Nunzio said they were going to keep everybody out for a while. Maybe someone . . ."

The door burst open, and Queen Hemlock stood framed in the entryway. Behind her my bodyguards stood, and as they caught my eye gave exaggerated shrugs. Apparently royalty was harder to stop than your average assassin . . . a thought that did little to cheer me realizing some of the rumors surrounding the current matriarch of Possiltum.

"There you are, Skeevie," the Queen exclaimed striding into my room. "I was looking all over for you when I saw those thugs of yours loitering about outside and . . . Who's this?"

"Your Majesty, this is Bunny. Bunny, this is Queen Hemlock."

"Your Majesty," Bunny said, sinking into a deep bow.

It occurred to me that as worldly as she was in some ways, Bunny had never met a member of royalty before, and seemed to be quite awed by the experience.

Queen Hemlock, on the other hand, was not at all over-awed by meeting another commoner.

"Why Skeeve! She's lovely!" she said, cupping Bunny's chin in her hand and raising her head to view her face. "I was starting to wonder a bit about you, what with that monstrous apprentice of yours, not to mention that lizard thing you brought back with you from wherever, but *this* . . . It's nice to know you *can* find a yummy morsel when you set your mind to it."

"Bunny's my administrative assistant," I said, a bit stiffly.

"Why of *course*!" the Queen smiled, giving me a broad wink. "Just like my young men are bodyguards . . . on the kingdom budget, anyway."

"Please, Your Majesty, don't misunderstand," Bunny said. "Skeeve and I are really just . . ."

"There there, my dear," Hemlock interrupted, taking Bunny by the hands and drawing her to her feet. "There's no need to worry about me being jealous. I wouldn't dream of interfering in Skeeve's personal life before or after we're married, any more than I'd expect him to in-terfere in mine. As long as he does the heir thing to keep the rabble happy, it doesn't really matter to me what he does with the rest of his time."

I really didn't like the way this conversation was going, and hastened to change the subject.

"You said you were looking for me, Your Majesty?"

"Oh yes," the Queen said, releasing her hold on Bunny's hands. "I wanted to tell you that Grimble was waiting to see you at your earliest convenience. I told him that you'd be giving him a hand straightening out the kingdom's finances, and he's ready to give you whatever information or assistance you need."

Somehow, that didn't sound like the J. R. Grimble I knew, but I let it slide for the moment.

"Very well. We'll be along presently."

"Of course." The Queen smiled, winking at me again. "Well, I'll just be running along then."

As she reached the door, she paused to sweep Bunny once more with a lingering gaze. "Charming," she said. "You really are to be congratulated, Skeeve."

There was an uncomfortable silence after the Queen left. Finally, I cleared my throat.

"I'm sorry about that, Bunny. I guess she just assumed . . ."

"*That's* the woman you're supposed to marry?" Bunny said as if I hadn't spoken.

"Well, it's what she wants, but I'm still thinking it over-"

"And if somebody kills her, you'd feel you had to take over running the kingdom?"

"Uh . . . well, yes."

There was something in Bunny's voice I didn't like. I also found myself remembering that while she had never met royalty before, her uncle was none other than Don Bruce, the Mob's Fairy Godfather, and that she was used to an entirely different brand of power politics.

"I see," Bunny said thoughtfully, then she broke into her usual smile. "Well, I guess we'd better go and see Grimble and find out what kind of a mess we're really in."

"Okay. Sure," I said, glad that the crisis had passed . . . if only for the moment.

"Just one question, Skeeve."

"Yes, Bunny?"

"How do *you* feel about 'the heir thing' as her majesty so graciously put it?"

"I don't know," I admitted. "I guess I don't mind."

"You don't?"

"Not really. I just don't understand what having a haircut has to do with being a royal consort."

III:

"A good juggler can always find work."

—L. PACCIOLI*

J. R. Grimble, Chancellor of the Exchequer for the kingdom of Possiltum, had changed little since I first met him. A little more paunch around the waist, perhaps, though his slender body could stand the extra weight and then some, and his hairline had definitely progressed from the "receding" to the "receded" category, but aside from that the years had left him virtually unmarked. Upon reflection, I decided it was his eyes that were so distinctive as to render his other features inconsequential. They were small and dark, and glittered with the fervent light of a greedy rodent . . . or of someone who spent far too many hours pouring over the tiny scribbled figures which noted the movement of other peoples' money.

"Lord Skeeve!" he exclaimed, seizing my hand and

[*I'll give you this one . . . Luca Paccioli—inventor of double-entry accounting, "Father of Bookkeeping"—R.L.A.]

pumping it enthusiastically. "So good to have you back. And Aahz! Couldn't stay away, eh?" He gave a playful wink at my partner. "Just kidding. Glad to see you again, too."

"Have you been drinking, Grimble?" Aahz said bluntly.

In all honestly, I had been wondering the same thing myself, but had been at a loss as to how to ask the question diplomatically. Fortunately, my partner's characteristic tactlessness came to my rescue.

"Drinking?" the Chancellor blinked. "Why, no. Why do you ask?"

"You seem a lot more cheerful than normal, is all. As a matter of fact, I don't recall your ever being happy to see either of us before."

"Now now, let's let bygones be bygones, shall we? Though I'll admit we've had our differences in the past, we're going to be working together now . . . and frankly, gentlemen, I can't think of anyone I'd rather have in my corner during our current financial crisis. I never felt at liberty to admit it before, but I've always secretly admired your skills when it came to manipulating monies."

"Uh . . . thanks, Grimble," I said, still unsure of exactly how to take his new attitude.

"And who do we have here?"

He turned his attention to Bunny, devouring her with his eyes like a toad edging up on a moth.

I suddenly recalled that Aahz and I had first become embroiled in the workings of Possiltum after Grimble had picked Tananda up in a singles bar. It also occurred to me that I didn't like Grimble much.

"This is Bunny," I said. "She's my administrative assistant."

"Of course," Grimble shot me a sidelong, reptilian glance, then went back to leering at Bunny. "You always did have exquisite taste in ladies, Skeeve."

Still annoyed at Bunny's treatment by Queen Hemlock, I wasn't about to let the Chancellor get away with this.

"Grimble," I said, letting my voice take on a bit of an

edge. "Watch my lips. I said she's my administrative assistant. Got it?"

"Yes. I . . . Quite."

The Chancellor seemed to pull in on himself a bit as he licked his lips nervously, but he rallied back gamely.

"Very well. Let me show you our expanded operation."

While Grimble might have been essentially unchanged, physically or morally, his facilities were another matter entirely. He had formerly worked alone in a tiny, cramped cubicle filled past capacity with stacks and piles of paper. The paper was still there, but that's about all that remained the same. Instead of the cubicle, it seemed he was now working out of a spacious, though still windowless, room . . . or, at least, a room that would have been spacious if he had it to himself.

Instead, however, there were over a dozen individuals crammed into the space, apparently preoccupied with their work, which seemed to entail nothing more than generating additional stacks of paper, all covered by columns and rows of numbers. They didn't look up as we came in, and Grimble made no effort to halt their work or make introductions, but I noticed that they all had the same fevered glint to their eyes that I had originally assumed to be unique to Grimble.

"It seems that the current financial crisis hasn't caused many cutbacks in your operation," Aahz said dryly.

"Of course not," Grimble replied easily. "That's only to be expected."

"How's that?" I said.

"Well, Lord Skeeve," the Chancellor smiled, "you'll find that accountants are pretty much like vultures . . . we thrive when things are worse for other people. You see, when a kingdom or company is doing well, no one wants to be bothered with budgets, much less cost savings. As long as there's money in the coffers, they're happy. On the other hand, when the operation is on the skids, such as is currently the case with Possiltum, *then* everyone wants answers . . . or miracles . . . and it's up to us irritating bean-counters to provide them. More analysis means more man-hours, which in turn means a larger staff and expanded facilities."

"Charming," Aahz growled, but Grimble ignored him.

"So," he said, rubbing his hands together like a blow-fly, "what would you like to address first? Perhaps we could discuss our overall approach and strategy over lunch?"

"Umm . . ." I said intelligently.

The horrible truth was that, now that I was actually confronted by Grimble and his paper mountains, I didn't have the foggiest notion of how to proceed.

"Actually, Grimble," Bunny said stepping forward, "before we think about lunch, I'd like to see your Operating Plan for the current year, the calendarized version, as well as the P and L's and Financial Statements for the last few months . . . oh yes, and your Cash Flow Analysis, both the projections and the actuals, if you don't mind."

The Chancellor blanched slightly and swallowed hard.

"Certainly. I . . . of course," he said, giving Bunny a look which was notably more respectful than his earlier attentions. "I'll get those for you right now."

He scuttled off to confer with a couple of his underlings, all the while glancing nervously back at our little group.

I caught Aahz's eye and raised an eyebrow, which he responded to with a grimace and a shrug. It was nice to know my partner was as much in the dark as I was regarding Bunny's requests.

"Here we are," Grimble said, returning with a fistful of paper which he passed to Bunny. "I'll have the Cash Flow for you in a moment, but you can get started with these."

Bunny grunted something non-committal, and began leafing through the sheets, pausing to scrutinize each page intently. More for show than anything, I eased over to where I could look over her shoulder. In no time flat, my keen eye could tell without a doubt that the pages were filled with rows and columns of numbers. Terrific.

"Um . . . I do have some spreadsheets to support some

of those figures if you'd like to see them," Grimble supplied uneasily.

Bunny paused in her examinations to favor him with a dark glance.

"Maybe later," she said. "I mean, you *do* know the origin of spreadsheets, don't you?"

"Umm . . ." the Chancellor hedged.

"They were named after the skins used by trappers," Bunny continued with a faint smile. "You know, the things they dragged after them to hide their tracks?"

For a moment Grimble stared at her, bewildered, then he gave a sudden bark of laughter, slapping her playfully on the shoulder.

"That's good!" he exclaimed. "I'll have to remember that one."

I glanced at Aahz.

"Accountant humor, I guess," he said with a grimace. "Incomprehensible to mere mortals. You know, like 'We'll make it up on volume' jokes?"

"Now *that's* not funny," Grimble corrected with mock severity. "We've had that line dumped on us all too often . . . in complete sincerity. Right Bunny?"

I couldn't help but notice that he was now treating Bunny with the deference of a colleague. Apparently her joke, however nonsensical it had been to me, had convinced the Chancellor that she was more than my arm ornament.

"Too true," my *assistant* said. "But seriously, Grimble, getting back to the problem at hand, we're going to need complete, non-camouflaged figures if we're going to get the kingdom's finances back on course. I know the tradition is to pretty things up with charts and studies of historic trends, but since we'll be working with insiders only, just this once let's try it with hard, cold data."

It sounded like a reasonable request to me, but the Chancellor seemed to think it was a radical proposal . . . and not a particularly wise one, at that.

"I don't know, Bunny," he said, shooting a look at Aahz and me one normally reserves for spies and traitors.

"I mean, you know how it is. Even though we usually get
cast as the villains of bureaucracy, we don't have any *real*
power to implement change. All we do is make recommendations to those who *can* change things. If we don't
sugarcoat our recommendations, or slant them so they're
in line with what the movers and shakers wanted to hear
all along, or clutter them up until the Gods themselves
can't understand what we're really saying, then there's a
risk that *we* end up being what gets changed."

"Nobody *really* wants to hear the truth, eh?" Aahz said,
sympathetically. "I suppose that's typical. I think you'll
find it's different this time around. Grimble. If nothing
else, Skeeve here has full power to implement whatever
changes he thinks are necessary to bring things in line."

"That's right," I said, glad to finally be able to contrib-
ute to the proceedings. "One of the things I think we
should do as soon as possible is cut back on the size of
the army . . . say, maybe, by one-half?"

Knowing the Chancellor's long-time feud with military
spending, I thought he'd leap at this suggestion, but to
my surprise, he shook his head.

"Can't do it," he said. "It would cause a depression."

"I don't care if they're happy or not!" Aahz snarled.
"Let's get 'em off the payroll. The Queen's agreed to stop
her expansionist policies, so there's no reason we should
keep paying for an army this size."

Grimble gave my partner a look like he was something
unpleasant on the bottom of his shoe.

"I was referring to an economic depression," he said
tersely. "If we dump that many ex-soldiers on the job mar-
ket at the same time we're cutting back on military spending, it would create massive unemployment. Broke, hungry
people, particularly those with prior military training, have
a nasty tendency to revolt against those in power . . .
which, in this case, happens to be us. I think you'll agree,
therefore, that, in the long run, huge cutbacks in the military force is *not* the wisest course to follow."

I was rapidly developing a greater respect for Grimble.

Obviously there was more to this bean-counting game than I had ever imagined.

"We might, however, achieve some savings through attrition," the Chancellor continued.

"Attrition?" I said. I had decided that, if I was going to be any help at all in this effort, it was time I admitted my ignorance and started learning some of the basic vocabulary.

"In this case, Lord Skeeve," Grimble explained with surprising patience, "the term refers to cutting manpower by not rehiring as people terminate at the normal rate . . . or, for the army, that we stop adding new recruits to replace those whose term of enlistment is up. It will still cut the size of the army, but at a slower rate more easily absorbed by the civilian work force."

"Can we afford to do it slowly?" Aahz said, seemingly unfazed by his earlier rebuke. "I was under the impression the kingdom was in dire straits financially."

"I believe I had heard some rumor that we might be raising our tax rate?" The Chancellor made the statement a question as he looked at me pointedly.

"I'm not sure that will do any good," Bunny said from where she was reviewing the figures Grimble had passed her.

"Excuse me?" the Chancellor frowned.

"Well, from what I'm seeing here, the big problem isn't income, it's collections," she said, tapping one of the sheets she was holding.

Grimble sighed, seeming to deflate slightly.

"I'll admit that's one of our weak suits," he said, "But . . ."

"Whoa! Time out!" I interrupted. "Could someone provide a translation?"

"What I'm saying is that the kingdom actually has a fair amount of money," Bunny said, "but it's all on paper. That is, people owe us a lot on back taxes, but it isn't being collected. If we could make some inroads into converting these receivables . . . that's debts owed to us . . . into cash, which we can spend, the kingdom would be in pretty good shape. Not stellar, mind you, but enough to ease the current crisis."

"The problem is," Grimble said, picking up the thread of her oration, "the citizens are *extremely* un-cooperative when it comes to taxes. They fight us every inch of the way in admitting how much they owe, and when it comes to actually *paying* their tax bill . . . well, the variety of excuses they invent would be amusing, if we weren't going bankrupt waiting for them to settle their accounts."

"I can't argue with them there," Aahz smirked.

"It's the duty of every citizen to pay their fair share of the cost of running the kingdom through taxes," the Chancellor said testily.

"And it's the right of every individual to pay the lowest possible amount of taxes they can justify legally," my partner shot back.

For a moment, it sounded like old times, with Aahz and Grimble going head to head. Unfortunately, this time, we all had bigger fish to fry.

"Check me on this," I said, holding up a hand to silence them. "What if we see if we can kill two birds with one stone?"

"How's that?" Grimble frowned.

"Well, first, we implement your suggestion of reducing the army by attrition . . . maybe hurrying it along a little by offering shortened enlistments for anyone who wanted out early . . ."

"That might help," the Chancellor nodded, "but I don't see . . ."

"And," I continued quickly, "convert a portion of those remaining in the service into tax collectors. That way they can be helping to raise the cash necessary to cover their own pay."

Grimble and Bunny looked at each other.

"That might work," Grimble said, thoughtfully.

"It can't do much worse than the system that's already in place," Bunny nodded.

"Tell you what," I said loftily. "Kick it around between the two of you and maybe rough out a plan for implementing it. Aahz and I will go discuss it with the Queen."

Actually, I had no intention of visiting Hemlock just now, but I figured it was as good a time as any to escape from this meeting . . . while I had at least a small victory to my credit.

IV:

"I'm getting paid how much?"

—M. JORDAN

The next several days were relatively uneventful. In fact, they seemed so much alike that I tended to lose track of which day was which.

If this sounds like I was more than a little bored, I was. After years of adventuring and narrow escapes, I found the day to day routine of regular work to be pretty bland. Of course, the fact that I didn't know what I was doing contributed greatly to my mood.

I mean, within my own areas of specialization . . . such as running from angry mobs or trying to finagle a better deal from a client . . . I was ready to admit that I was as good or better than anyone. At things like budgets, operating plans, and cash flows, however, I was totally out of my depth.

It was more than a little spooky when I realized that, even though I didn't know what I was doing, the recommendations I was making or approving, like converting part of the army into tax collectors, were becoming law nearly as fast as I spoke. Still, it had been impressed on me that we had to do *something* to save the kingdom's finances, so I repeatedly crossed my fingers under the table and went with whatever seemed to be the best idea at the time.

Before I get too caught up in complaining about my situation, however, let me pause to give credit where credit is due. As bad as things were, I would have been totally lost without Bunny.

Though I didn't plan it that way, my administrative assistant ended up doing double duty. First, she would spend long hours going over numbers and plans with Grimble in their high speed, abbreviated jargon while I sat there nodding with a vacant look on my face, then an equal or greater amount of time with me later patiently trying to explain what had been decided. As mind numbing as it was, I found it preferable to my alternate pastime, which was trying to figure out what to do about Queen Hemlock's marriage offer.

Every so often, however, something would pop up that I felt I DID know something about. While it would usually turn out in the long run that I was (badly) mistaken, it would provide a break from the normal complacency. Of course, I wasn't that wild about being shown to be *specifically* stupid as well as generally ignorant, but it was a change of pace.

One conversation in particular springs to mind when I think back on those sessions.

"Wait a minute, Bunny. What was that last figure again?"

"What?" she said, glancing up from the piece of paper she was reciting from. "Oh, that was *your* budget."

"My budget for what?"

"For your portion of the financial operation, of course. It covers salaries and operating expense."

"Whoa! Stop the music!" I said, holding up my hand. "I officially retired as Court Magician. How did I end up back on the payroll?"

"Grimble put you back on the same day you came back

from Perv," Bunny said patiently. "But that has nothing to do with this. This is your budget for your *financial* consulting. Your magical fees are in a whole separate section."

"But that's ridiculous!"

"Oh Skeeve," she grimaced, rolling her eyes slightly. "I've explained all this to you before. We *have* to keep the budgets for different kingdom operations on separate records to be able to track their performance accurately. Just like we have to keep the types of expenses within each operation in separate accounts. Otherwise . . ."

"No, I didn't mean that it was ridiculous to keep them in separate sections," I clarified hastily, before she could get settled into yet another accounting lesson. "I meant the budget itself was ridiculous."

For some reason, this seemed to get Bunny even more upset rather than calming her down.

"Look, Skeeve," she said stiffly. "I know you don't understand everything Grimble and I are doing, but believe me, I don't just make these numbers up. That figure for your budget is a reasonable projection, based on estimated expenses and current pay scales . . . even Grimble says it's acceptable and has approved it. Realizing that, I'd be *very* cautious to hear the exact basis by which you're saying it's ridiculous."

"You don't understand, Bunny," I said, shaking my head. "I'm not saying the number is ridiculous or inaccurate. What I mean is that it shouldn't be there at all."

"What do you mean?"

I was starting to feel like we were speaking in different languages, but pressed on bravely.

"Com'on, Bunny. All this work is supposed to be *saving* money for the kingdom. You know, turning the finances around?"

"Yes, yes," Bunny nodded. "So what's your point?"

"So how does it help things to charge them *anything* for our services, much less an outrageous rate like *this*. For that matter, I don't think I should charge them for my magical services, either, all things considered."

"Um, Partner?" Aahz said, uncoiling from his customary seat in the corner. If anything, I think he was even more bored by these sessions than I was. "Can I talk to you for a minute? Before this conversation goes any further?"

I *knew* what that meant. Aahz is notorious when it comes to pushing our rates higher, operating under the basic principle that earning less than possible is the same as losing money. As soon as I started talking about not only reducing our fees, but eliminating them completely, it was only to be expected that Aahz would jump into the fray. I mean, talk about money in general, and about our money specifically, would bring Aahz out of a coma.

This time, however, I wasn't about to go along with him.

"Forget it, Aahz," I said, waving him off. "I'm not going to back off on this one."

"But *Partner*," he said menacingly, reaching out his hand casually for my shoulder.

"I said 'No!' " I insisted, ducking out of his reach. I've tried to argue with him before when he has gotten a death grip on my shoulder, and was not about to give him that advantage again. "*This* time I know I'm right."

"*What's right about working for FREE?*" he snarled, abandoning all subtlety. "*Haven't I taught you ANYTHING in all these years?*"

"*You've taught me a lot!!*" I shot back at him. "And I've gone along with a lot . . . and it usually turned out for the best. But there's one thing we've never done, Aahz, for all our finagling and scrambling. To the best of my knowledge, *we've never gouged money out of someone who couldn't afford it*. Have we?"

"Well, no. But . . ."

"If we can beat Deveels or the Mob out of some extra money, well and good," I continued. "They have lots of money, and I got most of it swindling other people. But with Possiltum we're talking about a kingdom that's on the ropes financially. How can we say we're here to help them when at the same time we're kicking them in the head with inflated fees?"

Aahz didn't answer at once, and after a moment, he dropped his eyes.

"But Grimble's already approved it," he said finally, in a voice that was almost plaintive.

I couldn't believe it! I had actually won an argument with Aahz over money! Fortunately, I had the presence of mind to be magnanimous in my victory.

"Then I'm sure he'll approve of cutting the expense even more," I said, putting my hand on Aahz's shoulder for a change. "Aside from that, it's just a clerical adjustment. Right, Bunny?"

"No."

She said it softly, but there was no mistaking her answer. So much for my victory.

"But Bunny . . ." I began desperately, but she cut me off.

"I said 'No' and I meant it, Skeeve," she said. "Really, Aahz. I'm surprised you've let this go on for as long as it has. There are greater principles at stake here than basic greed!"

Aahz started to open his mouth, then closed it without speaking. It's probably the only time I've seen Aahz agree, even by silence, that there *existed* any higher principles than greed. Still, Bunny was arguing his side of the fight, so he let it ride.

"Your heart may be in the right place, Skeeve," she said, turning back to me, "but there are factors here you're overlooking or don't understand."

"So explain them to me," I said, a little miffed, but nonetheless willing to learn.

Bunny pursed her lips for a moment, apparently organizing her thoughts.

"All right," she said, "let's take it from the beginning. As I understand it, we're supposed to be helping the kingdom get out of it's current financial crisis. What Grimble and I have been doing, aside from recommending emergency expense cuts, is to come up with a reasonable budget and operating plan to get things back on an even keel. The emphasis here is on *'reasonable.'* The bottom line is that it is *not* reasonable to expect anyone . . . you, me, or Grimble . . . to provide such a crucial service for nothing. *Nobody* works for free. The army doesn't, the farmers don't, and there's no reason we should."

"But because of that very crisis, the kingdom *can't* afford to pay us!" I protested.

"Nonsense," Bunny snapped. "*First of all*, remember that the Queen got the kingdom into this mess all by herself by pouring too much money into the army. We're not the problem. We're the imported experts who are supposed to get them out of the hole they dug for themselves."

"Second," she continued before I could interrupt, "as you can see from the sheets I'm showing you, we *can* save enough in expenses and generate sufficient revenues from taxes to pay our own fees. That's part of the job of a bean-counter . . . to show their employer how to afford to pay themselves. Not many professions do that!"

What she was saying made sense, but I was still unconvinced.

"Well, at the very least can't we cut our fees a bit?" I said. "There's no real reason for us to charge as much as you have us down for."

"Skeeve, Skeeve, Skeeve," Bunny said, shaking her head. "I told you I didn't just make up these numbers. I know you're used to negotiating deals on what the client will bear, but in a budget like this, the pay scale is almost dictated. It's set by what others are getting paid. Anything else is so illogical, it would upset the whole system."

I glanced at Aahz, but he had his eyes fixed on Bunny, hanging on her every word.

"Okay. Let's take it from the top," I said. "Explain it to me in babytalk, Bunny. Just how are these pay scales fixed?"

She pursed her lips for a moment while organizing her thoughts.

"Well, to start with, you have to understand that the

pay scale for any job is influenced heavily by supply and demand." she began. "Top dollar jobs usually fall into one of three categories. First, is if the job is particularly unpleasant or dangerous . . . then, you have to pay extra just to get someone to be willing to do it. Second are the jobs where a particular skill or talent is called for. Entertainers and athletes fall into this category, but so do the jobs that require a high degree of training, like doctors."

"And magicians!" my partner chimed in.

"Bear with me, Aahz," Bunny said, holding up a restraining hand to him. "Now, the third category for high pay are those who have a high degree of responsibility . . . whose decisions involve a lot of money and/or affect a lot of people. If a worker in a corporation makes a mistake, it means a day's or a week's work may have to be redone . . . or, perhaps, a client is lost. The president of the same corporation may only make three or four decisions a year, but those decisions may be to open or close six plants or to begin or discontinue an entire line of products. If *that* person makes a mistake, it could put hundreds or thousands of people out of work. Responsibility of that level is frightening and wearing, and the person willing to hold the bag deserves a higher degree of compensation. With me so far?"

"It makes sense . . . so far," I nodded.

"Moving along then, within each profession, there's a pecking order with the best or most experienced getting the highest rates, while the newer, lower workers settle for starting wages. Popular entertainers earn more than relative unknowns who are still building a following. Supervisors and managers get more than those reporting to them, since they have to have both the necessary skills of the job *plus* the responsibility of organizing and overseeing others. This is the natural order of a job force, and it provides incentive for new workers to stick with a job and to try to move up in the order. Got it?"

"That's only logical," I agreed.

"Then you understand why I have you down in the

budget for the rather substantial figure you've been protesting," she concluded triumphantly.

"I do?" I blinked.

I thought I had been following her fine, step by step.
Somewhere along the way, however, I seemed to have
missed something.

"Don't you see, Skeeve?" she pressed. "The services
you're providing for Possiltum fall into *all three* of the
high pay requirements. The work is dangerous *and* unpleasant, it definitely requires special skills from you and
your staff, and, since you're setting policy for an entire
kingdom, the responsibility level is right up there with the
best of them!"

I had never stopped to think about it in those terms,
mostly to preserve my nerves and sanity, but she *did* have
a point. She wasn't done, however.

"What's more," she continued, "you're darn-near at the
top of your profession *and* the pecking order. Remember,
Grimble's reporting to *you* now, which makes your pay
scale higher than his. What's more, you've been a hot
magical property for some time now . . . not just here on
Klah, but at the Bazaar on Deva which is pretty big
league. Your Queen Hemlock has gotten the kingdom in
a major mess, and if she's going to hire the best to bail
her out, she's bloody well going to pay for it."

That last part had an unpleasant sound of vindictiveness
to it, but there was something that was bothering me even
more.

"For the moment, let's say I agree with you . . . at least
on the financial side," I said. "I still don't see how I can
draw pay as a financial consultant *and* a court magician."

"Because you're doing both jobs," Bunny insisted.

". . . But I'm not working magically right now," I shot
back.

"Aren't you?" she challenged. "Come on, Skeeve. Are
you trying to tell me that if some trouble arose that required a magikal solution, that you'd just stand by and
ignore it?"

"Well, no. But . . ."

"No 'buts,' " Bunny interrupted. "You're in residence here, and ready to throw your full resources into any magikal assignment that arises . . . just like you're doing at the Baazar. *They're* paying you a hefty percentage just to be on standby. If anything, you're giving Possiltum a break on what you're charging them. Make no mistake, though, you are doing the job. I'm just making sure they pay you for it. If they want a financial consultant and a court magician, then it's only fair that it shows in their budget and is part of the burden they have to raise money to pay."

She had me. It occurred to me, however, that if this conversation lasted much longer, she'd have me believing that black was white.

"I guess it's okay then," I said, shrugging my shoulders. "It still sounds high to me."

"It is," Bunny said, firmly. "You've got to remember though, Skeeve, that whole amount isn't just for you. It's M.Y.T.H. Inc. the kingdom is paying for. The fees have to cover the expense of your entire operation, including overhead and staff. It's not like you're taking the whole amount and putting it in your pocket."

I nodded casually, but my mind was racing. What Bunny had just said had given me an idea.

If nothing else, I had learned in these sessions that there was a big difference between a budget or operating plan and the actual money spent. Just because I was *allowed* to spend an astronomic figure didn't mean I was compelled to do it!

I quietly resolved to bring my sections in well under budget . . . even if it meant trimming my own staff a bit. I loved them all dearly, but as Bunny had just pointed out, part of my own job was to be highly responsible.

V:

"What you need is a collection agency."

—D. SHULTZ

My session with Bunny had given me food for thought. Retreating to the relative privacy of my room, I took time to reflect on it over a goblet of wine.

Usually, I assigned people to work on various assignments for M.Y.T.H. Inc. on a basis of what I thought it would take to get the job done and who I thought would be best to handle it. That, and who was available.

As Bunny had pointed out, our prices were usually set on a basis of what the traffic would bear. I suppose I should have given more thought in the past to whether or not the income from a particular job covered the expense of the people involved, or if the work warranted the price, but operating the way we had been seemed to generate enough money to make ends meet . . . more than enough, actually.

The recent two projects, my bringing Aahz back from Perv and the rest of the team trying to stop Possiltum's army, were notable exceptions. These were almost personal missions, undertaken on my own motivations or suggestions, without an actual client or revenue.

Now, however, I was confronted by an entirely new situation.

Everyone in the crew was hanging around the castle . . . with the exception of Tananda, who was minding the offices back on Deva. The question was, did they have to be here?

I had a hunch that they were mostly staying here because they were worried about me . . . not without some justification. They all knew I was in a spot, and wanted to be close at hand if I needed help.

While I appreciated their concern, and definitely wanted the moral support, I also had to admit that there wasn't whole bunches they could do. Bunny was invaluable in turning the kingdom's finances around, but aside from holding my hand though this crisis, there was relatively little the others could do.

The trouble was, by simple arithmetic, while they were here on Possiltum, they weren't out working other assignments, making money for M.Y.T.H. Inc. and therefore for themselves . . . for a whole month! On top of the work time they missed while stopping Hemlock's army as a favor to me. If this organization was going to be a functioning, profit-making venture and not a humanitarian "bail-Skeeve-out" charity, we had to get back our bottom-line orientation. What's more, both as president and the one who had led us off on this side trip, I had to seize the initiative in setting things right again. That meant that I either had to trim the force, or go along with Bunny's plan of charging the kingdom for all our time.

The question was, who to trim?

Aahz had to stay. Not only had I just gone through a lot of trouble to get him back from Perv, but I genuinely valued his advice and guidance. While I had gotten into immeasurably more trouble since we first met, I had also become very aware that he was unequaled at getting us *out* of trouble as well.

Bunny was a must. Even though it had been Tananda's

idea originally to deal her in on this mess, I was very aware that without her expertise and knowledge, we didn't have a chance at bailing out the kingdom financially. Besides, judging by her greeting when we were reunited, I wasn't sure she'd be willing to go back to the Bazaar and leave me to face this dilemma alone.

As to my three bodyguards . . . after a moment's thought I decided to hold judgment on that one. First of all, I had just convinced Pookie to stay, which would make me look like a fool if I suddenly changed my mind. Second, I wasn't altogether sure I wouldn't need them. When I went off to Perv, I did it without Guido and Nunzio . . . over their strong protests . . . and ended up having to hire Pookie in their absence. Before I thought seriously about sending them all away again, I'd want to have a long talk about how *they* viewed my prospective danger here. While I wanted to save the kingdom money, I wasn't so generous as to do it if it meant putting myself in danger.

That left Massha and Chumley.

Massha came to me as an apprentice, and though I hadn't been very diligent in teaching her magik, I still had a responsibility to her that couldn't be filled if she were on Deva and I was here. Despite the fact I hadn't let her accompany me to Perv, I knew full well from my own experience that an apprentice's place is with his or her teacher.

I was suddenly confronted by the fact that the only one remaining on the list to be trimmed was Chumley . . . and I didn't want to do it. Despite the hairyknuckled, muscle-bound illiterate act the troll liked to put on when he was working, Chumley was probably the levelest head in our entire M.Y.T.H. Inc. crew. Frankly, I trusted his judgment and wisdom a lot more than I did Aahz's fiery temper. The idea of trying to make up my mind about Queen Hemlock's proposal without Chumley's wisdom was disquieting at best. Maybe *after* I had reached my decision . . .

As much as I had tried to avoid thinking about it, the

problem popped into my head and the potential ramifications hit me with a chilling impact.

Nervously, I gulped down the remaining wine in my goblet and hastily refilled it.

After I reached my decision . . .

All my thoughts and energies were focused on the immediate problems and short term plans. What was going to happen *after* I made my decision, whatever that decision was?

Things were never going to be the same for me.

Whether I married Queen Hemlock or, if refused, she abdicated and left me to run the kingdom on my own, I was going to be committed to stay in Possiltum a long time. A *very* long time.

I couldn't do that and maintain an office on Deva!

Would we have to move our operation here to Klah?

For that matter, could I be either a consort or a king and still do a responsible job as the president of M.Y.T.H. Inc.?

If I was uneasy about charging the kingdom for my crew for a month, how could I justify putting them all on the payroll *permanently*?

What about our other commitments? if we moved to Klah, it would mean giving up our juicy contract with the Devan Merchant's Association as magicians in residence. Could I charge Possiltum enough to make up for that kind of an income loss?

. . . Or would I have to step down as president of M.Y.T.H. Inc. entirely? Despite my occasional complaining, I had grown to like my position, and was reluctant to give it up . . . particularly if it meant losing all my friends like Aahz and . . .

AAHZ!

However it went, would Aahz want to hang around as a partner constantly standing in the shadow of my being consort or king? Having just recently dealt with his pride head to head, I doubted it very much.

Whatever my decision, the odds were that, once I reached it, I was going to lose Aahz!

A soft rap on my door interrupted my thoughts.

"Say, Boss. Can you spare a minute?"

Not only could I spare it, I was glad for the break.

"Sure Guido. Come on in. Pour yourself some wine."

"I never drink when I'm workin', Boss," he said with a hint of reproach, "but thanks anyway. I just need to talk to you about something."

My senior bodyguard took a chair and sat fidgeting with the roll of parchment he was holding. It occurred to me how seldom I just sat and talked with my bodyguards. I had rather gotten accustomed to their just being there.

"So, what can I do for you?" I said, sipping my wine casually, trying to put him at his ease.

"Well, Boss," he began hesitantly, "it's like this. I was thinkin' . . . You know how Nunzio and me spent some time in the army here?"

"Yes, I heard about that."

"Bein' on the inside like that, I get the feelin' I probably know a little more'n you do about the army types and how they think. The truth is, I'm a little worried about how they're gonna handle bein' tax collectors. Know what I mean?"

"Not really," I admitted.

"What I mean is," Guido continued earnestly, "when you're a soldier, you don't have to worry much about how popular you are with the enemy, 'cause mostly you're tryin' to make him dead and you don't expect him to like it. It's different doin' collection work, whether it's protection money or taxes, which is of course just a different kind of protection racket. Ya gotta be more diplomatic 'cause you're gonna have to deal with the same people over and over again. These army types might be aces when it comes to takin' real estate away from a rival operation, but I'm not sure how good they are at knowin' when to be gentle with civilian types. Get my drift?"

While I had never shared Guido's experience of being *in* an army, I had faced one once during my first assignment here at the court of Possiltum, and even earlier had been lynched by some soldiers acting as city guardsmen.

Now, suddenly, I had visions of army troops with cross-bows and catapults advancing on helpless citizens.

"I hadn't really thought about it," I said, "but I see your point."

"Well, you know I don't care much for meddlin' in management type decisions," Guido continued, "but I have a suggestion. I was thinkin' you could maybe appoint someone from the army to specifically inspect and investigate the collectin' process. You know, to be sure the army types didn't get too carried away with their new duties."

I really appreciated Guido's efforts to come up with a solution, particularly as I didn't have one of my own. Unfortunately, there seemed to be a bit of a flaw in his logic.

"Um . . . I don't quite understand, Guido," I said. "Isn't it kind of pointless to have someone from the army watching over the army? I mean, what's to say our inspector will be any different from the one's he's supposed to be policing?"

"Two things," my bodyguard replied, flashing his smile for the first time since he entered the room. "First, I have someone specific in mind for the inspector . . . one of my old army buddies. Believe me, Boss, this person is not particularly fond or tolerant of the way the army does things. As a matter of fact, I've already had the papers drawn up to formalize the assignment. All you gotta do is sign 'em."

He passed me the scroll he had been clutching and I realized he had actually been thinking out this suggestion well in advance.

"Funny name for a soldier," I said, scanning the document. "Spyder."

"Trust me, Boss," Guido pressed. "This is the person for the job."

"You said there were two things?" I stalled. "What's the other?"

"Well, I thought you could have a couple personal envoys tag along. You know, reportin' directly to you. That way you could be doubly sure the army wasn't hidin' anything from you."

"I see," I said, toying with the scroll. "And I suppose you have a couple specific people in mind for the envoys, as well?"

"Um . . . As a matter of fact . . ."

"I don't know, Guido," I said, shaking my head. "I mean, it's a good idea, but I'm not sure I can spare both you and Nunzio. If nothing else, I want Nunzio to do a little work with Gleep. I want to find out for sure if there's anything wrong with him."

"Ah . . . Actually, Boss," my bodyguard said, carefully studying his massive hands, "I wasn't thinkin' of Nunzio. I was thinkin' maybe Pookie and me could handle it."

More than anything else he had said, this surprised me. Guido and his cousin Nunzio had always worked as a team, to a point where I practically thought of the two of them as one person. The fact that Guido was willing to split the team up was an indication of how concerned he was over the situation. Either that, or a sign of how far he was willing to go to get some time alone with Pookie.

"Really, Boss," he urged, sensing my hesitation. "There ain't a whole lot to do here for three bodyguards. I mean, the way I see it, the only one here in the castle who might want to do you any bodily harm is the Queen herself, and I don't think you have to worry about her until after you've made up your mind on the marriage thing. I'm just lookin' for a way that we can earn our keep . . . something useful to do."

That did it. His point about reassigning my bodyguards played smack into my current thinking about trimming the team or expanding their duties. Then, too, I wasn't eager to prolong any discussion which involved my making up my mind about what to do about Hemlock.

"Okay, Guido," I said, scribbling my signature across the bottom of the scroll. "You've got it. Just be sure to keep me posted as to what's going on."

"Thanks, Boss," he grinned, taking the scroll and looking at the signature. "You won't regret this."

It hadn't occurred to me at all that I might regret it . . . until he mentioned it. I mean, what could go wrong?

VI:

"Money is the root of all evil. Women need roots."

—D. TRUMP

Though the various administrative hassles of trying to straighten out Possiltum's finances weighed heavily on my mind, there was another, bigger worry that ran like an undercurrent through my head whenever I was awake.

Should I or shouldn't I marry Queen Hemlock?

Aahz kept saying that I should go along with it, become the royal consort with an easy (not to mention well-paying) job for life. I had to admit, in many ways it looked more attractive than having her abdicate and ending up holding the bag for running the kingdom all by myself. I had that "opportunity" once before courtesy of the late King Roderick, and *really* didn't want to repeat the experience.

So why was I dragging my feet on making my decision?

Mostly, my indecision was due to my reluctance to accept the obvious choice. As much as I was repelled by the known quantity of being king, I was as much or more terrified of the unknown factors involved in marriage.

Time and time again, I tried to sort out if it was the idea of getting married that scared me, or if it was Queen Hemlock specifically that I couldn't picture as my wife.

My wife!

Every time that phrase crossed my mind, it was like an icy hand grabbed my heart hard enough to make it skip a beat.

Frankly, I was having trouble picturing *anyone* I knew in that role. In an effort to get a handle on my feelings, I forced myself to review the women of my acquaintance in that light.

Massha, my apprentice, was out of the question. While we were close enough as friends, as well as teacher/student, her sheer size was intimidating. The truth was, I had trouble thinking of her as a woman. Oh, I knew she was female all right, but I tended to see her as a friend who was female . . . not as a *female*, if you can see the difference.

Bunny . . . well, I supposed that she could be considered a candidate. The problem there was that she was the first woman who had made a solid pass at me, and it had scared me to death. When her uncle, Don Bruce, first dumped her on me, she was all set to play a gangster's moll. Once I got her straightened out, however, she had settled into being my administrative assistant like a duck takes to water, and the question of anything intimate developing between us never came up again. Thinking of her in terms of a life partner would mean completely restructuring how I viewed her and worked with her, and right now she was far too valuable as my assistant for me to rock the boat.

Tananda . . . I had to smile at the thought of the Trollop assassin as my wife. Oh, she was friendly enough, not to mention very attractive, and for a long time I had a crush on her. It eventually became apparent, however, that the hugs and kisses she bestowed on me were no different than those she gave the rest of the team . . . including her brother Chumley. She was just a physically friendly person, and the affection she showed me was that shown for a co-worker, or maybe a kid brother. I could accept that, now. Besides, I somehow couldn't see her giving up her own career to settle down keeping house for me. No, as much as I loved her, Tananda would never fit as my wife. She was . . . well, Tananda.

That left Queen Hemlock, who I had no real feeling for at all except, perhaps a sense of uneasiness every time she was around. She always seemed extremely sure of herself and what she wanted . . . which made her almost my exact opposite. Of course, that in itself was an interesting thought. Then, too, she was the only one who had ever expressed a desire to be paired with me . . . and seemed to want it badly enough to fight for it. Even Bunny had backed off once I rebuffed her. I had to admit that it did something to a man's ego to have a woman determined to bag him . . . even if he wasn't all that drawn to the woman in the first place.

Unfortunately, that was pretty much it for my list of female acquaintants. Oh, there were a few others I had come into contact with over the years, like Markie . . . and Luanna . . .

Luanna!!

She had almost slipped my mind completely, but once I thought of her, her face sprang into focus as if she were standing in front of me. Luanna. Lovely Luanna. Our paths had only crossed a couple times, most notedly during my adventure in the dimension of Limbo, and the last time we met the parting hadn't been pleasant. In short, I really didn't know her at all. Still, in many ways, she epitomized everything that was feminine in my mind. Not only did she radiate a soft, vulnerable beauty, her manner was demure. That may not seem like much to you, but it was to me. You see, most of the women I work with can only be called aggressive . . . or, less politely, brassy. Even Hemlock, for all her regal blood, was very straightforward about stating her mind and wishes. Bunny had cooled it a bit, once I got her off her moll kick, but had replaced her blatant suggestiveness with a brusk efficient manner that, at times, could be every bit as intimidating as her old sex kitten routine.

In contrast, Luanna always seemed very shy and hesitant in my presence. Her voice was usually quiet to a point I sometimes had to strain to hear her, and she had a habit of looking down, then peering up at me through her lashes . . . as if she felt I could bully her physically or verbally, but trusted me not to. I can't speak for other men, but it always made me feel ten feet tall . . . very powerful and with an overwhelming urge to use that strength to protect her from the hardships of the world.

Thinking of her while trying to appraise what I would want in a wife, I found myself dwelling on the image of finding her waiting for me at the close of each day . . . and realized the image wasn't all that objectionable. In fact, once she surfaced in my memory, I found myself thinking of her quite a bit whenever I tried to sort out my current position, and more than occasionally wished I could see her again before I had to make my final decision.

As it turned out, I got my wish.

I was in my room, making another of my feeble attempts to make head or tail of the stack of spreadsheets that Bunny and Grimble kept passing me on an almost daily basis. As those of you who have been following these adventures from the beginning may recall, I *can* read . . . or, at least, I had *thought* that I could. Since undertaking the task of sorting out the kingdom's finances, however, I had found out that reading text, which is to say, words, is a *lot* different than being able to read numbers.

I mean, we were all in agreement as to our goal, which was to eliminate or lessen the kingdom's debt load without either placing a staggering tax burden on the populace *or* cutting so much off the operating budget that the necessary administrative operations became non-functional. As I say, we were all in agreement . . . verbally . . . with words. Any time there was a disagreement between Grimble and Bunny on particulars, however, and they came to me to cast the deciding vote or make a decision, they would each invariably support their side of the argument by passing me one or more of those cryptic sheets covered with numbers and not much else, then wait expectantly as I scanned it, as if their case had just become self-explanatory.

Now, for those of you who have never been placed in this situation, let me offer a little clarification. When I say I can't read numbers, I don't mean that I can't decipher the symbols. I *know* what a two is and what it stands for and how it differs from, say, an eight. The problem I was confronted with in these arguments was trying to see them in relation to each other. To do a "word analogy," if the numbers were words, both Bunny and Grimble could look at a page full of numbers and see sentences and paragraphs, complete with subtleties and innuendos, whereas I would look at the same page and see a mass of unrelated, individual words. This was particularly uncomfortable when they would pass me two pages of what to them was a mystery novel, and ask my opinion on who the killer was.

Even though I *knew* they knew I was a numeric illiterate, I had gotten awfully tired of saying "Duh, I don't know" in varying forms, and, in an effort to salvage a few shreds of my self-respect, had taken to saying instead "Let me look these over and get back to you." Unfortunately, this meant that at any specific point in time, I had a batch of these "mystery sheets" on my desk that I felt obligated to at least *try* to make sense of.

Anyhoo, that's what I was doing when a knock came at my door. In short, I was feeling inept, frustrated, and desperately in need of diversion.

"Yes?" I called eagerly, hoping beyond hope that it was news of an earthquake or attacking army or something equally disastrous that would require my immediate attention. "Who is it?"

The door opened, and Massha's head appeared.

"You busy, Hot Stuff?" she said with the respect and

deference she always shows me as my apprentice. "You've got a visitor."

"Nothing that can't wait," I replied, hastily stacking the offensive spreadsheets and replacing them in their customary spot on the corner of my desk. "Who's the visitor?"

"It's Luanna. You remember, the babe who almost got us killed over in Limbo."

In hindsight, I can see that Massha was both expressing her disapproval and trying to warn me with her description of Luanna, but at the time it didn't register at all.

"Luanna?" I said, beaming with delight. "Sure, bring her in. Better yet, *send* her in."

"Don't worry," Massha sniffed, disdainfully. "I wouldn't *dream* of intruding on your little tête-à-tête."

Again, her reaction escaped my notice. I was far to busy casting about the room quickly to be sure it was presentable . . . which, of course, it was. If nothing else, the maid service in the castle was stellar.

And she was there . . . standing in my room, as lovely and winsome as I remembered.

"Uh . . . Hi, Luanna," I said, suddenly at a loss for words.

"Skeeve," she said in that soft, low voice that seemed to make the simplest statements an exercise in eloquence.

We looked at each other in silence for a few moments.

Then, suddenly, it occurred to me that the last time we saw each other, she had left in a huff under the misapprehension that I was married and had a kid.

"About the last . . ." I began.

"I'm sorry about . . ." she stated simultaneously.

We both broke off abruptly, then looked at each other and laughed.

"Okay. You first," I said finally, with a half bow.

"I just wanted to apologize for the way I acted the last time we were together. What I heard later from the rumor mill at the Bazaar convinced me that things weren't what they seemed at the time, and I felt terrible about not having given you a chance to explain. I should have looked you up sooner to say how sorry I was, but I wasn't sure you'd even want to talk to me again. I . . . I only hope you can forgive me . . . even though there's no real reason you should . . ."

Her voice trailed off as she dropped her eyes.

Looking the way she did, so demure, so defenseless, I could have forgiven her for being a mass murderess, much less for any minor misunderstanding between us.

"Don't worry about it," I said, in what I hoped was an offhand manner. "Truth to tell, Luanna, I was about to apologize to you. It must have been terrible for you . . . coming to me for help and walking into the . . . ah . . . situation you did. I've been thinking that I should have handled it a lot better than I did."

"That's so sweet of you, Skeeve," Luanna said, stepping forward to give me a quick hug and a peck of a kiss. "You don't know how glad I am to hear you say that."

Not surprisingly, her brief touch did strange things to my mind . . . and metabolism. It was only the second time she had kissed me and the other time I had been in the middle of conning her out of a handkerchief so I could get Aahz out of jail. All of which is to say I was far from immune to her kisses, however casual.

"So . . . ah . . . What brings you to Possiltum?" I said, fighting to keep my reactions from showing.

"Why, you of course."

"Me?"

Despite my feigned surprise, I felt my pulse quicken. I mean, I could have assumed that she was here to see me, but it was nice to have it confirmed that I was the sole purpose of her visit rather than a polite afterthought.

"Sure. I heard about your new position here, and figured it was too good a chance to pass up."

That didn't sound quite so good.

"Excuse me?"

"Oh, I'm getting it all turned around," she said, cutely annoyed with herself. "What I'm trying to say is that I have a proposal for you."

That was better. In fact, it was a little too good to be

true. While I had been indulging my fantasies about
Luanna as a possible wife, I never dared to think that she
might be thinking the same thoughts about me . . . as a
husband, I mean, not a wife.

"A proposal?" I said, deliberately stalling to organize
my thoughts.

"That's right. I figure that you've probably got a bit of
discretionary funds available now that you're on the kingdom payroll, and the kind of scams I run have a good
return on investment, so I was hoping that I could get a
little start-up money from you and . . ."

"Whoa! Stop the music!"

It had taken a few beats for what she was saying to
sink in, obsessed as I was with my own expectations of
the conversation. Even now, with my pretty dream-bubble
exploding around me, I was having trouble changing gears
mentally to focus on what she was actually getting at.

"Could you back up and take it from the top? You're
here to ask for money?"

"Well . . . Yes. Not much really . . . maybe fifty or
seventy-five in gold should do," she clarified hastily. "The
nice thing with scams is they don't really need much up-
front capital."

"You mean you want to borrow money from me so you
can run a swindle? Here, in Possiltum?"

The look she leveled on me was, to say the least, cold
and appraising. Not at all the coy, shy, averted gaze I was
used to from her.

"Of course. That's what I do," she said levelly. "I
thought you knew that when you offered me a job. Or are
you just miffed because I prefer to operate independently?
I suppose this is pretty small potatoes to you, but it's the
best I can do."

As she spoke, my mind was racing back over the previous times I had seen or spoken with her. While I was
aware then that she was always involved in or running
from the results of some swindle or other, I had always
assumed that she was a sweet kid who was going along
with her partner, Matt. I realized now that I had no basis

on which to make that assumption, other than her innocent looks. In fact, beyond her looks, I really didn't know her at all.

"Is it?" I said. "Is it really the best you can do?"

"What do you mean?"

"Well, couldn't you do as well or better trying your hand at something legitimate? What if I passed you enough money to start and run a normal business?"

The last vestige of my idealized fantasies regarding Luanna died as her lip curled in a sneer.

"You mean run a little shop or grocery store? Me? No thanks. That's *way* too much like work. Funny, I always thought that if *anyone* would understand that, *you* would. You didn't get where you are today by hard work and sweat, you did it by fleecing the gullible and flim-flamming the ignorant, just like Matt and I did . . . just on a larger scale. Of course, we didn't have a demon helping us along, like you did. Even now, as rich and respectable as you're supposed to be, I'll bet you're pulling down a healthy skim from this kingdom. It's got to be real easy, what with having the Queen in your pocket and everybody doing whatever you say. All I'm trying to do is to cut myself in for a piece of the action . . . and a little piece, at that."

I was silent for a few moments. I thought of trying to tell her about the long hours and work I and my team were putting in trying to straighten out the kingdom's finances. I even considered showing her some of the cryptic spreadsheets on my desk . . . but decided against it. She might be able to decipher them, and if she could would doubtless ask some embarrassing questions about the hefty fee I was taking for my services. I was having trouble justifying that to myself, much less to her.

The inescapable conclusion, however, was that no matter what I had *thought* lovely Luanna was like, we were worlds apart in our views of people and how they should be treated.

Reaching into our petty cash drawer, I started counting some coins.

"Tell you what, Luanna," I said, not looking up. "You said you needed fifty to seventy-five in gold? Well I'm going to give you a hundred and fifty . . . double to triple what you asked for . . . not as a loan or an investment, just as a gift."

"But why would you . . ."

". . . There *are* two conditions, though," I continued, as if she hadn't spoken. "First, that you use some of the extra money for travel. Go off dimension or to another part of Klah . . . I don't care. Just so long as when you start to run your swindle, it's not in Possiltum."

"Okay, but . . ."

"And second," I said, setting the stack of coins on the edge of the desk near her, "I want you to promise that you will never see or speak to me . . . ever again . . . starting now."

For a moment, I thought she was going to speak. She opened her mouth, then hesitated, shrugged, and shut it again. In complete silence she gathered up the coins and left, shutting the door behind her.

I poured myself another goblet of wine and moved to the window, staring out at the view without really seeing anything. Dreams die hard, but whatever romantic thoughts I had ever had involving Luanna had just been squashed pretty thoroughly. I couldn't change that, but I could mourn their passing.

There was a soft knock at the door, and my heart took a sudden leap. Maybe she had changed her mind! Maybe she had thought it over and decided to return the money in favor of a legitimate business loan!

"Come in," I called, trying not to sound to eager.

The door opened, and a vampire walked in.

VII:

"You just don't know women."

—H. HEFNER

"**W**ine? No thanks. Never touch the stuff."

"Oh. That's right. Sorry, Vic," I said, refilling my own goblet.

"You know," my guest said, settling himself more comfortably in his seat, "it's women like Luanna that give vampires a bad name. *They're* the ones who will mercilessly suck someone dry, and the concept sort of slopped over onto us!"

In case you're wondering (or have neglected to read the earlier books in this series), Vic is the one who walked into my room at the end of the last chapter, and yes he *is* a vampire. Actually, he's a pretty nice guy ... about my age and a fairly successful magician in his own right. He just happens to come from Limbo, a dimension that's primarily "peopled" by vampires, werewolves, and the like.

Apparently he had stopped by our office on Deva looking to invite me out for lunch. When Tananda, who was currently minding the fort for us, told him where I was, he decided to pop over for a visit. (As an aside, one of his Limbo-born talents is the ability to travel the dimension without mechanical aid . . . something I've always envied and wanted to learn.)

Truth to tell, I was more than a little glad to see Vic. He was one of the few in my acquaintance who was familiar with the trials and tribulations of being a professional magician, yet wasn't an actual member of our crew. Not meaning any disrespect or criticism of my colleagues, mind you, but . . . well . . . they were more like family and my actions and future definitely affected them, whereas Vic was a bit more able to stand apart and view things objectively. This made it a lot easier to express my feelings and problems to him, which I had proceeded to do, starting with Queen Hemlock's proposal and running it right up through my recent rather disheartening meeting with Luanna.

Until he brought it up, I had forgotten that he had met Luanna. In fact, he had worked with her and Matt, and consequently gone on the lam with them . . . which was when I met him in the first place. As such, he knew the lady under discussion far better than I did, and my new analysis of her seemed more in line with his earlier formed opinions than with my own cherished daydreams.

"I can't say much about what you're doing with the kingdom's budgets and stuff," the vampire said with an easy shrug. "That's out of my league. It *does* occur to me, though, that you're having more than your share of woman problems."

"You can say that again," I agreed, toasting him with my goblet.

"I'll admit I'm a bit surprised," Vic continued. "I would have thought that someone with your experience would have been able to sidestep some of these tangles . . . and definitely spotted a gold digger like Luanna a mile away."

I hesitated for a moment, then decided to level with him.

"To be honest with you, Vic, I haven't had all that much experience with women."

"Really?" The vampire was gratifyingly surprised.

"Let's just say that while Aahz and the others have been fairly diligent about teaching me the ins and outs of business and magik, there have been certain areas of my education that have been woefully and annoyingly neglected."

"Now *that* I might be able to help you with."

"Excuse me?"

I had been momentarily lost in my own thoughts, and had somehow missed a turn in the conversation.

"It's easy," Vic said with a shrug. "You're having trouble making up your mind whether or not you should get married at all . . . much less to Queen Hemlock. Right?"

"Well . . ."

"Right?" he pressed.

"Right."

"To me, the problem is that you don't have enough information to make an educated decision."

"You can say that again," I said heavily, gulping at my wine. "What's more, between the workload here and Queen Hemlock's timetable, I don't figure I'm going to get any, either."

"*That's* where I think I can help you," my guest smiled, leaning back in his chair again.

"Excuse me?" I said, fighting off the feeling that our conversation was caught in an unending loop.

"What would you say to a blind date?"

That one caught me totally off guard.

"Well . . . the same thing I'd say to a date that could see, I imagine," I managed at last. "The trouble is, I haven't had any experience with either . . ."

"No, no," the vampire interrupted. "I mean, how would you like me to fix you up with a date? Someone you've never seen before?"

"That would have to be the case," I nodded. "I don't recall ever having *met* a blind person . . . male or female. Not that I've consciously avoided them, mind you . . ."

"Hold it! Stop!" Vic said, holding up one hand while pressing the other to his forehead.

It occurred to me that, in that pose, he looked more than a little like Aahz.

"Let's try this again . . . from the top. We were talking about your needing more experience with women. What I'm suggesting is that I line you up with a date . . . someone I know . . . so you can get that experience. Got it?"

"Got it," I nodded. "*You* know someone who's blind. Tell me, should I act any different around her?"

"No. . . . I mean, yes! NO!"

Vic seemed to be getting very worked up over the subject, and more than a little confused . . . which made two of us.

"Look, Skeeve," he said finally, through clenched teeth. "The girl I'm thinking about is *not* blind. She's perfectly normal. Okay?"

"Okay," I said, hesitantly, looking for the hook. "A perfectly normal, average girl."

"Well . . . not all *that* normal, or average," the vampire smiled, relaxing a bit. "She's a *lot* of fun . . . if you get what I mean. And she's a real looker . . . knock your eyes out beautiful."

"You mean *I'll* go blind?"

Out of my merciful nature and in the interest of brevity (too late), I'll spare you the blow by blow account of the rest of the conversation. Let it suffice to say that, by the time Vic departed, it had been established that he would arrange for me to step out with a lovely lady of his acquaintance . . . one who was in full command of her senses . . . sort of (that part still confused me a little) . . . and who would not adversely affect my health or senses, but would, if Vic were to be believed, advance my education regarding the opposite sex to dizzying heights.

It sounded good to me. Like any healthy young man, I had a normal interest in women . . . which is to say I didn't think of them more than three or four times a day. My lack of firsthand experience I attributed to a dearth of opportunity, which apparently was about to be remedied. To say I was looking forward to my date would be an understatement . . . a VAST understatement.

However the events of the day weren't over yet.

There was a knock at the door, but this time I wasn't going to get caught making any assumptions.

"Who is it?" I called.

"General Badaxe," came the muffled response. "I was wondering if you could spare me a moment?"

I was more than a little surprised. The General and I had never been on particularly good terms, and it was rare if ever that he called on me in my personal quarters. Casting about for an explanation, it occurred to me that he was probably more than a little upset at the cutbacks I had made in the army and military budget. In the same thought, it occurred to me that he might be out to murder me in my own room . . . or, at least, mess me up a little. As fast as the idea surfaced, however, I discarded it. Whatever else the General was, he was as straightforward and non-scheming as anyone I had ever met. If he meant to do me harm, it would doubtless be on the spur of the moment when we encountered each other in the halls or courtyard of the castle . . . not by stealth in my room. In short, I felt I could rule out premeditated mayhem. If he were going to kill me, it would be spontaneous . . . a thought that didn't settle my mind as much as I hoped it would.

"Come in," I called . . . and he did.

It was, indeed, the General of Possiltum's army, and without his namesake massive axe, for a change. Not that it's absence made him noticeably less dangerous, mind you, as Badaxe was easily the largest man I had ever met. Upon viewing him, however, I was a bit embarrassed by my original worries. Rather than the stern, angry countenance I was accustomed to, he seemed very ill at ease and uncomfortable.

"Sorry to interrupt your work, Lord Magician," he said, nervously looking about the room, "but I find it necessary to speak to you on . . . a personal matter."

"Certainly, General," I said, trying to put him at his

ease. Strangely, I found that his obvious discomfort was
making me uneasy. "Have a seat."

"Thank you, I'd rather stand."

So much for putting him at ease.

"As you wish," I nodded. "What is it you wanted to
see me about?"

I realized with some chagrin that I was falling into a
formal speech pattern, but found that I couldn't help it.
Badaxe seemed bound and determined to be somber, and
I felt obligated to respond in kind.

"Well . . . I'd like to speak to you about your apprentice."

"Aahz?" I said. As far as the kingdom was concerned,
Aahz was my loyal student.

"What's he done now?"

"No . . . not Aahz." the General clarified hastily. "I was
referring to Massha."

"Massha?" I blinked. This was truly a surprise. As far
as I knew, Massha and the General had always gotten
along fine. "Very well. What's the problem?

"Oh, don't misunderstand me, Lord Magician. There's
no problem. Quite the contrary. I wanted to speak to you
taking her hand in marriage."

On a day of surprises, this announcement caught me
the most off guard.

"Why?" I sputtered, unable to think of anything else to
say.

The General's brow darkened noticeably.

"If you're referring to her less than slender appearance,
or perhaps the difference in our age . . ." he began in a
deep growl.

"No, you misunderstand me," I said hastily, cutting him
off . . . though once he mentioned them, both points were
worth reflecting on. "I meant, why should you want to
speak to *me* about such a matter?"

"Oh. That."

For the moment, at least, Badaxe seemed mollified. I
mentally made a note to table any discussion of the two
points he had raised until another time.

"It's really rather simple, Lord Magician," the General was continuing. "Though I suppose it's rather old-fashioned of me, I felt I should follow proprieties and establish my good intentions by stating them in advance. Normally I'd speak to her father, but, in this case, you seem to be the closest thing to a father she has."

Now I was truly flabbergasted. Mostly because, try as I might, I couldn't find a hole in his logic. He was right. Even though she was older than me, Massha had never spoken of her family at all . . . much less a father. What was more, this was one I couldn't even fob off on Aahz. Since she was *my* apprentice, I was responsible for her care and well-being as well as her training. If there was anyone the General should speak to on matters regarding Massha's future, it was me!

"I see," I said, stalling for time to think. "And what does Massha have to say about this?"

"So far, I haven't spoken to her directly on the subject," Badaxe admitted uneasily, "though I have reason to believe the idea wouldn't be totally unwelcome to her. Frankly, I felt that I should attempt to gain your approval first."

"And why is that?"

I was getting better at this stalling game, and questions were a handy weapon.

The General eyed me levelly.

"Come, come, Lord Magician," he said. "I thought that we had long since agreed there was no need to bandy words between us. You know as well as I that Massha has a great deal of affection for you. What's more, there is the added loyalty of an apprentice to her teacher. While I have never shied from either battle or competition, I would prefer to spare her any unnecessary anguish. That is, I feel it would aid my case immensely if, at the same time I asked her to be my wife, I could state that I had spoken with you and that you had no personal or professional objections to such a match. That is, of course, assuming you don't."

I was silent for a few moments, reflecting on what he

had said. Specifically, I was berating myself for being so selfish in my thinking, of only considering the consequences to *me* in my decision of whether or not to marry Queen Hemlock. Even when I had been thinking of my friends and colleagues, I had been looking at it in terms of *my* loss of their friendship, not what it might mean to them.

"Then again, perhaps I was wrong in my assumption."

The General's words interrupted my thoughts, and I was suddenly aware that he had been waiting for a response from me.

"Forgive me, General . . . Hugh," I said hastily. I had to think quickly to recall his first name. "I was simply lost in thought for a moment. Certainly I have no objections. I've always held you in the highest regard, and, if Massha is amenable, I would be the last to stand between her and happiness. Feel free to proceed with my approval . . . and best wishes."

Badaxe seized my hand and pumped it hard . . . unfortunately before I could pull it away in alarm.

"Thank you, Lord . . . Skeeve," he said with an intensity I had only seen him express in battle planning. "I . . . Thank you."

Releasing my hand, he strode to the door, opened it, then paused.

"Were it not for the fact that, assuming she agrees, of course, I expect Massha will ask you to give the bride away, I'd ask you to honor me by standing as my best man."

Then he was gone . . . which was just as well, as I had no idea what to say in response.

Massha and Badaxe. Married.

Try as I might, I couldn't get my mind around the concept . . . which is a comment on the limits of my imagination and NOT on their respective physical sizes, individually or as a twosome.

Finally, I abandoned the effort completely. Instead, I poured myself another goblet of wine and settled back for the far more pleasant exercise of speculating on my own upcoming date.

VIII:

"Love is blind. Lust isn't!"

— D. GIOVANI

I found myself experiencing mixed feelings as I prepared for my date that evening. On the one hand, I wasn't real sure about how much fun it would be spending an entire evening with a woman I had never met before. While I had a certain amount of faith in Vic not to stick me with a real loser, it occurred to me that it would be nice to have some vague idea of what she was going to look like. Heck, if she turned out to be a lousy conversationalist, the evening could still turn out okay if she was at least fun to look at.

Despite my nagging concerns, however, there was no denying I felt a certain measure of excitement as the time drew near. As Vic had observed, I didn't really have a lot of experience with dating. Specifically, this was going to be my first date . . . ever. Now don't get me wrong, I knew a fair number of women, but I had met all of them in the course of business. Before I met Aahz, I had been living alone with Garkin in a shack in the woods . . . which is

not the greatest way to meet females. Since tying on with
Aahz, my life had gotten noticeably more exciting, but
there was little time for a social life. What off time I did
have was usually spent with other members of our crew,
and while they were good company for the most part, it
left little room for outsiders. Consequently, the idea of
spending an entire evening with a strange woman *just to
be spending time together* was a real treat . . . and more
than a little scary.

The one variable in the whole situation *I could* control
was me, and I was bound and determined that if anything
went wrong with the evening, it wouldn't be because I
hadn't put enough effort into my preparations. Money was
easy. While I wasn't sure where we would be going, I
figured that two or three hundred in gold would cover our
expenses . . . though I made a note to bring along my
credit card from Perv just to be on the safe side.

Wardrobe was another matter. After changing my outfit
completely a dozen times, I finally settled on the same
clothes I had worn when I had my match with the Sen-
Sen Ante Kid . . . the dark maroon open-necked shirt with
the charcoal gray slacks and vest. I figured that if it had
impressed people on Deva, it should be impressive no
matter where we went. Of course, on Deva, I had also
been traveling with an entourage of bodyguards and assistants . . . not to mention a quarter of a million in gold.

I was just considering changing my clothes one more
time, when there was a knock at the door. This surprised
me a little, as I had somehow expected that my date would
simply appear in the room. As soon as that thought occurred to me, however, it also occurred to me that there
had been an excellent chance that she would have appeared while I was changing outfits. Slightly relieved at
having escaped a potentially embarrassing situation, I
opened the door.

"Hi, Skeeve," Bunny said, sweeping past me into the
room. "I thought I'd stop by and brief you on the latest
budget developments and maybe do dinner and . . . Hey!
You look nice."

Needless to say, this was an unexpected . . . and unpleasant . . . surprise.

"Um . . . Actually I was just getting ready to go out," I managed politely.

She took it well. In fact, she seemed to brighten at the news.

"That's a great idea!" she said. "Hang on a few and I'll duck back to my room and change and we can go out together!"

"Um . . . Bunny . . ."

"To tell you the truth, I've been starting to go up the walls a little myself. It'll be wonderful to get out for a while, especially with you, and . . ."

"BUNNY!"

She stopped and cocked her head at me.

"What is it, Skeeve?"

"I . . . actually . . . well . . . I have a date."

The words hung in the air as she stared at me with eyes that had suddenly gotten very large.

"Oh," she said finally in a small voice. "I . . . Then I guess I'd better be moving along."

"Wait a minute, Bunny," I said, catching her as she started for the door. "Maybe tomorrow we can . . ."

There was a soft *bampf* in the room behind us, and we turned to discover that my date had arrived . . . at least, I assumed she was my date. I could think of no other reason for a creature appearing in my room that looked like that.

She was pale, even paler than Queen Hemlock, which only served to accent the deep red lipstick she wore. She was short, though her hair nearly made up for it as it rose from the top of her head in a thick dark wave before cascading all the way down her back well past her rump. Her body was heart-stopping, abundant to the point of exaggeration on top, narrowing to an unbelievably tiny waist before flaring into her tidy hips. It would have been noticeable in any situation, but her dress made sure it wouldn't be overlooked.

It was sparkly black, and hugged her curves like it was tattooed on. The neckline plunged daringly nearly to her navel, actually lower than the slit up the side of her dress, which in turn displayed one of the shapeliest legs it's ever been my privilege to view first hand. To say the least it was a revealing outfit, and most of what it revealed was delectable.

About the only thing that wasn't visible or easily imaginable were her eyes, which were hidden by a pair of cats-eye sunglasses. As if in response to my thoughts, she removed them with a careless, graceful motion, setting them carefully atop her hairdo. I would have watched the action more carefully if I hadn't been staring at her eyes. It wasn't the heavy purple eye shadow that held my attention, it was the fact that the whites of her eyes were, in fact, blood red.

My date was a vampire.

I guess I should have expected it. I mean, what with Vic being a vampire, it was only predictable that he would line me up with another vampire for a date. It just hadn't been predicted by me!

"Hi!" the vision of loveliness smiled, showing a pair of sharp canine teeth. "I'm Cassandra. You must be Vic's friend."

"Good God!" Bunny said, the words escaping from her in a gasp as she stared at my visitor.

"And who's this?" Cassandra said, sweeping Bunny with a withering gaze. "The warm-up act? You must be quite a tiger to book two dates, one after the other . . . or is she coming along with us?"

"Cassandra, this is Bunny . . . my administrative assistant," I intervened hastily. "We were just going over some office matters."

This seemed to mollify Cassandra somewhat. At least enough so that she stepped forward and coiled around my arm, pressing close against me. Very close.

"Well, don't wait up for him, Sugar," she said with a wink. "I figure on keeping him up for a long time . . . if you get what I mean."

"Don't worry. I won't."

Chumley had once tried to describe something called

"dry ice" to me. At the time, I had trouble imagining something cold enough to burn. Bunny's tone and manner as she spun on her heel and marched out of the room went a long way toward clarifying the concept for me. I might not be the most perceptive person in all the dimensions when it comes to women, but it didn't take a real genius to realize that she didn't approve of my choice of dates . . . even though I hadn't really made the choice.

"Alone at last," Cassandra purred, pressing even closer against me. "Tell me, Tiger, what are your thoughts for the evening?"

As I said, I hadn't really settled on anything. Still, I had an overwhelming urge to get this particular bombshell out of the castle, or, at least, out of my bedroom, and as far away from Bunny as possible.

"I don't know," I said. "I was thinking of maybe doing dinner or getting a couple of drinks and kind of letting the evening take care of itself."

"Sounds good to me," my date declared, giving a little shiver that seemed to take her entire body. "Are there any good clubs on this dimension?"

It only took me a second to realize she was talking about nightclubs, not the kind of club you beat people across the head with. I DO catch on eventually.

"I'm not sure," I admitted. "My work doesn't leave me much time to check out the nightlife."

"Hey! When it comes to nightlife, I'm your girl. I know some GREAT places over on Limbo."

Limbo! The dimension of werewolves and vampires. I had only been there once, and the memory wasn't all that pleasant.

"Um, I'd rather not if you don't mind."

"Really? Why not?"

"Well . . . if you must know, my dimension traveling skills aren't all they could be," I said, blurting out the first thing that came into my mind. Actually, my ability to travel the dimensions without the mechanical aid of a D-Hopper was non-existent, but I saw no need to be too honest.

"If that's the only hitch, no problem," Cassandra said. "Just leave the driving to me, Tiger."

So saying, she hooked one arm in mine, did something I couldn't see with her other hand, and, before I had the chance to protest further, we were there!

Now, for those of you who have never been there (which, I assume, includes most of my readers), Limbo isn't much of a dimension to look at. That is, it's hard to see much of anything because it's DARK. Now, I don't mean "dark," I mean **DARK!!** Even when the sun is up, which it currently wasn't, it doesn't push much light through the perpetually overcast sky. Then, too, the predominant color of the architecture, roads, etc. is black, which does nothing toward brightening up the landscape. That in itself might make things look bleak, but when you added in the decorative flourishes the place looked positively *grim*.

Everywhere you looked there were gargoyles, dragons, and snakes . . . stone ones, fortunately . . . peering back at you from rooftops, balconies, and window ledges. Normally I don't mind such creatures. Heck, as you know I have a dragon of my own, and Gus is one of my best friends even though he is a gargoyle. It should be noted, however, that those individuals manage to maintain their relationship with me without constantly displaying their teeth in bloodthirsty glee, a courtesy which their stone counterparts here in Limbo did NOT extend.

Then, too, there were the bats.

For every one of the aforementioned frightful creatures, there must have been ten or twenty bat decorations on display. They came in all sizes, shapes, and poses, and seemed to have only one characteristic in common . . . none of them looked friendly. It was an unnerving reminder that a goodly proportion of the dimension's inhabitants were vampires.

"Umm . . . Is this Blut, by any chance?" I said, ostensively studying the buildings around us while, in actuality, sneaking sideways peeks at Cassandra, trying to get another peek at her teeth.

"As a matter of fact, it is!" my date confirmed. "Don't tell me you've heard of it?"

"Actually, I've been here before."

"Really? That's strange . . . but then again, Vic *did* say that you were better traveled and informed than most off-worlders." Cassandra seemed genuinely impressed. "So, what did you think of the place?"

"I didn't really get to see much of it," I admitted. "I was sort of here on business and didn't have much time for socializing or sightseeing."

Again, this was a bit of an understatement. I had been here trying to bust Aahz out of jail before they executed him for murder. It occurred to me, however, that it might not be wise to go into too many details of my previous visit. Fortunately, I needn't have worried.

"Well we can fix that right now," Cassandra declared, grabbing my hand and pulling me along behind her as she started off. "There's a little club around the corner here that's all the rage currently. It's as good a place as any to start our expedition."

"Wait a minute," I said, digging in my heels a bit. "What about me? I mean, if I recall correctly, off-worlders in general and humans specifically aren't all that welcome here. In fact, don't most vampires consider us humans to be monsters?"

"Oh, that's just the superstitious old fuddy-duddies," my date insisted, continuing to tow me along. "The kind of folks that hang out at the clubs are pretty open-minded. You'll see."

Somehow, the phrase "pretty open-minded" didn't suffice to calm all my fears. I was all too aware that I was a long way from home with no independent means to get back there if anything went wrong and I got separated from my date. Just to be on the safe side, I started casting about for force lines . . . the energy source I was trained to tap into for my magik. Limbo was notoriously short on them, which had caused me no small amount of problems during my last visit, and if I was going to have to do anything on "reserve power," I'd be wise to start mustering it well in advance of any trouble.

"There it is now!" Cassandra chirped, interrupting my concentration.

The place she had selected was easy to spot. It had a line of customers out front that stretched to the corner and around it. It also, however, had a strong force line running right over it, which made me much more willing to agree to it as a relaxing stop on our tour.

"Darn it!" my date said, slowing slightly. "I was afraid this would happen, what with us showing up so late and all. How are you fixed for cash, Tiger? A little palm grease could cut our wait time a bit."

"Well, all I have is a couple hundred in gold," I said hesitantly. "If that's not enough, we can always . . ."

"Whoa!" Cassandra stopped in her tracks. "Did you say a couple *hundred?*"

"That's right," I nodded, letting go of her hand to reach for my belt pouch. "I wasn't sure how much . . ."

"Don't show it around here!" my date gasped, quickly stopping my hand with her own. "Geez! Do you want to get mugged? What are you doing, carrying your whole bankroll around with you? Don't you believe in banks?"

"Sure I do," I said, a little hurt. "This is just mad money. I wasn't sure how much this evening was going to cost, so I brought a long a couple hundred . . . that and a credit card."

"Really?" she said, obviously impressed. "How much do you . . . never mind. None of my business. Vic never said you were *rich*, though. I've never even *known* someone with a credit card before."

I had only recently acquired my credit card while looking for Aahz on Perv, and hadn't had a chance to use it yet. (Frankly, except for a few dimension travelers like my colleagues and me, I don't think anyone on my home dimension of Klah has even *heard* of a credit card. I know I hadn't until I hit Perv.) If anything, I had tended to down play it, since it seemed to upset Aahz. My partner wasn't here, though, and my impressionable date was. If nothing else over the years, I've learned to go with the flow.

"Oh, it comes in handy," I said loftily, producing the item under discussion with a flourish. "Keeps me from having to carry *too* much cash, you know."

The card disappeared from my fingertips as Cassandra seized it and gaped at it in open awe.

"A solid gold card!" she exclaimed breathlessly. "Wow! You sure know how to show a girl a good time, Tiger. Are we going to party tonight!!"

Before I could stop her, she had grabbed my hand again and plunged into the crowd, holding the card aloft like a banner.

"Excuse us! Coming through!"

The people in line who we were elbowing our way past didn't like it. A few went so far as to bare their fangs in annoyance. The card seemed to have some magik effect, though, because, after one glance, they all stepped back and cleared a passage for us . . . or, rather, for Cassandra. I just trailed along in her wake.

There was a velvet rope barring the door, and a big guy beside it whose only function seemed to be to admit people a few at a time as others left . . . that, and be intimidating. I mean, he was *BIG* . . . and that's coming from someone who has his own bodyguards. As soon as he spotted the card, however, he snatched the rope from the door, shoving a few of the line people back to open a path for us, and actually tried to twist his features into a smile as we swept past.

It was occurring to me that there might be more to this credit card business than I imagined. This didn't seem to be the time to ask, however, and a moment later we were in the club . . . and I lost all ability to think of anything else.

IX:

"I love the nightlife."

— V. DRACULA

I don't know what I had expected for the interior of a vampire nightclub, probably because it never occurred to me that I might visit one someday, but this definitely wasn't it.

First and foremost, it was bright. I don't mean bright, I mean **BRIGHT!!!**

The lighting level was so intense the glare was almost blinding, particularly coming in from the darkness outside. Even squinting, it was so bright I could barely make out the features of the room and even had to grope a bit to keep from tripping over things.

"Whatdaya think?" Cassandra shouted over the music as she clung to my arm.

"Hard to tell!" I called back. "It's kinda bright!"

"I know! Isn't it *great*!" she said, flashing a smile that shone through the light. "Real spooky, isn't it?"

For some reason, that made sense. In fact, suddenly the whole club did. Humans were primarily daylight lovers.

When they wanted to feel daring or be scared, they went to dark places. Vampires on the other hand, normally tended to shun the light. As such, I supposed it was only natural that a place lit up like a flare would be scary to them.

"Oh, it's not too bad . . . once your eyes adjust to it," I said loftily.

It was the truth. My eyes were slowly getting used to the glare, allowing me to look around the place.

What it lacked in size, it made up for in noise and customers.

What seemed like hundreds of people were packed around an expanse of tiny tables, each table having a small umbrella to provide limited relief from the bright lights like . . . well, like candles on tables in a dark room back where I came from.

The only portion that seemed even more crowded than the tables was a small space I took for a dance floor. I made this assumption based on the fact that the customers packed in there cheek to jowl were all moving rhythmically in unison to the music which was blaring through the place at a volume level to match the Big Game. I couldn't see a source for the music, unless it was from the one weird-looking guy who was ensconced behind a table overlooking the dance floor. Every so often, there would be a break in the music and he would shout something, whereupon the crowd would shout back at him and a new tune would start. From this, I guessed that he had something to do with the entertainment, but exactly what I couldn't be sure, as there was no sign of an instrument. Just stacks and stacks of shiny discs he kept feeding into a machine in front of him.

The music itself was beyond description . . . unless that description is "loud." Mostly, it sounded like jarring crashes of noise repeated endlessly to a driving beat. I mentioned that there would be pauses and new tunes, but in truth they seemed remarkably alike to me. I mean, whether one is repeatedly hitting a sackful of tin cans or a sackful of pots and kettles, or alternating between the two, the overall sound effect is the same for all intents and purposes. The crowd seemed to enjoy it, though, or, at least, it was sufficient to keep them cheering and gyrating with apparently limitless energy.

With all the noise and activity that was going on, I was almost surprised that I managed to notice the decorations hanging on the walls. Perhaps they caught my eye with their sheer incongruity.

There were strings of garlic—fake, to look at it—as well as vials of water and strings of beads, all marked with various religious symbols. Not exactly what I'd pick to have around while I was trying to relax . . . if I were a vampire. Then again, the objective of the place didn't seem to be to provide relaxation.

"Interesting decor," I said, still looking at the stuff on the walls. "What's the name of this place, anyway?"

"It's called The Wooden Stake," Cassandra supplied, giving a mock shudder as she hugged my arm even tighter. "Isn't it a gas?"

"Uh-huh," I managed noncommittally.

Actually, her little shudder was quite distracting . . . particularly crowded as close to me as she was.

"Quite a crowd here," I added, forcibly pulling my eyes away from her to look around again.

"I *told* you it was the hottest club around," she said, giving my arm a small shake. "Look. *Everybody's* here."

If it seems that I've been dwelling on the physical description of the club, it's because I've been hesitant to tackle the job of describing the patrons. They were like something out of your worse nightmare . . . literally.

As might be expected, there were vampires. If their red eyes and flashy clothes didn't give them away, there was always the minor detail that they tended to float above the dance floor and along the ceiling to get away from the crush of the other dancers.

The list didn't stop there, however.

There were "weres" around. Not just werewolves, but were-tigers, were-bears, and were-snakes as well. There were also mummies, lizard men, a night-shambler or two, and even a couple ghosts. At least, you could see through them so I supposed they were ghosts.

Just your average, run of the mill, neighborhood bar crowd . . . if your neighborhood happens to be the intersection of half a dozen horror movies.

"I don't see the Woof Writers anywhere," I said, just to be cantankerous. I didn't know many people here on Limbo, but the few I knew weren't here, so obviously *everybody* wasn't in attendance.

"Oh, Idnew is probably around somewhere," Cassandra said absently, scanning the crowd. "Don't expect to see Drachir, though. He's usually holed up somewhere quieter talking business or . . ."

She broke off suddenly and looked at me sharply.

"You know the Woof Writers?"

"Like I said," I smiled, squeezing *her* arm for a change. "I've been on Limbo before."

"*Look! There's a table!*" She grabbed my wrist and took off through the crowd, towing me along behind. If I had been hoping to impress her, I'd have to work more on my timing.

We barely beat out a vampire couple for the table, who favored us with dark glares before continuing their search. I watched their departure with a vague sense of relief. I *really* didn't want to get into a fight tonight . . . and *especially* not here in The Wooden Stake. I hadn't felt so much like an outsider since I returned from Perv.

The view from our table was notably much more restricted than the one we had when we were standing, due to the crush of people around us. The only real advantage to having a table, that I could see, was that we didn't have to hold our drinks . . . except we didn't have any drinks.

"What'll you have?"

For a moment, I thought the question had come telepathically in answer to my thoughts. Then I realized there was a ghost hovering next to me, nearly translucent, but carrying a solid enough tray. I supposed it made sense. A ghost to pass ethereally through the crowds, and a solid tray to carry the drinks on. Maybe if other bars and restaurants used the same idea, service would be faster.

"Hi, Marley. I'll have a Bloody Mary," Cassandra said. "What do you want, Tiger?"

I'll spare you the image which my mind came up with to associate with the name of her ordered drink. While I knew from my earlier visits that vampires don't necessarily drink human blood exclusively, the idea of imbibing *any* kind of blood was pretty low on my list for taste treats.

"Um ... What all do they have?" I stalled. "I'm pretty much just used to wine."

"Don't worry, it's a full service bar," she informed me brightly. "They've got pretty much ... Oh! I get it!"

She threw back her head and laughed, then gave my arm a playful slap.

"Don't get uptight, Tiger. They do have drinks for off-worlders."

Again I was relieved, but at the same time, I wasn't wild about being laughed at. I seemed to be losing ground in the "impress your date" department.

"No, I'm serious, Cassandra," I said. "I really *don't* have much experience drinking except for wine."

"Hey. No problem. I'll order for you."

That wasn't exactly what I had in mind, but she had turned to our waiter before I could stop her.

"Bring him a Bloody Mary, too, Marley. A regular one, not the local version," she said. "Oh, and we'll be running a tab. Here's his *credit card* so you can make an imprint."

The waiter accepted the card without batting an eye ... apparently waiters are harder to impress with credit cards than doormen ... and moved off through the crowd. And I do mean *through* the crowd.

Truth to tell, I had been so busy ogling the club, I had completely forgotten that Cassandra still had my card until she handed it to the waiter. Inexperienced though I was with credit cards, I was aware that losing track of one's card is *not* the wisest idea, and I resolved to reclaim it when the waiter brought it back.

In the meantime, there was one minor matter I wanted to take care of . . . to wit, my outfit.

As you may recall, I spent a certain amount of time choosing my ensemble for this date, but that was before I knew we were headed for Limbo. The clothes I was wearing were fine for Klah, or even Deva, but here on Limbo they were conservative to the point of looking drab. Normally, I wouldn't squander my magik on something so trivial, particularly on Limbo, but I had already scouted a strong force line directly over the club and . . . what the heck, I *was* still trying to impress my date.

At the moment, she was busy chatting with some friends of hers who had stopped by the table, so I figured now was as good a time as any. Closing my eyes, I went to work on my outfit courtesy of my good old trusty standby . . . the disguise spell.

Since I wasn't really all that dissatisfied with the outfit I was wearing, I didn't go for any radical change, just a few adjustments here and there. I deepened the neckline on both my shirt and vest to show a bit more of my chest . . . such as it was. Then I lengthened the points of my collar and added a bit more drape to the sleeves to be more in line with some of the more billowy outfits the other men in the club were wearing. As a final touch, I added a sparkly undertone to my shirt so that it would match my date's dress . . . in texture, at least.

Like I said, not much of a change. Just enough so I wouldn't look dowdy sitting in a club with flashy vampires. I couldn't see the changes myself, of course, which is one of the few drawbacks of a disguise spell, but I had enough confidence in this, one of my oldest spells, to know it was effective. I knew my date would be able to see the changes. The only question was, would she notice?

I needn't have worried.

Not that she noticed right away, mind you. Cassandra's friends had moved on, but she was still quite busy waving and calling to others in the crowd. Apparently she was quite a popular young lady. Not surprising, really.

The fun started when the waiter brought our drinks to

the table. Setting them them carefully in front of us, he leaned over to speak directly into my ear.

"This first round is compliments of the manager, *sir*," he said, with notably more deference than he had shown when taking the order originally. "He asked me to tell you he's honored you're visiting our club, and hopes you enjoy it enough to make it a regular stop."

"What?" I said, genuinely taken aback. "I don't understand."

"*I said, the manager . . .*" the ghost started to repeat, but I cut him off.

"No. I mean, *why* is he buying us a round of drinks?"

"He saw your name on the credit card," the ghost said, handing the item in question back to me. "I didn't recognize you on sight, myself . . . I hope you aren't offended."

"No. It's . . . no. No offense," I managed, still trying to figure out what was going on.

"What was that all about?" Cassandra said, leaning close again. She had noticed my conversation with the waiter, but hadn't been able to hear the exact words over the music.

"It's nothing," I explained. "The manager just bought us a round of drinks."

"Really?" she frowned. "That's odd. They don't usually do that here . . . at least, not for the first round. I wonder who's on duty?"

She started craning her neck trying to get a clear look at the bar. While she was doing that, I turned my attention to our drinks.

They appeared innocent enough. Basically an opaque red fluid over ice cubes with some kind of greenery sticking out of it. Hers was a darker red than mine, but aside from that, they looked the same. Cautiously, I took a sip . . . and discovered, to my relief, it tasted sort of like tomato juice.

"Hey! This is pretty good," I declared. "What's in it, anyway?"

"Hmm?" Cassandra said, turning her attention to me

again. "Oh. Yours is just tomato juice and vodka."

I didn't know what vodka was, but tomato juice I could handle. The first sip had reminded me how thirsty I was after all our running around, so I downed most of the glass with my next swallow.

"Hey! Take it easy, Tiger," my date admonished. "Those things can pack a wallop if you aren't used to them . . . and it can leave a stain, so don't drip any on your . . ."

She stopped in mid-sentence and stared at my outfit.

"Say. Weren't you wearing a different shirt before?"

"Oh, it's the same shirt," I said, as casually as I could. "I just changed it a little bit. I think this is more appropriate for this place, don't you?"

"But how could you . . . I get it! Magik!"

Her reaction was everything I could have hoped for . . . except she wasn't done.

"Wait a minute. You're a friend of Vic's from Klah, and you know magik . . . right?" she said, eagerly. "Do you know a magician there named the Great Skeeve?"

This *really* surprised me, but the pieces were starting to fall into place. The picture was incredible, but I managed to keep my cool.

"As a matter of fact, I know him rather well," I said with a faint smile.

"Whatdaya know!" Cassandra declared, slapping the table with her palm. "I thought Vic was just trying to impress me when he said he knew him. Tell me, what's he like?"

That one threw me.

"Vic? He's a nice enough guy. I thought you . . ."

"No, silly. I mean Skeeve! What's he like as a person?"

This was just getting better.

"Oh, he's a lot like me," I said. "I'm just surprised you heard of him."

"You've *got* to be kidding!" she declared, rolling her eyes. "He's about the hottest thing going as far as magicians go. *Everybody's* talking about him. You know, he engineered a jailbreak right here on Limbo!"

"I think I heard about that," I admitted.

"And just a while back, he got barred from the Dimension of Perv. Can you believe that? Perv?"

"It was a bum rap," I grimaced.

"So you really *do* know him! Come on, tell me more. When you say he's like you, do you mean he's young or what?"

As much fun as this was, I figured it was time to stop before it got out of hand.

"Cassandra," I said, carefully. "Watch my lips. He's a *lot* like me. Get it?"

She frowned, then shook her head.

"No. I don't. You make it sound like you're twins or something. Either that, or . . ."

She suddenly stared at me, her eye's widening.

"Oh, *no*," she gasped. "You don't mean you're . . ."

I held my credit card up in front of her so she could read the name on it, then favored her with my widest smile.

"Oh no!" she shrieked, loud enough to draw attention from the neighboring tables. "*You're him!!!* Why didn't you *tell* me!!"

"You never asked," I shrugged. "Actually, I thought that Vic . . ."

But by that time, I was speaking to her back . . . or, to be more specific, her rump. She was on her feet calling triumphantly to the other patrons.

"*Hey, everybody! You know who this is? This is SKEEVE THE GREAT!!!*"

Now, at different times, various people have tried to tell me that I was building a rep through the dimensions. Most recently, Bunny had brought it up when explaining how she set the prices for the services of M.Y.T.H. Inc. I guess I was sort of aware of it, and had even kind of accepted it, but for the most part I didn't really see where it made any difference in my normal day to day life. Sitting in The Wooden Stake in the dimension of Limbo, however, was not part of my normal day to day life . . .

and neither was the reaction of the crowd when it learned who I was.

At first, heads turned, then drew together in whispered conversation as the whole room stared at me as if I had grown another head.

"I hope I didn't embarrass you, Skeeve . . . can I call you Skeeve? . . . but I'm just so excited." Cassandra was back in her seat, focusing all her attention on me. "Imagine, me out on a date with *the Great Skeeve!*"

"Umm . . . that's all right, Cassandra," I assured her, but now my attention was elsewhere.

Over her shoulder . . . heck, from all around us . . . I could see people starting to make their way towards our table. Now, as I've mentioned, I've been chased by mobs before, but never starting surrounded! Still, they didn't look particularly hostile or angry. If anything, they all seemed to have exaggerated smiles on their faces . . . which considering the array of teeth in the room, wasn't all that pleasant to behold.

"Excuse me, Cassandra," I said, eyeing the incoming people, "but I drink . . . I mean, I think we're about to have company."

The slip of the tongue was because I had just tried to take another sip of my drink, only to find the glass was empty except for the ice cubes . . . strange, because I didn't remember finishing it. Then the first person reached the table.

It was a male vampire, all decked out in a fine set of evening clothes which he wore with enviable grace.

"Excuse me for interrupting, Mr. Skeeve," he said with a smile, "but I wanted to shake your hand. Always wanted to meet you, but never thought I'd get the opportunity."

"Uh, sure," I said, but he had already seized my hand and was pumping away.

"I was wondering . . . could I have your autograph?" a young lady said, trying to edge around the first gentleman.

"What? I suppose so . . ."

Unfortunately I couldn't seem to get my hand loose from the vampire who was still shaking it, though he seemed to be looking elsewhere at the moment.

"Hey! Waiter!" I heard him call. "Another round of whatever Mr. Skeeve and his guest are drinking . . . and put it on my tab!"

"Umm . . . thank you," I said, extracting my hand and turning to the girl who had asked for an autograph. "Do you have a pen?"

"Gosh no!" she exclaimed. "But I'll go get one. Don't go away, I'll be right back."

I really didn't know what to think. I had been nervous about coming back to Limbo because of my near criminal activities during my last visit, and here they were treating me like a celebrity!

"Mr. Skeeve. If you don't mind. It's for my little girl."

This last was from a were-tiger who thrust both paper and pen at me. Fortunately, after the last visitor, I knew what he was after, and hastily scribbled my signature on the page.

Our ghost waiter materialized through the growing crowd and set our drinks on the table . . . except there were three of them! From the color, one for Cassandra, and two for me.

"What's with the extra?" I said.

"Compliments of the table over there, sir," the waiter said, pointing somewhere off to my left.

I tried to look where he was indicating, and almost put my nose in the navel of another young lady who was crowding up beside me. Actually, she was one of three, any one of whom would be eye-catching under normal circumstances, but were just part of the crowd here.

"Where are you going from here, Mr. Skeeve?" the taller one purred. "There's going to be a party at our place later if you want to come by."

"Wipe your chin, Sweetheart," Cassandra smiled, slipping her arm around my shoulder. "He's *my* date . . . and I plan to keep him busy all night."

That had an intriguing sound to it, but just then someone else started tugging on my sleeve.

"Excuse me, Mr. Skeeve," said an awesome set of teeth

from a point too close to focus on. "I was wondering if I might interview you sometime at your convenience?"

"Well . . . I'm kind of busy right now," I hedged, trying to lean back far enough to get a better look at my questioner . . . which unfortunately pressed the back of my head up against one of the party girls.

"Oh, I don't mean *now*," the teeth said, matching my retreat with a move forward so I *still* couldn't see what or who was talking. "If you can stop by our table over there later, we'll set up an appointment. I'll have a drink waiting for you . . . Bloody Mary, right?"

"Right. I mean, okay. But . . ."

But by that time the person was gone. I only hoped that they'd recognize me if I got into the general vicinity. Right now, my attention was caught by the fact that whoever I was pressing backward against was now pressing forward against the back of my head . . . far too insistently for it to be an accident.

"Say, Skeeve," Cassandra said, giving me an excuse to break contact, which I took, pausing only to take a gulp of my drink before I leaned toward her.

"Yes, Cassandra?"

"If you don't mind, can we head out of here after you finish your drink? There are a couple other places I'd like to hit tonight . . . you know, to show you off a little?"

"No problem," I said, "but it might take a while."

Somehow, during the last flurry of discussions, my two drinks had multiplied into four.

"Oh, I'm in no hurry," she said, giving me a quick kiss. "I know you've got to deal with some of these people now that they know who you are. It goes with the notoriety. It may be old hat to you, but I'm having a blast!"

To say the least, it wasn't old hat to me. Maybe if it was, I would have handled it better.

I remember signing my name a lot . . . and some more drinks being delivered . . . and kissing Cassandra . . . and, I think, another club . . . or two other clubs . . . and more drinks . . .

X:

"Happiness is defined by one's capacity for enjoyment."

—BACCHUS

Opening my eyes, I suffered a brief moment of disorientation, then things started swimming into focus.

I was in my room . . . in my own bed, to be specific, though the covers seemed to be twisted and disheveled. I was naked under the covers, though I had no recollection of getting undressed. I assumed it was morning, as there was sunlight streaming through the window. In short, everything looked normal.

So why did I feel there was something wrong?

I was lying on my side, and I realized my sinuses had flooded, making it impossible to breathe out of the nostril on the "downhill" side. In an effort to alleviate this situation, I rolled over and . . .

It hit me!!!

A pounding headache . . . a nauseous stomach . . . the works!

There had been times in the past when I had gotten sick, but nothing like this! At first I was afraid I was going to die. Then I was afraid I'd live. Misery such as I was feeling should have a finite end.

Groaning slightly and burrowing into my pillow, I tried to gather my thoughts.

What was going on here? What happened to make me feel . . .

Suddenly, the memory of the previous night flashed across my mind . . . or, at least, the beginning of it.

The blind date . . . The Wooden Stake . . . the admiring crowds . . . *Cassandra!*

I sat bolt upright and . . .

Big mistake. *BIG* mistake.

Every pain and queasiness I had been feeling slammed into me threefold. With a moan, I fell limply back onto my pillow heedless of the new unpleasant sensations this move caused. You could only feel so miserable, and I had bottomed out. Nothing could make me feel worse. Forget any effort at rational thought. I was just going to lie there until my head cleared or I died . . . whichever came first.

A knock sounded at the door.

Disoriented as I was, I had no difficulty deciding what to do: I was going to ignore it. I was certainly in no condition to see or talk to anyone!

The knock came again, a little louder this time.

"Skeeve? Are you awake?"

It was Bunny's voice. From what I could recall of the beginning of last evening, I *really* didn't want to talk to her right now. All I needed to make my misery complete was to have her carping on me about my taste in dates.

"Go away!" I called, not even bothering to try to make it sound polite.

As soon as I uttered the words, however, I realized I would have been better off just staying quiet. Not only had the effort increased the pounding in my head, I had inadvertently let her know I was awake.

As if in response to my afterthought, the door opened and Bunny came in, a big tray of food in her hands.

"When I didn't see you at breakfast *or* at lunch, I fig-ured you might be a little worse for wear from last night," she said crisply, setting the tray on my desk. "I had the kitchen put together a tray for you to help you back to the land of the living."

Food was definitely low on my list of priorities at the moment. If anything, I was more concerned with things going the other way through my digestive tract. It *did* however, suddenly occur to me that I was thirsty. In fact, VERY thirsty.

"Have you got any juice on that tray?" I managed weakly, not wanting to sit up far enough to look myself.

"Do you want orange or tomato?"

The mention of tomato juice brought memories of last night's Bloody Marys to mind, and my stomach did a slow roll and dip to the left.

"Orange, will be fine," I said through gritted teeth, trying hard to talk, keep my mouth shut, and swallow at the same time.

She favored me with a speculative glance.

"Well, it wasn't Screwdrivers or Mimosas."

"Excuse me?"

"Never mind. Orange juice, coming up."

I could have done without the "coming up" comment, but the juice tasted fine. I downed it in two long swallows. Strangely enough, it left me even more thirsty. Not that the juice wasn't a welcome input of cool moisture, but it made me realize just how dehydrated I was.

"Any more of that?" I said hopefully.

"Got a whole pitcher here," Bunny replied, gesturing toward the tray. "I had a hunch you were going to need more than one glass. Take it slow, though. I don't think it would be a good idea to gulp down a lot of cold liquid just yet."

I resisted the urge to grab the entire pitcher from her, and instead simply held out my glass for a refill. With a major effort, I did my best to comply with her suggestion and sipped it slowly. It lasted a little longer that way, and did seem to have a greater effect.

"That's better," she said, refilling the glass again without being asked. "So. Did you have a good time last night?"

I paused in mid-sip, trying to force my brain to function.

"To be honest with you, Bunny, I don't know," I admitted at last.

"I'm not sure I follow you."

"What I remember was okay," I said, "but after a certain point in the evening, everything's a blank. I'm not even sure exactly when that point was, for that matter. Things are a bit jumbled in my mind still."

"I see."

For a moment, Bunny seemed about to say something else, but instead she pursed her lips and wandered over to the window where she stood staring out.

My head was clearing now, to a point where I felt almost alive, and I decided it was time to try to set things right.

"Um . . . Bunny? About last night . . . I'm sorry I left you standing like that, but Vic had set up the date for me, and there was no real way to back out gracefully."

"Of course, the fact that she was quite a dish had nothing to do with it," Bunny commented with a grimace.

"Well . . ."

"Don't worry about it, Skeeve," she said quickly, waving off my reply. "That's not what's bothering me, anyway."

"What is?"

She turned to face me, leaning back on the windowsill.

"It's the same thing that's been bothering me ever since I arrived for this assignment," she said. "I haven't wanted to say anything, because it's really none of my business. But if what you say about last night is true . . ."

She broke off, biting her lip slightly.

"Go on," I said.

"Well . . . Simply put, I think you're developing a drinking problem."

That one caught me off guard. I had been half expecting her to make some comment about how little I was helping on the kingdom's finances, or even the parade of women I seemed to be suddenly confronted with. It had never occurred to me that she might be taking affront at my personal habits.

"I . . . I don't know what to say, Bunny. I mean, sure, I drink. But everybody drinks a little from time to time."

"A little?"

She came off the windowsill in one easy motion and came to perch on the edge of my bed.

"Skeeve, every time I see you lately you've got a goblet of wine in your hand. It's gotten so that your idea of saying 'Hello' to someone is to offer them a drink."

I was really confused now. When she first mentioned my drinking, my immediate reaction was that she was being an alarmist. The more she talked, however, the more I found myself wondering if she might have a point.

"That's just being hospitable," I said, stalling for time to think.

"Not when you're making the offer first thing in the morning," she snapped. "Definitely not when you go ahead and have a drink yourself, whether they join you or not."

"Aahz drinks," I countered, starting to feel defensive. "He says the water on most dimensions isn't to be trusted."

"This is your home dimension, Skeeve. You should be used to the water here. Besides, Aahz is a Pervect. His whole metabolism is different from yours. He can handle drinking."

"And I can't. Is that what you're trying to say?"

The misery I had been feeling since I awoke was now taking the form of anger and annoyance.

"Check me on this," she said. "From what I've heard, during your recent trip to Perv, you got into a fight didn't you? After you'd been drinking?"

"Well . . . Yes. But I've been in fights before."

"From what I hear, if Kalvin, the Djinn, hadn't sobered you up, you might not have survived this one. True?"

She had a point there. The situation *had* been a bit

hairy. I had to admit that my odds of surviving the brawl would have gone way down if I hadn't been jerked back to sobriety by Kalvin's spell.

I nodded my agreement.

"Then there's last night," she continued. "You really wanted to make a good impression on someone. You dressed up in one of your spiffiest outfits, probably dropped a fair hunk of change, and then what? From the sounds of it, you got carried away with the drinking until you can't even remember what happened. You don't even know what went on, much less whether or not your date had a good time. That doesn't sound like you . . . at least, the you that you'd like people to remember."

I was starting to feel really low, and not just from the aftereffects of the night before. I had always thought my drinking was a harmless diversion . . . or, more lately, a way to ease the pressures of the problems confronting me. It had never occurred to me how it might look to others. Now that I was thinking about it, the picture wasn't very pleasant. Unfortunately, I was still a little reluctant to admit that to Bunny.

"One of the things I *do* remember about last night is that people kept buying me drinks," I said defensively. "It kind of caught me by surprise, and I thought it would be rude to refuse."

"Even if you *have* to accept drinks to be social, there's nothing that says what you drink has to be alcoholic," Bunny shot back. "There *are* other things to drink, you know. You could always just have a soft drink or some fruit juice."

Suddenly, I was very tired. Between my hangover and the new thoughts that had been thrust upon me, what little energy I had when I awoke was now depleted.

"Bunny," I said, "I'm really not up to arguing with you right now. You've raised some interesting points, and I appreciate your bringing them to my attention. Give me some time to think about them. Okay? At the moment, all I want to do is curl up and die for a while."

To her credit, Bunny didn't continue to push her case. Instead, she became extremely solicitous.

"I'm sorry, Skeeve," she said, laying a hand on my arm. "I didn't mean to jump you like that while you were still drying out. Is there anything I can get you? A cold washrag, maybe?"

Actually, that sounded like a wonderful idea.

"If you would, please. I'd really appreciate it."

She hopped off the bed and made for the washstand while I tried to find a more comfortable position.

After rearranging the pillows, I glanced over to see what was keeping her, only to find her standing stock-still, staring at the wall.

"Bunny? Is there something wrong?" I called.

"I guess I was wrong," she said in a strange tone, still staring at the wall.

"How's that?"

"When I said you probably left a bad impression on your date . . . I think I should have kept my mouth shut."

"What makes you say that?"

"I take it you haven't seen this."

She gestured at the wall over the washstand. I squinted slightly and focused my still-bleary eyes on the spot she was indicating.

Written on the wall, in bright red lipstick, was a note.

Skeeve,
Sorry to go, but I didn't want to wake you. Last night was magic. You're as good as your rep. Let me know when you want to play some more.
                                        Cassandra

I found myself smirking as I read the note.

"Well, I guess she wasn't too upset with my drinking. Eh, Bunny?"

There was no answer.

"Bunny?"

I tore my eyes away from the message and glanced

around the room. The tray was still there, but Bunny wasn't. With the door standing open, the only logical conclusion was that she had left without saying a word.

Suddenly, I didn't feel so smug anymore.

XI:

"If labor and management communicated better, there would be fewer terminations."

—J. HOFFA

"Hi, Buttercup. How's it going, fellah?"
The war unicorn raised his head and stared at me for a moment, then went back to eating from his feed bin.

"Com'on, fellah. You know me," I urged.

The unicorn continued eating, ignoring me completely.

"Don't worry, Boss," came a squeaky voice from behind me. "Unicorns are like that."

I didn't have to look to see who the voice belonged to, but turned to face my bodyguard anyway.

"Hi, Nunzio," I said. "What was that about unicorns?"

"They're temperamental," he explained with a shrug. "War unicorns like Buttercup are no exception. He's just giving you a rough time because you haven't been visiting him much."

One of the assorted things I had learned about Nunzio's past was that at one time he had been an animal trainer, so I tended to believe him. I was a little disap-

pointed, however. I had been hoping that Buttercup's reaction to me would provide a confirmation as to what did
or didn't happen between Cassandra and me the night
before, but it seemed there were other, more rational, possible reasons for his standoffishness.

Of course, fast on the heels of my disappointment came
a surge of guilt. I *had* been neglecting my pets badly . . .
along with a lot of other things.

"That reminds me, Nunzio," I said, eager to shift the
guilt, "how are you doing with Gleep?"

My bodyguard frowned and wiped a massive hand
across his mouth and chin in thought.

"I dunno, Boss," he said. "I can't quite put my finger
on it, but there's somethin' wrong there. He just don't *feel*
right lately."

Strangely enough, that made sense. In fact, Nunzio had
managed to put into words my own nebulous concerns
about my pet . . . he didn't *feel* right.

"Maybe we're going about this wrong," I said. "Maybe
instead of trying to pin down what's wrong with him *now*,
we should try to backtrack a bit."

"I don't quite follow you," my bodyguard scowled.

"Think back, Nunzio," I urged. When did you first notice that Gleep wasn't acting normal?"

"Well . . . he seemed okay when Markie was around,"
he said thoughtfully. "In fact, if you think about it, he was
the first of us to figure she wasn't on the up and up."

Something flitted across my mind along with that memory, but Nunzio kept talking and it disappeared again.

"I'd have to say it was right after that job when him
and me was guarding that warehouse. You remember?
With the forged comic books?"

"Was he all right on that assignment?"

"Sure. I remember talkin' with him quite a bit while
we was sittin' around doin' nothin'. He was fine then."

"Wait a minute," I interrupted. "You were talking *with*
Gleep?"

"I guess it was more like talkin' *to* him, since he

doesn't really answer back," Nunzio corrected himself easily. "You know what I mean, Boss. Anyway, I spent a lot of time talkin' *to* him, and he seemed okay then. In fact, he seemed to listen real close."

"What did you talk to him about?"

My bodyguard hesitated, then glanced away quickly.

"Oh . . . this and that," he said with an exaggerated shrug. "I really can't remember for sure."

"Nunzio," I said, letting a note of sternness creep into my voice, "if you can remember, tell me. It's important."

"Well . . . I was goin' on a bit about how worried I was about you, Boss," Nunzio admitted hesitantly. "You remember how you was right after we decided to incorporate? How you was gettin' so wrapped up in work that you didn't have much time for anything or anyone else? I just unloaded on Gleep a bit about how I didn't think it was healthy for you, is all. I didn't think it would hurt nothin'. That's why I did my talkin' in front of him and not anyone else on the team . . . even Guido."

There were clear images dancing in my head now. Pictures of Gleep breathing fire at Markie . . . who only escaped narrowly when Nunzio intervened . . . and of my pet throwing himself in front of me when another, larger dragon was on the brink of making me extinct.

"Think carefully, Nunzio," I said slowly. "When you were talking to Gleep, did you say anything . . . anything at all . . . about the possibility of Tananda or anyone else on the team being a threat to me?"

My bodyguard frowned thoughtfully for a moment, then shook his head.

"I don't remember sayin' anything like that, Boss. Why do you ask?"

Now it was my turn to hesitate. The idea that was taking shape in my mind seemed almost too silly to voice. Still, since I was turning to Nunzio for advice and expertise, it was only fair to share my suspicions with him.

"It may be crazy," I said, "but I'm starting to get the feeling that Gleep is a lot more intelligent than we ever suspected. I mean, he's always been kind of protective of me. If he *were* intelligent and got it into his head that someone on the team was a threat to me, there's a chance he might try to kill them . . . just like he went after Markie."

My bodyguard stared at me, then gave a short bark of laughter.

"You're right, Boss," he said. "That *does* sound crazy. I mean, Gleep's a dragon! If he was to try to whack someone on the team, we'd know it pretty fast, know what I mean?"

"Like when he tried to burn Tananda?" I pressed. "Think about it, Nunzio. If he *were* intelligent, wouldn't part of his conclusions be that I would be upset if anything happened to anyone on the team? In that case, wouldn't he do his best to make any mishap look like an accident rather than a direct attack? I'll admit it's a wild theory, but it fits the facts."

"Except for one thing," my bodyguard countered. "For him to be doin' what you say, puttin' pieces together and comin' up with his own conclusions, much less organizing a plan and executing it, would make him more than intelligent. It would make him smarter than us! Remember, for a dragon he's still real young. It would be like sayin' a baby that could hardly walk was planning a bank heist."

"I suppose you're right," I sighed. "There must be another explanation."

"You know, Boss," Nunzio smiled, "folks say that, after a while, pets start takin' on the traits of their masters and vice verses. Takin' that into consideration, I think it's only logical that Gleep here acts a bit strange from time to time."

For some reason, that brought to mind my earlier conversation with Bunny.

"Tell me, Nunzio, do you think I've been drinking too much lately?"

"That's not for me to say, Boss," he said easily. "I'm just a bodyguard, not a babysitter."

"I was asking what you thought."

"And I'm sayin' I'm not supposed to think . . . at least,

not about whoever it is I'm supposed to be guardin'," he insisted. "Bodyguards that comment on their clients's personal habits don't last long. What I'm supposed to be doin' is guardin' you while you do whatever it is you do . . . not tellin' you what to do."

I started to snap at him, but instead took a long breath and brought my irritation under control.

"Look, Nunzio," I said carefully, "I know that's the normal bodyguard/client relationship. I like to think, though, that we've progressed a little past that point. I like to think of you as a friend as well as a bodyguard. What's more, you're a stockholder in M.Y.T.H. Inc., so you have a vested interest in my performance as president. Now, this morning Bunny told me that she thought I was developing a drinking problem. I don't think that I am, but I'm aware that I may be too close to the situation to judge properly. That's why I'm asking your opinion. . . . as a friend and fellow worker whose opinions and judgment I've grown to value and respect."

Nunzio rubbed his chin thoughtfully, obviously wrestling with a mental dilemma.

"I dunno, Boss," he said. "It's kinda against the rules . . . but then again, you're right. You do treat Guido and me different from any other boss we've had. Nobody else ever asked our opinion on nothin'."

"Well I'm asking, Nunzio. Please?"

"Part of the problem is that it's not that easy a question to answer," he shrugged. "Sure, you drink. But do you drink too much? That's not as clear-cut. You've been drinking more since you brought Aahz back from Perv, but 'more' doesn't necessarily mean the same as 'too much.' Know what I mean?"

"As a matter of fact, no I don't."

He sighed heavily. When he spoke again, I couldn't help but notice that his tone had the patient, careful note that one takes, or should, when one is explaining something to a child.

"Look, Boss," he said. "Drinkin' affects the judgment. Everybody knows that. The more you drink, the more it affects your judgment. Sayin' how much is too much isn't easy, though, seein' as how it varies from individual to individual depending on such factors as weight, temperament, etc."

"But if it affects your judgment," I said, "how can you tell whether or not your judgment is right when you say it's not too much?"

"That's the rub," Nunzio shrugged. "Some say if you have the sense to question it, you aren't drinkin' too much. Others say that if you have to ask, then you ARE drinkin' too much. One thing I do know is that a lot of people who drink too much are sure they don't have a problem."

"So how do you tell?"

"Well," he said, rubbing his chin, "probably the best way is to ask a friend whose judgment you trust."

I closed my eyes and fought for patience.

"That's what I THOUGHT I was doing, Nunzio. I'm asking YOU. Do YOU think I'm drinking too much?"

"That isn't important," he said, blandly. "It isn't a question of if I think you're drinkin' too much, it's if YOU think you're drinkin' too much."

"NUNZIO," I said through gritted teeth. "I'm asking what YOUR opinion is."

He averted his eyes and shifted uncomfortably.

"Sorry, Boss. Like I say, this isn't easy for me."

He rubbed his chin again.

"One thing I WILL say is that I think you're drinkin' at the wrong time . . . and I don't mean too early or late in the day. I mean at the wrong time in your life."

"I don't understand," I frowned.

"Ya see, Boss, drinkin' usually acts like a magnifyin' glass. It exaggerates everything. Some people drink tryin' to change their mood, but they're kiddin' themselves. It don't work that way. It don't change what is, it emphasizes it. If you drink when you're happy, then you get REAL happy. Know what I mean? But if you drink when you're down, then you get REAL down, REAL fast."

He gave another heavy sigh.

"Now, you've been goin' through some rough times lately, and have some tough decisions to make. To me, that's not a real good time to be drinkin'. What you need right now is a clear head. What you DON'T need is somethin' to exaggerate any doubts you've got about yourself or your judgment."

It was my turn to rub my chin thoughtfully.

"That makes sense," I said. "Thanks, Nunzio."

"Hey. I just had an idea," he said brightly, apparently buoyed by his success. "There's a real easy way to tell if you're drinkin' too much. Just lay off the sauce for a while. Then see if there's any big change in your thinkin' or judgment. If there is, then you know it's time to back off. Of course, if you find out that quittin' is harder than you thought, then you'll have another signal that you've got trouble."

A part of me bristled at the thought of having to ease up on my drinking, but I fought it down . . . along with my flash of fear at what that bristling might imply.

"Okay, Nunzio," I said. "I'll do it. Thanks again. I appreciate how hard that was for you."

"Don't mention it, Boss. Glad I could help you."

He reached out and laid a hand on my shoulder in a rare display of comradeship.

"Personally, I don't think you have that much to worry about. If you've got a drinkin' problem, it's marginal at best. I mean, it's not like you've been blackin' out or anything."

XII:

"Let's see the instant replay on that!"

—H. COSSELL

"**H**ey, Partner! How's it going?"

I had been heading back toward my room with the vague thought of getting a little more sleep. The hail from Aahz, however, reduced my odds of success noticeably.

"Hi Aahz," I said, turning toward him. That put the sun in my eyes, so I stepped back slightly to find some shade.

He drew up close to me and peered at me carefully. I, in turn, tried my best to look relaxed and puzzled.

Finally he nodded to himself.

"You look okay," he declared.

"Shouldn't I?" I said, innocently.

"I heard you had quite a time last night," he explained, shooting me another sidelong glance. "Thought I'd better look you up and survey the damage. I'll admit you seem to have weathered the storm well enough. Resilience of youth, I guess."

"Maybe the reports were exaggerated," I suggested hopefully.

"Not bloody likely," he snorted. "Chumley said he saw you and your date when you rolled back into the castle and, as you know, if anything, he's prone to understatement."

I nodded mutely. When he wasn't in his working persona of Big Crunch, the troll was remarkably accurate in his reports and observations.

"Whatever," Aahz waved. "Like I say, you seem to have survived pretty well."

I managed a weak smile.

"How about a hair of the dog? A quick drink to perk you up," he suggested. "Com'on partner. My treat. We'll duck into town for a change of pace."

A moment's reflection was all it took to realize that a stroll through the town around the castle sounded good. Real good if Bunny was on the warpath.

"Okay, Aahz. You're on," I said. "But as to the hair of the dog . . . I'll stick to regular stuff if you don't mind. I had enough of strange drinks last night."

He gave off one of those choking noises he used to make during my days as an apprentice when I said something really dumb, but when I glanced at him, there wasn't a trace of a smile.

"Aren't you forgetting something, partner?" he said without looking at me.

"What?"

"If we're heading out among the common folk, a disguise spell would be nice."

He was right of course. Even though I was used to seeing him as he actually was, a Pervect with green scales and yellow eyes, the average citizen of Possiltum still tended to react to his appearance with horror and fear . . . which is to say much the same way I reacted when I first met him.

"Sorry, Aahz."

Closing my eyes, I quickly made the necessary adjustments. Manipulating his image with my mind, I made him look like an ordinary castle guard. If anything, I made him a bit more scrawny and undernourished than average. I mean, the idea *was* not to intimidate people, wasn't it?

Aahz didn't even bother checking his reflection in any of the windows we passed. He seemed much more interested in prying details of my date out of me.

"Where did you find to go on this backwater dimension, anyway?" he said.

"Oh, we didn't stick around here," I said loftily. "We ducked over to Limbo. Cassandra knew a couple clubs there and we . . ."

I suddenly noticed Aahz was no longer walking beside me. Looking back, I realized he had stopped in his tracks. His mouth was working, but no sound came out.

"Limbo?" he managed at last. "You went bar crawling on Limbo? Excuse me, partner, but I was under the impression we were *persona non grata* in that neck of the woods."

"I was a little worried at first," I admitted casually, which was only a little lie. As you'll recall, I had been a LOT worried. "Cassandra said she could blip us back out fast if there was any trouble, though, so I figured what the heck. As it turned out, nobody seems to be holding a grudge there. In fact, it seems I'm . . . I mean, *we're* . . . minor celebrities over there. That's partly why the evening ran as long as it did. Half the people we ran into wanted to buy me a drink for putting one over on the local council."

"Is that a fact?" Aahz said darkly, starting to move again. "Just who is this Cassandra person, anyway? She doesn't exactly sound like a local."

"She's not," I confirmed. "Vic set me up with her. She's a friend of his."

"Nice to know he didn't set you up with an enemy," my partner quipped. Still in all, it seems to me . . ."

He broke off and did another double take.

"Wait a minute. Vic? The same vampire Vic that you hang around with over at the Bazaar? You mean this Cassandra babe is . . ."

"A vampire," I said with a careless shrug. The truth was, I was starting to get a bit of a kick out of shocking Aahz. "Oh, she's okay. No one you'd want to take home to mother, but . . . what's wrong?"

He was craning his head around to peer at my neck from different angles.

"Just checking for bite marks," he said.

"Com'on, Aahz. There wasn't any danger of that. She was drinking her blood out of a glass last night."

"Those weren't the kind of bite marks I was checking for," he grinned. "Vamps have a rep of being pretty wild women."

"Um . . . speaking of destinations," I said eager to change the subject, "where are *we* going?"

"No place special," my partner said. "These local bars and inns are pretty much all the same. This one should do us fine."

With that, he veered through the door of the place we were passing, leaving me to follow along behind.

The inn was refreshingly ordinary compared to what I could remember of the surreal clubs I had been to on Limbo. Ordinary, and more than a little dull.

Dark wooden tables and chairs were the main feature of the decor, with occasional candles scattered here and there to supplement the light which streamed in through windows and the open door.

"What'll you have, Skeeve?" Aahz called, heading for the bar.

I started to say "Wine," but changed my mind. Whether or not Bunny was right about my drinking getting out of hand, it wouldn't hurt to ease up a bit. Besides, Nunzio's comment about blacking out had me more than a little uneasy.

"Just some fruit juice for me," I waved.

Aahz paused, cocking his head at me.

"Are you sure you're all right, partner?" he said.

"Sure. Why do you ask?"

"Awhile back you were talking about looking forward to having your usual, and now you're switching drinks."

"All right. Have it your way," I grimaced. "A goblet of wine, then. No need to make a big thing of it."

I leaned back and looked around the room, though it was mostly to break eye contact with Aahz before he realized I was upset. It was funny, but I found myself somehow reluctant to tell my partner my worries about my drinking. Still, it was difficult to change my drinking patterns around him without raising questions that would require an explanation. I figured that, for the moment, the easiest thing to do would be to go on as before . . . at least, while I was around Aahz. Later, more privately, I'd start tapering off.

One thing I noticed about the inn was that there seemed to be a lot of young people hanging around. Well, to be honest, they were about my age, but I spend so much time with the team, I tend to think of myself as older.

One table of girls in particular caught my attention, mostly because they seemed to be talking about me. At least, that was my guess, as they kept glancing my way, then putting their heads together and giggling, then glancing over again.

Not long ago, this would have made me nervous. My recent excursion to Limbo, however, had gotten me a bit more used to notoriety.

The next time they glanced over, I looked directly back at them, then gave a brief, polite nod of acknowledgment with my head. This, of course, caused another hurried huddle and burst of giggles.

Ah, fame.

"What are you smiling at?" Aahz said as he set my wine in front of me and slid onto the bench across the table, cradling his own outsized drink.

"Oh, nothing," I smiled. "I was just watching that table of girls over there."

I indicated the direction with a tilt of my head, and he leaned sideways to scope them out himself.

"Kind of young for you, aren't they, partner?"

"They're not that much younger than I am," I protested, taking a long swallow of wine.

"Don't you have enough problems already?" Aahz said, settling back. "Last time I checked, you were suffering from an overabundance of women . . . not a shortage."

"Oh, relax," I laughed. "I wasn't figuring to *do* anything with them. Just having a little fun, is all. They were looking at me, so I let them see me looking back."

"Well don't look now," he grinned back, "but at least one of them is doing more than looking."

Needless to say, I looked.

One of the girls had stood up and was approaching our table. When she saw me looking in her direction, she seemed to gather her courage and closed the distance in a rush.

"Hi," she said brightly. "You're him, aren't you? The wizard from the castle?"

"That's right," I nodded. "How did you know that?"

"I thought I heard him call you Skeeve when he went to fetch your drink," she gushed.

"Probably because that's my name," I smiled.

Okay, so it wasn't the wittiest thing I'd said. In fact, it was pretty lame compared to the usual banter that goes on within the team. You'd never tell it, though, from her reaction.

She covered her mouth with one hand and shrieked with laughter loud enough to draw the attention of everyone in the room . . . in the town, for that matter.

"Oh! That's *priceless*," she declared.

"That's where you're wrong," I corrected. "Actually, my rates are rather high."

This, of course, set off another gale of laughter. I caught Aahz's gaze and winked. He rolled his eyes in disgust and turned his attention to his drink. That seemed like a good idea, but when I went to sip my wine, the goblet was empty. I started to ask Aahz to get me another, but changed my mind. That first one had disappeared with disturbing speed.

"So, what can I do for you?" I said, as much to take my mind off the wine as to get an answer.

"Well, everyone in town has been talking about you,"

the girl chirped, "and my girlfriend . . . the cute one over there . . . has a *real* thing for you since she saw you in court when you first came back. Anyway, it would just make her whole incarnation if you'd come over to our table so she could meet you personally."

"I don't know," I said. "There are things to be said for meeting people im-personally as well."

"Huh?" she said, giving me a blank look, and I realized I had pushed beyond her sense of humor.

"Just tell her I'll be over in a few moments, as soon as I finish my conversation here."

"Great! She'll *die!*"

I watched her scamper off to tell her friends, then turned back to Aahz.

"I *may* throw up," he announced.

"You're just jealous," I grinned. "Keep an eye on my drink for me, will you?"

With that I rose and headed for the girls' table. At least, I started to.

There was a gangly youth blocking my way. I started to move around him, but he stepped sideways, deliberately putting himself in my path again.

I stopped and looked at him.

I'd been in fights before. Sometimes against some pretty tough customers when I wasn't sure I would survive it. This joker, however, was different.

He couldn't have been more than my age. Probably a few years younger. What's more, he didn't hold himself with the confident poise of a brawler or even a soldier. In fact, if anything, he looked scared.

"Leave them alone," he said in a shaky voice.

"I beg your pardon?"

"I said leave them alone!" he repeated, his voice gaining a bit of strength.

I let the ghost of a smile play across my face.

"Young man," I said gently, "do you know who I am?"

"Oh, I know all right," he nodded. "You're Skeeve. The big bad wizard from the castle. What's more, I know you can make me sorry I ever breathed, much less got in your way. You can turn me into a toad or make my hair burst into flame, or even whistle up some nasty creature to tear me apart if you don't want to get your own hands dirty. You can squash me or anyone else you want just to get your way . . . but it doesn't make it right. Maybe it's about time someone stood up to you even if it means getting killed just for trying."

I couldn't help but notice there were some nods and mutterings of support for the youth at the other tables in the inn, and no few dark looks cast in my direction.

"All right," I said levelly. "You're standing up to me. Now make your point."

"The point is you can't just waltz in here and put moves on our women. What's more, if you try, you'll be sorry."

To emphasize his words, he reached out and gave me a shove that knocked me back. I had to take a step to recover my balance.

It was suddenly very quiet in the inn. The moment seemed to hang in the air as everyone tensed and waited to see what would happen next.

Blood was pounding in my ears.

I heard the bench behind me slide as Aahz started to get up, and I signaled behind me with my hand for him to stay out of it.

"I have no intention of putting any 'moves' on these women either now or in the future," I said carefully. "The young lady there came to *my* table and said that her friend wanted to meet me. I was about to comply. Period. That's it. It was an effort on my part to be polite. If, as it seems, it is somehow offensive to you or anyone else here, I'll forego the pleasure."

I looked past him to where the girls were watching.

"Ladies," I nodded. "Another day, perhaps."

With that, I turned on my heel and marched out of the place . . . angry and embarrassed, but confident that I had correctly handled a dubious situation.

It didn't help, however, that as I passed through the door, a shout from the youth came wafting after me.

"And don't come back!"

XIII:

"The secret of popularity is confidence."

— W. ALLEN

"Hold up a minute, partner. We're still together, you know."

I slowed my pace a bit, and Aahz caught up with me, falling in step beside me.

"If you don't mind the observation," he said, "that little scene back there seems to have gotten you a little upset."

"Shouldn't it have?" I snapped.

"Don't let it bother you," my partner said easily. "Locals always get upset with outsiders ... especially when their women start flirting with them. It's a problem as old as the hills. Just ask any soldier or carny person. Don't take it personally."

He gave me a playful punch on the arm, but, for a change, I wasn't reassured.

"But they weren't reacting to an outsider, Aahz. They were reacting to *me*. I live here, too. What's more, they knew it. They knew who I was and that I work at the castle, but they still treated me like an outsider."

"As far as they're concerned, you are."

That one stopped me.

"How's that again?"

"Take a look at the facts, Skeeve," Aahz said, more serious now. "Even ignoring your travels through the dimensions, you aren't the same as them. Like you say, you work at the castle . . . and not as a chambermaid or a kitchen worker, either. You're one of the main advisors to the Queen, not to mention a possible consort . . . though I doubt they know that. Things you do and say on a daily basis affect everyone in this kingdom. That alone puts you on a different social . . . not to mention economic . . . level from the folks here in town."

That made me pause and think.

My new life and lifestyle had sort of grown up around me over the years. Socializing and/or clashing with kings or mayors had become pretty commonplace, though I had never stopped to consider it. Rather, I had always assumed that it sort of went with the territory when one was a magician. Then again, how many magicians had I met while I was growing up?

Aahz was right. My work with the team *had* cocooned me away from the rest of society to a point where I took things for granted. The extraordinary had become so ordinary to me, that I had ceased to be aware of, or even consider, how it must seem to the ordinary citizens.

I shook my head abruptly.

"No. There's more to it than that, Aahz. Those people back there didn't like *me*."

"Uh-huh," my partner nodded. "So what's your point?"

"What's my point?" I echoed a little shrilly. "Maybe you didn't understand me. I said . . ."

". . . They didn't like you," Aahz finished. "So what?"

"What do you mean 'So what'?" I said. "Don't you want to be liked?"

My old mentor frowned slightly, then gave a shrug.

"I suppose it would be nice," he said. "But I really don't give it much thought."

"But . . ."

"And neither should you."

There was a levelness and firmness, almost a warning, in his tone that brought me up short.

Instead of protesting, I struggled for several moments trying to understand what he was trying to tell me, then surrendered with a shake of my head.

"I don't get it, Aahz. Doesn't everyone want to be liked?"

"Maybe at some level," my partner said. "But most people realize it's a wistful hope at best . . . like it would be nice if it only rained when we want it to. The reality is that it rains when it bloody well feels like it, and that some people aren't going to like you no matter what you do. The up side is that there are also people who will *like* you no matter what you do."

"I can't accept that," I said, shaking my head. "It's too fatalistic. If you're right, then there's no point in trying at all."

"Of course there is," Aahz snapped. "Just don't take everything to extremes. Okay? Reality always lies somewhere between the extremes. Not trying at all to have people like you is as silly as trying too much."

"Is that what I've been doing? Trying too much?"

My partner waggled his hand in front of him in a so-so gesture.

"Sometimes you drift dangerously close," he said. "I think that sometimes you let your desire to be liked get out of proportion. When that happens, it starts to warp your perception of yourself and the world."

"Could you give me an example or two?"

"Sure," he said easily. "Let's start with an easy one . . . like taxes. Part of your job right now is to be a consultant on the taxes being levied on the citizens. Right?"

I nodded.

". . . Except that people don't *like* to pay taxes. If they had their druthers, they would get the protection and services of the kingdom without paying a cent. Of course, they also realize that something for nothing is an unrealistic situation, so they accept the necessary evil of taxes.

They accept it, but the don't like it. Because they don't *like* it, there is going to be an ongoing level of resentment and grumbling. Whatever the tax assessment is, it's too high, and whatever the level of services is, it's too low. That resentment is going to be forced on anyone involved with setting the taxes, which includes you and everyone else who works at the castle."

He shook his head.

"What I'm saying is that if you're in a position of decision making and power, such as you are now, you can forget about being *liked* by the people who are affected by your decisions. The best you can hope for is *respect*."

"Wait a minute," I said, "are you saying that people can respect you without liking you?"

"Sure," Aahz said easily. "That one I can give you dozens of examples on. Since we're on the subject of taxes and finances, consider Grimble. You respect his skill and dedication even though you don't particularly like him as a person. Right?"

I had to admit that he was right there.

"Better still," he continued, "think back to when you and I first paired up. I was pretty rough on you with the magik lessons, and made you practice even when you didn't feel up to it. You didn't like me for drilling you constantly, but you did respect me."

"Um . . . Well, I didn't know you as well then as I do now," I said uneasily. "At the time, though, I guess I had to believe that you knew what you were doing, and that what you were putting me through was necessary for the learning process . . . whether I liked it or not."

"Precisely," Aahz nodded. "Don't feel bad. It's the normal reaction to an authority figure, whether it's a parent, a teacher, a boss, or a government representative. One doesn't always *like* what they make us do, but even in the midst of disliking being forced to do something, one can still admire and respect the fairness and expertise with which they do their job."

He shrugged easily.

"I guess that's it in a nutshell," he said. "You're a

likeable young man, Skeeve, but sometimes I think you should worry less about being liked and more about being respected. If nothing else, it's a more realizable goal."

I thought about what he had said for a few minutes.

"You're right, Aahz," I said finally. "Being respected *is* more important than being liked."

With that, I veered off to head in a different direction than the one we had been walking.

"Where are you going, partner?"

"I'm going to see Bunny," I called back. "There's a conversation we started this morning that I think we should finish."

I had a fair amount of time to think about what I wanted to say before I reached Bunny's room. It didn't help. When I got there, I was still as much at a loss of how to express my thoughts as when I started out.

I paused for a few moments, then rapped lightly on her door before I lost my nerve. Truth to tell, I was half hoping she was out or asleep, which would let me off my self-imposed hook.

"Who is it?"

So much for half-hopes. Maybe next time I should try a whole one.

"It's me, Bunny. Skeeve."

"What do you want?"

"I'd like to talk to you, if it's all right."

There was a silence that lasted just long enough for me to both get my hopes up, and to start seriously worrying.

"Just a minute."

As I waited, I could hear occasional sounds of metallic clanking, as if someone was moving stacks of iron plates . . . *heavy* iron plates, from the sound of it. This puzzled me, as I could think of no reason why Bunny would have metal plates in her room.

Then it occurred to me that she might have someone else in there with her.

"I can come back later, if this is a bad time," I called, shutting my mind on trying speculate who might be in my assistant's quarters at this hour . . . and why.

In response, the door flew open, and Bunny stood framed in the doorway.

"Come on in, Skeeve," she said, rather breathlessly. "This is a surprise."

It certainly was.

Silhouetted against the light, at first I thought she was stark naked. Then she turned, and I realized she was actually wearing a brightly colored outfit that was skintight and hugged her body like it was painted on.

"Umm . . ." I said smoothly, unable to tear my eyes from her form.

"Sorry I'm such a mess," she said, grabbing up a towel and beginning to dab the sweat from her face and throat. "I was just working out."

Now, as you know, I've gotten pretty intense while working out my own problems in the past, but I've never felt the need to wear a special outfit while doing it. Then again, I've *never* worked up the kind of sweat doing it that Bunny seemed to. Whatever her problems were, they must be dillies.

"Is there anything I can do to help?" I said, genuinely concerned.

"No thanks," she smiled. "I was pretty much done when you knocked. Maybe sometime you can come in and spot for me, though."

Now she had lost me completely. Spot what? And how would spotting anything help her work things out?

"So what's up?" she said, perching on the edge of her bed.

Whatever her problems were, they didn't seem to have her particularly upset. I decided to hold off on trying to sort them out, at least, until I had settled what I came here to do.

"Basically, Bunny," I said, "I wanted to apologize to you."

"For what?" she seemed genuinely puzzled.

"For how I acted this morning . . . or whenever it was that I woke up."

"Oh that," she said, looking away. "There's no need to apologize. Everyone gets a bit out of sorts when they have a hangover."

It was nice of her to say that, but I wasn't about to let it slide.

"No, there's more to it than that, Bunny. You tried to raise some valid concerns about my health and well being, and I gave you a rough time because I wasn't ready to hear what you were saying. I guess I didn't want to hear it. With everything else I've been trying to sort out, I really didn't want one more problem to complicate things."

I paused and shook my head.

"I just wanted you to know that since then, I've been thinking about what you said. I've decided that you may be right about my having a drinking problem. I'm not sure, mind you, but there's enough doubt in my mind that I'm going to try to ease up for a while."

I sat down on the bed beside her, and put my arm around her shoulders.

"Whether you were right or not, though, I wanted to thank you for your caring and concern. That's what I *should* have said this morning instead of getting defensive."

Suddenly, she was hugging me, her face buried in my chest.

"Oh Skeeve," came her muffled voice. "I just get so worried about you. I know you're in the middle of making some rough decisions, and I try not to add to your problems. I just wish there was something more I could do to ease things for you, but it seems that when I try to help, I just make things worse for you."

Gradually, I became aware that she was crying softly, though I wasn't sure why. Also, I became *very* aware that there weren't many clothes between me and the body she was pressing against me . . . and that we were sitting on a bed . . . and . . .

I shut the door on that portion of my thoughts, vaguely ashamed of myself. Bunny was obviously upset and concerned for me. It was ignoble of me to taint the moment by entertaining thoughts of . . .

I shut the mental door again.

"Come on, Bunny," I said softly, stroking her hair with one hand. "You *are* a big help to me. You know and I know that I'd be lost trying to straighten out the kingdom's finances without your knowledge. You've taken that whole burden on yourself."

I took her by the shoulders and held her away from me so that I could look into her eyes.

"As to doing more," I continued, "you're already trying harder which is probably wise. Like this morning when you talked to me about my drinking problem. I appreciate it . . . I really do. Some things I just have to work out for myself, though. That's the way it should be. Nobody else can or should make my decisions for me, since I'm the one who is going to have to live with the repercussions. All that you can do . . . all that anyone can do . . . to help me right now is to be patient with me. Okay?"

She nodded and wiped her eyes.

"Sorry about the waterworks," she said wryly. "Gods. The first time you come to my room, and I look like a mess."

"Now *that* is silly." I smiled, touching my finger to the end of her nose in mock severity. "You look terrific . . . like you always do. If you *don't* know that, you should."

After that, it was only natural to kiss her . . . a short, friendly kiss. At least, that's the way it started out. Then it started to last longer, and longer, and her body seemed to melt against mine.

"Well, I better say good night now," I said, pulling away from her. "Big day tomorrow."

That was a blatant lie, as tomorrow promised to be no more or less busy for me than any other day. I realized, however, that if I didn't break things up, and our physical involvement grew, I'd have trouble convincing myself that the reason I had come to Bunny's room was to apologize and thank her for her concern.

For a mad moment, I thought she was going to protest

my leaving. If she had, I'm not sure the strength of my resolve would have been sufficient to get me out the door.

She started to say something, then stopped and drew a deep breath instead.

"Good night, Skeeve," she said finally. "Come and see me again sometime . . . soon."

To say the least, there were many distracting thoughts dancing in my head as I made my way back to my room.

Bunny had come on to me pretty strong when we first met, and I had backed her off. Having made such a big thing out of keeping our relationship on a professional basis, could I now reverse my stance without making a complete fool of myself? Would she let me? She seemed to still be interested, but then again I might simply be kidding myself.

Then, too, there was the question of whether or not I had any right to be shopping around for a new relationship while I was still making up my mind on Queen Hemlock's proposal. The night with Cassandra had been an adventure and a learning experience, but even I couldn't kid myself that getting involved with Bunny would be a brief fling.

What was it exactly that I wanted . . . and from who?

Still lost in thought, I opened the door to my room . . . and found a demon waiting for me.

XIV:

"Take a walk on the wild side."

—G. GEBEL-WILLIAMS

Now, those of you who have been following my adventures are aware that there is nothing new about my finding a demon in my room. It's not all that unusual these days, though I still have trouble from time to time getting used to it.

Of course, some demon visitors are more welcome than others.

This one was a cute little number. She had close-cropped brown hair which framed a round face with big, wide-set almond-shaped eyes, a pert little nose, and small, heart-shaped lips. She also had a generous number of curves in all the right places, which the harem outfit she was wearing showed off with distracting clarity. The only trouble was, she was tiny. Not "small," mind you . . . tiny.

The figure in front of me, delectable as it might be, was only about four inches high and floated in midair.

"Hi!" the diminutive lady chirped in a musical voice. "You must be Skeeve. I'm Daphnie."

There was a time when I would have found the effect
unsettling. Courtesy of my recent travels, however, I had
seen it before.

"Don't tell me, let me guess," I said in my most off-
worldly, casual manner. "You're a Djin. Right? From
Djinger?"

"Well . . . a Djeanie, actually. But if we're going to be
friends, no wisecracks about the Djeanie with the light
brown hair. Okay?"

I stared at her for a moment, waiting for her to provide
the rest of what was obviously supposed to be a joke.
Instead of continuing, though, she simply looked back at
me expectantly.

"Okay," I agreed finally. "That shouldn't be hard."

She peered at me for a moment longer, then shook her
head.

"You must be the only one in the known dimensions
who doesn't know that song," she said. "Are you *sure*
you're Skeeve? The Great Skeeve?"

"Well . . . yes. Do we know each other?"

Realizing how stupid the question was, I hastened to
modify it before she could answer.

"No. I'm sure I would have remembered if we had met
before."

For some reason, my clumsy recovery seemed to please
her.

"That's sweet," she said, floating forward to run a soft
hand along my cheek, light as a butterfly's touch. "No. I
haven't had the pleasure. We have a mutual acquaintance,
though. Do you remember a Djin named Kalvin?"

"Kalvin? Sure. He gave me a hand a while back when
I was on Perv."

"On Perv, eh?" she said, looking lost in thought for a
moment, but then she brightened. "Well he mentioned you
and said that if I was ever out this way, I should drop in
and say 'Hi' for him."

"Really? That's nice of him . . . I mean, you."

I was pleasantly surprised by Kalvin's thoughtfulness.
I don't get many social visitors from off world, mostly

just those who are looking for help on one thing or another. It also occurred to me that I had never thought of dropping in to pay social calls to any of the various people I had met on my many adventures, and made a mental note to correct that situation.

"So, how's Kalvin doing? Is he fitting back into life on Djinger okay after being gone so long?"

"Oh. He's okay," the Djeanie said shrugging her shoulders . . . which had an interesting effect on a shapely body in a harem outfit. "You know how it is. It always takes a while to get back in stride after a sabbatical."

"Say . . . if we're going to be talking for a while, would you mind enlarging to my size? It would make conversation easier."

To be honest with you, after having watched what happened when she shrugged her shoulders, I was interested in seeing her body on a larger scale. If nothing else, it would get rid of the uncomfortable feeling that I was getting physically interested in a talking doll.

"No problem," she said, and waved her arms.

The air rippled and shimmered, and she was standing in front of me at my size. Well, actually, a little less than a head shorter than me, which placed me in the tantalizing position of looking down at her.

"Say, is this a monastery or something?"

"What? Oh. No, this is the Royal Palace of Possiltum." I said. "Why? Do I look like a monk?"

That was, of course, supposed to be a trick question. I was really rather proud of my wardrobe these days, and any monk who dressed the way I did was way out of line with his vows of poverty.

"Not really," she admitted. "But you seem to be showing an awful lot of interest in my cleavage for someone who's supposed to be as well traveled as the Great Skeeve. Don't they have women on this dimension?"

I guess I had been staring a bit, but hadn't expected her to notice . . . or, if she did, to comment on it. However if there's one thing my years with Aahz have taught me, it's how to cover my shortcomings with words.

"Yes, we have women here," I said with an easy smile. "Frankly, though, I think your cleavage would be stared at no matter what dimension you visited."

She dimpled and preened visibly.

"As starable as it is, however," I continued casually, "my actual interest was professional. Aside from Kalvin, you're the only native of Djinger that I've met, and I was wondering if that stunt you do changing size is a disguise spell, or if it's true shape shifting."

Not bad for a quick out from an embarrassing situation, if I do say so myself. Anyway, Daphnie seemed to accept it.

"Oh that," she said, shrugging her shoulders again. This time, however, I managed to maintain eye contact. No sense pushing my luck. "It's the real thing . . . shape shifting, that is. It's one of the first things a Djin . . . or, especially a Djeanie . . . has to learn. When your whole dimension is in the wish biz, you've got to be able to cater to all kinds of fantasies."

My mind went a little out of focus for a moment as it darted across several unprintable fantasies I could think of involving Daphnie, but she was still going.

"It's not just size either . . . well, height, I mean. We can shift to any proportions necessary for the local pinup standards. Check this out."

With that, she proceeded to treat me to one of the most impressive arrays of female bodies I've ever seen . . . except they were all her! In quick succession, she became willowy, then buxom, then long-legged, while at the same time changing her hair length and color, as well as changing her complexion from delicately pale to a darker hue than her normal cinnamon hue. I decided then and there that wherever this pinup dimension was, I should make a point of dropping in for a visit . . . soon.

My other reaction was far less predictable. Maybe it was because I had been thinking so much about women and marriage lately, but, while watching her demonstrating her shape shifting skills, it popped into my head that she would be an interesting wife. I mean, think of it: a

woman who could assume any size, shape, or personality
at will! It would certainly ease the fears of being bored
living with one woman for the rest of your life.

"Very impressive," I said, forcing my previous train of
thought to a halt. "Tell me, have you ever considered a
career in modeling?"

Daphnie's eyes narrowed for a moment, then her face
relaxed again.

"I'll assume that was meant as a compliment. Right?"
she said.

That one had me really confused.

"Of course," I said. "Why? Isn't it?"

"I'm so attractive, I could make a living at it. Is that
what you were thinking?"

"Well . . . Yes. Even though when you put it that way,
it *does* sound a little dubious."

"You don't know the half of it," the Djeanie said, rolling her eyes.

"Look, Skeeve. I tried that game once . . . and you're
right, I can do it and there's good money in it. It's what
goes with it that's a pain."

"I don't understand," I admitted.

"First of all, even though the job may look glamourous
from the outside, it isn't. It's long hours in uncomfortable
conditions, you know? I mean, it's fun for most people
to go to the beach, but try sitting in the same spot for six
hours while waves break over you so the jerk photographer can get 'just the right look and lighting' . . . and even
then more often than not they don't use the shot."

I nodded sympathetically, all the while wondering what
a photographer was and why she would hold still while
he shot at her.

"Then again folks think there's a lot of status attached
to being a model," she continued. "There's about as much
status as being a side of beef on a butcher's block. You
may be the center of attention, but to the people working
with you, you're just so many pounds of meat to be po-
sitioned and marketed. Now mind you, I like having my
body touched as much as the next woman, but I like to

think that while it's going on, whoever's doing it is thinking of *me*. The way it is, it's like you're a mannequin or a puppet being maneuvered for effect."

"Uh-huh," I said, thinking that if I ever got a chance to touch her body, I'd certainly be keeping my mind on her in the process.

"Of course, there's always the job of keeping the equipment in shape. Most women feel they'd look better if they lost a couple pounds or firmed up the muscle tone . . . and they even work at it occasionally. Well, let me tell you, when your livelihood depends on your looks, keeping the bod in shape is more than a leisure-time hobby. It's a full-time project. Your whole life is centered around diets and exercise, not to mention maintaining your complexion and hair. Sure, I have an advantage because I can shape shift, but believe me, the less you have to do magikally, the less strain you put on the system and the longer the machine lasts.

"Which brings up another point: Whatever you do to maintain your looks, it's a losing fight with time. Djeanies may have a longer life span than some of the women from other dimensions, but eventually age catches up with everyone. Strategic features that once used to catch the eye start to droop and sag, the skin on the neck and hands starts to look more and more like wet tissue paper, and faster than you can say 'old crone,' you're back out the door and they've replaced you from the bottomless pool of young hopefuls. Terrific, huh?"

That one made me think a bit. One thing about being a magician was that age wasn't a prime factor. Heck, for a while when I was starting out, I used my disguise spell to make myself look older because no one would believe that a young magician would be any good. The idea of losing one's job simply because one had grown older was a terrifying concept. I found myself being glad that most jobs didn't have the age restrictions that modeling seemed to.

"Then, just to top things off," the Djeanie said, "there's the minor detail of how people treat you. Most men are intimidated by your looks and won't come near you on a bet. They'll stare and drool, and maybe fantasize a little, but they won't try to date you. Unless they have stellar looks themselves or an iron-clad ego, they're afraid of creating a 'Beauty and the Beast' comparison. The ones who do come on to you usually have a specific scenario in mind . . . and that doesn't involve you either talking or thinking at all. They want an ornament, and if there's actually a person inside that glamourous package, they're not only surprised, they're a little annoyed."

She sighed and shook her head.

"Sorry to ramble like that, but it's a pet peeve of mine. When you stop to think about it, it's a little sad to think of women who feel that all they have to offer the world is their looks. Personally, I like to think I have more to offer than that."

Taking a deep breath, she blew it all out noisily, then smiled and cocked her head at me.

"Um . . . How about if I just say that I think you look fantastic, and forget about speculating on your potential as a model?" I said cautiously.

"Then I'd say 'Thank you, kind sir'. You aren't so bad looking yourself."

She smiled and made a small curtsey. I successfully resisted an impulse to bow back to her.

Mostly, I was trying to think of what we could talk about next, having exhausted the subject of beauty.

"So, how do you know Kalvin?" Daphnie said, solving the problem for me. "He made it sound like the two of you were old buddies."

Now we were back on familiar footing.

"Actually, I bought him over at the Bazaar at Deva. Well, to be accurate, I bought his bottle. I only was en- titled to one wish from him . . . but I don't need to explain that to you. You probably know the drill better than I do. I didn't get to know him until a couple years later when I got around to opening the bottle."

"I don't understand," she said, frowning prettily. "Why

did you buy his bottle if you weren't going to use it for several years?"

"Why I bought it in the first place is a long story," I said, rolling my eyes comically. "As to why I didn't use it for so long, I'm part of a fairly impressive team of magik users . . . the head of it, actually. We do a pretty good job of handling most problems that come up on our own without calling on outside help."

Okay. So I was blowing my own trumpet a bit. Even though I didn't know if anything would ever develop between us, she was cute enough that I figured that it couldn't hurt to impress her a little.

"So he was with you the whole time? From when you purchased his bottle until his discharged his duty on Perv? When was that, exactly?"

She didn't seem very impressed. If anything, it was as if she was more interested in asking questions about Kalvin than in learning about me, a situation I found slightly annoying.

"Oh, it wasn't all that long ago," I said. "Just a couple weeks back, in fact. Of course, time doesn't advance at the same rate on all the dimensions . . . as I'm sure you know."

"True," she said, thoughtfully. "Tell me, did he say he was going straight back to Dijinger? Or was he going to stop somewhere along the way, first?"

"Let me think. As I recall, he didn't . . . Wait a minute. Didn't he make it back to Djinger? I thought you said that he was the one who told you to look me up."

I was both concerned and confused. If Daphnie was looking for Kalvin, then how had she found out about me? I didn't know any other Djins . . . or anyone who traveled to Djinger on a regular basis.

"Oh, he made it back all right," she shrugged. "I was just a little curious about . . ."

There was a soft BAMF, and a second Djin materialized in the room. This one I recognized immediately as Kalvin, who I had just been speaking to Daphnie about. I could tell at a glance, though, that something was wrong.

XV:

*"Blessed are the peacemakers, for they
shall take flack from both sides."*

—UNOFFICIAL UN MOTTO

I had gotten to know Kalvin pretty well during my trip
to Perv, and all through that adventure he had been as
unshakable in a crisis as anyone I had ever known. Now,
however, he was exhibiting all the classic symptoms of
someone who was about to lose control of his temper . . .
clenched teeth, furrowed brow, tight expression, the
works.

Fortunately, his anger seemed to be directed at my
guest rather than at me.

"I should have known!" he snarled, without so much
as a nod to acknowledge my presence. "I should have
checked here first as soon as I found out you were gone."

It occurred to me that, as little as I knew about Djins,
that it could be markedly unhealthy to have one upset with
you. Realizing that magik, like a knife, could be used both
benevolently *or* destructively, my first instinct probably
would have been to try to calm him down quickly . . . or
to vacate the premises.

To my surprise, however, the Djeanie spun around and leveled what seemed to be an equal amount of anger back at him.

"Oh, I see," she spat back. "It's all right for *you* to disappear for years at a time, but as soon as I step out the door, you've got to come looking for me!"

The interest I had been feeling in Daphnie came to a screeching halt. In the space of a few seconds her personality had changed from a flirtatious coquette to a shrill shrew. Then, too, there seemed to be more to her relationship with Kalvin than just an "acquaintance" as she had billed it.

"That was business," the Djin was saying, still nose to nose with my visitor. "You know, the stuff that puts food on the table for our whole dimension? Besides, if you were just going out to kick up your heels a bit I wouldn't care. What I DO mind is your sneaking off to check up on me."

"So what? It shouldn't bother you ... unless you haven't been telling me *everything*, that is."

"What bothers me is that you can't bring yourself to believe me," Kalvin shot back. "Why do you even bother asking me anything if you aren't going to believe I'm telling you the truth?"

"I *used* to believe everything you told me. YOU taught me how stupid that was. Remember?"

This seemed to be going nowhere fast, so I summoned my courage and stepped forward to intervene.

"Excuse me, but I thought you two were friends."

Kalvin broke off his arguing to spare me a withering look.

"Friends? Is that what she told you?"

He rounded on the Djeanie again.

"You know, babe, for someone who keeps accusing me of lying, you play pretty fast and loose with the truth yourself!"

"Don't be silly," the Djeanie said. "If I had told him I was your wife, he would have just covered for you. You

think I don't know how you men lie to protect each
other?"

"Wait a minute," I interrupted. "Did you say 'wife'?
Are you two married?"

Whatever was left of my interest in Daphnie died without a whimper.

"Sure," Kalvin said with a grimace. "Can't you tell by
the loving and affection we shower on each other? Of
course we're married. Do you think either of us would
put up with this abuse from a stranger?"

He gave a brief shake of his head, and for a moment
seemed to almost return to normal.

"By the way, Skeeve, good to see you again," he said,
flashing a tight smile. "Sorry to have forgotten my manners, but I get . . . Anyway, even though it may be a bit
late, I'd like to introduce you to my wife, Daphnie."

"Well, at least now I know what it takes to be intro-
duced to one of your business friends."

And they were off again.

There was a knock on the door.
       I answered it, thinking as I did that it was nice to
know at least a few people who came into my room the
normal way . . . which is to say, by the door . . . instead of
simply popping in unannounced.

"Is everything okay, Boss? I thought I heard voices."

"Sure," I said, "it's just . . . Guido?"

My mind had to grapple with several images and concepts simultaneously, and it wasn't doing so hot. First was
the realization that Guido was back from his mission as
a special tax envoy. Second, that he had his arm in a sling.

The latter probably surprised me more than the former.
After all our time together, I had begun to believe that
my bodyguards were all but invulnerable. It was a little
unsettling to be reminded that they could be hurt physically like anyone else.

"What are you doing back?" I said. "And what happened to your arm?"

Instead of answering, he peered suspiciously past me at the arguing Djins.

"What's goin' on in there, Boss?" he demanded. "Who are those two jokers, anyway?"

I was a little surprised that he could hear and see my visitors, but then I remembered that it's only while a Djin is under contract that he or she can only be seen and heard by the holder of their bottle.

"Oh, those are just a couple friends of mine," I said. "Well . . . sort of friends. I thought they were dropping by to say 'Hi,' but, as you can see, things seem to have gotten a little out of hand. The one with the beard is Kalvin, and the lady he's arguing with is his wife, Daphnie."

I thought it was a fairly straightforward explanation, but Guido recoiled as if I had struck him.

"Did you say 'his wife'?"

"That's right. Why?"

My bodyguard stepped forward to place himself between me and the arguing couple.

"Get out of here, Boss," he said quietly.

"What?"

At first I thought I had misunderstood him.

"Boss," he hissed with aggravated patience. "I'm your bodyguard. Right? Well, as your bodyguard and the one currently responsible for the well bein' of your continued health, I'm tellin' you to get out of here!"

"But . . ."

Apparently Guido wasn't willing to debate the point further. Instead, he scooped me up with his good arm and carried me out the door into the corridor, where he deposited me none too gently against the wall beside the doorway.

"Now stay here," he said, shaking a massive finger in my face. "Got that? *Stay here!*"

I recognized the tone of his voice. It was the same as when I tried to give Gleep a simple command . . . for the third or fourth time after he had been steadfastly ignoring me. I decided I would try to prove that I was smarter than my pet by actually following orders.

"Okay, Guido," I said, with a curt nod. "Here it is."

He hesitated for a moment, eyeing me as if to see if I was going to make a break for the door. Then he gave a little nod of satisfaction, turned, and strode into my room, closing the door behind him.

While I couldn't make out the exact words, I heard the arguing voices cease for a moment. Then they were raised again in angry chorus, punctuated by Guido's voice saying something. Then there was silence.

After a few long moments of stillness, the door opened again.

"You can come in now, Boss," my bodyguard announced. "They're gone."

I left my post by the wall and re-entered my room. A quick glance around was all it took to confirm my bodyguard's claim. The Djins had departed for destinations unknown. Surprisingly enough, my immediate reaction was to be a little hurt that they hadn't bothered to say goodbye.

I also realized that I wanted a goblet of wine, but suppressed the desire. Instead, I perched on the side of the bed.

"All right, Guido," I said. "What was that all about?"

"Sorry to barge in like that, Boss," my bodyguard said, not looking at all apologetic. "You know that's not my normal style."

"So what were you doing?"

"What I was doin' was my job," he retorted. "As your bodyguard, I was attemptin' to protect you from bein' hurt or maybe even killed. It's what you pay me for, accordin' to my job description."

"Protecting me? From those two? Com'on, Guido. They were just arguing. They weren't even arguing with me. It was a family squabble between the two of them."

"*Just arguing?*" my bodyguard said, looming over me. "*What do you think . . .*"

He broke off suddenly and stepped back, breathing heavy.

I was genuinely puzzled. I couldn't recall having seen

Guido more upset, but I really couldn't figure out what was bothering him.

"Sorry, Boss," he said finally, in a more normal tone. "I'm still a little worked up after that close call. I'll be all right in a second."

"What close call?" I pressed. "They were just . . ."

"I know, I know," he said, waving me to silence. "They were just arguing."

He took a deep breath and flexed his arms and hands.

"You know, Boss, I keep forgettin' how inexperienced you are. I mean, you may be tops in the magik department, but when it comes to my specialty, which is to say rough and tumble stuff, you're still a babe in the woodwork."

A part of me wanted to argue this, since I had been in some pretty nasty scrapes over the years, but I kept my mouth shut. Guido and his cousin Nunzio were specialists, and if nothing else over the years I've learned to respect expertise.

"You see, Boss, people say that guys like me and Nunzio are not really all that different from the cops . . . that it's the same game on different sides of the line. I dunno. It may be true. What I am sure of, though, is that both we and our counterparts agree on one thing: The most dangerous situation to stick your head into . . . the situation most likely to get you dead fast . . . isn't a shoot-out or a gang war. It's an ordinary D&D scenario."

"D&D," I frowned. "You mean that game you were telling me about with the maps and the dice?"

"No. I'm takin' about a 'domestic disturbance.' A family squabble . . . just like you had goin' on here when I came in. They're deadly, Boss. Especially one between a husband and wife."

I wanted to laugh, but he seemed to be utterly serious about what he was saying.

"Are you kidding, Guido?" I said. "What could happen that would be dangerous?"

"More things than you can imagine," he replied. "That's what makes them so dangerous. In regular hassles,

you can pretty much track what's going on and what
might happen next. Arguments between a husband and
wife are unpredictable, though. You can't tell who's
gonna swing at who, when or with what, because they
don't know themselves."

I was beginning to believe what he was saying. The
concept was both fascinating and frightening.

"Why do you think that is, Guido? What makes fights
between married couples so explosive?"

My bodyguard frowned and scratched his head.

"I never really gave it much thought," he said. "If I had
to give an opinion, I'd say it was due to the motivation-
als."

"The motives?" I corrected without thinking.

"That too," he nodded. "You see, Boss, the business-
type disputes which result in violence like I am normally
called upon to deal with have origins that are easily com-
prehended . . . like greed or fear. That is to say, either
Boss A wants somethin' that Boss B is reluctant to part
with, as in a good-sized hunk of revenue generatin' territory, or Boss B is afraid that Boss A is gonna try to
whack him and decides to beat him to the punch. In these
situationals, there is a clear-cut objective in mind, and the
action is therefore relatively easy to predict and counter.
Know what I mean?"

"I think so," I said. "And in a domestic disturbance?"

"That's where it can get ugly," he grimaced. "It starts
out with people arguin' when they don't know why
they're arguin'. What's at stake there is emotions and hurt
feelin's, not money. The problem with that is that there
is no clear-cut objective, and as a result, there is no way
of tellin' when the fightin' should cease. It just keeps es-
calatin' up and up, with both sides dishin' out and takin'
more and more damage, until each of 'em is hurt so bad
that the only important thing left is to hurt the other one
back."

He smacked his fist loudly into his other hand, wincing
slightly when he moved his injured arm.

"When it explodes," he continued, "you don't want to

be anywhere near ground zero. One will go at the other, or they'll go at each other, with anything that's at hand. The worst part is, and the reason neither us or the cops want to try to mess with it, is that if you try to break it up, chances are that they'll both turn on you. You see, mad as they are, they'll still reflexively protect each other from any outside force ... into which category will fall you or anyone else who tries to interfere. That's why the best policy, if you have a choice at all, is to get away from them and wait until the dust settles before venturin' close again."

This was all very interesting, particularly since I was in the middle of contemplating marriage myself. However, my bodyguard's wince had reminded me of the unanswered question originally raised by his appearance.

"I think I understand now, Guido," I said. "Thanks. Now tell me, what happened to your arm? And what are you doing back at the palace?"

Guido seemed a little taken aback at the sudden change of topic.

"Sorry I didn't check in as soon as I got back, Boss," he said, looking uncomfortable. "It was late and I thought you were already asleep ... until I heard that argument in process, that is. I would have let you know first thing in the morning."

"Uh-huh," I said. "No problem. But since we're talking now, what happened?"

"We ran into a little trouble, is all," he said, looking away. "Nothin' serious."

"Serious enough to put your arm in a sling," I observed. "So what happened?"

"If it's okay with you, Boss, I'd rather not go into details. Truth is, it's more than a little embarrassing."

I was about to insist, then thought better of it. Guido never asked for much from me, but it seemed right now he was asking that I not push the point. The least I could do was respect his privacy.

"All right," I said slowly. "We'll let it ride for now. Will you be able to work with that arm?"

"In a pinch, maybe. But not at peak efficiency," he admitted. "That's really what I wanted to talk to you about, Boss. Is there any chance you can assign Nunzio to be Pookie's backup while I take over his duties here?"

Realizing how infatuated Guido was with Pookie, it was quite a request. Still, I was reluctant to go along with it.

"I don't know, Guido," I said "Nunzio's been working with Gleep to try to figure out what's wrong with him. I kind of hate to pull him off that until we have some answers. Tell you what. How about if I talk to Chumley about helping out?"

"Chumley?" my bodyguard frowned. "I dunno, Boss. Don't you think that him bein' a troll would tend to scare folks in these parts?"

Realizing that both Guido and Nunzio relied heavily on intimidation in their work, this was an interesting objection. Still, he had a point.

"Doesn't Pookie have a disguise spell or something that could soften Chumley's appearance?" I suggested. "I was assuming that she wasn't wandering around the country-side showing the green scales of a Pervect."

"Hey! That's right! Good idea, Boss," Guido said, brightening noticeably. "In that case, no problem. Chumley's as stand up as they come."

"Okay, I'll talk to him first thing in the morning."

"Actually, Chumley's a better choice than Nunzio," my bodyguard continued, almost to himself. "Pookie's still kinda upset over shootin' me, and Nunzio would probably . . ."

"Whoa! Wait a minute! Did you say that *Pookie* shot you?"

Guido looked startled for a moment, then he drew himself up into a wall of righteous indignation.

"Really, Boss," he said. "I thought we agreed that we wasn't gonna talk about this. Not for a while, anyway."

XVI:

*"Marriage is a fine institution . . . if one
requires institutionalizing."*

—S. FREUD

"Hi, Chumley. Mind if I come in?"
The troll looked up from his book, and his enor-
mous mouth twisted into a grin of pleasure.

"Skeeve, old boy!" he said. "Certainly. As a matter of
fact, I've been expecting you."

"Really?" I said, stepping into his room and looking
around for somewhere to sit.

"Yes. I ran into Guido this morning, and he explained
the situation to me. He said you were going to be calling
on me for a bit of work. I was just killing time waiting
for the official word, is all."

I wondered if the briefing my bodyguard had given
Chumley was any more detailed than what he had told
me.

"It's all right with you, then?" I said. "You don't
mind?"

"Tish tosh. Think nothing of it," the troll said. "Truth
to tell, I'll be glad to have a specific assignment again.

I've been feeling a bit at loose ends lately. In fact, I was starting to wonder why I was staying around at all."

That touched a nerve in me. It had been some time since I had even stopped by to say "Hello" to Chumley.

"Sorry if I've been a bit distant," I said guiltily. "I've been . . . busy . . . and . . ."

"Quite right," Chumley said with a grin and a wink. "Caught a glimpse of your workload when you rolled in the other night. Bit of all right, that."

I think I actually blushed.

"No really," I stammered. "I've been . . ."

"Relax, old boy," the troll waved. "I was just pulling your leg a bit. I know you've been up against it, what with the Queen after you and all. By the by, I've got a few thoughts on that, but I figured it would be rude to offer advice when none had been asked for."

"You do? That's terrific," I said, and meant it. "I've been meaning to ask your opinion, but wasn't sure how to bring it up."

"I believe you just have, actually," Chumley grinned. "Pull up a chair."

I followed his instructions as he continued.

"Advice on marriage, particularly when it comes to the selection of the partner to be, is usually best kept to one-self. The recipients usually already have their minds made up, and voicing any opinion contradictory to their decision can be hazardous to one's health. Since you've actually gotten around to asking, however, I think you might find my thoughts on the matter to be a tad surprising."

"How's that?"

"Well, most blokes who know me . . . the real me, that is, rather than Big Crunch . . . think of me as a bit of a romantic."

I blinked, but kept a straight face.

While I have the utmost respect for Chumley, I had never thought of him as a romantic figure . . . possibly something to do with his green matted hair and huge eyes of different sizes. While I suppose that trolls have love lives (otherwise, how does one get little trolls?) I'd have to rate their attractiveness in relation to dwellers of other dimensions to be way down near the bottom. Their female counterparts, the trollops, such as his sister Tananda, were a whole different story, of course, but for the trolls themselves . . . on a scale of one to ten, I'd generously score them around negative eighteen.

This particular troll, however, old friend though he might be, was currently sitting within an arm's length of me . . . his arm, not mine . . . and as that arm was substantially stronger than two arms of the strongest human . . . which I'm not . . . I decided not to argue the point with him. Heck, if he wanted to say he was the Queen of May I'd probably agree with him.

"For the most part, they'd be right," Chumley was continuing, "but on the subject of marriage, I can be as coldly analytical as the best of them."

"Terrific," I said. "That's what I was really hoping for. . . . An unemotional, unbiased opinion."

"First, let me ask you a few questions," the troll said.

"All right."

"Do you love her?"

I paused to give the question an honest consideration.

"I don't think so," I said. "Of course, I really don't know all that much about love."

"Does she love you?"

"Again, I don't think so," I said.

I was actually enjoying this. Chumley was breaking things down to where even I could understand his logic.

"Well, has she said she loves you?"

That one I didn't even have to think about.

"No."

"You're sure?" the troll pressed.

"Positive," I said. "The closest she's come is to say she thinks we'd make a good pair. I *think* she meant it as a compliment."

"Good," my friend said, settling back in his chair.

"Excuse me?" I blinked. "For a moment there, I thought you said . . ."

"I said 'Good,' and I meant it," the troll repeated.

"You lost me there," I said. "I thought marriages were supposed to be . . ."

". . . Based on love?" Chumley finished for me. "That's what most young people think. That's also why so many of their marriages fall apart."

Even though he had sort of warned me in advance, I found the troll's position to be a bit unsettling.

"Um, Chumley? Are we differentiating between 'analytical' and 'cynical'?"

"It's not really as insensitive as it sounds, Skeeve," the troll said with a laugh, apparently unoffended by my comment. "You see, when you're young and full of hormones, and come in close contact for the first time with someone of the opposite sex who isn't related to you, you experience feelings and urges that you've never encountered before. Now since, despite their bragging to the contrary, most people are raised to think of themselves as good and decent folks, they automatically attach the socially correct label to these feelings: Love. Of course, there's also a socially correct response when two people feel that way about each other . . . specifically, marriage."

"But isn't that . . ." I began, but the troll held up a restraining hand.

"Hear me out," he said. "Now, continuing with our little saga, eventually passions cool, and the infatuation has run it's course. It might take years, but eventually they find that 'just being together' isn't enough. It's time to get on with life. Unfortunately, right about then they discover that they have little if anything in common. All too often they find that their goals in life are different, or, at the very least, their plans on how to achieve them don't coincide. Then they find, instead of the ideal partner to stand back to back with while taking on the world, they've actually opened a second front. That is, they have to spend as much or more time dealing with each other as they do the rest of the world."

Despite myself, I found I was being drawn in, almost mesmerized, by his oration.

"What happens then?" I said.

"If they are at all rational . . . notice I said 'rational,' not 'intelligent' . . . they go their separate ways. All too often, however, they cling to the concept of 'love' and try to 'make it work.' When that happens, the result is an armed camp living an uneasy truce . . . and nobody's happy . . . or actually achieving their full potential."

I thought about the bickering I had recently witnessed between Kalvin and Daphnie, and about what Guido had told me about domestic disturbances and how they can explode into violence. In spite of myself, I shuddered involuntarily.

"That sounds grim," I said.

"Oh, it is," the troll nodded. "Trying to 'make it work' is the most frustrating, depressing pastime ever invented. The real problem is that they've each ended up with the wrong person, but rather than admit that, they try to gloss things over with cosmetics."

"Cosmetics?"

"Surface changes. Things that really don't matter."

"I don't get it."

"All right," the troll said. "I'll give you an example. The wife says she needs some new clothes, so her husband gives her some money to go out shopping. That's a rather simple and straightforward exchange, wouldn't you say?"

"Well . . . yes."

"Only on the surface," Chumley explained. "Now look at it a little deeper . . . at what's *really* going on. The husband has been getting caught up in his work . . . that's a normal reaction for a man when he gets married and starts feeling 'responsible,' by the way . . . and his wife is feeling unhappy and ignored. Her solution is that she needs some new clothes to make her more attractive so her husband will pay more attention to her. A surface solution to her unhappiness. Now, when she says she needs new clothes, the husband is annoyed because she seems to have a closet full of clothes that she never wears, but rather than argue with her, he gives her some money for shopping . . . again, a surface solution. You'll notice that he simply gives her the money. He doesn't *take* her shopping and help her find some new outfits."

The troll leaned back in his chair and folded his arms.

"From there, it goes downhill. She gets some new clothes and wears them, but the husband either doesn't notice or doesn't comment . . . possibly because he still resents having to pay for what he thinks is a needless purchase. Therefore, buying new clothes . . . her surface solution . . . doesn't work because she still feels ignored and unhappy . . . and a little angry and frustrated that her husband doesn't seem to appreciate her no matter how hard she tries. Her husband, in the meantime, senses that she's still unhappy so that giving her money . . . *his* surface solution . . . didn't work. He feels even more bitter and resentful because now it seems that his wife is going to be upset and unhappy even if he 'gives her everything she's asked for.' You see, by trying to deal with the problem with surface, cosmetic gestures without acknowledging to themselves the real issues, they've actually made things worse instead of better."

He smiled triumphantly as I considered his thesis.

"So you're saying that marriages don't work," I said carefully, "that the concept itself is flawed."

"Not at all," the troll corrected, shaking his head. "I was saying that getting married under the mistaken impression that love conquers all is courting disaster. A proper match between two people who enter into a marriage with their eyes open and free of romantic delusions can result in a much happier life together than they could ever have alone."

"All right," I said. "If love and romance are bad bases for deciding to marry someone because it's too easy to fool yourself, what would you see as a *valid* reason to get married."

"There are lots of them," Chumley shrugged. "Remember when Hemlock first arrived here? Her marriage to Roderick was a treaty and a merger between two kingdoms. It's common among royalty, but you'll find similar matches in the business world as well. In that case, both sides knew what they wanted and could expect, so it worked out fine."

"Sorry, but that seems a bit cold to me," I said, shaking my head.

"Really?" the troll cocked his head. "Maybe I'm phrasing this wrong. What you *don't* want is a situation where there is a hidden agenda on either or both sides. Everything should be up front and on the table . . . like with the Hemlock/Roderick marriage."

"What's a hidden agenda?"

"Hmmm . . . That one's a little hard to explain. Tell me, if you married Queen Hemlock, what would you expect?"

That one caught me totally unprepared.

"I don't know . . . nothing, really," I managed, at last. "I guess I figure that it would pretty much be a marriage in name only, with her going her way and me going mine."

"Good," the troll said emphatically.

"Good?" I echoed. "Com'on, Chumley."

"Good in that you aren't expecting anything. You aren't going into it with the notion of reforming her, or that she'd give up her throne to hover around you adoringly, or any one of a myriad of other false hopes or assumptions that most grooms have on the way to the altar."

"I suppose that's good," I said.

"Good? It's vital," the troll insisted. "Too many people marry the person they *think* their partner will become. They have some sort of idea that a marriage ceremony is somehow magical. That it will eliminate all the dubious traits and habits their partner had when they were single. That's about as unrealistic as if you had expected Aahz to stop being a money-grubber or to shed his temper just because you signed on as an apprentice. Anyway, when their partner keeps right on being the person he or she has been all along, they feel hurt and betrayed. Since they believe that there *should* have been a change, the only conclusion they can reach is that their love wasn't enough to trigger it . . . or, more likely, that there's something wrong with their partner. *That's* when marriages start getting bloody. At least with Queen Hemlock's proposal, nobody's kidding anybody about what's going to happen."

I mulled over his words for a few moments.

"So you're saying that you think I should marry Queen Hemlock," I said.

"Here now. Hold on," the troll said, leaning back and holding up his hands. "I said no such thing. That's the kind of decision that only you can make. I was just commenting on what I see as the more common pitfalls of marriage, is all. If you *do* decide to marry the Queen, there are certain aspects that would weigh in favor of it working . . . but you're the one who has to decide what you want out of a marriage and whether or not this is it."

Terrific. I had been hoping that Chumley's analytic approach would simplify things for me. Instead, he had simply added a wagon load of other factors to be considered. I needed that like Deva needed more merchants.

"Well, I appreciate the input, Chumley," I said, rising from my seat. "You've given me a lot to think about."

"Think nothing of it, old boy. Glad to help."

"And you're all set with the assignment? Guido told you how to hook up with Pookie?"

"Right-o."

I started to go, but paused for one more question.

"By the way, Chumley. Have you ever been married yourself?"

"Me?" the troll seemed genuinely surprised. "Gracious no. Why do you ask?"

"Just curious," I said, and headed out the door.

XVII:

*"What am I supposed to do with all this
gold?"*

—MIDAS, REX

At this point, I had to admit that I was more confused
than ever. It seemed that everyone I talked to had a
different view of marriage, which wasn't making my decision any easier. One thing everyone seemed to agree on,
though: A bad marriage could be a living Hell.

Of course, defining what a good marriage was and how
to avoid a bad one seemed to defy simple explanation . . .
or, at least, one simple enough that I could grasp.

The problem was, as limited as my experience with the
opposite sex was, my knowledge of marriages, good or
bad, was even sketchier. I could barely remember my own
family, I had left home so long ago. The only married
couple I had met on my adventures was the Woof Writers,
and realizing they were werewolves I somehow didn't
think they were a valid role model for me. Then again,
Massha and Badaxe were talking about getting married.
Maybe they could provide some insight for me.

I was considering this possibility as I wandered across

the palace courtyard, when a voice interrupted my thoughts.

"Hey, Partner!"

I had to look around for a moment before I spotted Aahz waving at me from one of the palace's upper windows.

"Where were you this morning? We missed you at the session with Grimble."

"I had to talk to Chumley," I called back. "Guido got hurt, and I had to ask Chumley to stand in for him."

"Whatever," my partner waved. "Go see Grimble. It's important!"

That sounded vaguely ominous, but Aahz seemed chipper enough.

"What's up?"

"Day of the eagle," he yelled, and disappeared from sight.

Terrific!

As I redirected my steps toward Grimble's office, I couldn't help but feel a little annoyed. I mean, with all the other problems plaguing me, I really didn't need the added distraction of talking to Grimble about some bird sanctuary.

"**H**i, Grimble. Aahz said you wanted to see me?"

The Chancellor glanced up to where I was leaning against the doorway.

"Ah. Lord Skeeve," he nodded. "Yes. Come in. This shouldn't take long."

I eased into the room and plopped down in the offered chair.

"What's the problem? Aahz said something about eagles?"

"Eagles? I wonder what he was referring to. No, there's no problem," Grimble said. "If anything, quite the contrary. In fact, the new tax collection process is working well enough that we're now in a positive cash flow situation. What's more, I think that except for dotting a few

I's and crossing a few T's we've got the new budget pretty well nailed down."

He leaned back and favored me with one of his rare smiles.

"Speaking of 'tease,' that's quite a little assistant you have there. I'll admit I'm very impressed with *all* her qualifications. Take my advice and don't let her go . . . as if I had to tell you that."

This was, of course, accompanied by a smirk and a wink.

While I had grown to expect this sort of comment from Grimble whenever the subject of Bunny came up, I found I was no more fond of it than when they had first met. At least now, he was refraining from such behavior in her presence . . . which was a victory of sorts, I suppose. Still, I was annoyed and decided to take another shot at it.

"I'm surprised to hear you talk that way, Grimble," I said. "Are you really so hung up on hormones that you can't just acknowledge her worth as a colleague *without* adding sexual innuendos?"

"Well . . . I . . ." the Chancellor began, but I cut him off.

" . . . Especially realizing that the Queen . . . you know, your employer? . . . is also female. I wonder if she's aware of your slanted views regarding her gender, or, if she isn't, how she'd react if she found out. Do you think she'd just fire you, or would she want to see if you were bluffing, first? From what I can tell, she's as interested in playing around as you claim to be."

Grimble actually blanched which, realizing how pale his complexion was to start with, was quite a sight.

"You wouldn't tell her, would you, Lord Skeeve?" he stammered. "I meant no disrespect to Bunny. Really. She has one of the best financial minds it's been my privilege to work with . . . male or female. I was just trying to make a little joke. You know, man to man? It's one of the rituals of male bonding."

"Not with all males," I pointed out. "Relax, though. You should know me well enough by now to realize it's not my style to go running to the Queen with reports or complaints. Just don't push it so hard in the future. Okay?"

"Thank you, Lord Skeeve. I . . . Thanks. I'll make a point of it."

"Now then," I said, starting to rise, "I assume we're done here? That the report on the collections and budget was what you wanted to see me about?"

"No, that was just a casual update," Grimble corrected, back on familiar ground now. "The real reason I had to see you was this."

He reached somewhere on the floor behind him and produced a large bag which jingled as he plopped it onto his desk.

"I don't understand," I said, eyeing the bag. "What is it?"

"It's your wages," he smiled. "I know that normally you let your assistants handle these matters, but realizing the amount involved due to your promotion, I thought you might like to deal with it personally."

I stared at the bag uncomfortably. It was a very big bag.

Even though I had been persuaded by Aahz and Bunny to accept a sizable wage for my services, looking at a number on a piece of paper was a lot different than actually seeing the equivalent in hard cash.

Perhaps it wouldn't seem like so much after I had paid the others their share . . .

"Your assistants have already picked up their wages," Grimble was saying, "so this is the last payment to complete this round of payroll. If you'll just sign here?"

He pushed a slip of paper across the desk at me, but I ignored it and kept staring at the money bag.

It was a *very* large bag. Especially considering how little I was actually doing.

"Is something wrong, Lord Skeeve?"

For a moment, I actually considered telling him what was bothering me, which is a sign of how upset I was. Grimble is not someone you confide in.

"No. Nothing," I said instead.

"Would you like to count it?" he pressed, apparently still unconvinced.

"Why? Didn't you?"

"Of course I did," the Chancellor bristled, his professional pride stung. I forced a smile.

"Good enough for me. Checking your work would be a waste of both our time, don't you agree?"

I quickly scribbled my name on the receipt, gathered up the bag, and left, carefully ignoring the puzzled look Grimble was leveling at me.

"**Y**ou gonna need us for anything, Boss? You want we should hang around out here?"

"Whatever, Guido," I waved absently as I shut the door. "I'm going to be here for a while, though, if you want to get something to eat. I've got a lot to think over."

"Oh, we already ate. So we'll just . . ."

The door closed and cut off the rest of whatever it was he was saying.

Guido and Nunzio had materialized at my side somewhere during my walk back from Grimble's. I wasn't sure exactly when, as I had been lost in thought and they hadn't said anything until we reached my room. If I had realized they were there, I probably would have had one of them carry the bag of gold for me. It was heavy. Very heavy.

Setting the burden down on my desk, I sank into a chair and stared at it. I had heard of bad pennies coming back to haunt someone, but this was ridiculous.

I had been so absorbed in trying to make up my mind about Queen Hemlock that I hadn't gotten around to my self-appointed task of trying to cut back on my staff or otherwise reduce the M.Y.T.H. Inc. bill to the kingdom. Now, I had the money in hand, and all I felt was guilty.

No matter what Aahz and Bunny said, it still felt wrong to me. Here we were, cutting corners on the budget and squeezing taxes out of the populace to try to shore up the kingdom's financial woes, while I siphoned money out of the treasury that I didn't really need. What was more, since it was my procrastinating on staff cuts that had resulted in the inflated payday, I certainly didn't think I should be rewarded for it.

The more I thought about it, the more determined I became to figure out some way to give the money back. Of course, it would have to be done quietly, almost secretly, or I'd suffer the wrath of both Aahz and Bunny. Still, to me it was necessary if I was going to be able to live with myself.

Then, too, there was the problem of how to reduce our payroll. Actually, if what Grimble had just told me was accurate, that situation might take care of itself. If the budget was coming into balance, and if the collection process was now flowing smoothly, then I could probably send Bunny back to Deva, as well as one or more of my bodyguards. What was more, I could then insist on removing my own payment as financial counselor. All that should reduce the M.Y.T.H. Inc. bill substantially.

That still left me with the problem of how to deal with the disproportionate payment I had already received.

Then an idea struck me. I'd do what any other executive would do when confronted with a problem: I'd delegate it to someone else!

Striding to the door, I opened it and looked into the hall. Sure enough, my two bodyguards were still there, apparently embroiled in conversation with each other.

"Guido! Nunzio!" I called. "Come in here for a second."

I re-entered the room and returned to my desk without waiting to see if they were responding. I needn't have worried.

By the time I had re-seated myself, they were standing in front of me.

"I have a little assignment for you boys," I said, smiling.

"Sure, Boss," they chimed in chorus.

"But first, I want to check something. As long as I've

known you, you've both made it clear that, in the past, you've had no qualms about bending the rules as situations called for it, working outside the law as it were. Is that correct?"

"That's right."

"No problem."

I noticed that, though to the affirmative, their answers were slower and less enthusiastic than before.

"All right. The job I have for you has to be done secretly, with nobody knowing that I'm behind it. Not even Aahz or Bunny. Understand?"

My bodyguards looked even more uncomfortable than before, but nodded their agreement.

"Okay, here's the job," I said, pushing the bag of money towards them. "I want you to take this money and get rid of it."

The two men stared at me, then exchanged glances.

"I don't quite get you, Boss," Guido said at last. "What do you want us to do with it?"

"I don't care and I don't want to know," I said. "I just want this money back in circulation within the kingdom. Spend it or give it to charity."

Just then an idea hit me.

"Better still, figure out some way of passing it around to those people who have been complaining that they can't pay their taxes."

Guido frowned and glanced at his cousin again.

"I dunno, Boss," he said carefully. "It don't seem right, somehow. I mean, we're supposed to be collectin' taxes from people . . . not givin' it to them."

"What Guido means," Nunzio put in, "is that our speciality is extracting funds from people and institutions. Givin' it back is a little out of our line."

"Well then I guess it's about time you expanded your horizons," I said, unmoving. "Anyway, that's the assignment. Understand?"

"Yes, Boss," they chorused, still looking uneasy.

"And remember, not a word about this to the rest of the team."

"If you say so, Boss."

As I've said, the bag was heavy enough to have given me trouble carrying it, but Guido gathered it up easily with his one good hand, then stood hefting it for a moment.

"Umm . . . Are you *sure* you want to do this, Boss?" he said. "It don't seem right, somehow. Most folks would have to work for a lifetime to earn this much money."

"That's my point," I muttered.

"Huh?"

"Never mind," I said. "I'm sure. Now do it. Okay?"

"Consider it done."

They didn't quite salute, but they drew themselves up and nodded before they headed for the door. I recalled they had been working with the army for a while, and guessed that it had rubbed off on them more than they realized.

After they had gone, I leaned back and savored the moment.

I actually felt *good!* It seemed that I had found a solution to at least one of my problems.

Maybe that had been my difficulty all this time. I had been trying to focus on too many unrelated problems at once. Now that the whole money thing was off my back, I could devote my entire attention to the Queen Hemlock situation without interruptions or distractions.

For the first time in a long while, I actually felt optimistic about being able to arrive at a decision.

XVIII:

"It's so easy, a child could do it!"

—THE LEGAL DISCLAIMER FOUND ON
THE INSTRUCTION SHEET OF ANY
"ASSEMBLE IT YOURSELF" KIT

"Blah blah blah flowers, blah blah blah protocol. Understood?"

"Uh-huh," I said, looking out the window.

When I had agreed to hear the plans for the upcoming marriage between Massha and General Badaxe, I had done it without realizing how long it would take or how complex the ceremony would be. After several hours of this, however, I realized that my own part was going to be minimal, and was having a great deal of difficulty paying attention to the myriad of details.

"Of course, blah blah blah . . ."

And they were off again.

A bird landed on a branch outside the window and began gobbling down a worm. I found myself envying him. Not that I was particularly hungry, mind you. It was just that the way my life had been going lately, eating a worm seemed like a preferable alternative.

"Have you got that? Skeeve?"

I jerked my head back to the task at hand, only to find my massive apprentice peering at me intently. Obviously, I had just missed something I was supposed to respond to.

"Umm . . . Not really, Massha. Could you summarize it again briefly so I can be sure I have it right?"

I didn't mean to emphasize the word "briefly," but she caught it anyway.

"Hmmm," she said, fixing me with a suspicious stare. "Maybe we should take a break for a few minutes," she said. "I think we could all do with a good stretch of the legs."

"If you say so, my dear," the General said, rising obediently to his feet.

I admired his stamina . . . and his patience. I was sure that this was as tedious for him as it was for me, but you'd never tell it to look at him.

I started to rise as well, then sank back quickly into my seat as a wave of dizziness hit me.

"Hey Skeeve! Are you all right?"

Massha was suddenly more concerned than she had been a moment before.

"I'm fine," I said, trying to focus my eyes.

"Would you like some wine?"

"*No!!* I mean, I'm all right. Really. I just didn't get much sleep last night is all."

"Uh-huh. Out tom-catting again, were you, Hot Stuff?"

Normally, I kind of enjoyed Massha's banter. Today, though, I was just too tired to play.

"Actually, I went to bed fairly early," I said, stuffily. "I just had a lot of trouble getting to sleep. I guess there was just too much on my mind to relax."

That was a bit of an understatement. Actually, I had tossed and turned most of the night . . . just as I had for the two previous nights. I had hoped that once I had dealt with the money problems I had been wrestling with, I could concentrate on making up my mind about whether or not to marry Queen Hemlock. Instead, all the factors and ramifications kept dancing in my head, jostling in my head, jostling each other for importance, until I couldn't focus on any of them. Unfortunately, I couldn't put them aside, either.

"Uh-huh," she said, peering at me carefully.

Whatever she saw, she didn't like. Pushing two chairs together, she sat down next to me a put a motherly hand on my shoulder.

"Come on, Skeeve," she said. "Tell Massha all about it. What is it that's eating you up lately?"

"It's this whole thing about whether or not to marry Queen Hemlock," I said. "I just can't seem to make up my mind. As near as I can tell, there isn't a clear-cut right answer. Any option I have seems to be loaded with negatives. Whatever I do is going to affect so many people, I'm paralytic for fear of doing the wrong thing. I'm so afraid of doing something wrong, I'm not doing anything at all."

Massha heaved a great sigh.

"Well, I can't make that call for you, Skeeve. Nobody can. If it's any help, though, you should know that you're loved, and that your friends will stand by whatever decision you reach. I know it's rough right now, but we have every faith that you'll do the right thing."

I guess that was supposed to be reassuring. It flashed across my mind, however, that I really didn't need to be reminded of how much everyone was counting on me to reach the right decision . . . when after weeks of deliberation I still didn't have the foggiest idea of what the right decision was! Still, my apprentice was trying to help the only way she knew how, and I didn't want to hurt her for that.

"Thanks, Massha," I said, forcing a smile. "That does help a bit."

"Ahem."

I glanced up to see General Badaxe stepping forward. He had been so quiet I had forgotten he was in the room until he cleared his voice.

"Will you excuse us, my dear? I'd like to have a word with Lord Skeeve."

Massha glanced back and forth between the General and me, then shrugged.

"Sure thing, Hugh. Gods know I've got enough to keep me busy for a while. Catch you later, Hot Shot."

The General closed the door behind her, then stood regarding me for several moments. Then he came over to where I was standing and placed both of his hands on my shoulders.

"Lord Skeeve," he said. "May I be permitted the privilege of speaking to you, of treating you for a few moments as if you were my own son . . . or a man under my command in the Army?"

"Certainly, General," I said, genuinely touched.

"Fine," he smiled. "Turn around."

"Excuse me?"

"I said 'Turn around.' Face in the other direction, if you will."

Puzzled, I turned my back on him and waited.

Suddenly, something slammed into my rear end, propelling me forward with such force that I nearly fell, saving myself only by catching my weight with my hands and one knee.

I was shocked.

Incredible as it seemed, I had every reason to believe the General had just kicked me in the rump!

"You kicked me!" I said, still not quite believing it.

"That's right," Badaxe said calmly. "Frankly, it's long overdue. I had considered hitting you over the head, but it seems that lately your brains are located at the other end."

Grudgingly, I began to believe it.

"But why?" I demanded.

"Because, Lord Skeeve, with all respect and courtesies due your station and rank, it is my studied opinion that you've been acting like the north end of a south-bound horse."

That was clear enough. Surprisingly poetic for a military man, but clear.

"Could you be a bit more specific?" I said, with as much dignity as I could muster.

"I'm referring to your possible marriage to Queen Hemlock, of course," he said. "Or, more specifically, your difficulty in making up your mind. You're agonizing over the decision, when it's obvious to the most casual observer that you don't want to marry her."

"There are bigger issues at stake here than what I want, General," I said wearily.

"Bullshit," Badaxe said firmly.

"What?"

"I said 'Bullshit,' " the General repeated, "and I meant it. What you want is the only issue worth considering."

I found myself smiling in spite of my depression.

"Excuse me, General, but isn't that a little strange coming from you?"

"How so?"

"Well, as a soldier, you've devoted your life to the rigors of training and combat. The whole military system is based on self-sacrifice and self-denial, isn't it?"

"Perhaps," Badaxe said. "Has it occurred to you, though, that it's simply a means to an end? The whole idea of being prepared for combat is to be able to defend or exert what *you* want against what someone else wants."

I sat up straight.

"I never thought of it that way."

"It's the only way *to* think of it," the General said, firmly. "Oh, I know a lot of people see a soldier's life as being subservient. That it's the role of a mindless robot subject to the nonsensical orders and whims of his superior officers . . . including Generals. The fact is that an army has to be united in purpose, or it's ineffectual. Each man in it *voluntarily* agrees to follow the chain of command because it's the *most effective way* to *achieve a common goal*. A soldier who doesn't know what he wants or why he's fighting is worthless. Even worse, he's a danger to anyone and everyone who's counting on him."

He paused, then shook his head.

"For the moment, however, let's consider this on a

smaller scale. Think of a young man who trains himself
so that he won't be bullied by older, larger men. He lifts
weights to develop his muscles, studies various forms of
armed and unarmed combat, and practices long hard hours
with one objective in mind: To harden himself to where
he won't *have* to knuckle under to anyone."

The General smiled.

"What would you say, then, if that same young man
subsequently let every pipsqueak and bravo shove him
around because he was afraid he'd hurt them if he pushed
back?"

"I'd say he was a bloody idiot."

"Yes," Badaxe nodded. "You are."

"Me?"

"Certainly," the General said, starting to look a little
vexed. "Didn't you recognize yourself in the picture I just
described?"

"General," I said, wearily, "I haven't gotten much sleep
for several days now. Forgive me if I'm not tracking at
my normal speed, but you're going to have to spell it out
for me."

"Very well. I spoke about a young man building himself up physically. Well, you, my young friend, are probably the most formidable man I know."

"I am?"

"Beyond a doubt. What's more, like the young man in
my example, you've built yourself up over the years . . .
even in the time I've known you. With your magikal skills
and wealth, not to mention your allies, supporters, and
contacts, you don't have to do anything you don't want
to. What's more, you've proved that time and time again
against some very impressive opposition."

He smiled and laid a surprisingly gentle hand on my
shoulder.

"And now you tell me that you have to marry Hemlock
even though you don't want to? I don't believe it."

"Well, the option is that she abdicates and I'm stuck
with being king," I said, bitterly. "I want that even less."

"Then don't do that, either," the General shrugged.

"How is anyone going to force you to do *either* if you don't voluntarily go along with it? I know I wouldn't want the job."

His simple analysis gave me a thread of hope, but I was still reluctant to grab for it.

"But people are counting on me," I protested.

"People are counting on you to do what is right for *you*," Badaxe said firmly. "Though it's hard for you to see, they're *assuming* that you'll do *what you want to do*. You should have listened more closely to what my bride to be was saying to you. If you *want* to marry Queen Hemlock, they'll support you by not standing in the way or giving you grief. Do you really think, though, that if you firmly state that you *want* to continue working with them, that they won't support that with as much or more enthusiasm? *That's* what Massha was trying to say, but I think she was saying it too gently for you to hear. Everyone's been too gentle with you. Since you don't seem to know what you want, they've been walking on eggshells around you to let you sort it out. In the meantime, you've been straining to hear what everyone else wants rather than simply relaxing and admitting what *you* want."

I couldn't suppress my smile.

"Well, General," I said, "if there's one thing no one could accuse you of, it would be of not treating me overly gently."

"It seemed appropriate."

"That wasn't a complaint," I laughed. I was feeling good now, and didn't bother trying to hide it. "It was admiration . . . and thanks."

I extended my hand. He gathered it into his own and we exchanged a single, brief shake that sealed a new level in our friendship.

"I take it that you've reached your decision then?" Badaxe said, cocking an eyebrow at me.

"Affirmative," I smiled. "And your guess as to what it is would be correct. Thank you, sir. I hope it goes without saying that I'd like to return the favor sometime, should the opportunity present itself."

"Hmmm . . . If you could, perhaps, show a little greater interest in the plans for the wedding," the General said. "Particularly if you could come up with a way to shorten the planning procedure?"

"I can shorten today's session," I said. "Give Massha my apologies, but I feel the need to meet with Queen Hemlock. Perhaps we can continue the session tomorrow."

"That isn't shortening the process," Badaxe scowled. "It's prolonging it."

"Sorry, General," I laughed, heading out the back door. "The only other suggestion I'd have is to convince her to elope. I'll hold the ladder for you."

XIX:

"There must be fifty ways to leave your lover!"

—P. Simon

My mind finally made up at last, I set out to give the news to Queen Hemlock. I mean, since she was waiting for a decision from me, it wouldn't be right to delay sharing it once it had been made. Right? The fact that if I waited too long, I might chicken out entirely had nothing to do with it. Right?

Suddenly, I was very aware of the absence of my bodyguards. When I had given them their assignment to distribute my unwanted cash, it had been under the assumption that I was in no particular danger while here at the palace.

Now, I wasn't so sure.

I had noticed back when we first met, when I was masquerading as King Rodrick, that Queen Hemlock had a nasty, perhaps even a murderous streak in her. There had been no evidence of it lately, but then again, I wasn't aware of her having received any bad news of a degree such as I was bringing her, either.

I shook my head and told myself I was being silly. At her worst, the Queen was not taken to open, unpremeditated violence. If it looked like she was taking the news badly, I could simply gather the crew and skip off to another dimension before she could get around to formulating a plan for revenge. There was absolutely no reason for me to need bodyguards to protect me from her. Right?

I was still trying to convince myself of this when I reached the Queen's chambers. The honor guard standing outside her door snapped to attention, and it was too late for a graceful retreat.

Moving with a casualness I didn't feel, I knocked on her door.

"Who is it?"

"It's Skeeve, Your Majesty. I was wondering if I might speak to you if it's not inconvenient?"

There was a pause, long enough for me to get my hope up, and then the door opened.

"Lord Skeeve. This is a pleasant surprise. Please, come right in."

Queen Hemlock was dressed in a simple orange gown, which was a pleasant surprise. That she was dressed, that is, not the color of it. The first time she had entertained me in her quarters, she had been naked when she opened the door, and it had put me at an uncomfortable disadvantage for that conversation. This time around, I figured I was going to need all the advantages I could muster.

"Your Majesty," I said, entering the room. I looked about quickly as she was shutting the door, and, when she turned, gestured toward a chair. "Please, if you could take a seat?"

She raised a questioning eyebrow at me, but took the indicated seat without argument.

"What's this all about, Skeeve?" she said. "You look so solemn."

There was no way of stalling further, so I plunged in.

"I wanted to let you know that I've made my decision regarding marrying you," I said.

"And that is?"

"I . . . Your Majesty, I'm both honored and flattered that you would consider me worthy of being your consort. I had never dreamed that such a possibility existed, and, when it was suggested, had to take time to examine the concept."

"And . . ." she urged.

I realized that no amount of sugarcoating would change the basic content of my decision, so I simply went for it.

"My final conclusion," I said, "is that I'm not ready for marriage at this time . . . to you or anyone else. To try to pretend otherwise would be a vast disservice to that person . . . and to myself. Between my work and studies as a magician, and my desire to travel and visit other dimensions, I simply have no time or interest in settling down right now. If I did, I would doubtless end up resenting whoever or whatever had forced me to do so. As such, I fear I must decline your kind offer."

Having said it, I braced myself for her reaction.

"Okay," she said.

I waited for a moment for her to continue, but when she didn't, I felt compelled to.

"As to your abdicating the throne to me . . . Your Majesty, I beg you to reconsider. I have no qualifications or desire to be the ruler of a kingdom. At best, I'm a good advisor . . . and even that's only with the considerable help of my colleagues and friends. I fear that if I were to attempt to undertake such a responsibility, the kingdom would suffer badly . . . I know I would . . . and . . . and . . ."

My oration ground to a halt as I saw that she was laughing.

"Your Majesty? Excuse me. Did I say something funny?"

"Oh Skeeve," she gasped, coming up for air. "Did you really think . . . Of course I'm not going to give up the throne. Are you kidding? I *love* being Queen."

"You do? But you said . . ."

"Oh, I say *lots* of things," she said, waving a negligent

hand. "One of the nice things about being royalty is that you get to decide for yourself which of the things you say are for real and which should be ignored."

To say the least, I was confused.

"Then why did you say that if you didn't intend to follow through?" I said. "And how about your marriage proposal? Didn't you mean that, either?"

"Oh, I meant it all right," she smiled. "But I didn't really expect you to want to marry me. I mean, why should you? You've already got wealth and power *without* being tied down to a throne or a wife. Why should you want to stay here and play second banana to me when you could be off hopping around the world or wherever it is that you go as the one and only Great Skeeve? It would have been fabulous for me and the kingdom to have you tied into us permanently, but there weren't any real benefits for you. That's why I came up with that abdication thing."

"Abdication thing?" I echoed weakly.

"Sure. I knew you didn't want to be a king. If you had, you would have kept the throne back when Roddie had you pose as him. Anyway, I figured that if you didn't want it bad enough, it just might make a big enough threat to lure you into playing consort for me instead."

She made a little face.

"I know it was weak, but it was the only card I had to play. What else could I do? Threaten you? With what? Even if I managed to come up with something that would present a threat to you and that menagerie of yours, all you'd have to do is wave your hands and blink off to somewhere else. It simply wouldn't be worth the effort and expense to keep tracking you down . . . no offense. Going with the abdication thing, I at least had a *chance* of getting you to consider marrying me . . . and if nothing came of it, no harm done."

I thought of the days and nights I had been spending agonizing over my decision. Then I thought about throttling the Queen.

"No harm done," I agreed.

"So," she said, settling back in her chair, "that's that. No marriage, no abdication. At least we can still be friends, can't we?"

"Friends?" I blinked.

Even though I had met her some time back, I had never really thought of Queen Hemlock as a friend.

"Why not?" she shrugged. "If I can't have you as a consort, I'm willing to give it a try as a friend. From what I've seen, you're pretty loyal to your friends, and I'd like to have *some* tie to you."

"But why should that be important to you? You're a Queen, and the ruler of a fairly vast kingdom to boot."

Hemlock cocked her head at me curiously.

"You really don't know, do you Skeeve? You're quite a powerful man yourself, Skeeve. I'd much rather have you as an ally, to the kingdom and for myself, than as an enemy. If you check around, I think you'll find a lot of people who would."

That sounded remarkably like what Badaxe had pointed out to me earlier.

"Besides," the Queen added, "you're a nice guy, and I don't really have many friends. You know, people I can talk to as equals who aren't afraid of me? I think in the long run, we have more problems in common than you realize."

"Except I'm in a better position to still be able to do what I want," I finished thoughtfully.

"Don't rub it in," Hemlock said, wrinkling her nose. "Well, what do you say? Friends?"

"Friends," I smiled.

On an impulse, I took her hand and kissed it lightly, then stood holding it for a few moments.

"If I may, Your Majesty, let me add my personal thanks to you for taking my refusal so well? Even if you more than half expected it, it still must have stung your pride a bit. It must have been tempting to make me squirm a little in return."

The Queen threw back her head and laughed again.

"It wouldn't be real smart of me to give you a rough

time, now, would it?" she said. "As I said before, you can
be a real help to the kingdom, Skeeve, even if it only
means hiring you occasionally as an independent contrac-
tor. If I made you feel too bad about not marrying me,
then you wouldn't ever want to see me or the kingdom
again."

"I really don't know," I admitted. "The court of Possiltum gave me my first paying job as a magician. I'll
probably always have a bit of a soft spot for it. Then, too,
Your Majesty is not without charm as a woman."

That last bit sort of slipped out, but the Queen didn't
seem to mind.

"Just not quite charming enough to settle down with,
eh?" she smiled. "Well, let me know when you have some
leisure time on your hands, and maybe we can explore
some alternatives together."

That *really* took me aback.

"Ahh . . . certainly, Your Majesty. In the meantime,
however, I fear it's nearly time for my colleagues and I
to take our leave of Possiltum. From what Grimble tells
me, the kingdom is nearly back on solid financial footing,
and there are pressing matters which require our attention
elsewhere."

"Of course," she said, rising to her feet. "Go with my
personal gratitude, as well as the fees you so richly de-
serve. I'll be in touch."

I was so uncomfortable about the reference to our fees,
that I was nearly to the door before her last comment sank
in.

"Umm . . . Your Majesty?" I said, turning back to her.
"One more thing. Next time you need me, could you just
write a note like everyone else instead of sending me a
finger? It was a bit unnerving when it arrived."

"No problem," she said. "By the way, could I have the
finger back? If nothing else, I'd like to have the ring to
remember Roddie by."

"I thought you had it." I frowned. "I haven't seen it
since our conversation when I first got back here."

"Hmm . . . I wonder where it's gotten to. Oh well, I'll

put the maids to work looking for it. If you happen to come across it in your things, be a dear and send it back to me?"

"Certainly, Your Majesty. Goodbye."

With that, I gave her my deepest bow and left.

XX:

"Meanwhile, back at reality..."

—G. LUCAS

Ifelt as if a huge weight had been lifted from my back! For the first time since my return from Perv, I was in control of my own destiny!

No more wondering about what I should or shouldn't do about marrying Queen Hemlock for the good of the kingdom, or the good of the team ... or the good of civilization, for that matter. Things were back in perspective! My future was mine to do with as I wished, without the pressure of trying to sort out what was best for others.

I found myself whistling to myself as I strode through the castle corridors, something I hadn't done in a long while, and had to fight the temptation to break into a jig.

As soon as that realization hit, that I was resisting a temptation, I immediately did a little hop-skip.

I was through trying to judge everything I did on whether or not other people thought it was proper ... or, more specifically, whether I *thought* other people would think it was proper. From now on, I was going to do what

I wanted to do . . . and the rest of the world, *or* the dimensions at large, could just bloody well adapt!

With that decision, I threw in an extra high kick. It may not have been classic dance, but it felt good. Heck! *I* felt good. Better than I could ever remember feeling.

I became aware of a couple people staring at me from afar, and a few more craning their necks for a better look. Rather than feeling embarrassed or self-conscious, I waved at them gaily and continued my prancing.

I had to tell someone! Share my newfound happiness with my friends. They had all stood by me through the bad times. Now I wanted to be with them when I felt *good!*

I'd tell Bunny . . . no, Aahz! I'd tell Aahz first and *then* Bunny. My partner deserved to be the first to know.

"Hey Boss! Skeeve!"

I turned to see Nunzio beckoning me from the other end of the corridor. I was surprised to see him, and started to wave. Then it dawned on me that this was the first time he had ever called *me* to join *him* instead of the other way around. A feeling of alarm swept away my earlier euphoria.

"Come quick, Boss! It's important!"

My fears were confirmed. Something was wrong. Something was *very* wrong.

I hurried to join him, but he moved off down the corridor ahead of me, looking back from time to time to see if I was following.

"Wait for me, Nunzio!" I called.

"Hurry, Boss!" he replied, not slackening his pace.

I was starting to get a bit winded trying to catch up with him, but if anything he seemed to be increasing his speed. Then he ducked down a flight of stairs, and an idea came to me.

When I reached the stairs, instead of descending normally, I vaulted over the railing and used my magik to fly (which is really levitation in reverse) after him. This seemed to be a bit faster than running, and certainly a lot easier on the lungs, so I kept it up. I managed to catch

my breath *and* catch up with my bodyguard just as we
were emerging into the palace courtyard.

"What's this all about, Nunzio?" I said, slowing my
speed to match his pace.

Instead of answering, he pointed ahead.

There was a group of people gathered in the courtyard.
Some were guards or other people I had seen around the
palace, but there also seemed to be a batch of costumed
characters with them. Then I saw Guido and Pookie in
the group . . . and Aahz!

"Hey Aahz! What's happening?" I called.

At the sound of my voice, the whole group looked in
my direction, then fell back slightly and . . .

And then I saw what they were gathered around.

"GLEEP!"

My pet dragon was lying on his side, showing no sign
of his usual energy and life.

I don't recall landing . . . or of moving at all. I just remember crouching at my pet's side and gathering his head
into my lap.

"What's wrong, fellah?" I said, but got no response.
"Aahz? What's the matter with him?"

"Skeeve, I . . ." my partner began, but then I saw it.

Protruding from Gleep's side, just behind his leg, was
an arrow!

At that moment, I felt my pet stir in my arms, weakly
trying to raise his head.

"Take it easy, fellah," I said, trying to sound soothing.

Gleep's eyes found mine.

"Skeeve?" he said faintly, then went limp, his head falling back on my lap.

He had said my name! The first thing he had ever said
other than the sound that had given him his name.

I carefully eased his head onto the ground and rose. I
stood looking down at him for several moments, then
raised my eyes to the surrounding crowd. I don't know
what my expression was, but they all gave ground several
steps as my gaze passed over them.

When I spoke, I tried to keep my voice soft and level, but it seemed to come from far away.

"All right," I said. "I want to know what's been going on here . . . and I want to know *now!!*"

About the Author

Robert (Lynn) Asprin was born in 1946. While he has written some stand-alone novels such as *Cold Cash War*, *Tambu*, *The Bug Wars*, and also the *Duncan and Mallory* illustrated stories, Bob is best known for his series: *The Myth Adventures of Aahz and Skeeve*; the *Phule* novels; and, more recently, the *Time Scout* novels written with Linda Evans. He also edited the groundbreaking *Thieves World* anthologies with Lynn Abbey. His most recent collaboration is *License Invoked*, written with Jody Lynn Nye. It is set in the French Quarter, New Orleans, where he currently lives.